ANAERFELL

THE BLOOD OF DRAGONS
BOOK 1

THRICE NINE LEGENDS

Joshua Robertson
&
J.C. Boyd

CRIMSON EDGE PRESS

Acknowledgement

To any person who faces an enemy to conceal the war within themselves.

There once was a time when the gods were gods without question. When men were men without example. When heroes were only the frivolous dreams of lurid mortality. It was a time when truths and untruths were indistinguishable, hatred and love were equally excusable, and life and death regaled all of humanity in the same breath. Myths of old were realized and legends were born from the very dust man was formed of, to be told and retold until the grace of time altered them beyond knowing or forgot them completely. Still, some tales were preserved deep within the hearts of mankind, for reasons that could not be fathomed. Perhaps bearing the fruit of some profound truth or kept alive merely by the strength of the men who lived them. Some tales would never be forgotten.

Table of Contents

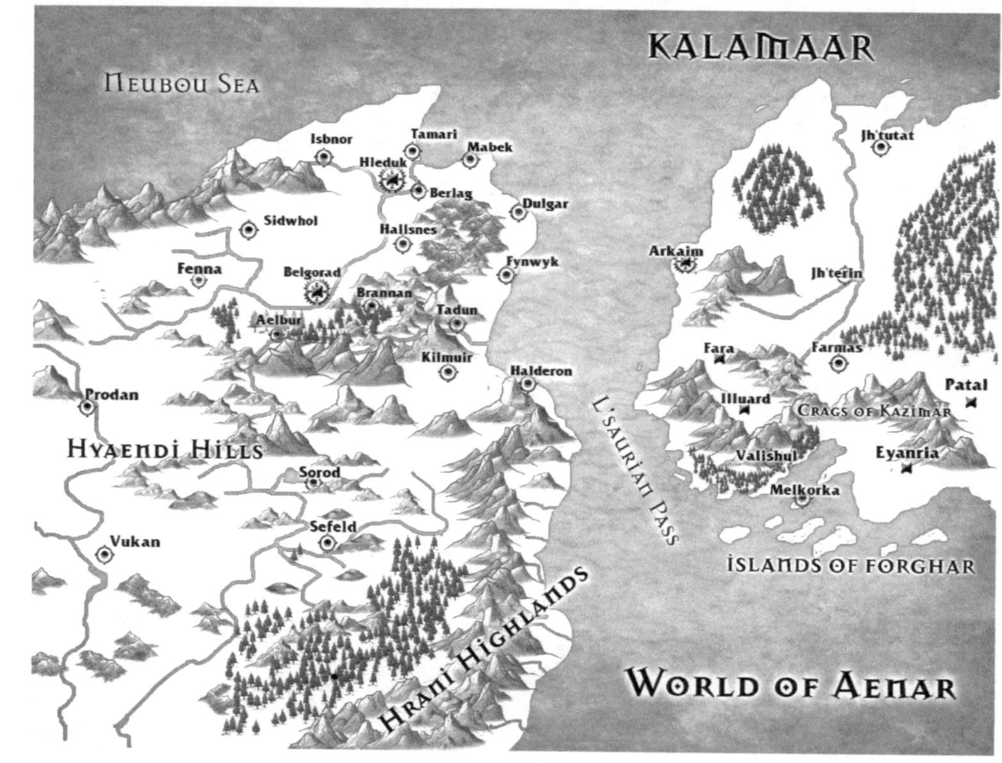

KALAMAAR
Neubou Sea
Isbnor
Tamari
Mabek
Hleduk
Berlag
Dulgar
Sidwhol
Hallsnes
Fynwyk
Fenna
Belgorad
Brannan
Tadun
Aelbur
Kilmuir
Halderon
Prodan
Hyaendi Hills
Sorod
Sefeld
Vukan
Hrani Highlands
Jh'tutat
Arkaim
Jh'terin
Fara
Farmas
Illuard
Patal
Crags of Kazimar
Valishul
Eyanria
Melkorka
L'Saurian Pass
Islands of Forghar
World of Aenar

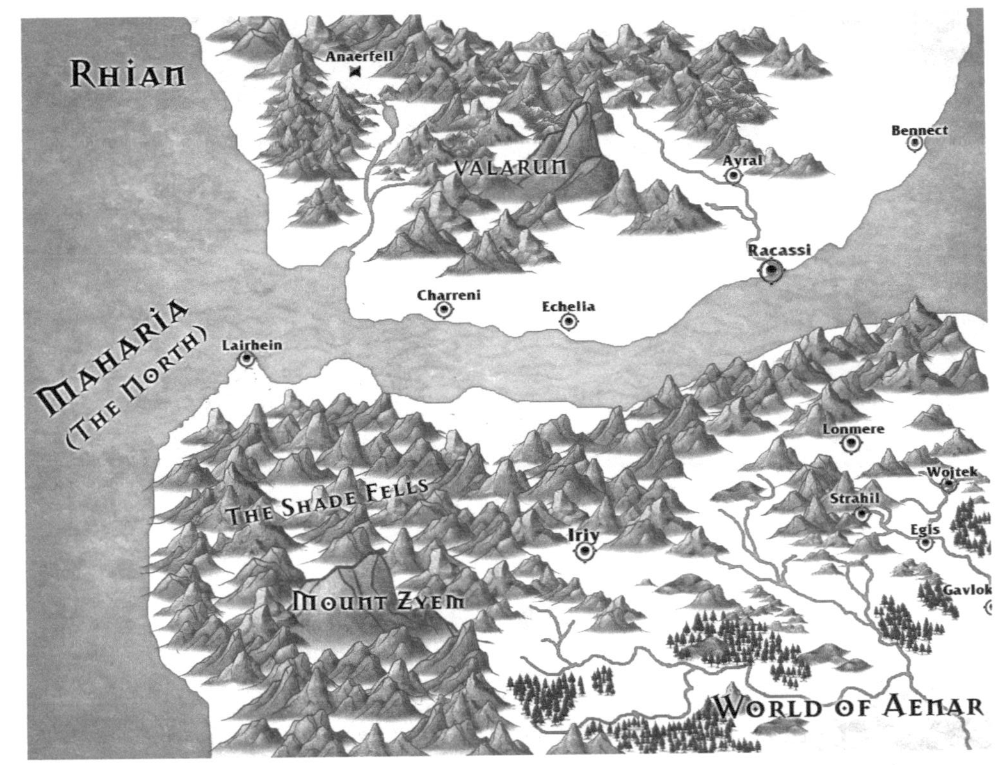

Rhian
Maharia (The North)
Anaerfell
VALARUN
Bennect
Ayral
Racassi
Charreni
Echelia
Lairhein
THE SHADE FELLS
Lonmere
Wojtek
Strahil
Egis
Iriy
Gavlok
MOUNT ZYEM
WORLD OF AENAR

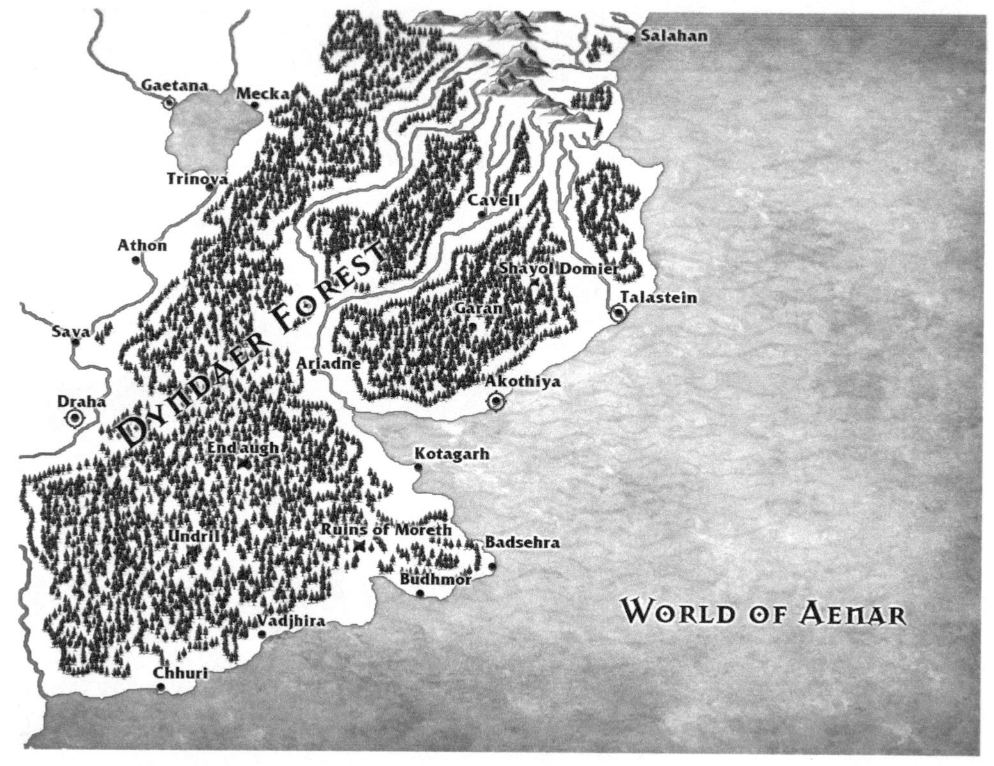

DYNDAER FOREST
WORLD OF AENAR
Salahan
Gaetana
Mecka
Trinova
Athon
Cavell
Shayol Domie
Talastein
Sava
Ariadne
Akothiya
Draha
Kotagarh
Undri
Ruins of Moreth
Badsehra
Budhmor
Vadjhira
Chhuri

World of Aenar
Mount Dvargen
Almdalir
Tundris Mor
Shade Fells
Sprague
Faldar
Tyrewen
Utolock
Raybin
Ohenvlast
Kalinov Desert

Thrice Nine Legends Saga

The Blood of Dragons by Joshua Robertson & J.C. Boyd
ANAERFELL*
HESHAYOL*

The Kaelandur Series by Joshua Robertson
MELKORKA*
DYNDAER*
MAHARIA*

Other Thrice Nine Legends Saga by Joshua Robertson & J.C. Boyd
STRONG ARMED*
WHEN BLOOD FALLS*
THE NAME OF DEATH*
WARDEN OF THE ASH TREE*
THE HIGHBORN LONGWALKER*
DEATH AT DUSK**

Additional Works

Legacy Series by Joshua Robertson & J.C.Boyd
BLOOD & BILE*

THE HAWKHURST SAGA*
GRIMSDALR*
THE PRINCE'S PARISH*
JACK SPRATT*

Published by Crimson Edge
**Forthcoming by Crimson Edge*

ANAERFELL

THRICE NINE LEGENDS

Chapter I

Bow in hand, Drast pushed a finger into the grisly wound of the dead body. The warmth had gone from the Vucari's blood despite the height of the springtime sun.

"Ser Drast?"

Flinching somewhat at the title, Drast pulled his hand free from the corpse. He stood. The shorter man next to him watched him with wide eyes. The man always had wide eyes, as if he was perpetually surprised at his own existence.

Drast smiled at him. "Yes, *Ser* Simon?"

Simon frowned, his eyes remaining wide. Drast could not imagine how the man managed such an expression. "There is no need for sarcasm, Ser Drast. We are both noble and should treat each other as such, even if your family doesn't have the purest of bloodlines."

Drast tightened his grip on the strung bow and thumbed the fletching of an arrow, one of three held loosely between the fingers of his other hand. He still smiled. "Noble or no, I prefer not to have empty words as a precursor to my name, if you please."

Simon continued to watch him. Drast swore the man didn't blink. "As you wish, *Drast*. So long as you recognize that I will be referred to as *Ser* Simon. After all, my father is the *Arkhon* and yours is but a *Serder*. You would do well to remember I am not one of your soldiers."

Drast maintained an amiable smile. Why did Simon choose to place so much emphasis on titles? "Of course, *Ser* Simon." He mimicked the oddly clipped tone of the man. "We are of an accord."

Averting his eyes to keep Simon from seeing him roll them, and more importantly, to keep himself from acting upon impulse, Drast kicked the dead Vucari. He knew if he had to keep looking at those wide blue-green eyes above that weak red mustache, he would need to jab an arrow in them. One arrow for each socket. If Simon held any less power, blood would already color the sand.

"I am well aware of your position, *Ser* Simon." He wondered if the Arkhon's son would notice his continued mockery. "And, as I may have mentioned before we left Lairhein, I am perfectly capable of retrieving my brother without you. Familial reunions should be kept private, you know?"

"I don't think so, and—more importantly—neither does my father."

Drast widened his grin, shouldering his bow and clapping the man on the shoulder. The Vucari blood still on his finger left a stain on Simon's coat. The Arkhon's son did not notice. "I am certain. I know your family is greatly concerned with the well-being of my own, for which we are eternally grateful." He really hated Simon. "It is such bonds that keep we Stuhia strong and unified, like a pack of wolves working together to bring down the mighty moose or elk."

The Arkhon and his fool of a son believed Drast's family was conspiring against the Arkhon's family. Which, of course, his family was, but there was no need to admit the truth. Hidden truths were best.

Releasing Simon's shoulder, Drast leaned over the naked corpse, examining it further, and mentally pushed the round-eyed man from his thoughts. The body had already begun to rot, stiffened and cold to the touch. It had a male shape with a shaven head and pale lips. He pulled back an eyelid to confirm the carcass had brown eyes. Vucari always had brown eyes.

The corpse did not bother him, but the creature itself sickened him. The Vucari were skin-switchers, and that kind of thing just seemed unnatural.

Ignoring the feeling of disgust, he took note of the ground. It had softened with the melting snows. The Vucari's weight had left an indentation against the budding grasses and in the soil. He inhaled the stench of the carcass while ignoring the handful of flies buzzing near his ear.

Definitely rotting.

He pulled back and stood. "It has been dead for at least a few days."

Simon asked, "Did your scouts do this?"

"No, *Ser* Simon. My scouts did not do this. It has been dead much too long and we only recently came into the region." Drast peered across the narrow distance between the mountains and the Neabou Sea. "I imagine my brother's pathfinders discovered this Vucari when they came out of the Shade Fells. It might have been an enemy scout. Tyran must have already returned from his adventure, though why they have not advanced closer to Lairhein, I cannot say. With any luck, we will find him farther up the coastline."

"*Ser* Tyran?" Simon said in a matter-of-fact tone, gifting Drast with a wide-eyed smirk. "He has been gone for many months. I hear he was after something important."

Drast held the grin, forcing his eyes to crease. Sometimes it was hard to remember to make the smile reach his eyes. Genuine. He had to seem genuine. "What else could possibly keep him away?"

The response caused Simon to lift an eyebrow, but he did not respond.

"Regardless, it is not our concern now. The weather is warming, which means the skin-switchers will be venturing near Lairhein again. It looks to be another year of war. Perhaps you should return now to make certain the Arkhon is aware?"

Simon ignored the question. "Their power is minimal compared to our own. Still, it is intriguing..." Simon traced his thin mustache, "the dragons leave the Vucari alone and attack the Stuhia."

Drast glanced at the Shade in the south. The dark mountains towered towards the thin clouds. The soil beneath the melting snow was blackened or grey with several dark green trees lining the base of the looming rocks. The mountains could have been their own vertical world, expanding as far as the eye could see. Drast chuckled, "Surely you are not expecting me to explain the motivations of dragons?"

Simon cocked his face to the side. "I assumed you would have some insight."

"Oh, I would imagine no more than you have yourself." Drast considered punching Simon in the face a couple of times and seeing if he could make him close his eyes. "We are Stuhia, *Ser* Simon. We are dragon-people. By definition, we are sacred to Wolos." Drast kept the conversation pinpointed on Simon. "You suggest dangerous things."

Simon started. "Oh, no, nothing of the sort. I am a faithful man, of course. But I cannot help but wonder—if we are favored by Wolos, why do the serpents, his creation, attack Lairhein and lay waste to the Stuhia? Why are the Vucari permitted to invade our lands?"

"Ah, *Ser* Simon, such questions are best asked of wiser men than I. Maybe you could consult the Ninth Council when we return to Lairhein."

Drast suddenly wished Tyran was with him. His brother never got himself into such situations, where he must think on his feet and come up with wily responses. No, Tyran would merely grunt, and then leave someone else to figure out what the grunt meant. Instead, Drast was stuck trying to determine the sincerity of Simon's concerns. Sincerity from a Kluk would be a first. He was likely attempting to egg Drast into a pitfall of self-condemnation for denying Stuhian beliefs. Not that he particularly cared what the man thought.

Maybe if he surprised Simon, then the perpetually surprised look would fall off Simon's face. Yes, fight fire with fire. He hardened his voice, "Are you testing me, *Ser* Simon?" He nearly smirked, ruining his fun before he started. How could the man not hear the mockery in his tone? "Did my father send you to see if I would be arrogant enough to guess at the will of Wolos?"

Simon's jaw fell. "No, Drast. Serder Dagmar Kaligula has nothing to do with this."

"Or, perhaps, it is your father?"

"No!" Simon cried.

"Then tell me why you challenge my faith!" Drast thundered forward to keep his false demeanor. When a moment passed without an answer, he raised his bow hand as if to strike him.

The man shrank backwards, cowering from him. If anything, his eyes became wider.

Drast fumed. "Tell me!"

"Please, Drast. I meant no harm. I—I was only echoing..."

"Echoing what? Your father?" Drast sneered to keep from laughing. "What does he want? Why are you really out here with me and my army? I lead these men to glory. That is my duty! I don't have time for games."

Pure terror filled Simon's face. Beautiful.

A shrug of Drast's shoulder sent his bow down his arm and into his grip. In a blink, he set one of the arrows to the string. The sinew pulled hard and the yew bent heavily. The copper tip gleamed in the springtime sun, leveled at the cowering man's unblinking, bulging left eye.

"Please, put down your bow, Drast," Simon pleaded, falling to the ground in a heap. His hands raised above his head, palms opened as wide as his eyes. "We don't have to mention this hiccup when we return. A simple misunderstanding."

Drast worked to keep his jaw shut. Why would Simon cower before him? The man was at least an equal in power with the magic of the Stuhia, *Koldovstvo*. Probably more powerful, actually.

Simon's eyes closed.

Drast grinned, releasing the tension on the string. "Come now, *Ser* Simon. You must develop a sense of humor." He twisted the bow in his grip. With a flip of his wrist and a jerk of his arm, he had hooked the bow over his shoulder again. "You also must learn not to question the gods. There are many who would take offense to such questions. Be glad the lesson was not harder to learn."

Simon's eyes widened again, bewildered at what had just occurred. Drast could not conceal the sigh that escaped his chest. Although fun, he did not have the time or energy to play this game all day.

A soldier approached from the rear. "Ser Drast! There is battle on the shoreline just beyond the bend. The pathfinder says it is Ser Tyran." The man paused as if realizing the tension between the two Sers. The soldier raised his voice, clarifying, "Your brother."

Delight boiled in his stomach, watching Simon. He recognized the soldier's voice without seeing him. The man was charged as his Voivode, a soldier who held the position to aid in the command of the other soldiers. "Excellent, Walstan. Move the spearmen to the front and the archers to the rear."

The Voivode complied. "As you wish, Ser Drast."

"Stop calling me Ser!" Drast hollered over his shoulder.

Walstan mumbled something inaudible and raced to prepare the army. Drast kept his gaze on Simon, who had not moved a muscle. It suddenly struck him that Simon could have an accident during the battle. A stray arrow, perhaps. Such an accident would surely please his father, Serder Kaligula; he was certain. The Arkhon's family, the imperial bloodline, had always been a thorn in his father's side. Removing Simon would be one less prick to worry about.

"Get a hold of your wits, you will need each one," Drast said.

Simon's voice shook like willows in the wind. "Yes…of course."

Without another word, Drast left Simon scrambling to follow. He walked away forcing himself to stare onward. The lessons learned from his father seldom left the forefront of his mind. Turning back would be a sign of weakness; in this case, a sign of guilt. He wanted to see the look on Simon's face. The concern, the uncertainty, the fear.

Gritting his teeth, he picked up his pace to reach the incline overlooking the camp of his small army. Eighty-six men were commissioned under his watch, and each of them valuable. His ability to keep them alive would determine his family's advancement in Lairhein. Unnecessary death often soured people, and his father never let him forget his duty to his family.

"Drast, how long has it been since you have seen *Ser* Tyran?" Simon asked from behind.

The question naturally put him in mind of his brother, and he grunted as a response.

"Do you worry for his death?"

Drast snorted. "I don't think death has the gall to face Tyran. It avoids him every chance it gets."

Drast felt surprised when the other Ser whispered, "We all die eventually. It is the one thing we cannot avoid."

He adjusted the arrows. "You think you have completed your charge, *Ser* Simon? Believe you will be taken to the Thrice Ten Kingdom?"

"One can only hope."

Drast grunted again. His brother's way of responding was undoubtedly easier.

He inspected the soldiers while he and Simon descended towards the army. Firm handshakes, guttural laughs, and ready smiles were passed freely about. Each soldier moved without hesitation, seemingly eager for a good fight. Was there such a thing as being too well trained?

The spear wall had nearly been organized before he reached the bottom of the hill. The men were in a convex formation, their leathern shields and stone-tipped spears at the ready. Meanwhile, the rear third of the men carried bows like Drast's, though not as high quality.

He hoped they were too well trained, because it was a far cry better than the reverse. If it was his brother's army ahead, he wanted the strength of his own army to be witnessed.

Walstan approached from the throng of soldiers. "The men are ready, Ser Drast."

He cursed silently at the title. If Walstan was less useful, he would consider having the man meet a similar accident as Simon on the battlefield. Lucky for him, Walstan maintained the army most of the time, freeing Drast for more compelling activities. "I can see that. Let's not waste time. Go on. Move them out."

The red-haired Voivode nodded. He rotated back the way he had come and shouted, "Move out!"

Drast had known Walstan while growing up in Lairhein. He found it strange to see the man holding the stone-tipped spear. Although they had played together as young children, they had grown apart as they matured. During their adolescence Drast had been told by his father that Walstan was unworthy to be called friend. Unequal was the better word. Afterwards, their playing had stopped.

He could not be certain, though—Walstan had seemed to try to prove himself since Drast's father had separated them. Even now, Walstan dashed ahead of the brigade at a half-jog to lead the attack. The man had earned the title of Voivode. He was certain his brother had a complex process to choose men for such a responsibility, but Drast merely found Walstan to be self-sufficient. Drast hated to deal with the details of leading an army.

Walstan's momentum generated grunts and battle roars throughout the small army. The lot of them advanced towards the shoreline at a matched speed.

He listened for Simon's footfalls. They were light, almost like raindrops falling behind him against the dirt. It only took a moment before the sound was drowned out by the din of weapons and death.

A war horn blew on the opposite side of the hill.

His army was only moments ahead of him, climbing over the remaining incline. Their ferocious exclamations resounded, rising as they charged towards the enemy. Drast hastened his feet to join his army. He was a leader, but a leader was only as strong as the men who followed him.

The Vucari flooded from the Neabou Sea and onto the shoreline straight into the *welcoming* hands of the Stuhia forces. The skin-switchers had their many long boats pulled to the shore. They vented from the shallow waters, mostly wearing nothing, and carrying weapons like those of his soldiers.

A second force of Stuhia men moved in sections, pressing the Vucari back into the Neabou Sea. They struggled in the waters to maintain their ground and fight with equal strength against the men on the land. Drast noticed at once how several of the Vucari shed their skins and transformed into more vicious beasts. Wolves, panthers, and bears swarmed forth as soon as they conquered the lashing waters. They growled and snarled, viciously charging the Stuhia.

He heard Walstan bellow from the ranks. He had used the magic of *Koldovstvo* to lift his voice. "Fire!"

The order echoed and the archers behind the spearmen let loose their stone-tipped shafts into the ranks of the enemy. Upon death, the creatures returned to their human form, naked and helpless. Others still in their human form flung spears and fired their own arrows towards his soldiers.

Drast hated the Vucari. Unnatural half-human, half-beast creatures that claimed connection with the dragons by whom the Stuhia were defined. The magical force of *Koldovstvo* bound them together, the single connection between the Stuhia and the

Vucari. Somewhere in the histories he had heard the suggestion that the Vucari were Stuhia before sullying their magic. Of course, it mattered little now.

If there had been a pause in the battle from his own soldiers suddenly advancing on the scene, he had missed the moment. The Vucari spread down the bank and stormed towards his spearmen like they had been formally invited to death.

He took only a moment to scan the terrain and the other army ranks for Tyran. Drast saw no sign of his younger brother. He knew he could not take the time to look for him now.

"Best to stay close, *Ser* Simon."

"I am not a stranger to battle, Drast."

"Perhaps not, but even acquaintances should be careful after long absences. Pay attention and I might teach you a few things." Drast winked at the man and set to work. He found something refreshing in being a simple soldier rather than playing at politics with his father.

The three arrows in his hand were put to the string and before the last struck its mark, three more filled his hand. No sooner had the first arrow been set on the right side of the smoothed yew and loosed than he replaced it with another. Against the naked Vucari invaders, the bow was certainly his weapon of choice. In less than the time it would take a man to swing a sword, Drast could fire three arrows and replenish the projectiles in his hand again.

"*Ser* Tyran is near the wagon." Simon had caught up with him.

Without responding, Drast glanced to the right. He had not even seen a wagon, but sure enough Tyran stood beside it, stalwart and unflinching.

A head taller than the men in his own militia, his younger brother had grown a full beard and head of hair in the year he had been gone. Their reddish color, the mark of any Stuhia, shown vibrant against his dark attire. Tyran looked as though he had aged several years, making him appear to be about the same age as Drast. Using *Koldovstvo* aged any man or woman who wielded it, and Drast had no doubt his brother had need of it in the Shade. Any Stuhia was more than willing to pay for such great power, no matter the cost. Their veins held the blood of dragons—the source of the mighty magic. All the same, Drast could barely recognize the man as the boy who had left Lairhein last spring.

"What in the Nine Lands is that?" Simon gasped from his side.

Drast stared in bewilderment at the wagon behind his brother. A bluish-grey beast hung halfway off the backside. The dirty white fabric covering the thing flapped loosely to the side. It only took a moment for Drast to distinguish the multiple crescent heads coiling limply from the singular body.

"A dragon…Father sent him to kill a dragon."

"The Stuhia will lose favor with Wolos for this travesty. The dragons are precious to him! It is no wonder the Vucari are allowed to invade our lands."

Drast blanched, nocking an arrow. *Ser* Simon's time to die had come.

Before he could act, Drast felt something strike his skull. He collided with the dirt and the world darkened.

Chapter II

Twenty-six soldiers had died in the Shade Fells. Their deaths hardened the wits of those who had survived. Yet the remaining men still fought like lilies instead of lions.

The strong center had collapsed and Tyran's army was being pushed back up the beach towards the mountains. The right flank had begun to separate from the center and the left pressed forward relentlessly, leaving their compatriots behind. His men had abandoned all semblance of a unified force, succumbing to exhaustion. Or…fear? Fear of death was a powerful motivator.

"The Vucari are gaining ground, Ser Tyran. The men need your direction," a voice spoke beside him.

"Mm." Tyran clicked his tongue, taking note of Drem's obvious declaration.

Drem tried again. "What are your orders?"

"I have already given my orders, Drem. It is not your place to make amends for the failings of your fellow Voivodes."

"But they are competent men."

"Only compared to the other soldiers I have to choose from." Tyran would never tell Drem he was the most useful Voivode among the four. Drem always followed his orders. He was a good soldier.

The army had battled through the Shade Fells against nightmares and worse, and now they were being overwhelmed by skin-switchers.

A moment passed. Tyran realized he had not finished his thought, having been stuck in his own head. "They should know how to control a battlefield. Clearly the men have not had their fill of death in the Shade, else they would have learned from their time there. We can spare a few more ill-spent lives before we go home."

The Voivode shifted his weight uncomfortably. "We are so close to home. I would hate to see any more die when their loved ones are this close."

"Don't challenge me with your pity, Drem. I have spent a year teaching these louts how to fight. Do you think I don't want to be home? Isolde is waiting for me and it is only now, with home on the horizon, that the fools forget how to lift their shield and thrust their spear. If they are weak, let them die."

"Ser…"

"As for those who survive, let their inner turmoil give them the sense to learn from their failings."

He held each of his men to the same standard to which he held himself. None of them, with their weakness, would keep him from reaching Isolde. She had waited for him. He would not betray her loyalty to him by dying here.

A war horn sounded from the Vucari. They were pressing the attack.

The man at his side shifted again. He noticed Drem looking towards the horizon where the sun would be setting in a couple of hours.

Tyran barely heard the commotion billowing from the western hill beyond the screams of dying Stuhia and roaring Vucari within his gaze. Though in mere moments, an army was silhouetted against the dimming sun rays. Not a single soldier slowed in their descent. The Stuhian spearman and bowman pummeled towards the shoreline like they would wipe the Vucari from existence in a single charge. The soldiers' lack of restraint told Tyran all he needed to know; it mirrored the leadership. As expected, within seconds, his elder brother, Drast, dashed over the hill following his troops.

Even at this distance, Tyran knew his brother. No other man would carry a bow and a handful of arrows, the weapons of a scout, and move with the carelessness of a front linesman. His brother wasted little time scanning the terrain before propelling himself into the heart of battle with his men, his bow working furiously.

Nothing changed. The man was as rash as rash could be. What good could an army be without a commander to lead them?

Drast's army would give Tyran enough distraction to reassemble his own forces. Tyran bellowed at his Voivodes over the battle din. "Eplich, Meran, Kormish, to me!"

The three Voivodes stumbled over the sand, retreating from the battle.

"Eplich, press forward! I want their left flank hit hard. Use Koldovstvo if you need to; a few years are better than death. Kormish, fall back. Get your men back in rank, keep them organized, and widen the gap. Make sure your men stay together, and don't falter. If any one of those bastards breaks rank or file, you personally put your spear through his skull."

Kormish nodded.

Tyran pressed on. "Meran, hold fast. You are the pivot and you cannot move. Do *not* press the attack, but keep them in place. When Eplich pushes and Kormish retreats, rotate your unit with them. I want the Vucari with their backs to our allies and their flank to the sea. Thin out their ranks, crush them, but leave them a way out. We want them fleeing, not fighting to the death. Now, go."

Drem spoke again from beside him, clear relief on the tip of his tongue. "Very wise, Ser Tyran. You will force them to use their magic while driving them into the sea."

"War is eternal. If we can weaken them today, they will stumble tomorrow." The Voivodes maneuvered the troops and Tyran watched his plan begin to unfold. "Battles between Stuhia and Vucari are not about who can use *Koldovstvo* better. They are about who can use it last."

"Do the Vucari even use *Koldovstvo*?"

Tyran was on the verge of snorting in derision, but soon realized that he had never actually heard that they *did*. In fact, Tyran had no idea how they managed to change into beasts as they did. He was not sure if he could turn into a wolf or bear with *Koldovstvo*. Maybe it was not even possible.

Drem seemed to sense his disquiet and continued. "I am not sure your brother recognizes the same tactical ploy."

"Mm." From the corner of his eye, Tyran glimpsed magic flashing and swirling from the joining army.

"There is no question why your father sent you into the Shade instead of Ser Drast," Drem said. "The campaign required a sound mind that could strategize and scheme without losing sight of the goal."

"Do *not* insult my brother."

Drem said nothing for a time. Finally he said, "I just wonder at the numbers of Vucari."

Tyran appreciated the change of topic. "How so?"

"We kill scores every year and still they come here. How great is their civilization? How do they replenish their ranks so swiftly?"

Maybe they shapeshift into rabbits. The thought brought a smile to his lips.

"Ser Tyran."

Tyran tried to turn his smile into a sneer, acutely aware it was likely the wrong expression to have on his face while watching his men die. Only Drast laughed in battle. Drast was always laughing. He forced his tone flat. "What?"

"There!" The Voivode pointed to the sky where three hawks were diving towards him.

Tyran slipped his mace out of the leather throng at his side—a two-foot yew haft with a heavy bronze ball at the end, the size of his fist—and unslung his shield from his back. Yew and hardened bull's hide, the rectangular buffer protected him from knee to shoulder.

Some men had commented on his choice of yew instead of oak or elm for his weaponry, but he had found the flexibility coupled with yew's unique hardness preferable. Better to bend than to break.

Tyran could see similar birds of prey swooping towards his troops. He had to restrain himself from calling for his men to look to the skies. Such a distraction might give the Vucari the opening they needed to gut more than a few of his men.

"Drem, tell the archers to focus fire at the skies, then get to my commanders. Make the men aware. But I want the front line focused on the front line, not finding shapes in the clouds. With haste!"

Tyran focused on the three hawks nearly upon him. The first two swooped in, slashing, his great shield more than capable of deflecting their talons. The third transformed mid-flight into a great black cat with claws as long as his fingers latching into his shield.

It was all Tyran could do to keep his arm from being ripped off by the momentum of the Vucari. He twisted with the weight, spinning around so he landed on top of the animal, his shield providing a barrier against the beast. Using his girth, he crushed it into the sand of the beach. A yowl transformed to a roar as the cat became a bear, claws shifting to paws bigger than Tyran's head.

A wild swing of his mace awkwardly connected with the bear's paw, crushing bone. He rolled away, tucking his shield close. The flapping of wings reverberated in his ears and the other two Stuhia swooped where he had been with tearing talons.

The bear bellowed, rolling upright, one of its paws held gingerly above the sand. Tyran met the Vucari's brown-eyed gaze, now on its feet as well. With a cry, he threw his mace at the creature, charging with his shield held before him. He did not look to see where his weapon hit, but the audible growl told him to reach with *Koldovstvo* to pull the weapon through space and time back into his hand.

Tyran felt his shield connect with the torso of the bear, now on its hind legs, and gripped his mace hard. He swung the mace overhead with all his strength to strike the skin-switcher in the skull, blood and brain showering over him. Lowering his shield, he saw the Vucari crumpled on the ground in its humanoid form.

Turning away, he saw the other two Stuhia had landed and transformed. One a wolf and the other humanoid, a female, stark to the sunbeams. A gut-wrenching scream filled the air at the sight of the dead woman behind Tyran. A relation of some kind, he had no doubt, but with *Koldovstvo's* aging affects, the elderly woman could have been anything from a daughter to her mother. That is, if *Koldovstvo* worked the same way for the Vucari.

The wolf bounded towards him, and Tyran did not hesitate to let his mind reach *Koldovstvo* once again. The magic sapped at his youth. He could feel his fingers stiffen and his joints grow weak from the effort.

When the wolf's paws touched down again, Tyran transformed the sand from golden to black. The ground became a swampy, heinous pit filled with dead, grasping hands. The wolf tried to spring forward but could do no more than whine. Corpse fingers fastened around its legs, intertwined in its fur, and dragged it downwards into the pit. When the wolf disappeared beneath the surface, Tyran released his magic and allowed the ground to solidify, burying the creature in a tomb of sand.

The female Vucari let out a cry but was cut short by three arrows in quick succession decorating her bare chest. Tyran snorted a contemptuous laugh. So much for vengeance.

Tyran slung his shield onto his back and turned to face Drem, who was lowering his bow.

"The Vucari are retreating to the sea, Ser Tyran, as you predicted."

"How many dead?"

Drem handed him a cloth to wipe the head of his mace. "We are still counting, Ser, but rough estimates put us at no more than ten or fifteen with another ten wounded."

"Good." Tyran clenched his jaw and continued, "And, Drem, see that you focus on those who can be saved this time. We don't have the time or the resources to make men comfortable. This campaign has nearly come to an end."

"Of course, Ser Tyran."

"Enemy dead?"

"Perhaps twice as many. Throat-cutters will give us a better idea of the numbers soon enough."

Tyran nodded, watching his Stuhia walk about the field gathering their injured and killing the Vucari bleeding into the sand. "Where is my brother?"

"Reports are that he was struck in the head with a stone and collapsed." Drem hesitated.

Tyran raised his hand to silence the Voivode. He did not even consider the possibility Drast would be dead. Not because it would not break him to learn of it, but because Drast had the uncanny ability to keep his chestnuts out of the fire. The man's luck matched that of Wolos himself.

"Find him."

Chapter III

Drast touched the lump on the back of his head and grimaced. He had come to learn he had been dropped by a stone and sling. He could think of nothing worse than being taken down by the weapon of a shepherd.

He knew he needed to wear a helm, but he had yet to find one that did not restrict his eyesight unnecessarily. But those simple shepherd weapons could be just as deadly as his bow—he had once seen a man's skull caved in from a fist-sized rock launched from fifty feet. He sighed heavily, hooking his bow over his shoulder.

"Ser Drast?"

"Don't call me that!" Drast snarled. The pain in the back of his head was not doing him any favors.

Walstan bowed. "My apologies."

Drast worked to clear his face of anger. "What is it you need, Walstan?"

"I am here to provide you with a count of the dead and injured."

Drast nodded, still rubbing the back of his head.

"Thirteen dead. Sixteen severely injured. I would guess perhaps four will likely die before morning."

Drast forestalled him. "We will not be staying long enough to find out. If arrangements cannot be made for them to travel with us, see that their passing is quick and painless."

"Of course, Ser Drast."

Drast raised an eyebrow at him and he dipped his head again as an apology. "Did Simon survive?"

Walstan cocked his head. "Yes, Se...Drast."

"Just my luck," Drast muttered.

"Would you like me to…?" He let the question hang.

Drast paused a moment to rub the stubble on his chin, eyeing Walstan. Could he trust him? He had known Walstan for a long while, but trust was a hard thing to come by. "No, Walstan. I am not sure the Arkhon would appreciate that."

Walstan smiled conspiratorially. "Yes, but perhaps that lack of appreciation would create unique opportunities for your family."

"Walstan, the politics of Lairhein are like using Koldovstvo."

His Voivode lifted an eyebrow, clearly confused by the analogy.

"Before you start to fuss," Drast smirked, placing his hand on Walstan's shoulder to secure the man's attention, "consider what you know about Koldovstvo. Do all Stuhia use Koldovstvo in the same way? My brother or Simon? You or I?"

"Certainly not," Walstan dithered, his eyes darting back and forth. Drast squeezed the man's shoulder, encouraging him to continue. After a short hesitation, he elaborated, "There are eight cruxes of Koldovstvo and each of us is well-practiced in one *sort*, maybe two."

"No, it is not practice."

Walstan hurried to explain himself. "It is determined by our bloodline, I meant. Each Stuhia is stronger in a specific crux, dependent on what blood is in our veins. We all age to a lesser degree when we use the magic that comes most naturally."

"Yes. That is the more correct thing to say, Walstan."

Walstan dipped his head like a child who had pleased his father. "Yes, Ser Drast."

He snorted at the title. "See, it is not practice which makes the Stuhia gifted with a particular type. The Kaligula family can easily touch the void, whereas the Arkhon's family, including Simon, manipulates stone."

"And my family can wield—"

"Yes, yes," Drast sighed, cutting off Walstan, "but there is more to consider. Do you and I shape Koldovstvo in the same way? Does it stir in you as it does in me? Can you produce Koldovstvo, mold it, or impress it on the world around you like me?"

"No," Walstan said, "how could we? I am not even certain my bloodline would allow me to touch the crux of the void. I do not have the skill."

"Mm." Drast grunted as Tyran might when something so profound was stated. Drast could not help but think of other bloodlines—or individuals—who could touch other cruxes as healers might, when he could not. Drast could not spend time on the point and filled the silence with another question to guide his Voivode along. "And do you think that Tyran or I experience Koldovstvo in the same way?"

"I suppose not."

"Of course not," Drast corrected, squeezing Walstan's shoulder again. The man was captivated by the conversation. He supposed he had been fascinated too, when his father had first explained it to him. "Koldovstvo is formed by my own perception, created in my own mind." Drast finally released Walstan and pointed at his temple for emphasis. "Koldovstvo is not only specific—distinct—to my being—for me—but it flows naturally through my veins; the craft is imprinted upon me in such a way that I have no choice but to be who I am."

"But wielding Koldovstvo still impacts the world around you and yourself. Every action has a consequence, which could bring a bloody and untimely end to either your enemy or yourself."

"And in that way," Drast drove his point home, slapping Walstan on the shoulder, "the politics of Lairhein are the same. The players in governance perceive politics differently, viscerally, and if your instincts are wrong...well—" Drast moved his finger across his neck to signify the impending result.

"Drast," Tyran grunted.

He had not heard his brother approach, but hearing his name, Drast turned his head to face Tyran. The man stepped quickly across the sands towards him. Seeing Tyran close swept away any thoughts of pain, duty, or the dead littering the shoreline around them. He waved a dismissive hand towards Walstan.

"Tyran." Drast lifted his hand to clasp Tyran's when he approached. Drast pulled him close. He wrapped an arm around the man's shoulder in an awkward embrace. Neither of them was much for any kind of display of affection, and Tyran less so. The large man self-consciously stepped away from him. "I should say something dramatic but no words come to mind."

"Mm."

Drast noticed his brother's deeper tone. "You have changed." He frowned—what he said was not what he meant.

Tyran grumbled, "No man goes into the Shade and expects to stay the same. How is Father? It has been a week since I saw him in Klukas."

Drast paused. He had not traveled within the shadow plane of Klukas for some time. Although he had mastered walking through the thin fabric of space between this world and the next, most Stuhia did not use this skill often, especially within the parameters of the city. It left the physical body too vulnerable. The Stuhia normally used Klukas for communication with each other over a long distance.

"Father is fine," Drast answered. "He has not said much about you until recent weeks, but that is not unusual. He rarely speaks to me."

"And Isolde?"

Drast raised an eyebrow at the mention of Tyran's betrothed. Of course, Tyran would want to know about her well-being, but his brother had to know their father was not any keener about

Tyran being smitten now than when he had left for the Shade. "Surely you have spoken with her within Klukas?"

He shook his head. "For a month or so, we did. It became too risky the farther into the Shade we traveled. It is the same reason you and I did not speak often."

Drast shrugged. His dismissal from Tyran in Klukas was expected and hardly considered a second time. Drast imagined Tyran had been firmer in quieting Isolde from contacting him in the shadow plane. "She still waits for you, if that is what you need to hear. I have not spoken with her much. I cannot say I have had much reason for it."

"She is a good woman. For her to wait for me after all this time," he paused, "I cannot help but be bound to her."

"Is that all it takes? Waiting?" Drast raised an eyebrow. "Because I am pretty sure you are going to find a herd of women waiting at the gates of Lairhein."

Tyran grunted, which Drast took as satisfaction with the response. With his brother, however, it was hard to tell. Still, he hoped Tyran would finally get rid of the naïve, whiny woman.

Drast glanced over Tyran's shoulder to take in the rolling cart carrying the three-headed serpent. The fabric had been hooked again, keeping the beast hidden from sight. He could only imagine the reaction from the Stuhia within the city if the monster had remained unconcealed.

Walstan was counting the men and resetting the ranks for a march back to Lairhein. No one was within earshot. This might be the only time for conversation before seeing their father.

Drast eyed his brother in silence. Tyran stood vigilant and stone-faced, scanning the world around them. Drast suddenly felt inferior to his younger brother. While he had been forced to play servant to his father's whims in Lairhein, Tyran had become a warlord in the Shade.

Drast no more than opened his mouth when he caught sight of Ser Simon speeding towards them, his eyes widening with each step.

"What is it for?" Simon said, breaking up the reunion. He balanced his spear at his side, his other hand pulling at his thin mustache.

"What is what for?" Tyran's words were quick, as though he had been expecting the question to come. His steady, green gaze locked onto the Arkhon's son.

Drast recognized a film of coldness set in his brother's face. Masking a grin, he reflected a similar position and squared off to face Simon.

"Ser Tyran, we don't have time for games."

"True."

A few beats passed while Simon awaited more, but Tyran made no move to speak.

Finally, Simon spoke. "Do you know who I am?"

Tyran stepped forward. He pulled back his shoulders, showing off the breadth of his muscle. "I don't much care."

Drast nearly stepped back at the frankness of his brother. A blanket *no* or *yes* would have sufficed. Drast could not conceal his surprise when Tyran took another step forward, casting a shadow over Simon with his height. The Arkhon's son barely reached Tyran's chest.

His brother had never been any good at remembering faces, and a year away guaranteed he saw the small man as just another soldier. An impudent soldier, who needed to be put in his place. Drast knew he should intervene. He should make Tyran aware Simon was the Arkhon's son. But then again, it could be interesting to see where this would go.

Simon cocked his chin and blinked. Drast scowled. He could not believe Tyran had gotten the man to close his eyes only by stepping forward and puffing his chest.

"Hold—"

Tyran interrupted Simon. "Go find your place in the ranks before I pick you up and put you there myself. I have traveled to the Shade and back and don't have the patience to deal with boys who don't recognize their betters."

Drast struggled to withhold a smile. His brother never let his emotions show. He bolstered Tyran's suspicions. "I saw you skulking about. Why did you wait so long to approach?"

Tyran snorted at the comment, not giving Simon time to respond. "Skulking, eh? Mice skulk. Weasels skulk. Rats skulk. It is time you skulked back to where you came from and hope I don't take a mind to step on you."

Drast felt a grin slip onto his face. Tyran paid no attention to him, focused on Simon. And Simon's eyes stayed locked on his brother. He never got the chance to play up on Tyran, his brother was usually too in control to fall for his manipulations. Stone to the head or not, it was a good day.

Simon sneered. "You are that much a fool to insult me, Ser Tyran! When we return to Lairhein, you will learn what it means to speak ill towards *your* betters." The man snorted before turning away from them and marching back across the sands.

Tyran turned his head with a jolt, jaw opening slightly.

Drast barked a laugh. "He is Simon Kluk, the Arkhon's son. He was sent to oversee your return."

"I see." Any light in Tyran's eyes deadened. He rarely got angry. Usually, he seemed bored, but Drast knew his brother had retreated into his head. Somewhere in there the wheels were turning and he would not get him back for some time.

Drast watched Simon stalk among the soldiers, casting angry looks towards Tyran. Still chuckling, Drast shifted his eyes between the Arkhon's son and Tyran. But his smile slipped when he saw Walstan meet with Simon and the two put their heads together before walking on.

He was not sure what Walstan was doing, but he did not like it. Could he trust him?

He turned his attention back to his brother. "What is the dragon for, Tyran?"

Tyran spoke in a half-whisper. "Father will use it to give us the power to rule over Lairhein. We will kill Arkhon Kluk and the rest of the royal bloodline. Knowing Father, he has other plans."

"Doesn't he always?" Drast muttered. "But I suppose we need to get the dragon back to our estate first? And before Simon returns to his *royal* father, of course."

Tyran nodded.

Drast grinned. "We can prevent that little mishap right now." He quickly unshouldered his bow, nocked an arrow briefly touched with Koldovstvo, drew, and fired. The arrow flew straight up into the air. In a blink, he had returned his bow to his shoulder.

His brother's eyes bulged. "What are you doing?"

"Disposing of a problem." Drast shrugged. "A stray arrow happened to slay the Arkhon's son. Freak accident, is all. No way to say where it came from."

"You cannot simply kill him. I am not saying he should not die, but we need a plan first." Tyran hissed. "Plausible deniability!"

Cries erupted in the distance, soldiers scrambling to and fro. Drast showed his teeth. "Too late. Problem solved."

Chapter IV

"Eplich is dead, Ser Tyran. Who would you like to take his place?" Drem's voice added to the cacophony of the marching soldiers and creaking of the wagon.

Tyran blinked several times, trying to stop the burning in his eyes. Each step was a chore. Lairhein could not be much farther. He cast a reproachful glance at the sun.

"Ser?"

"You can!" Tyran snarled.

The Voivode's jaw clenched, the blood draining from his face. "Yes. Yes, Ser Tyran. Of course." He bowed jerkily before turning to take his place by the wagon that carried the dragon.

Drem had left as quickly as he came.

Tyran wanted nothing more than to think of Isolde. Her eyes—her smile—her laugh. Her...

Drast was a fool for killing Simon Kluk. His brother only thought about himself and never gave any thought to his actions or the consequences. Tyran would be the one who must answer to their father for Drast's rashness when they reached Lairhein. After a year, nothing had changed.

Feeling eyes on him, Tyran turned to meet Drast's gaze. "What?"

Drast snorted. "You did not hear a word I said, did you?"

Tyran grunted.

"I *said*," Drast wet his lips as if preparing to start again, "Father is probably scheming for something more than ruling Lairhein. I cannot imagine the rulership of the Stuhian people will be enough for him. Nothing ever is," he scoffed.

"Mm," Tyran mumbled, looking at his feet. Drast had the tendency to start pointless conversations in a vain attempt to make amends. His brother was likely second-guessing himself. He had no interest in indulging Drast. Tyran wanted to be angry.

For several paces, he continued to feel Drast's eyes on him. His brother would not leave him be until Tyran forgave him. Drast persisted. "Anyway, I thought you liked Drem? Good soldier and all that? I am surprised that you would ask him to waste away his years purifying the serpent."

"He will be fine."

"If you say so."

Tyran grunted. Among his soldiers, Drem was one of the few men worth knowing. The man followed orders. No questions, no balking, and no blaming. Drem was a good soldier, but someone had to use Koldovstvo to keep the serpent from rotting before it reached Lairhein.

"He could use some extra grey in his hair," Tyran added.

Drast only nodded. Knowingly. Like he knew…something. Tyran hated when Drast acted like he could read him. For all he knew, he could, but he did not need to act like it.

Tyran averted his eyes and held his neck, muscles as stiff as a washboard. He would not show signs of weakness around Drast. He should not have to remind himself that there had been much worse within the Shade. He could handle his brother's piercing eyes.

He needed sleep. He could barely understand his own thoughts. Which, of course, begged the question of how Drast thought *he* could.

He stifled a yawn that made his jaw crack.

"You wanted to kill him too," Drast said.

Tyran did not turn his eyes from the ground. He did not flinch. He made sure his face appeared as solid as stone pressed between stone.

"Mm."

He had good reason to be angry with Drast's lack of restraint. Killing Simon pushed their plans ahead, and Father would be less than pleased. Invariably, Tyran would be caught in the whirlwind of his father's wrath, all because Drast could not wait to kill a man for a few more days. He knew how this story unfolded. It had been told and retold throughout their childhood.

"I will take that as an affirmative."

Tyran frowned. "Don't mock me. I spent too long in the Shade for you to mess this up."

His brother slowed, clearly taken aback by Tyran's tone. He ran a hand through his red hair, disheveled and out of place against his pale skin. "Mess it up? I have done nothing more than simplify the matter. If the pieces are in place—as you have said—then I have left nothing to chance. You know well enough that Simon could have been a dangerous enemy in Lairhein. If worse comes to worst, we tell the Arkhon that Simon died in the battle."

"There were plenty who witnessed a different story."

"My men are loyal to me and our family, Tyran. They would string any man up who spoke against my word."

Tyran fixed his brother with a steady gaze. Drast acted as if rules did not apply to him. As if men did as they were told. "You don't know how they would behave when offered silver or land. No man is that loyal."

"You and I have a bond that is not swayed by worldly things."

"We are not the norm. I would think you had figured that out by now. You are naïve, Drast."

His brother rolled his shoulders. "Maybe we are not and maybe I am, but why do you think others don't have the same capacity? You speak of people as though you are not one yourself. I don't question your reason to err on the side of caution, but some things are meant to be. Father's quest will be done. Nothing will stop that."

Tyran grimaced. Drast's argument was inscrutable. The man was a fatalist, hoping for things as though they were already inscribed in the stars. He could try to point out the lack of reason behind such a claim. For instance, the two of them were only scarcely aware of what their father's plan truly was, but he did not have the energy to argue with the man.

"I hope you are right."

Drast grinned. "Of course, I am right. Did you forget that you killed a dragon?"

"It doesn't mean much if we don't get it to the estate," Tyran smirked.

"I don't envy you, Tyran," Drast said matter-of-factly. "Living in your head with all that naysaying has to be exhausting."

"You have no idea."

"Honestly, I must admit that I am a bit envious, Tyran." Drast shuffled next to him. The smile was still painted on his face. "It had to be something trekking through the Shade Fells."

"Envious, why?" Tyran glowered. "It was a terrible experience. The Shade is murky, gloomy, and with caverns that twist every which way. With the winter months, it was hard to tell which way was what, especially when the snow began to stick. For weeks, I thought we would die without ever finding a way out, or we'd be eaten by a dragon."

Drast may have actually been rubbing his hands together with excitement. "Sure, sure. But did you see the entrance to the Netherworld?"

Tyran glanced at his brother for only a moment before setting his eyes back to the ground ahead of him. "No. But I cannot say that I was looking for it either. There were enough beasts running about. I was not about to go out searching for more."

His brother's shoulders slumped noticeably. "I was hoping for better stories."

Tyran grimaced. "I am sorry to disappoint. You are lucky I have returned with any story to tell. If spring had not come, I might still be traipsing around among the rocks."

"Yes," Drast responded. "The spring equinox came right on time this year. Strega, the God of the Nine Winds, was victorious in the fight against Marheena."

"I am aware of the mythos of the gods and the seasons," Tyran said.

Drast shrugged. "The Temple of Wolos has been preaching the cycle of seasons for the past month in full accord." Drast tilted his chin, mocking the priests who would tell the tale. "Marheena, the Seamstress of Nightmares, brings the cold and the darkness of winter, tormenting the living for months. Wolos, the Horned God, the Protector of the Eternal Spring and the Ash Tree, prevents Marheena from ruling over Aenar from winter solstice til spring equinox, until Strega the White-Bearded comes to kill the Goddess of the Netherworld."

"And then Gero, Marheena's brother, defies his sister's love even more by bringing the harvest and vegetation," Tyran said. "It is strange people think that the way of the world will ever change. The cycle of the seasons is as affirmed as the cycle of life and death."

"So it seems."

"Mm."

Drast lifted his hand towards the horizon. "Welcome home."

A chilled wind swept from the north, touching Tyran's skin. Ignoring the sensation, he examined his home city. He felt as though it had been ages since he had seen the mighty towers of Lairhein glimmering on the coast of the Neabou Sea. Within the red granite walls, eight hundred men, women, and children were well into their day. Tyran was glad his father had avoided the common fishing industry and instead chosen to build his trade in war.

Ignoring his fatigue, Tyran pressed towards the front of the armies. "Hold. Hold."

He heard his Voivodes echoing him. Drem yelled the loudest. "Hold!"

The armies slowed to a halt. Tyran stepped quickly to the front of the mass.

Tyran towered above most of the men. He looked beyond those within his reach and lifted his voice with Koldovstvo.

"Brothers, a year ago, we departed swearing fidelity to our campaign and our people, and I remind each of you, it is your duty to uphold that oath. What we have felt. What we have heard. What we have seen—is for us alone. Our struggles in war are what bind us as brothers. Don't forsake those who have fought to return you home. Don't forget!"

Whispers and sliding glances towards the wagon sifted through the throng of men. Yet there were none who spoke a word in opposition.

Tyran harshened his tone. "There will be no forgiveness to those who do."

Drast's voice whispered behind him. "Well done. You have scared the piss right out of them."

He released Koldovstvo. "Out of all the things worth fearing in this world, they should learn to fear the Kaligula name most."

The Kaligula estate was built on the southern side of the city and decorated with the same red granite as the city walls. Tyran looked on his childhood home feeling calmer than he thought he would. Although not large, by any means, the estate's courtyard housed the recruits for both the soldiers among Tyran and Drast's armies and the soldiers who made up the town watch. The training yard and barracks sat along the south end of the courtyard and the stables along the north. The sounds of clashing swords nearly drowned out the creaking wagon following behind him. The sounds of home were comforting to hear.

Tyran glanced over his shoulder at the handful of men that guarded the covered dragon. Finally, the long campaign had come to an end.

Drast had not moved from his side. "Our home has not changed much. I swear the incoming conscripts grow more ignorant and less coordinated every day."

Drem, who guided the wagon, was within earshot. "Ser Drast, a soldier is only as skilled as he is taught to be, much like a child who learns discipline from a parent."

"Don't call me that!" Drast growled. "Soldiers with mush for brains are better off being fishermen."

Tyran fingered the bronze head of his mace and snorted. He had no interest in arguing about how a man became learned. "Men are who they are, and nothing more. It is the job of their betters to determine how best to use what skills they have."

"A valid point," Drast responded. "Though it seems most men have far more worth being a practice dummy than an actual soldier."

"I can only wonder if such things were said of me when I had gone through training," Drem muttered.

"Mm."

"Very reassuring, Tyran," Drast laughed.

Tyran snorted, realizing his grunt had been taken for agreement. "Every man who wants to join the army is measured. He would not be here if he was not superior to the other soldiers."

"Ah, yes," Drast snickered, "Drem is a fool among idiots. Or an idiot among fools. I can never remember which, but I doubt either is terribly flattering."

"Don't taunt him. He is a good soldier."

Drast turned his ear upward mockingly. "Tyran, did you just give a compliment? The Shade did change you."

Drem spoke beneath his breath. "Ser Tyran, your father comes."

Tyran and Drast both faced forward with the precision of a brigand falling into line. They dipped their heads while Drem fell to a knee in recognition. The trainees, instructors, and any man in the courtyard immediately dropped to the ground as Drem did. Not even the Arkhon demanded such respect.

Serder Dagmar Kaligula was a broad man, though shorter than both of his sons. With deliberate haste, he marched across the courtyard towards Tyran and Drast. The deep red color of his beard and the way his locks of hair fell below his ears reflected the appearance of his sons. The hints of grey that patched his mane like a mended cloak were the exception. Ripples in the man's threaded robe, red as splattered blood, shattered any sense of serenity, much like the firestorm of the leviathans within the Shade.

His father spoke; of this, Tyran was sure. But he could only hear silence, taking in the warming sun, the sea breeze, and the sudden stillness of practice swords.

"Father, it is not as if there was a back entrance to wheel it through," Drast sighed. Apparently, his brother had heard the question that Tyran had missed. "We assured that the wagon was well covered and maintained. No one has given us more than a second glance, and the gate guard was not about to ask us any questions when we came through with two armies at our backs."

Dagmar scoffed, "You aim to tell me, Drast, that there is no concern of Arkhon Kluk coming to knock at our gate? He has plenty of people in the city watching our estate. You know this better than any other. I did not train you to be so blind."

Drast's eyes flashed. "There is always threat of the Kluks coming into our courtyard, Father." He shrugged. "But if it *were* today, then it would put an end to all this dancing about."

"No, we are not ready," the Serder said, "and besides, the courtyard of my estate is not the place to discuss such matters." The man squinted at the soldiers kneeling around the wagon. He seemed to measure their life, their loyalty.

Tyran thought his father was deciding whether to slaughter everyone within the courtyard to silence them. To do so was not beyond the man's reach.

His father had not welcomed him back, but Tyran felt a moment of recognition and reunion pass between them. "Well, there is a pretty good chance that today is the day. Ser Simon Kluk is dead."

"The Arkhon's son?" Serder Kaligula's face reddened. He had been pulled suddenly from whatever thoughts he may have been contemplating. "How?"

Tyran forced his gaze to stay on his father and worked to keep his voice even. "He fell during battle. We were ambushed by the Vucari on the shoreline beyond the Shade. Drast's army provided ample support to overcome them, but...Simon did not survive the encounter."

"Is that so?"

Tyran noticed the Serder look to Drast. The word of one son was never good enough. Their father perpetually looked for weakness between the two, for some indication of falsity.

Drast shrugged as if he had as much interest in the topic as counting scales on a fish. Still, Tyran saw his brother tightening his jaw to conceal a grin from splitting his face.

Drem spoke from where he knelt. "It is, Serder Kaligula. Many of us witnessed his death on the battlefield."

"The Arkhon will never believe that story," their father grumbled. "We must start the ritual immediately. Pull the wagon to the stables in the back. I will gather the book."

"As you wish, Father," Tyran said.

Serder Kaligula nodded. Pivoting and muttering under his breath, he stormed back towards the house as hastily as he had come.

Tyran turned away from the wicked smile that erupted on Drast's face.

Drast smacked him in the shoulder and pointed back towards Drem. "You are right. He is a good soldier."

Chapter V

Men flitted to and fro in the courtyard, Tyran shouting orders in anticipation of the Arkhon's arrival, and the dragon's corpse being pulled laboriously through the mix to the stables were all concert in the madness. In Tyran's absence, Drast had been forced to do much of the legwork, and letting someone else do the yelling and commanding came as something of a relief. Drast knew he could yell as well as Tyran, but it became tedious. If he started giving orders, then men started expecting orders, and he wanted no part of such nonsense.

As soon as Tyran had set all the wheels in motion, the two walked towards the stables themselves. Tyran walked with his head down, his visage unreadable. His brother remained, as ever, truly difficult to read. Drast could usually call a man's mood from a hundred yards, but there were times when he thought Tyran had simply blown out his emotions like blowing out a candle.

"It will work out, Tyran," he suggested after a moment.

His brother did not even look up. "We will see."

"Are you still angry? Simon needed to die. You know that."

"Mm."

The famed grunt. Perfect. How was a grunt even a response? It was like trying to talk to a horse. "So, what is this ritual Father spoke of?"

His brother cast a glance his way, sighing as if speaking were a chore. "I am not sure. I think we drink the blood, but I don't know what else there could be."

Drast blinked. Drink dragon blood? "Well, fantastic."

Tyran met his eye. "Mm."

The wagon had already been drawn into the stables, dragon in tow. The structure was not quite large enough to accommodate much more than the wagon with the dragon itself. Stables lined the walls on either side, allowing for up to six horses, but the Kaligulas owned only four—two for the cart and two for riding. The stables smelled like straw and horse manure.

Drast sneezed.

He could never get used to the stink, and it would be stuck in his clothes the rest of the day.

Tyran began untying the canvas covering the dragon, pulling it back to reveal the creature. It was Drast's first good look at the thing. He had heard tales of dragons, certainly, but reality did not compare to fiction.

Three heads. That revelation alone kept Drast occupied for several moments. He had seen a two-headed sheep once, but it had shared a neck. With the dragon, each head had its own long neck connecting to the wedge-shaped torso. Leathery wings folded against the sides, twice as long as the frame. A long tail curled around its body, and four legs, short but thicker than the necks, were folded beneath it. Though quite long, it could not have been any heavier than a horse.

"Don't touch its hide," Tyran said as he tossed the canvas to the side. "It looks dry and scaly like a snake's, but it secretes an oily substance when touched. It burns like fire, and water just causes it to spread. One of my men nearly died from it and another nearly killed himself saving him with Koldovstvo."

Drast retracted the hand that had been unconsciously edging towards the creature. "That is…good to know."

"Mm."

Serder Kaligula strode into the stable, dark purple robes swirling with each decisive step, a great book hugged against his chest in one arm, the *Varkolak*. The ancient tome held the history of the Stuhia, and their father claimed his copy was the last. Other copies had been destroyed with the fall of the Carian Council.

"Why are you not prepared?" their father asked.

"I see you dressed for the occasion," Drast snorted.

Drast's vision blurred as his father's hand collided with his face, knocking him to his knees. The sharp edges of his house ring bit through Drast's cheek. "Don't be smart."

"What needs to be done, Father?" Tyran spoke evenly. Showing concern was a sign of weakness. Tyran knew as well as Drast that a hint of alarm would have resulted in him receiving a portion of their father's wrath as well. That is, unless he decided Drast should administer the punishment; an eventuality not entirely uncommon. Half of the scars Drast had earned in his life had come from his brother's hand.

"Don't smile at me like a fool!"

Drast realized his father had been talking to him and replaced his smile with a grimace. He did not even recognize when he was smiling sometimes. He had a grin on his face constantly—even when angry. He had no control over it. While his smiling simply unnerved most, it sparked his father's anger.

"We need silver goblets. Silver," Serder Kaligula enunciated emphatically. "A strong bull, a budding flower, the fangs of a snake, black earth, and a clay mug filled with clear water."

Drast bit his tongue against another remark. Their father was testing them after Tyran's long absence. Father wanted to see if Tyran's resolve had waned while away. Drast straightened his back.

"I suppose these things have been prepared, Father?" Tyran said, as if the ritual was common course.

Dagmar nodded and motioned to a rear stall in the stables. "Yes. The bull is here. The rest needs to be retrieved from my study."

"Drem!" Tyran called at once.

"No! This is not a task for your Voivodes or soldiers," Father snapped. He eyes turned to Drast. "Go retrieve the items. A tray on my desk holds all that is needed. I wish to speak with your brother."

"Yes, Father." Drast bowed.

As soon as Drast exited the stables, he began searching for his brother's right-hand man. Drem, having heard Tyran call his name, rapidly approached. Trustworthy, his brother had said. He hoped Tyran was correct.

"Drem." Drast spoke evenly, trying to import the seriousness of the matter. "I need you to retrieve some items from my father's study."

As soon as his brother's Voivode departed towards the estate, Drast sleuthed to the entrance of the stables.

He could not help but think his father *forgetting* the items in the study was merely an excuse to get Drast out of the way so he could speak with Tyran.

"…seems to have done well. You don't need me, Father. Why not let me pursue my own ends?"

"You think of that trollop you were chasing after before I sent you after your destiny? You lose sight of the larger world when your mind is on her and forget that you are Ser Tyran, Dragon Slayer!"

Drast tried not to snort a giggle at the epithet. Did that make him Drast the Simon Slayer?

"Please, Father, I…"

"Such loose women will come and go and give you nothing but anguish and agony. If you stay true to the path I have set for you, if you heed your father—your *wise* father—you will have immortality in your grasp; eternal life, and such women will sprout about you like flowers in spring because when you cannot die, life is eternal spring, my son. But you must stay true!"

"I understand, Father, but…"

"No. If you understand, then there is nothing else to add or to contradict. Obey the will of your father."

"Yes, Father."

Sometimes he wished Tyran would simply do as their father asked. Drast tried his best to do so, even if he did have a smart lip sometimes. Tyran needed to act more like Drem in relation to their father.

Drast nodded to himself. Yes, if Tyran had one weakness, it was a lack of loyalty to their father. For all that he went to the Shade and back, he did so from being forced rather than in obeisance to their father's will.

"Now, assist me in preparing for the ritual. Fetch the bull."

Drast stopped listening and stepped away from the stables to intercept Drem when he came along. Always more of the same. Tyran longing for a normal life and Father demanding something exceptional. He could understand Tyran's want, but he could never compete against Father's will. Whatever faults he might hold, he would remain a dutiful son. Oftentimes, he simply wished his father would recognize that much.

Drem came along shortly with a silver tray. Drast eyed the items and determined everything was present from his father's list. Dismissing the man, he turned and entered the stables.

"Here you are, Father." Drast set it down on a nearby bench used for tack and harness repair.

"We are short on time. I would think you would show a little haste for want of utility."

"I apologize, Father."

Serder Kaligula spat. "I have no use for apologies! Words are nothing. Less than nothing. Spend your sweat assisting your brother instead of testing my forbearance!"

Drast turned to Tyran, whose stony gaze said volumes about his own conversation with their father. Together, they brought the bull from the stable to stand before the cart. The animal was uncommonly amenable to their direction and Drast suspected their father had already touched its mind with Koldovstvo, rendering the beast dumb.

When the bull stood dully in place, Dagmar handed Drast a knife, the entirety of the weapon carved from a single piece of bone. "This blade was made from the thigh bone of a dragon by the Carian Council more than a millennium ago for this ritual. The bull is helpless. Castrate it."

Drast could feel his lips pulling away from his teeth in a smile, but turned his gaze quickly from his father, catching Tyran's eye as he knelt beside the bull. Tyran's eyes were still stony. His brother was likely in his head; he probably did not even hear what their father had said. The joke would be on him when Drast popped up with the bull testicles in his hand.

He could hear his father muttering beneath his breath, speaking the words of the ritual as he set to work. The bull did not seem to notice him as he worked, not even a snort or a stamped hoof. Drast suddenly wanted very much to know exactly what his father had done to the bull to put it in this state. He knew some tricks with Koldovstvo, but nothing like this.

When he stood with the bull's testicles, his father had stopped reading from the *Varkolak*. Tyran had moved from the bull, the black earth from the tray now on the dragon's head. He had not even heard his father give his brother the direction.

Drast began to wonder if their father concealed parts of the ritual so neither brother saw the entire thing. It made perfect sense as to why Drast could not understand his father's words and why he could not remember having seen Tyran move. Of course, he did not know if Tyran had heard the bit about the bull testicles. His brother was in such a mood he probably would not blink if the bull suddenly caught fire and ran from the stables.

"Place them on the black earth, Drast." His father spoke in a humming, emotionless voice.

He obeyed his father's direction. The sound of more incomprehensible words followed from his father. Looking about revealed Tyran cutting the bud from the flower with the bone knife. Drast did not remember giving him the knife after using it on the bull.

Drast looked down at his bloody hands. How had their father hidden parts of the ritual from them? It made no sense. He felt as if he were in a dream, leaping from moment to moment.

The bull testicles were on fire, a snake fang sticking out from each. Drast nearly jumped out of his skin, seeing the odd image with the bull's bits burning in a pile of dirt on top of a dragon's face. He was definitely missing something out of this entire ritual, maybe something about rejuvenation and life? That had to be part of it. Strength? Maybe the fire. What did the fangs represent? Where did the bud from the flower go? Where did the moon go on black nights? Why did the sea rise?

Drast shook his head. His thoughts were a jumbled mess.

A silver chalice in his hands, covered in blood.

"Drink," his father said.

The cup of water had been dumped on top of the fire.

"Drink," his father said.

The fire was out.

"Drink," his father said.

The earth had been washed away.

"Drink," his father said.

The dragon's blood pooled on the ground.

"Drink," his father said.

The bull was dead.

"Drink," his father said.

Drast drank.

Salt and metal. All he could taste was salt and metal.

He blinked and looked about, his head finally cleared. He did not feel anything. "Is that it?" He thought he would feel the power of the dragon's blood after drinking it. A reinvigoration, a burning in his stomach. Stronger. Something, at least. Instead, he felt like washing his mouth of the taste of salt and metal.

His father furiously scanned the book. The vellum pages of the *Varkolak* threatened to tear with each turning. Tyran did not look impressed by the ritual either. His brother had blood covering half of his body, and when Drast looked down, he saw he was not much different. The blood from the two animals covered the stable floor. The horses in the stable were stamping their hooves and rolling their eyes.

Drast shook his head. "We tried, Father. Perhaps something went wrong. We can get another dragon."

"No, fool!" His father sneered, the blood staining his lips and teeth giving him a malevolent appearance. "We cannot. For good or ill the ritual can only be performed once. Only those with an adequate bloodline can benefit from it. Our blood is too weak!"

"How do we know we were not successful?"

Their father's eyes leapt from the book. "Yes. Yes, how do we know?" He licked his bloody lips. "A test. We need a test." His eyes fell on Drast. "Fly."

"What?"

"You are my son, Drast. You are loyal to my will. Use Koldovstvo to leave the ground."

Tyran's voice raised. "You cannot ask this. If the ritual failed, the effort alone might add enough years to him to kill him."

Serder Kaligula's eyes pierced Tyran. "Then he will die in service to his father's will. Call it a test of loyalty. Call it what you will, but when I ask one of my sons to do a thing, he should be pleased to do it!"

"Of course, Father," Drast said at once. "I will do as you ask."

He closed his eyes. The power of Koldovstvo welled up inside of him until he overflowed with the raw energy. Such power could be devastating, and simple tasks, such as flying, could kill a man. His father once told them of a young Stuhian who had attempted to walk across the sea. After only a few hundred feet, the man had aged so much he could not maintain his connection to Koldovstvo. The effort weakened the Stuhia, causing him to fall beneath the surface and drown. The effort involved in flying was tenfold.

Drast felt his feet lift from the blood-soaked earth. He waited to feel his life waste away, the ever-present sensation of his joints stiffening, his skin sagging, his muscles weakening.

The sensation did not come.

At least, not in the way he expected. Only slightly were those effects felt, when the effort of flying alone should have turned him into a husk.

Opening his eyes, he saw a wide smile on his father's face and could not help but smile himself. He descended to the ground. "It worked, Father."

A horn in the courtyard interrupted any celebration which might have come. Tyran grunted, "The Arkhon's horn."

Serder Kaligula, now in excellent spirits, chuckled gaily, his eyes flashing with fire. "Let us go and meet him, yes?"

With a wave of his hand, Koldovstvo surged through the space to clear the filth and blood from the three of them, leaving them as pristine as if they were fresh from a bath. The wanton use of Koldovstvo did not add so much as a grey hair to his father's head.

"There is no reason to reveal our newfound power." Taking his great book, he used Koldovstvo to reduce its size and slide it into one of the voluminous pockets of his robe. "Nor its source."

Drast nodded and responded in unison with his brother. "Of course, Father."

Serder Kaligula left the stables, flanked by his two sons, his purple robes flowing grandly behind him. Drast made a conscious effort to ensure he walked with the same slow, confident, measured steps of his father and brother. He held his head straight, looking down his nose. The three of them were taller than nearly any other man in Lairhein. With their chests puffed and shoulders pulled back, their height was all the more emphasized.

The Arkhon stood inside the gate to the courtyard with his three remaining sons at his back. Beyond the gate were a dozen or so honorary guards from his house. The Arkhon appeared a grand man with a grey beard and a head full of white hair. He stood with a silent, fatherly dignity, making the slow approach of the Kaligulas seem childish. He was thick about the middle, stout in the chest, and his age, rumor said, had come from the use of Koldovstvo in battle, unlike Serder Kaligula, who had garnered his many years seeking immortality and power in rituals and sacraments.

The three came to a stop twenty feet from the Arkhon and his entourage. The ruler of Lairhein spoke in a deep, heavy voice. "Serder Kaligula. I have come to speak to you of my son, Simon."

Dagmar bowed his head slightly. "I had concluded as much, Jonafel." Their father's failure to use his superior's title did not go unnoticed by Drast. A wave of murmurs erupted from the soldiers. "It is my sad duty to inform you of his death in a conflict with the Vucari."

The Arkhon tilted his head. "A conflict with the Vucari? My understanding of the matter was that his death came sometime after the battle, *Dagmar*." The aged Stuhia emphasized their father's name, imitating the lack of respect.

Serder Kaligula glanced over his shoulder. His recent joy over his newfound power appeared to be waning rapidly. "Is that so?"

Drast chewed the inside of his cheek. How far should the lie be taken? Tyran was, of course, correct. Men could be bought, their loyalty sold to the highest bidder. He could never count on his men to remain true to him. Perhaps he could kill a few as an example for future issues of trust. Shaking the thought from his head, he understood such lines of consideration did not resolve their trouble at the moment.

"Forgive me, Arkhon," Drast spoke quickly, "it was indeed after the main conflict with the Vucari. However, his death was still a direct result of that encounter, you can be assured."

"Assured?" His grey eyebrows rose. "I find nothing assuring in your account of events, young Drast. Indeed, what should a father find *assuring* in the death of a son? How should a father feel *assured* in the knowledge that where once he had a piece of his own flesh and blood, he now has a grave?" The Arkhon's voice began to rise. "Of what, pray tell, should I be *assured* against? Of what other alternative do you wish to *assure* me my son did not fall victim?"

Drast winced. Maybe assured was not the word he wanted. His attempt to help ameliorate the situation had utterly failed. He tried to work moisture into his suddenly dry mouth.

Before he could respond, his father snapped his fingers to silence him. "Jonafel, you are grieving and put too much stock in the poor choice of words of Drast. I am sure he merely wished to ensure you understood it is not our intention to withhold the truth of how your son met his untimely end."

"Forgive me if I do not find *assurance* in your proffered intentions." The Arkhon took a step forward, his three sons stepping forward with him. "However, I will not conceal my intentions from you. Nor will I leave the question of your son's fate unanswered. As Arkhon, I…"

"I challenge you to *Claduk*," Serder Kaligula cried. "It is my right! Until my challenge has been answered and the rite completed, you may lay claim to nothing I possess."

The Arkhon said nothing as he stared at the Kaligula family. "You have taken my son from me, a brother from my children, and now desire to take my throne and take a father from his family? You are a dishonorable line. You suspend justice for your own greed." He shook his head. "I am a man of honor, however, and I will follow the law, even if you lack the will to do so. Rest *assured* that after your sons lose their father, they will lose each other as well."

Chapter VI

Tyran held Isolde's silken hand, unwilling to let go while he led her into the pine glade beyond the town and outer fields. It had always been their reserved place, where they could escape even during adolescence to relish each other's company. She stumbled behind him laughing while he tugged her along.

Her hand squeezed his with the same force he held his mace in battle. Tyran met her eyes for a moment and smiled his best smile. Grinning was difficult—unnatural. Tyran knew Drast and he were different. His brother always had his teeth showing, but enjoyment did not come as easily to Tyran, and if it did, he was not accustomed to showing it.

"I cannot believe you have finally come back!" she gleamed. "The days I have wondered, the moments I have worried, the tears I have—"

"It is done," Tyran said. "There is nothing more to worry about. I am home now." He pulled her along, speaking with authority. "I told you before I left that nothing, not even the Shade, could keep me from you, Isolde. You believe me now? You know you can trust me?"

Isolde tittered. Tyran winced at the sound, doing his best to turn the expression into a smile. Isolde had waited for him. He would be here for her, too. Though the sound of her laugh was not quite what he had remembered.

Her eyes sparkled. "Yes! But I always trusted you, Tyran. Don't fault me for thinking your promises were beyond your control."

"Mm."

"My aunt had warned me…"

"About?"

Isolde kept the smile, despite her words, like Drast. "She said that war changed men. Those who have been in war would come out only thinking of survival, to kill or be killed. She said war did more than destroy the enemy—it would destroy a man's sense of self." Her voice became a whisper. "His sense of love."

Tyran tensed his shoulders. He did not like to think anything would ever be "beyond his control." Weak men and women did not have control, and Tyran knew he was not weak.

"Mm."

Suddenly, Tyran recalled something Drast had said years ago. *It would be better if you left Isolde aside. She will change you for the worse. Love is not meant for you and me.*

Drast did not disapprove of his relationship with Isolde—not as Isolde's aunt and his father did. No, Drast feared for Tyran's well-being. He knew his brother too well to doubt his intentions. Drast was an eternal optimist, and for him to worry about Tyran's dear Isolde vexed him.

"Tyran?" He realized Isolde was staring at him. The smile had disappeared. "Are you okay? You look…like you are somewhere else."

He did not answer.

"What is it?" Her unforgiving tone grated on him.

Tyran swallowed. He was glad she could not tell when he lied. "You are more beautiful than I remember."

"Oh." Isolde blushed, her hand fiddling with his red locks. She wriggled comfortably in his embrace. "If I knew a year apart would make you so sweet, I might have been more welcoming to it."

He forced a smile again. Was he really so cold that he never offered compliments? First Drem and now her. Perhaps he became a better man by being away from anyone he cared about.

"Clearly, my aunt was wrong."

"Yes," Tyran said, "she was."

Isolde gave Tyran something he had never known before, something he had thought his mother might have provided had she survived his birthing. Acceptance.

His brother knew him as a steadfast man. His army saw him as a formidable leader. His father knew him to be an unwavering son, loyal and bound by reason. Still, no one accepted him, not the way Isolde did; she loved him.

"What are you thinking about, Tyran?" Isolde asked.

"My father," he said.

"Oh." She pushed off his chest and stepped back to look him over. He could not help but notice her tone was as light as when he called her *beautiful* moments ago. "I heard he challenged Arkhon Kluk to *Claduk*. Does your father really want to hold the position of the imperial family?"

"I don't know," he lied again. Tyran had an inkling his father's ambition of becoming Arkhon was only the beginning.

"You just got home, Tyran. I cannot begin to think what it was like in the Shade. Battle after battle. I don't understand how you can support your father. Is death and bloodshed all you think about?"

Tyran tried to look away, but he found himself glaring into Isolde's eyes.

"The Kluks are a strong family. If your father dies..." she paused, tilting her head and letting her words sink in. "You and your brother are next." She leaned forward, gripping his hand, as though it might ease his anger. "I love you, Tyran. I do not want to see you dead."

"I am not going to die."

Isolde shuddered. Her eyes held water in the crevices.

"Don't cry, Isolde. Not today." Tyran could not shake the anger from his tone. He had to love her. She had waited for him. "Forget my father. Forget my brother. Forget Lairhein. Only think of us."

"I—"

He was quick to silence her pestering. "Quit! My father will not fail. He has never failed in anything." Tyran heard himself using the fatalistic language he often heard from Drast. It sounded fake coming from his mouth.

"I cannot bear to lose you again. I have only gotten you back," she cried.

"I am not going to die!" Tyran squeezed her hand, towering over her small frame.

"Tyran." She pulled her hand back. "You are hurting me."

He did not care, grabbing her shoulders. "You need to hear me. I will not die."

"Are you sure?" she whispered, looking up at him and cradling her injured hand.

"Yes," he growled.

"Then," she straightened her back, "marry me."

The words numbed him. Tyran dropped his hands to his sides. He could do nothing but stare at her. The smell of pine caused his stomach to churn. How could she ask him that *now*?

Isolde exhaled. "Say something."

Tyran had no response. He had responsibilities to his father and his brother. Isolde had done nothing but pick at him since he returned and now she wanted to marry him? Marriage was the farthest thing from his mind.

She challenged him. "Did you not ask me to be your wife before you left? Did you find some Vucari girl out there in the wilderness who has stolen your heart? Or are you still bound to me?"

Tyran had to forcibly close his mouth. He nearly choked at the mention of a Vucari. How could he ever love one of those beasts? She was forcing his hand. Trapping him. He tensed. "There is no other but you, Isolde." He tried to think of a reason—any reason—why they could not marry. "We cannot be married without ceremony; without permission from your aunt and my father. There are rules we must follow."

"I have known you for a long time, Tyran Kaligula," she contended, growing quiet. "Rules only apply to you when they serve you."

Tyran gritted his teeth, wanting to shake her.

She continued, pleading, "We could wed in secret."

"No!" Tyran's voice resounded deeper than he had intended. Fear surfaced on Isolde's face. He reminded himself she was not one of his soldiers.

The woman shrank away from him.

"No," he repeated in a softer tone. "We cannot run away and we cannot marry in secret." He reached out and touched her face. His hand shook. "But I *will* marry you."

Isolde did not smile.

Tyran struggled to find the words to reassure her. "I will speak to my father and see what can be done."

The light in her eyes diminished entirely. "You cannot live in his shadow forever, Tyran. At some point, you have to think for yourself."

Isolde turned from him. Lifting her skirts, she ran from him. Her sobs stayed with him long after she was gone from his sight.

Chapter VII

Drast trailed thirty feet behind his soldiers in secret. He had been listening to their directionless banter for most of the morning and he was still no closer to figuring out who had betrayed him. One of the four had told the Arkhon he had murdered Simon.

"Ser Drast wants us to throw the dragon's corpse into the sea, then?" Legan asked for the fifth time since leaving Lairhein. The man had a nasally voice that buzzed in Drast's ears.

The nasally voiced man had not left the rear of the wagon since leaving Lairhein. Skell, who marched beside Legan, constantly twitched the canvas to the side to peer at the corpse.

Walstan walked near the front of the wagon with the last of the four, L'ubu.

Drast's Voivode sighed. "Yes, Legan, we are throwing the accursed corpse into the sea. If that is too difficult for you to grasp, please, by all means, sit down and mull it over."

L'ubu and Skell snorted, chuckling. Drast could not help but smile himself. He had not gotten the chance to spend much time with Walstan since his father had severed his connections with those he deemed his lesser. He had forgotten the man's sense of humor.

Drast yawned, his jaw threatening to break off. Ambition filled his father to the brim after the success of the ritual, and Drast had not had much sleep in the last few days. How his father managed to continue with such mind-breaking discussions day after day baffled him. The only thing his father wanted to do was talk strategy about the upcoming contest with the Arkhon and how to manipulate the battle to ensure victory.

Drast appreciated portions of those conversations. The fact that his father wanted to talk with him was a pleasant change of pace. And, because Tyran tended to be a bit rule-bound at times, Drast had been given the chance to prove himself to his father by discovering how they could cheat their way to victory in Claduk if possible.

But he needed a break. He reminded his father that they had a rotting dragon in their stables needing to be disposed of before someone noticed it or attempted to recreate the ritual. Being a menial task, he had been assigned to dispose of the corpse at once. And again, being a menial task, Drast had assigned the task to his Voivode and a few other soldiers he did not particularly trust. Not that he trusted any of them, despite what he had led Tyran to believe.

Tyran's tale of the poison covering the skin of the thing intrigued him, and he hoped he would get the opportunity to see it in action. Drast had given specific instructions to Walstan to ensure the Voivode did not make the mistake of touching the thing or doing anything foolish enough to result in his death. Walstan was a decent soldier, and while Drast did not fully trust the man, he did not want to lose him by accident.

Thirty feet or so above the four men on a rise paralleling the track that led to the ocean's edge, Drast had plenty of opportunities to listen to the men's conversation. Their talk mostly consisted of families, the war, and anticipation of what the upcoming Claduk would mean for Lairhein. Drast could have done away with all of it. His real interest was discovering who had betrayed the truth of Simon's death to the Arkhon.

Drast knew Walstan did not have any ties to Arkhon Kluk's family, but his Voivode gave him reason to pause. He often would find Walstan standing at doorways where he should not be or lingering too long after Drast had dismissed him.

However, accompanying Walstan were men like Legan, a narrow-eyed fox of a man who had worked in the Arkhon's home for several years. Drast had worked hard to learn that information. Much in the same way he had worked to discover the weakling L'ubu had a bit of heartache for one of the Arkhon's daughters, Maelili, and wide-mouthed Skell had a few outstanding debts to settle.

"What else would we do with the corpse? The thing was kept fresh with Koldovstvo for nigh a month while Ser Tyran's men brought it down out of the Shade, but it has been rotting in the stables for three days." Walstan motioned to the now putrid creature covered by canvas, not bothering to turn his head back to look at Legan. "Would you like to carve it up and serve it to your wife and kids? Maybe skin it and wear a dragon skin cloak about Lairhein? I am sure the smell will make you popular with the trollops you frequent. Naught else can be done with the thing other than tossing it into the sea. More is riding on this body than you can likely grasp. This decaying corpse will determine the fate of Lairhein."

Legan slammed his fist into the side of the wagon, startling the horse pulling it and forcing L'ubu to tighten his hold on its harness to keep it from upsetting the whole affair. "No need to be snide! I'm just saying that a dragon has not been seen in our lifetime, and now that we have one, we are tossing it out like yesterday's rubbish."

"Ah, so you do understand what we are doing?" Walstan said acerbically, stopping and turning to face the soldier. L'ubu halted the horse. "Thank Wolos, because you had me afraid I was going to have to toss you off with the condemned dragon, because I refuse to command fools in battle."

"I feel the same way about being led by them."

Legan seemed as surprised by his words as Drast felt, but Walstan reacted quickly enough. A fist to Legan's face sent the narrow-eyed man to the ground and a series of kicks from the stocky Voivode likely broke a few of the foxy man's ribs.

Drast chuckled.

He was beginning to like Walstan a bit more. He found it hard not to and suddenly wished his father was not so opposed to letting him share a few drinks with the man.

Drast's commander breathed in gulps, his deep chest heaving. "I do not know if that remark was towards me or towards the Kaligulas, but I will give you the benefit of thinking it was me. If I thought for a moment you were talking ill of the men who are putting bread in your belly, you would be eating your own intestines right now." He spat at him. "I will spend the rest of our journey inventing some way to punish you for your cheek. Pray that you give me no more."

The Voivode walked forward, L'ubu being quick to follow with the horse and wagon. Skell stayed back to help Legan to his feet. When the two caught up to the wagon, Legan leaned heavily on the sideboard to keep himself upright and moving forward.

Silence ensued for a time as Drast paced himself above them to stay within earshot but out of eyesight, careful of their newfound silence. But he was certain each man was too caught up in his own thoughts to think anyone would be following them. The silence rode on for a time and the men approached the cliff's edge that fell into the Neabou Sea.

"He has a point, does he?" Walstan suddenly snapped at L'ubu, turning mid-stride.

Drast was not close enough to hear what the man had said, but he did not have a hard time guessing. He had been waiting for this: betrayal. Would they give in to the temptation of the power of the dragon? They were considering it, and the fact that two out of the four men had voiced their thoughts meant it was only a matter of time. Any man who willingly disobeyed simple rules would not balk at betraying him and his brother.

L'ubu seemed to understand what Walstan had inferred. "Oh, no…no, not that! No, please, I did not mean to say anything against you or the Kaligulas at all. I meant the dragon." He gestured back towards the cart shakily. "There is no reason to waste it."

"Waste it?" Walstan nearly shouted. "It is waste! It is rotten! Can you not smell the thing? Or have you gone as dull as Legan?"

Skell spoke up. "I think he means to say that we all know the Kaligulas gained something from this dragon; no reason why we cannot as well. It is already going to be tossed out."

Drast smiled. That was three.

When Walstan did not respond, Skell spoke louder, gaining confidence. "When a fellow throws a perfectly good piece of crockery in the rubbish heap, there is no reason to let it lie there. You might as well pick it up."

"Aye," Walstan nodded, "but we are not dealing with a piece of crockery, are we? We are dealing with someone who is throwing out a three-day-rotten corpse." He strode back to the end of the wagon and flipped the canvas open to reveal the long-dead dragon. "Even if the thing did not smell like your unwashed skivvies, it is poison. Have you not heard the rumors from Ser Tyran's men?"

L'ubu left the horse to follow Walstan back. "Of course we have. But I also heard that drinking the thing's blood gives you power. You can use Koldovstvo without aging."

Walstan rubbed his eyes wearily. "How are you going to drink its blood without touching it?"

His question was met with silence by the three men. Legan's only working eye—the other now swollen shut—scanned the other two men in hopes that they might have an answer. Skell and L'ubu shrugged.

"Well, since we now have that resolved, we are at the spot to dump the creature, so what say we get our work done and head back to Lairhein for a drink?"

"Wait!" Skell said quickly. "I have to try. I have to see if it will work."

"Me too," L'ubu squeaked fervently.

Legan added a favorable grunt but still did not seem eager to speak in Walstan's presence.

Walstan shrugged. "Well, as they say, it is your burial." He chuckled. "Actually, just to be clear: when you die—and you will die—your body is going into the sea with the dragon. Your family will not know your fate, because they cannot know. The purpose of dragging the dragon out here is to conceal it, so don't think I will jeopardize that because you could not keep your lips off a corpse."

As the three men exchanged glances and nodded resolutely to each other, Walstan's eyes wandered in Drast's direction. Drast attempted to duck out of the way, but his Voivode seemed to know exactly where to find him. Walstan smiled at him and turned his gaze back to his men.

At first, Drast was slightly amused the man knew he was with them, but it quickly turned to a cold sweat with an uneasy lump in his stomach. How long had Walstan known Drast was following? Was his abuse of Legan all for show? Was he simply loyal and recognized his companions were expendable because of their lack of loyalty to the Kaligulas? Or was he trying to show he could one up Drast?

There were far too many questions about what Walstan knew and where he stood. Drast had known Walstan for many years and thought he knew him well, but he began to doubt that rapidly. Walstan, being this aware of the events and anticipating that Drast chose to test his men by sending them on this foray into the wilderness, was dangerous if the man himself could not be trusted.

Skell pulled his short copper sword from his belt and carefully examined the dragon while Legan and L'ubu watched eagerly. Upon seeing the slash at the beast's throat, he looked back to them for help.

"You will likely have to cut into a foot or something. Find a place where the blood has pooled." Legan pulled back the canvas further to reveal more of the body. "Its throat has been cut, so there is not much blood left in the thing."

"Don't touch it!" L'ubu said suddenly as Skell reached for a handhold to steady his cut. Skell fell back—his hands were now visibly shaking, the tip of his sword wavered and he grumbled nervously.

Walstan snorted. "Will you little girls hurry up; I don't intend to stay here all day while you try to decide if you plan to suck its fingers or its toes. I would like to make it back to Lairhein before dark."

"Give me that!" Legan took the sword, raised it up, and thrust it into a clawed foot near the edge of the wagon. The dragon was far from fully grown and its scales were not nearly thick enough to repel the weapon. For a moment, it appeared as though, despite the darker color of the claw wherein the blood had pooled, nothing would come from the wound. Then it began to ooze and drop in globs.

After a few globs fell, Walstan chuckled. "Well, who is first?"

The men exchanged glances. "I am," L'ubu said resolutely. "I need this."

He put his hand beneath the wound and let a few globs fall into his palm. Several deep breaths later, he put his mouth to his hand and the blood disappeared.

Drast, along with the others, watched eagerly, waiting to see what the result would be. L'ubu made a disgusted face for several moments, but finally grunted and smiled a bit. "That is probably the foulest thing I have ever tasted, but I feel fine other than wanting some water."

Skell took his place and repeated the process, holding out his hand, taking far more than L'ubu had, and cleaning his hand before wiping it on his trousers. "Ugh, that is disgusting. But I kind of feel good. Stronger, more aware."

L'ubu nodded. "Yes, I do too."

Drast could see something, but at his distance, he could not place it until Legan acknowledged it. "Your nose is bleeding, L'ubu."

"Huh?"

"Your nose is bleeding."

"It is." Walstan agreed.

L'ubu wiped his nose and chuckled. "Eh, not a problem." He cleared his throat. "My chest feels odd."

Skell let out a cry. "No!" He had blood on his hands from his nose. "What do we do?"

"A bloody nose is really nothing to sniff at," Walstan snickered.

"This is not funny!" L'ubu screamed, his hands shaking again. He appeared to be on the verge of tears.

Skell began coughing. Violently. L'ubu soon joined him. Legan stood back in silent surprise; Walstan leaned up against the wagon and merely watched.

The coughing lasted for a long while. It was nearly continuous, only interrupted by desperate intakes of breath and L'ubu's sobbing. When blood began to come with the coughing, Legan looked away and Walstan turned his gaze from the men to meet Drast's. His gaze was steady, unblinking as the two men before him colored the ground crimson. He was waiting for Drast to act.

It was time to address this nonsense. Drast stood and delicately made his way down the steep embankment to his soldiers. When he emerged from the brush lining the clearing on the edge of the cliff, Walstan greeted him.

"Ser Drast, it is a pleasure to see you!" He bowed. "As you can see, your men are not faring too well."

"Don't call me 'Ser,'" Drast snapped at him.

Legan's eyes and mouth fell wide open. "Ser…Drast! You are here!" He shook his head. "I tried to stop them, but they drank from the dragon. Drank its blood, I mean to say."

Drast met his eyes and slowly looked towards the bloody sword in Legan's hand. "Stop them, you say?"

The man's mouth suddenly appeared dry, as he worked his lips trying to generate a response. His one good eye darted between Drast, his coughing companions, and Walstan, hoping for an answer.

Drast idly picked at his fingernails. "Since you are prone to lying to me, perhaps it is you I have to blame for reporting the Arkhon's son's death."

Legan shook his head. "N-n-no. I would never do that. I am loyal, Drast."

"No?" Drast raised an eyebrow. "Well, forgive me if I have trouble believing you, but you also told me that you did not assist these men in drinking dragon's blood, and we both know the truth of that." He paused for a moment. "No response? Well, perhaps these men can answer me." Drast turned his gaze to the coughing men. "You are both dying, and you will die quite slowly, I can assure you. While you still have speech, tell me who told the Arkhon about his son's death."

Both men coughed loudly; it now appeared as though pieces of flesh had begun to come out along with the blood. Neither acknowledged him.

"Or perhaps you are past such a time already. I have it in my power to save whomever can tell the truth and," he looked at Legan, "kill whomever hides it."

A quick exchange of glances between the three men, and a trio of fingers were leveled at Walstan.

Drast turned to face him.

A quick burst of Koldovstvo snapped the necks of the three soldiers, and a subsequent burst of wind, powered by Drast, pulled all three men along with the dragon off the cliff and into the sea. He had still not gotten over how little Koldovstvo affected him after the ritual. It was quick and decisive, leaving Drast alone with Walstan on the cliff face.

The man's eyes were wide at the raw display of power. "The dragon's power? It worked."

Drast nodded silently, watching his stocky Voivode. Why would the man betray him? Why would he reveal the truth of Simon's death? Had he misread Walstan so badly? It was a betrayal that would not happen twice. Drast could guarantee that much.

"I had hoped. I thought you would gain the power, but I knew that the Claduk would result, regardless." He continued staring at Drast wide-eyed. "Your family can finally take its place as the rulers of the Stuhia!"

"What do you mean?" Drast could feel the doubt, the confusion in his tone. What was Walstan going on about?

"That was your plan: to murder Simon to cause the Claduk in order to rule Lairhein. When we spoke on the beach, you said you wanted Simon dead, but told me not to act. But then you killed him."

"How do you know?" Drast asked.

"I know your arrows, Ser Drast," Walstan rambled. "I figured you wanted to ensure the credit of his death went to you. Your father doesn't recognize your value, and now he must. But the men, they are too afraid, they thought you wanted the truth to remain hidden. And you could not say yourself."

"You are giving me a great deal of credit, Walstan. Why would I do all of this?"

"I know you, Ser Drast. Since we were young. I have always tried to help where I could. But I know you are the one who set everything in motion. Now Serder Kaligula will know he has you to thank. You prepared the stage while your brother was gone to ensure your father would become Arkhon, and killing Simon was the final piece before the Claduk could be called. No one will question your father's desire to protect his sons. If he had called it without cause, then the people of Lairhein would resist his rule. By killing Simon and throwing doubt on his demise, the Arkhon's hand was forced and now your father can rule unopposed."

Walstan was nearly feverish in his excitement. "I am here to serve, Ser Drast. I am your spear and I am your armor. Direct me as you will!"

Drast stroked his chin and grinned. Walstan was right. He had played it out perfectly. His father's plan had been to challenge the Arkhon when ready. The doubt and distrust present allowed him to call Claduk under the guise of self-preservation and love of his sons. "Come, Walstan, we have much to do."

Chapter VIII

Serder Kaligula sat at his great alder wood desk, turning the delicate pages of the ancient codex, the *Varkolak*. Tyran watched his father, genuinely surprised at the faded vellum within the worn leather casing. Even at a distance, he could make out the scribbles of pockmarked ink, written with the power of Koldovstvo. The Kaligula family kept the relic secret from the prying eyes of the other Stuhia.

Tyran asked, "Where did the *Varkolak* come from, Father?" Tyran had never touched the book or even glanced at the pages over his father's shoulder, but he knew the words written within motivated his father beyond any other thing in this world.

"The book passed through the hands of all in our lineage, from my father to me, but originally from the first bloodlines of the Stuhia people. Our ancestors have maintained it since the time of the Carian Council."

"I wonder why the Carian Council burned the other texts," Tyran said, continuing to stall off the real reason he had come to his father's study. He needed to talk to his father about marrying Isolde.

"Blind men become accustomed to not seeing. Even when they are granted with sight, their vision healed, they may gouge out their own eyes to escape back to a more familiar place," his father explained.

Tyran grunted in confusion. "So, the truth found in the *Varkolak* did not sit well with the Carian Council?"

His father turned another page. "No. The weak cannot handle the truth as much as they claim to desire it. The Carian Council could not comprehend the value of the truth. The fools were driven by fear, afraid of changing their profane traditions; that is, except your grandfather. He carved the path for the Kaligula bloodline to take our place as the imperial family."

Tyran knew the tome held secrets from an earlier age, which allowed for indescribable power in the right hands. Tyran did not doubt his father's hands were the right hands for such power.

"How can you be certain that this is the time for our advancement? Many Kaligulas have lived before us and have not elevated beyond the position of Serder," Tyran said.

"Because it is," Serder Kaligula huffed, flipping through several pages like he was looking for something particular. His eyes crumpled. "I hoped you would have been here earlier this morning."

Tyran did not respond. It was never wise to be cheeky with his father. Something Drast had never learned.

Dagmar moved on, apparently unconcerned with Tyran's lack of response.

"The talks we shared in Klukas have been a blessing to me this past year."

"Mm."

"As of late, I have been compelled to share my knowledge, to pass on what your grandfather shared with me, lest my charge was not done," Serder Kaligula said. "There is much more I must tell you before my battle with Jonafel Kluk."

"There will be time after," Tyran said.

His father glanced back to the codex. "We cannot guarantee that. Even with the ritual completed, every precaution must be taken."

Tyran winced. "Why me?"

His father tightened his hand into a fist on the table.

"And not Drast. Why has he been sheltered from the plans for our family?" Tyran clarified, rapping his fingers on the smooth wooden armrest. He had not considered it strange that his father and he had spoken in the shadow plane, in Klukas, while he was in the Shade. But when Drast asked about the dragon, Tyran realized his older brother was clueless to their father's schemes. And now, here Tyran stood, summoned to his father's chamber, and Drast was nowhere to be found.

"Your brother likes to think himself a leader, but he is far more suitable for other vocations."

Tyran attempted to keep his face emotionless. His gut roiled when his father spoke so openly of what he considered to be Drast's failings. In some way, Tyran longed to receive the same critique. Although, every compliment his father had was forked with an insult on the opposing end.

The Serder did not notice how the words impacted him. His father's face remained buried in *Varkolak*. Then again, a certain part of Tyran believed his father saw everything. At least the codex had not halted his father's perception when Tyran was a child.

"Drast has been involved in the politics of this city for the past year while I have been in the Shade. It seems he would know leadership better than I would."

"Yes, one would think as much," Serder Kaligula scoffed, "but his leadership is not your leadership. Drast is a man with the capability of being successful in nearly anything he sets his mind to accomplish. Though he will use others as stepping stools to achieve the task. Drast is remarkable but cannot teach other men to be remarkable. You can teach others greatness; that is the leadership this family needs. Don't misunderstand me. Drast has done well, using his tongue to keep the family out of the fire, so to speak, but a new era for the Kaligula bloodline is about to unfold. And with the recent events regarding Simon, it has become evident to me his talents are not far-reaching."

"Mm." Drast had been used as a puppet to distract the other Stuhia from his father's cunning and Tyran's campaign. Tyran could not help but think how he may be used as a puppet now that he had returned.

"You are a bright man, Tyran. I am proud knowing you have grown as you have—and I am equally impressed by your brother's skill sets. But we are not here to discuss the things we already know."

"I understand."

"Of course you do." The Serder nodded as he turned another page, and then lifted his blue eyes towards Tyran. "Mortality is a curse. Death is hard-pressed on the living by the gods—a bizarre joke, telling man to enjoy his life while knowing there is nothing waiting in the end except death. The thought of leaving this body and entering the staleness of the Netherworld is sickening to me. The constant threat of dying brings us misery in this life; without it, we would be free to enjoy each day equally."

"But the Stuhia don't age beyond young adulthood unless they touch Koldovstvo," Tyran asserted. "We bring death upon ourselves. Wolos gifted us with agelessness and we squander it by using our magic. Is that not what the temple teaches?"

"It is indeed. The matter is concerning how we should not be threatened with death at all. The gods wield unlimited power without constraint, and we are sentenced to death for doing the same. Tell me, why is that so?"

Tyran remained expressionless as best as he was able, looking at the wrinkles around his father's eyes. A voice inside his head screamed the answer: *Because they are gods!*

Serder Kaligula's red hair was thinning, patches of grey overtaking the strands. He could imagine how the man would consider death with the onset of age, using Koldovstvo through his lifetime. The only way any Stuhia died was through the overuse of Koldovstvo, sickness, or battle.

In the Shade, Tyran had been faced with death regularly but had never considered dying. His quest did not allow for it. Tyran supposed sitting behind stone walls, staring at vellum gave a man little to do but wonder at death.

"Do you think that this is fair?"

"I…" Tyran paused, realizing he had not heard a word his father had said, if he had said anything more at all. He searched for an acceptable response based on what he knew of the Serder. "I cannot see why mankind's suffering would be necessary to the glory of the gods."

His father nodded in agreement. "As was the concern of your grandfather. You share his wisdom. We will finally offset this atrocity."

Tyran sighed with relief. Paying attention to another person talking exhausted him. Tyran wished he knew how Drast did it while still finding the means to think for himself.

"Once we hold the power in Lairhein, there will be nothing stopping us from waging war against the Vucari. With absolute sovereignty, I will have the authority to send our armies to Rhian. There we will target the Vucari priests and their temples."

"And killing the priests will grant us immortality?" Tyran asked.

His father's eyes gleamed. "Yes. Immortality with absolute power."

Tyran rapped his fingers again. His father was bound to explain himself further. He and Drast shared the tendency to have more words than they did breath.

His father struggled to say his next words, staring hard at Tyran. "Wolos favors the Vucari, not the Stuhia."

Tyran held his fingers still. "What? We are the dragon-people…not them."

"Indeed," the Serder agreed, "but the *Varkolak* is clear. The Carian Council, the first of our kind, were dragon slayers; we were not blessed by the dragons or Wolos."

"But Wolos made us ageless." Tyran sat up straighter in his chair, debating. He reflected on the teachings of the temple. "Father, we have been taught to worship Wolos since we were children. The Ninth Council—everything and everyone—is structured to worship the God of the Dead."

Tyran stared at the *Varkolak* along with his father.

"And they are wrong. We are lucky our own bloodline, our ancestors, were brave enough to reserve the *Varkolak*."

"If we are not blessed by Wolos and the dragons," Tyran started, thinking aloud, "it means Koldovstvo is not channeled through the Horned God. Where does the power of the Stuhia come from?"

His father spoke at a whisper as he stroked the skin binding of the *Varkolak*.

"Marheena."

"The Seamstress of Nightmares?" Tyran scowled. "The Goddess of the Netherworld?"

"Yes," his father said. "She gave the Stuhia their power, and moreover, I can tell you Wolos's magic is a perversion. He is the one who allows the Vucari to shed their skin away to become beasts. He is also the one who demands the Stuhia die when they wield Koldovstvo. Wolos must die an eternal death if we are to have true immortality, not just agelessness."

"We are going to slay Wolos?" Tyran almost laughed out loud and then realized his father was solemn.

"Yes." His father's eyes focused on Tyran grimly. "If we destroy the God of the Dead, then there will be no death for us."

Tyran froze. Drast and he had often tried to discover their father's ambitions, but neither had dreamed they were so grand. The idea of fighting a god, not to mention killing a god, was unthinkable. Had his father gone mad? Tyran shuddered to think if Isolde should find out.

"What about Claduk?" asked Tyran.

His father dismissed the question. "Do not worry about the battle with Jonafel. Your brother and I have worked out the details."

Tyran said, "And what about Wolos? Does Drast know?"

"There is no need," Dagmar stated. "Your brother is impulsive. I will tell him what he needs to know when I need him. But you are the son I need now. You mind is for strategy, not for whimsy."

"I don't understand," Tyran said. "How am I supposed to find a god?"

Dagmar cleared his throat. "According to the *Varkolak*, the Vucari priests join Wolos each winter in Rhian to battle Marheena. By eliminating the priests, Wolos will be forced to face us."

Tyran frowned. "What about Isolde?"

His father ignored the question, repeating himself. "You must swear it, Tyran. This is your charge in life."

Tyran's stomach twisted in knots. Isolde had waited for him. If she waited a bit longer, he may gain his father's approval after all. "I will kill Wolos or die trying."

His father did not move his eyes from Tyran's.

Tyran conceded. "I swear it."

The hundreds of citizens of Lairhein gathered beyond the wall, beyond the pine grove, and walked two hours to the southwest shore along the mountainside to Tekorga. The ruins of the ancient arena had become piles of stone over the ages. Tyran was aware that history suggested that regular fights had once taken place among these scattered remains that were built with Koldovstvo, but no one had been here for this purpose in hundreds of years.

In all his life, Tyran had never seen such a great concourse of people. He supposed the tidings of Claduk had gone out into all parts of the city. This would be a spectacle among spectacles, watching a battle for the role of Arkhon in Lairhein. The outcome of this engagement would predict more than just the immediate authority within Lairhein, it would also impact the bloodlines, the perceptions of Koldovstvo, the retelling of their history, and the future of the world.

Whatever seating may have once surrounded Tekorga had crumbled from being anything recognizable long ago. As a result, the crowds of people had to traipse up the mountainside, out of harm's way, and watch from a distance. Only a select few would be allowed near the fighting area, including kin and the magistrates who made up the Ninth Council.

Tyran sat with his elbows on his knees on a stone slab next to Drast. Beside them were the imperial family, three sons and two daughters of Arkhon Jonafel Kluk. In addition were the nine magistrates from the Ninth Council. The lot of them were within an assortment of six stones, the *sharishka*. The golden egg-shaped stones, each the size of a human skull, were placed in a circle around them.

The sharishka were said to serve as a magical ward around the members, protecting them from physical harm and the Koldovstvo.

"Do you not think we should test these rocks out before the battle starts? I don't want Serder Kaligula's guts splattered on me." A man Tyran recognized as Kindel Kluk leered, absentmindedly digging the heel of his foot into the soft sands.

"They are activated and will prevent any impact from the outside, including the casting of Koldovstvo," Serder Grasil, one of the nine magistrates, said. The youngest of the men sounded confident.

"What about from the inside?" Maelili Kluk asked, keeping her green eyes fixated on the crowd that coated the mountainside. The daughter of the current Arkhon had the reddest hair of any Stuhia, even brighter than Isolde.

Tyran had known Maelili since they were children, and they had even had a *thing*, a liking for one another, early on in their youth. The attraction had been before Tyran really understood the division between the imperial family and his own bloodline. He had heard people say that a man never forgot his first kiss, and it was true in this case. His fascination with the girl had not waned much. She was easy on the eyes, sharp of mind, and compelling with her tongue.

Lucky for him, he did not have to think about Maelili. He had Isolde.

He turned his gaze to the mountainside while the councilmen behind him fudged around for an answer to her arresting question. *What if someone wielded Koldovstvo from inside the sharishka?*

Many of the women and children in the crowd were laden with flowers. He could hear those who had any sense of musical talent playing their flutes, horns, and viols. He could even hear some clear-voiced singers humming within the masses frolicking a safe distance from the designated arena. He almost wanted to enjoy this spectacle as much as the other Stuhia. It was likely a much different experience when a personal family member was not doing the fighting. They were probably more focused on the political outcome and the impact on their personal lives than who lived and who died.

Serder Malefej finally responded after the murmurings of the councilmen subsided. Even from behind, Tyran could imagine his white eyebrows shaking as he talked. "The sharishka were originally created for war, protecting those within and not those on the outside. That is their function. I am certain there are none within this conclave who would tamper with the outcome of the duel. It would be beyond dishonorable. Whatever would make you think of such a possibility, Maelili?"

The woman turned to scowl at Tyran and Drast. Those who claimed a woman looked pretty when angry had never met Maelili Kluk. Her beauty disappeared like dust flung into darkness. In that moment, his impression of her waned. "The competition."

The Ninth Council shifted on their slabs behind Tyran. Malefej stood with the ease of a young man, adjusted his dusky robe, and stepped out into the arena.

"Brothers and sisters, peoples of Lairhein," Malefej thundered, enriching his voice with Koldovstvo, "we come for Claduk."

Applause and hails resounded from the mountainside as the redheaded men and women stood in ovation. The sound was more deafening than battle.

Malefej continued once the roar subsided. "First, the challenger, Serder Dagmar Kaligula."

Again, the crowd cheered. Tyran watched his father step out from behind the stones on the opposite side of the battlefield, through makeshift pillars of rock. He had layered himself in hide armor from head to foot, made from the best quality available. Smooth and unscathed, the armor had never been worn in battle. The thick hide helmet was pulled securely over his head, hiding his features.

He marched forward over sands as though he were solid and unconquerable. The armor was not grand, but his father behaved as though it were constructed by magic. He bore a shield on his left arm that reached from knee to neck, and on his back he carried three sharpened spears. Tyran paid the most attention to the leather-corded flail strapped to his father's belt. He did not know that his father owned the weapon. One successful hit with the oversized stone secured in the leather holding would lob a man's head clean off his shoulders.

"And his competitor, the Arkhon," Malefej resumed, "Jonafel Kluk."

The cacophony of the crowd became even louder and Arkhon Kluk strolled into Tekorga. He approached from another angle, stepping lightly towards the middle to meet Serder Kaligula.

The Arkhon was a grand man in the glaring sunlight. Every step gave measure to his stout chest. Yet by the looks of the elderly Stuhia, it appeared as though Arkhon Jonafel Kluk had come to die. He wore a cloth robe and carried a crooked walking stick, which he may or may not have needed to hobble towards the center. He looked perplexed, like a sage who had lost his way. Tyran wondered if Simon's death still shocked him. Regardless, the Arkhon did not seem fit for battle.

Tyran must not have been the only one who thought so, because Serder Grasil raised concern from behind him

"Does the Arkhon know this is a fight to the death? He brought a stick!"

Kindel Kluk laughed. "That is not any old stick, magistrate. That is *Habërmani*. It has been in our family for a thousand years or more."

"We can remedy that," Drast muttered under his breath.

"Drast," Tyran warned.

Kindel's smile disappeared. "Many things will be remedied after this battle, Ser Drast."

Malefej disrupted any further conflict within the sharishka, calling the attention of all in the area with his voice. "The rules of Claduk have not changed since its origins and they will be respected here equally. Hark! Only the competitors may engage in the battle. Hark! All weapons and magic are permissible in combat. Hark! Only one fighter is permitted to leave Tekorga alive. Hark! The champion of Claduk will claim the property, titles, and authority of the deceased. As it was in the beginning, it also shall be now."

Tyran swallowed.

The crowd grew silent as the Serder and the Arkhon moved within an arm's length of one another. Tyran's father removed his helmet and the right rawhide gauntlet, with a silent suggestion to bring an end to the formalities.

Tyran could see the anticipation on his face.

"Before we begin, as the defender, the Arkhon will have the first ceremonious strike, followed by Serder Kaligula."

The Arkhon did not say a word to Dagmar, keeping his staff pressed solidly against the earth with his left hand. If Tyran were closer, he guessed he would see tears well up in the man's eyes. Stepping forward with his right foot, he struck, hitting the Serder squarely in the left eye with his fist.

There was no magic; no tricks. It was a blow holding the power of a man grieving the death of his son.

Dagmar stumbled back, swaying from the bearing. Tyran nearly stood to his feet, thinking his father might fall before the fight had even begun, but he held himself at bay. He realized in this moment that his father had likely never been in a real fight.

The Serder craned his neck back towards the Arkhon, standing upright once more. Blood oozed from above his eye socket and trickled down the side of his face. He reached up to touch it, and then looked at the crimson stain on his fingertips.

His father looked angry. Any control he may have held had been lost at the sight of his own blood.

Dagmar swung upwards from his waist, catching Jonafel under the jawbone. The old man's head rocked backwards, taking his feet out from underneath him.

The crowd barely had time to murmur.

Before the Arkhon landed, Dagmar had equipped his gauntlet and helmet, using Koldovstvo to hasten his actions, and advanced.

"Wai—" Malefej bade, backpedaling towards the sharishka, flinging himself within its protective wake.

In a heartbeat, the Serder's hand held a spear and threw it at Jonafel's gut. He had not come here for pretty words and tradition. Dagmar Kaligula had come with purpose—for war.

"Father!" Maelili cried out.

The older man threw up a handful of dirt that shaped into a stone barrier mid-flight, stopping the spear dead. Dagmar seemed unphased and countered by pulling the sand out from beneath the divider so it tumbled back onto Jonafel. Tyran watched as the Arkhon struggled to get to his feet on his side of the stone wall, but he did not act quickly enough. The stone partition of his own creation crushed him.

The Serder was not finished. He called lightning from the clear sky and struck the stone through its thickness. It cracked with the first strike and imploded with the second, breaking away.

Tyran found himself on his feet, whether in anticipation or to see over the children of Jonafel Kluk, he could not say.

"Gone," Drast whispered with skepticism.

Serder Kaligula shifted with uncertainty. The sands in front of him wafted like an undulating tide.

His helmet turned noticeably towards his sons within the sharishka. Tyran could feel his father's eyes upon him.

The gravel and grit erupted into the air. A figure formed of Koldovstvo, within the midst and struck Dagmar with a rock fist. Tyran watched his father soar backward through the air like a stone flung from a sling, slamming into the makeshift pillars he had stepped through at his introduction.

Repetitive boulders of equal size followed suit, slamming into the body of the Serder. Tyran turned his head away as the pillar fissured and swayed.

He looked again in time to see the Serder fall to the ground. The spears on his back had splintered and snapped, falling from their holdings. He landed among their remains. Tyran winced, forcing himself to watch the outcome. The hide armor was not strong enough. Every bone in his father's body was surely crushed from the blow.

The Serder tried to stand, but sprawled forward landing against his shield.

Tyran swallowed.

The dust settled. Jonafel Kluk stood calmly among the dissipating storm holding Habërmani valiantly, victoriously. The little stunt had cost the man; Tyran noted the additional wrinkles upon his visage.

Out of the corner of his eye, he also noticed Drast grinning.

"What in the Nine Lands, Drast?" Tyran wheezed under his breath. He heard a stirring of the councilmen behind him. He may have spoken too loudly.

Drast dipped his head towards their father with that knowing look. Tyran hated that look.

Still, Tyran turned to see his father standing upright, holding his shield steady. The Serder stumbled forward a few steps before halting his pace altogether. The man had feigned exhaustion.

It suddenly struck him as being odd that his father's armor remained unmarked. His first thought was that his father had forged armor with Koldovstvo, which would call for the protective covering to be destroyed and his father's immediate death.

As it were, the Stuhia were not allowed to make permanent weapons or armor with their gifted craft, Koldovstvo. The Ninth Council taught that long-lasting armaments made by magic would bring havoc to the world of the living. Be that as it may, his father's armor could not withstand such power without leaving a mark.

The only other explanation had to be that Drast had intervened. His brother must have imploded each sarsen before it struck their father, giving the impression to the crowd that Serder Kaligula had been struck.

Tyran struggled to remain stone-faced.

Serder Kaligula charged the Arkhon with the sudden speed and strength of a warrior fresh to battle. The gasps of astonishment echoed from the mountainside, but none seemed more surprised than the Arkhon himself.

Dagmar held his flail ready, his shield raised. With an audible roar, he swung the weapon for Jonafel's head and the old man ducked before it swung low to strike at his legs, which he skipped back from. But he could not dodge the full-sized shield that jutted forward against his frame.

He stumbled backwards from the bash, almost falling, reaching outward towards the sand. In an instant, a stone sword erupted, created magically, and entered his hand. He swung it at the flail, only to have it become ensnared in the leather strap and pulled from his grip. His weapon fell to pieces as quickly as it had been formed.

The Serder did not stop his progression. He swung a fist—still gripping the haft of the flail—at Jonafel as solidly in the face with his fist as he had with the ceremonial strike.

Skin split and blood spewed, the strike powered with magic.

Tyran felt himself hold back his own grin as the family members in front of him squirmed on their stone slabs.

Fire roared from the Serder's lips as if he had the lungs of a leviathan, scorching the old man in front of him. The flame burned bright and blue, searing layers of flesh without remorse.

The grandfatherly figure shrieked. His children let out sobs of frustration at the sight of their tortured father. The screams of the Arkhon lasted eternally, and even Tyran had to turn away his gaze.

Finally, an ocean wave swept away the fire. The Arkhon had pulled water from some distance, but it crashed into the arena, washing over the man and flinging Tyran's father back across the arena.

"Blood magic," Kindel alleged at a whisper, tears in his eyes.

Drast's fingers inched towards his boot. Tyran nudged his brother swiftly to stop him.

"It is almost over," Tyran said.

Maelili inhaled and exhaled heavily, her bright red hair glued to her flushed cheeks by the tears flowing from her bright eyes.

As the water summoned by the Arkhon settled into the sand, he shivered. His skin was crumpled, bloody, and liquified against the fabric of his robe. The old man tried to shuffle forward, but even pulling the water from the ocean to extinguish the flame had stolen years from his life.

Serder Kaligula made it clear to the gathered people of Lairhein that the battle had been won. He stood slowly, taking pause to stretch. With deliberate measure, he dropped his shield, let loose his flail, and threw away his helmet.

Rotating to take in those who accompanied the magistrates of the Ninth Council, and then the crowd, he lifted his voice using Koldovstvo. "A new age of leadership has come. Know that the Stuhia will be known for their restraint when merciful, and their *lack* when upholding justice."

Dagmar lifted his fist towards Jonafel Kluk and spread his fingers wide. The man had no time to register the shock. His body split and tore with unequal measure, limbs ripped from his torso. All that had once been the leader of the Stuhian people splattered the sands of the Tekorga.

Dagmar Kaligula raised his voice once more, eerily calm, "The Claduk is finished. I am your Arkhon. Are there any who wish to challenge me while we are all gathered?"

Silence answered him.

Month of Harvest

Fourth of Warmth

45 CE

Chapter IX

"A sickness pervades our city, my sons." Arkhon Dagmar Kaligula sat regally behind his great alder wood desk. Rich samite robes of dark blue, nearly black, fell heavily over his shoulders.

Their father had been wont to dress with abundance before his appointment as the ruler of Lairhein, though it now seemed there was a certain purpose behind his garb. The splendid samite seemed to make the weight of his speech all the more dire.

"A month has passed and the children of the former Arkhon still wander the city," he continued, "infecting it against me. Enough time has elapsed that their disappearances might go unnoticed if you are careful. I can no longer have such unrest within my city. *My* city will be a great city unified by *my* will and *my* purpose. The first step in securing such unity has been accomplished, my sons, for I am the Arkhon." He smiled at Drast and Tyran.

In all the years that Drast had worked to see his father's will done, he doubted whether he had ever seen a genuine smile from the man. It was not pleasant to behold. As genuine as it seemed, his eyes were still cold and black. Nothing seemed as though it could light the darkness therein.

"I will see that you are rewarded properly for your diligence in this matter. Women, wine, and a few delicacies I have been saving await you in your rooms." His smile was gone. "But, do not become greedy. Remember that my gains are your gains. Do not lose sight of your father's will now that our authority has increased."

He stood and walked to gaze out a nearby window. "Kill the Kluk children. I want my city to be healthy and whole, not divided against itself by the sickness and doubt these naysayers bring."

Drast and Tyran stood to leave.

"And," he turned slightly, "do not limit your scope to only the spawn of Kluk. Keep an open eye and a thoughtful ear for any others who doubt me. We do not have room in this city for such beasts."

When the two had reached the hallway with the door closed behind them, Drast chuckled. "Well, that was certainly cheerful."

Tyran nodded as if the two had just attended a funeral. "Mm."

Drast supposed that, to some degree, they had. At the very least, they had been preparing a funeral for the remainder of the Kluk family. He found himself to be thankful the family was not larger. Some of the families in Lairhein were quite extensive with aunts, uncles, cousins and so on. "I can take care of her, if you want, Tyran."

His brother stopped and turned. "Who?"

"Maelili Kluk." Drast shrugged and could not help but smile. He had tried to stop, but he always seemed to smile when he was nervous. Fortunately, Tyran understood. "I saw you looking at her at the Claduk—I thought I would offer."

"Mm," he grunted. "Well, I appreciate that, but I am sure I will be fine."

"Where are you off to?"

"I am meeting with Isolde to discuss wedding plans."

Drast felt his smile coming back into place. The conversation he overheard between Tyran and Dagmar in the stables came to mind. "Have you talked to Father about her? I don't think he will approve. In fact, I would imagine he will definitely disapprove. We must follow his will. It would be best if you put an end to things now before they get any worse, you know."

"No." Tyran's voice was hard. "I will not let him rule me and keep me from happiness. I have tried talking to him many times." He sighed heavily. "And it is useless. I hate speaking with him. I will do as I wish and he will have to accept that I am my own man."

"Are you not loyal to him any longer?"

"Loyal?" Any other man would have been yelling, but Tyran's anger took a slow, measured approach. His voice did not raise, but it became raw. "I killed a dragon for him, I parted from Isolde for a year for him—I performed some profane ritual for him. My entire life I have been at his beck and call. I have killed when and where I was told to kill and destroyed the lives of those for whom I have cared. I will keep something for myself."

"If you want to keep something, Tyran, you keep it close, in your pocket and not out where the world can see." Drast shrugged. His heart ached for his brother, but Tyran had to see the futility of defying their father. "Besides, he has spoken against it. You should do as he says."

Tyran's response was a steady, unwavering look; he turned and strode away determinedly.

"Tyran," he tried.

The man marched onward, ignoring Drast.

"Tyran!"

It was no use. For all the time Tyran spent in his head, one would think he would be logical. Yet there were times when his brother was beyond being reasonable, as stubborn as a mule during a thunderstorm. Drast sighed. It was his own fault. He should not have tried to approach him head-on. Drast should have wheedled him into what he really wanted, what he was looking for from Isolde.

In Drast's experience such wants were governed by ideals rather than by realities. Tyran saw freedom or love or some other nonsense in Isolde, but that did not mean he felt anything real for her. The best way to handle Tyran was not to tell him he should or should not do something, as he was likely to do the opposite. The best way was to reason him into it, but it was strenuous work because his brother spent all his time in his head, and it was difficult to beat him at any game of thinking.

With a sigh, Drast meandered towards the courtyard in the opposite direction. He was not going to chase Tyran, nor was he going to go near his own quarters anytime soon. He had no intention of partaking in his father's little reward. Such rewards came with lessons attached. The last time his father had left a woman in Drast's room, she was diseased, and when he had asked his father about it, he made some speech about roses having thorns and other nonsense. He would likely be finding somewhere else to sleep tonight.

Regardless, he had successfully upset his brother, which meant he would be speaking in grunts for the next week.

Yet Drast still wished he had the kind of resolve that Tyran had. Drast could never stand against Father's will. Dagmar Kaligula was so forceful about his *wants* that Drast found it difficult to have any *wants* of his own. Drast needed a few strong drinks.

He entered the courtyard with a sigh of relief. The summer heat felt good. He really hated the cold, and the warmth seemed to seep through the months of cold. Such days were rare in Lairhein, as rain was common more often than not, and a nice dry heat did wonders.

The streets were filled with men and women moving to and fro with their daily tasks. Drast was not particularly concerned with the happenings of the city, though it seemed like everyone was in decent enough spirits. He wandered about for a time, taking a circuitous route to the mead hall, enjoying the warmth of the sun and the chatter of the city. Drast recognized most of those he passed, but few bothered to return his friendly nod. He was generally well liked, but his family's recent rise to power had made several citizens uncomfortable.

A natural hierarchy existed within the city, governed by the amount of Koldovstvo in the veins of a given family. Most of the lower classes could either not wield the more powerful magics at all or could only do so at the cost of an early and untimely death. The Kaligulas were an old bloodline, long recognized for their power. However, it had been established throughout the years that the Kluks were far stronger. Drast had attempted to council his father to make his victory appear to be more of a struggle, instead of seeming so effortless. The easy victory had almost made the Kaligula name an expletive.

With one last glance at the sun, Drast entered the mead hall. There were smaller alehouses about town, but the mead hall was the official gathering place for many of the Stuhia living in Lairhein. If one wanted news, this was the place to go. Given the recent disquiet concerning his family, Drast was merely looking for a bit of visibility in case some fool took it into his mind that he wanted blood.

Sitting at one of the long benches that stretched the length of the hall, he contented himself with the variety of drinks the establishment had to offer. In the same way he enjoyed the sun and summer heat, he found himself enjoying the mead hall. Tall windows near the tiled roof were thrown open and a warm, pleasant breeze made the place downright comfortable.

He could not place how long he sat drinking, but the buzz and general feeling of warmth and contentment told him he had been sitting long enough to warrant moving on. He had started to feel slightly irascible when Peter Kluk entered.

Of the sons of the late Arkhon, Peter was the youngest. A bit thick about the middle and a bit thicker about the head. As soon as he entered the hall, his pudgy eyes locked on Drast's and he made a beeline towards him. His wide frame creaked on the bench across from Drast.

"Kaligula." He sneered, letting the name hang in the air for a moment.

Drast was feeling pretty good and could not help but smile at the portly fellow's solemnity. Peter had said his last name like it was a swearword.

"Kluk." He responded, purposefully pronouncing it as if imitating a chicken.

Peter's eyes narrowed. "How dare you mock me after what you have done to me and my family."

"Done?" Drast smacked his lips. "The Claduk was fairly won. We followed the law, young *Cluck*."

"Fair. Fair? Oh, that is rich. Since when has the noble Kaligula line done anything fair?"

A steady redness was rising up his neck into his cheeks. His pudgy, pudgy cheeks. Drast giggled.

"You murdered my brother. You cheated at the Claduk and murdered my father. My family is ruined and now we must decide if we will suffer under your despotic rule or flee."

"You know, when a wolf is in the hen house," he struggled to finish his sentence for laughing, "most of the *Clucks* will run as fast as they can."

Peter was on his feet, his voice squeaking. "How dare you laugh at me! How dare you laugh at my family! You murdered my kin, and it will not be ignored!"

The mead hall fell silent, watching. And Drast could not get the smile off his face. "Easy, *Cluck*, easy. Sit down, and let us discuss this as adults. No need to get worked up."

"I would sooner share a table with a dog."

Drast could not help himself. "I would expect most *Clucks* would not want to share a table with a dog any more than they would want to share a table with a wolf."

The redness had reached Peter's hairline, and a great inhale foretold a greater outburst on the man's part. Likely as squeaky as the last.

Drast forestalled him. "You wish this debt, this injustice—as you see it—be remedied?"

Peter, chest full of air, nodded briefly, refusing to exhale. It was as though releasing his pent-up outburst would prevent him from working up the gumption to start again.

"No doubt you feel your family has been wronged, Peter." He paused, making a point to say the man's name again. "Peter, you feel as though I and my own are to blame." He had to get the man to exhale. "Firstly, I must apologize for my disrespectful humor. Understand that I deal poorly with such heated times as these, and it is my means of becoming at ease." Drast's head was swimming. He wondered how long he could keep this going. Peter nodded his head impatiently, becoming slightly redder from holding his breath.

Drast raised a finger as if instructing the young Kluk. "You must understand, young *Cluck*," he fought back a snort of laughter, "we feel as though we were in the right in this matter. Justified, if you will. And your accusations are nearly as hurtful to me and my own as your perception that we have done ill towards your family. You see, I was there when your dear brother Simon passed, and I can assure you that it was most unfortunate, as if a bolt from the sky had taken his life. And you were present when the formal challenge of Claduk was offered by my father." He raised his hands, shrugging. "I don't know how this may be remedied. When two opponents are justified in their beliefs, only the truth of the matter can discern the difference, and, sadly, we don't have access to that truth."

Peter, nearly purple from holding his breath during Drast's long speech, exhaled to prevent any darker hue. He sat down, likely as much to indicate his willingness to talk as from a result of feeling dizzy from holding his breath. "What do you propose?"

"Well, Peter, it will not do to have the two most powerful families in Lairhein at each other's throats." Drast shook his head. "No, no, it would not do at all. We must make amends, and it can begin with you and me." He leaned forward conspiratorially. "You must know that you and I are the two most reasonable members of our respective lines. My brother is far too hot-headed after his recent adventures and my father is grossly offended by the lack of hospitality of your family after his rise to Arkhon."

Peter nodded knowingly. "Yes, yes, I see that."

"Of course you do, Peter, of course you do." It was like having a pissing contest with a woman. At least the young man did not make Drast call him Ser like Simon had. "Now, I don't propose any solution today, because I have had too much of the creature to think very clearly, and you, my friend, are certainly upset. Let us have a friendly game of drinks in fond memory of those you have lost, and tomorrow we will meet to discuss terms to bring this dark business to an end."

"Very well." He dipped his head sagaciously. "I agree."

Drast smiled. "Excellent. Drinks!" He cleared his throat roughly. "Now, the rules of this game are fairly simple. It has been in my family for years and you will be the first man who has an opportunity to play it outside of my family, so listen well. We take turns making wagers by tossing coins into our respective drinks. Whoever finishes their drink first wins the bet. If any of your coins fall, you lose. If you swallow any of your coins, you lose. But I am not going to wait to get them back, so make sure you have a few extra handy, yes?"

Peter's chubby face split into a grin. "That sounds like an excellent game. Start with one coin?" He tossed one in his drink as it was set before him.

"Sounds fine." Drast tossed one in his as well. "Consume!"

Drast tossed back his head, catching the coin with his tongue as he drank and spat it back into the mug before setting it down.

Peter belched. "Drat. I swallowed it."

Drast chuckled. "It takes a bit of practice. Let us try again."

He quickly lost count of how many drinks he had, and Peter had swallowed nearly half of the coins he had put into his drink.

He was not looking terribly cheerful any longer and was decidedly flush with drink.

"I am not sure about this, Drast." He belched again. "I am not feeling too well. I think I am done."

Drast smiled drunkenly. "Not a problem, Peter *Cluck*. Just give me the coins I am due and you can be on your way."

Peter's chubby, drunken fingers fumbled to dump coins on the table from his pouch. A few tumbled out and he frowned. "I think you may have to wait until tomorrow."

Drast shook his head. "No, I told you I was not going to wait. You need to pay up before you leave."

"Come now, Drast. I thought we were making amends."

"I know," he smiled. "But I want my due. And you were right the first time, *Clucks* should not share a table with dogs."

With a snarl, Drast used Koldovstvo to rip the coins free from Peter's stomach, erupting its contents in a bloody spray, eliciting a cry from Peter. The coins flew out of him about the mead hall, covered in his gore. "Or wolves."

Cries erupted about the mead hall, a cacophony led by Peter's screams. Drast smiled, attempting to lift his voice above the din. "Sorry! Sorry! I guess he cannot hold his ale!"

Chapter X

Tyran murmured, "I need to speak with you." He wanted to look away from his father, who stared intently at the book in front of him, but he needed to appear composed with a sense of absolution. Though his chin might drop and gaze avert if the Arkhon returned eye contact.

"Concerning what, exactly?"

The words were hastily spoken as though his father were paying little attention. If Tyran kept the emotion out of his voice, his father might actually be in a decent mood to respond positively.

Tyran kept his voice smooth, like a steady breeze through the pines. "Isolde and I would—"

His father lifted his gaze, noticing the pause. He wore an expression that made Tyran feel as though he were left to hang on tenterhooks.

Curses resounded in his head. He swallowed but praised himself for holding his frame steady.

"Isolde and I *are*," Tyran said with more authority, "planning to be married. It was our intent to do so when I returned from the Shade. I have put it off long enough."

"I see."

Tyran waited. He half expected an arrow to pierce his skull from the rear for merely suggesting the topic. He would not put it beyond his father's influence to convince even his brother to do such a thing.

He felt encumbered with emotion.

"Marriage will take commitment, and we have more pressing matters at hand. We have already discussed this issue."

"We have, Father," Tyran acquiesced. "Isolde is important to me." He sounded a hair more pleading than what he wanted, but he did notice his father adjust the way he sat in the chair. The man had to know something of love. He had married his mother after all.

"We will discuss this later," Dagmar said.

Tyran left his father's study no closer to securing his marriage with Isolde than he had been a month ago. He marched down the hallway and outside into summer's heat. He had only made it a few steps beyond the courtyard before Isolde was on his arm.

Of course, she had waited for him when he had told her to go home.

"How did it go?" Isolde asked. "Did he give his blessing?"

Tyran cleared his throat, unable to make eye contact. She had been pestering him for weeks to talk to his father. He told her what she wanted to hear. "It will be fine."

She clung to his arm a bit tighter. "I have never been so happy."

He turned his head, hoping she would take hint that he was not in the mood to discuss it further. She squeezed him closer, wrapping one arm around his waist. Her red hair traced against his bicep and her hands moved to clasp his wrist, causing him to perspire even more. He was sure that he stank like a sweltering hog. He hated the heat.

"Should we have yellow daisies or bluestars?" she pondered, leading him in and out of the city streets towards the market. "I originally wanted to do something with lilacs, but those might be hard to find this time of the year."

"Yellow is fine," he grimaced.

"You think so? If we go with the bluestars, it will bring out the color in your eyes. They really are your best feature."

"Blue it is."

Isolde lifted her chin to look at Tyran. "I am not sure you are even listening to me."

"I am," Tyran said. At least she was not accusing of him of not caring or lying. What did it matter what color their flowers were? They did not even have approval to get married.

"Good," Isolde said. "I don't want to make the decisions about our wedding all on my own, nor do I want you to simply agree with me. This is your day, too, you know?"

"Mm."

"My aunt already put in the order for the gown to be made. Have you gotten yourself measured by the tailor?"

"Not yet. I have been busy with…" Tyran paused, not wanting to refer to his father's tasks, "other commitments. I only spoke to my father today."

"Yes...a month later than you promised you would," her voice quivered.

He placed his hand on the small of her back, biting back the bile in his throat. Sometimes Isolde was too forward. "You have no need to worry. We will be married."

He noticed a shadowed figure under a grey cloak moving near the shops. Red hair, the brightest he had ever seen, slipped from the folds of the cloth.

"I only wish it were sooner," Isolde said. Tyran watched her from the corner of his eye. She looked at the marketplace before lifting her eyes towards him. "When we are married, I hope there will be some changes, Tyran."

"What changes?" he mumbled, standing a bit straighter. The figure in the cloak twisted to look in his direction and then stepped behind several bystanders.

Tyran increased their walking speed to keep an eye on the concealed person. It seemed that the figure was intentionally trying to stay out of his line of sight. He knew instinctively that it could only be Maelili Kluk. None other had hair that bright.

"For one," Isolde jutted her chin out, nearly falling from being dragged along, "I was hoping that I would become more of a priority in your life. I don't want to fight for your attention. I should not have to win you from your father and brother."

"Don't be ridiculous," Tyran said.

"Don't *call* me ridiculous!" Isolde shouted. "What a terrible thing to say. You know what I am saying is true."

Tyran bit his cheek, refusing to let the woman steal his attention away.

"Shut your mouth."

Isolde continued boldly, "Are you concerned it might make your father, the Arkhon, look poorly? He does a fine enough job of that on his own."

Tyran spun on her, clenching his jaw. "Don't speak of my father. You don't hear me belittling your precious aunt."

She trembled beneath his gaze. "Because there is nothing wicked to say about her. Do you not hear what they say about your family on the streets?"

"There is plenty to say about any family in Lairhein, including your own," he sneered. Tyran tore his hand away from Isolde, holding himself back from physically striking her.

His hand was shaking at the realization of what he had almost done. He hoped that it was merely the heat getting to him. How much in him was his father? He could *not* harm her.

"Tyran?" Isolde's look morphed from one of defiance to absolute fear.

He maintained his scowl, refusing to let his own panic steal from his argument. He needed to get rid of her before he did something he regretted. "You think that you are perfect. You think that I could not find someone prettier. Go find a feathered pillow and smother your tears. Go ahead and cry away the afternoon, woman. I have other things needing to be done besides listening to your persistent sniveling."

Gods! He hated himself.

Tyran rumbled, "If any soldier whined as much as you, I would cut out his heart and eat it with my wine."

Her eyes started to water. "You do not mean that."

Tyran turned to burn the image of her crying from his mind, swallowing any pain he might feel. He had to pursue Maelili Kluk. It was his duty. He did not have time for Isolde, weddings, or discussions of formal dresses and flowers.

This woman, with her lesser bloodline, understood nothing.

Tyran stormed towards the crowd of Stuhia to where he had last seen the cloaked figure.

Isolde's voice resonated from behind, "I am not one of your soldiers, Tyran!"

He ignored her. He ignored the crowd staring after him. He ignored his anger. Her fear. His hate. The sooner he did as his father asked, the sooner he would be free. Then he could make his amends. But he did not have the time to think about the consequences of his words to Isolde. Dear Isolde. He forced the entire event from his mind.

He had to find Maelili. He would not be held responsible for his family's downfall.

Out of the corner of his eye, a flash of grey danced between two buildings. Tyran hurried in the same direction, reaching for a weapon and shield that he did not have with him.

His breathing was heavy by the time he reached the gap between the buildings. The heat was stifling. He could see more buildings beyond the first, blocking anyone from viewing the alleyway. The pathway looked empty, but Tyran knew better.

The air was stale. Tyran swallowed a cough as he advanced forward, but choked back the dust in his throat.

He stared intensely at the red stone walls that made up either side of the pathway. Crates and barrels, but little else, allowed for few places to hide.

"There is no use in hiding." Tyran's monotone voice was unnatural for the intensity of the situation. He should have felt some sense of urgency behind his words.

Sometimes he hated how cold he sounded. It was a silly thing to notice, but he found himself often contemplating his own triteness.

He was a bit surprised when there was no response. He had not expected anything immediately, but after a moment, he felt foolish standing defensively without any sign of his quarry. His mind murmured uncertainties; it repeated echoes that he could not silence.

"You are persistent, Ser Tyran." The feminine voice of Maelili Kluk was sharp through her clenched teeth. She stepped out from behind a barrel, throwing her hood back with a hint of ferocity.

She was noticeably holding herself at bay. He could imagine the fury of the woman after her brother's and father's deaths.

She could have gotten the jump on him, burning him to ash with Koldovstvo before he had a moment to react. He took note that she had not.

Tyran nodded, glancing back at the street for passersby. The way was empty. He squared off to Maelili warily. "You think you know me?"

"I have known you long enough. We were friends before you left Lairhein, or have you forgotten the moments we have shared? Has the vileness of your father infected your memories as well?"

He said nothing. A man truly did not forget his first kiss. But the gentleness of children is as misplaced as it is misunderstood. He was not a child any longer.

She continued, "It doesn't matter what I used to know of you or what I know of you now. I know who your father is," she sneered. "It takes a certain type of man to follow other men blindly."

"You simply assume I am blind to my father's ways. What is to say I don't take concert in his desires?" Tyran knew he was stalling. Maybe Drast was right. Maybe he could not do this. "Where are the rest of your siblings? Where is Habërmani?"

Maelili's posture changed, giving sign of genuine interest. "Is that what you seek? My father's staff is well beyond your reach. It will never again be seen in Lairhein."

Tyran stared in bewilderment at her. "Who has taken it? Who has fled the city?"

He was surprised when she answered. "Kindel left with Habërmani moments after Claduk. Don't think that we are fools. We knew you would hunt us down one by one." She paused. "We would have done the same."

Tyran ground his teeth. "You should have left with your brother."

"Not all of us are cowards," she replied, unmoved.

"You are forcing my hand!"

"No, Tyran. Don't blame me for the choices you make."

His throat rumbled and he turned his head away, again taking a glimpse outside of the alleyway. Nothing stirred on the streets. Nothing prevented him from ending her here and now. Yet, for some reason, he hesitated.

Leniency had no place in war. Hesitation had no place in war. Tyran had learned these lessons well enough in his father's courtyards when younger and, more recently, in the Shade. Still, he wavered. He could not say why the thought of killing Maelili caused him to tremble. Perhaps it was because he had known her beyond the function of enemy.

The truth was on the edge of his tongue. He admired her.

"You should leave," Tyran bade.

"Leave?" she echoed. The uncertainty in her voice was unmistakable. She had every reason to be cautious. He was a commander of war. He did not know frailty.

Tyran was quick to respond. "Yes."

She stepped towards him, each strand of hair perfectly placed against her grey cloak. "What are you doing?"

"I—" Tyran moved away from her awkwardly. His feet did not want to move the way they should.

Maelili moved closer and closer, waiting for his response. She was soon within arm's reach.

His blood pulsed.

"Why?" Her eyes searched him. He felt them piercing through his stoic guise. "Are you not as evil, as vile, as you seem, Tyran Kaligula? Could it be that power doesn't corrupt absolutely?"

Koldovstvo touched his fingertips and his large hands swooped towards a broken crate at her rear. A thick hunk of wood settled within his hand in an instant. Maelili's eyes expanded.

Tyran did not wait for her outcry.

With the speed and accuracy of a practice sword to a dummy, Tyran bashed the woman across the head. Broken shards fell to their feet as Maelili lost consciousness. He caught her mid-fall, tossing the makeshift club from his grasp.

"You killed her..." the voice trembled from behind.

Tyran turned, holding the Koldovstvo at his fingertips. The way had been clear!

Isolde stood opposite him, wide-eyed and gaping. He released the magic.

He was not sure how long he stared blankly at his wife-to-be. The world stood still. He expected Isolde to appear angry, repulsed, or fearful by his action. Tyran would have even accepted a sense of disbelief. Instead, she looked upon him with compassion.

"What has your father made you?"

The words struck him deeply. His chest tightened. He squeezed his fists until his knuckles cracked beneath the weight of the body. He had to look away from Isolde and gulp air.

To his dismay, his eyes met the limp body in his hand. He answered in a tone softer than dandelions, as though it would mean something more. "She is not dead."

Isolde shook her head.

He thought she was relieved by the news. He hoped the simple fact that he had not yet killed this single girl could salvage the thing that he truly appreciated. Was he going to kill her?

"Her life doesn't mean anything to you, Tyran. Say what you mean!"

Tyran searched frantically, feeling his mind become peppered as it always did. He did not want to consider whether he cared for Maelili. "I love you, Isolde."

Her upper lip quivered, nostrils flaring. Tears welled in her eyes. It came all at once, overwhelming her pretty features. All that was attractive about the woman, all that he cherished, was washed away in a moment of emotional dishevelment. "Do you even know what love is?"

Tyran burbled unsuccessfully. He gently laid Maelili on the dirt and staggered forward.

"Don't come near me, Tyran."

He had never known words to sting him with the taste of a sword's edge, like blood in his throat.

"I…" he searched desperately for words, "want to be with you, Isolde. Don't simply think that because I returned to Lairhein with my shield and not on it, I did not lose something of myself in the Shade. To live, to return to you, I have had to endure nightmares within nightmares. Pain, hunger, loss…I have suffered."

He reached towards her and she withdrew. "Please. I need you to know my thoughts have always been about you. I could not be the man who returned to you had I not changed out in the Shade. Hear me when I tell you I can change again."

Isolde did not look at him. She only had eyes for the redheaded woman lying awkwardly on the ground. "You cannot do this and be with me."

"I will not." Tyran lifted his hands with open palms. He could not be certain the words were true, but he had every intention of seeing them through. "I swear to you, Isolde. I will not harm anyone ever again."

She lifted her gaze.

Tyran stretched out his hand. "Please, come to me."

Chapter XI

"What is it?" Drast muttered again. Walstan bobbed in front of him, darting back and forth before him like a hunting dog eager for his master to follow the trail it had found.

"This way, Ser Drast, this way." He ducked his head, attempting to bow and walk at the same time. "I have something for you. I know you will be pleased."

It was the same each time Drast tried to get more out of the man. He had been lying low for the past week or so after murdering Peter Kluk. He was not used to being so idle.

Drast had denied it all, of course, blaming any actions he took and his subsequent lack of memory on having had too much drink. His father was not terribly pleased about his means, being public as they were, but Peter was in the ground now, so he gave him grudging acceptance. Or, at least, Drast chose to perceive it that way. Moreover, his father's new status prevented people from asking too many questions. Walstan had been his eyes and ears, tracking the other Kluk children for him. His guess was that he had captured another.

"Not much farther, Ser Drast."

Drast could not help but smile. He could not understand it exactly, but for some odd reason he now found a sense of surety in Walstan's instance on calling him *Ser*. His father's lack of appreciation was somehow ameliorated by Walstan's near worship. Drast was generally not one to enjoy such behavior from his underlings, though his brother's recent return and his further slippage from his father's favor was starting to grate on his nerves to the point that he almost felt as though he deserved a little dotage.

Just a little.

They had traveled well beyond the walls of Lairhein to the coastline. A tepid sea breeze touched his right cheek and a thick expanse of alder, yew, and sour gum trees concealed the land on his left. The sun that Drast had so enjoyed last week was gone, replaced now by a grey mist. The air was wet and the sand, even high up on the beach, was damp. Light mist had fallen day after day for the past week or two, and the fog that now hung in the air made Drast want to strike something. He had probably missed the only remaining days of dry heat this summer would have to offer. The rain had come, and humidity could be stifling.

"Here," Walstan said eagerly.

A small fishing cabin stood just beyond the sands of the beach under the bows of the trees guarding the coast, a sturdy if somewhat dilapidated structure the Stuhian fishermen used when going whaling. Drast was surprised to see it empty at this time of the year. As he understood it, whaling extended from late spring to early fall, depending on the type of whale the fishermen were hunting. He expressed his concern to Walstan.

The stocky man nodded. "This cabin is used in the spring, primarily for hunting grey whales. For blue whales, the fishermen take to the western coast." He smiled back at Drast. "We should have no trouble today."

It took a bit of muscle on Walstan's part, but he managed to shoulder the swollen door of the cabin open. "Come in, Ser Drast. Quickly, if you please."

Drast followed while Walstan shut the door behind him with a heavy grunt. The cabin was composed of a single room with a small table and three mismatched chairs. It did not take long for Drast to notice Elena Kluk lying on the floor. The unconscious girl had her wrists and feet bound.

He chuckled warmly, slapping his Voivode on the back. "Well done, Walstan." Drast could have sworn the stocky man blushed.

"Thank you, Ser Drast. I was hoping you would be pleased."

Drast nodded. "Yes, yes, of course." He examined Elena closely as he leaned his bow in a corner beside the door. "I see you have taken appropriate precautions." A nail was driven through her hempen bonds to keep her immobile. Carved into the floorboards over her head to prevent her from touching Koldovstvo was a symbol known as a *Znaki*—a crude eye with a moon and a cross.

"Yes, Ser Drast."

Elena was pretty. Drast could not deny the fact. She was not quite a ravishing beauty as her sister Maelili, but pretty nonetheless. Instead of her sister's bright red hair, Elena had dark orange locks that hung to her waist. Her nose was slightly too large and her eyes slightly too small. But pretty.

He looked back to Walstan. "Wake her."

As the man set to waking the woman, Drast stretched and dragged a chair over to sit at her feet. He worked to calm his breathing, feeling the excitement welling up from his gut. He needed to practice restraint.

"Uh, Walstan? What is happening?" she murmured groggily. "My head. My head hurts."

Walstan stepped away from her, leaning against the wall. Drast made no move and sat watching her as she adjusted to her surroundings. It did not take her long to see Drast at her feet.

When she comprehended seeing him with her, her emerald eyes alit. Baring her teeth, she attempted to kick at him. The bonds about her feet were similarly nailed into the floor, and she managed to only flop awkwardly. "You! You killed Peter!"

Drast was beyond the reach of the woman's needless flailing and sat as calmly as he could. "Yes, dear Elena, I did. You would do well to remember as much."

"You filth! I should burn you where you sit!" Her eyes widened as if she were attempting to use Koldovstvo, and upon realizing that nothing happened, her eyes grew wider still. She craned her neck, twisting to look over her head, as if attempting to verify the existence of the Znaki that prevented her from accessing Koldovstvo. After a moment, she lifted her head so that she could see Drast. "You coward! Let me free of my bonds! Let me access Koldovstvo! You are weak! A sniveling cur to bind me and refuse me a chance to fight!"

Drast chortled. "I would think, dear Elena, you would have learned by now that I am not much in the habit of playing fair. I don't have the time to waste on your petty pride." He eased a foot along her ankle, slowly pushing her skirt up her leg. His eyes did not leave hers. "This will go much more easily if you answer my questions."

Elena shuddered at his touch. "Are you threatening to kill me or rape me?"

"Both." He withdrew his foot. "Although, the former is a forgone conclusion—let us dispense with make believe—the latter is at your discretion, dear Elena."

"Do you think you can simply do anything you want?" she asked, her voice breathy and quivering, the terror evident. "What gives you the right to treat me in this way? To treat my family in this way?"

Drast blinked. He glanced at Walstan briefly, somewhat confused by the question, and smiled. "Why, dear Elena, because I can."

"Power gives you authority?"

"What a ridiculous thing to say. Authority *is* power. Ability *is* power. Aptitude *is* power." He stood. "Do you doubt that I have control here? Do you doubt my proficiency in keeping you here, or my know-how?" He leaned forward over her. "If you do, then by all means, leave." He smiled. "Ah, you cannot? Well, then I suppose that my power gives me the *right* to treat you and yours however I so choose."

Elena had begun shaking, emotive and uncontrollable. Her voice quaked. "How can you be so vile? So evil? Do you not care for your fellow Stuhia? Do you possess no capacity for compassion? Our right to exist is not subject to your whim!"

Drast pulled his quiver from his shoulder and leaned it against his chair. "When I was eight years old, Tyran and I were sword training with sticks in the courtyard." He began unbuttoning the jacket covering his tunic. Her eyes followed his fingers, his hands, horrified. "My brother slipped and fell. I withdrew to let him regain his footing. My father was not pleased." He slipped off his jacket and began to take his tunic off over his head, speaking through the cloth. "He forced me to strike Tyran to show me the necessity of pressing the advantage. And then," he tossed the tunic to the side and turned around to show his back, "my father made my brother strike me to show me the cost of compassion."

"How?" He could hear her swallow. "How long did he force Tyran to hit you?"

Drast turned back to face her, unable to keep his teeth from showing. "Long enough for me to learn the lesson."

"That is monstrous!"

Drast sat back down in his chair, slowly and deliberately. "What is a monster, Elena? Are they born or bred? I am Stuhia, just as you are. I am of a noble line, just as you are." He shook his head. "No, I don't think I was born a monster. If I am a monster, then I was bred to be one—it is my father who made me this way."

"That makes you no less a monster."

"Perhaps," Drast said, easing her skirt up again with the toe of his boot. "But it means that the gods did not make me this way. My father reared me as a monster and I became a monster. I can change. I can leave. I can choose. The fact that I stay makes me more dangerous. I am a monster by choice, not by blood."

Elena's eyes overflowed with tears. She attempted to draw herself away from him, but the bonds about her feet, nailed into the floor, kept her in place. Lifting her head, she whispered, "Please!"

He withdrew his foot again. "If we understand each other, perhaps you will answer my questions."

She dropped her head back to the floor and turned it so that he could no longer see her eyes. "What do you want to know?"

"I want to know where your siblings are." He leaned back in the chair. "Let us begin with Kindel. I know that he took Habërmani after the Claduk." He knew that Tyran had already discovered where Kindel and Habërmani were, but tests were never amiss.

She gave him a grim smile. "Both are beyond your reach now. My brother took the staff from Lairhein and your vile fingers will never touch it."

"Good, good. I am glad you have elected to tell me the truth." He cleared his throat. "Now, where is your brother, Ghanimer?"

Her laugh was deep and throaty. "You don't understand. I am the only one left. After Kindel fled with Habërmani, you murdered Peter, and your brother nearly beat Maelili to death. Ghanimer would not stay. He took Maelili from Lairhein to keep her safe three days ago." She spat at him, "Our line will not be ended with your family's depravity!"

Drast was taken aback. Tyran had said Maelili was dead. He claimed he killed her the same day that Drast had killed Peter. He eyed Elena, scanning her face. She had no reason to lie about Maelili. If her sister were dead, she would be as forthcoming about that information as she was about Peter. If she were telling the truth about Kindel *and* Maelili, then what reason did she have to lie about Ghanimer?

Drast rubbed his chin.

No, she had no reason to lie. Of course, that meant that Tyran had either lied to him or mistaken Maelili for dead when she was not. Regardless, she was out of Lairhein, and that much was all that was really important for the time being.

Walstan suddenly jerked away from the wall and rushed towards one of the closed shutters along the southern wall of the cabin. He put his ear near the window before turning to Drast and drawing his sword.

He mouthed, "Someone is outside."

Drast shot to his feet as the door to the cabin was heavily pushed forward. The intruder stumbled as the door unstuck and gave way. Being on the wrong side of the opening door, Drast could not see who it was, but Walstan's snarl and the intruder's scream—comingled with Elena's—told him that whoever it was, was now dead.

Drast snatched his quiver, looped it over his shoulder, and took his bow from the corner. He nocked an arrow before pulling the door open the rest of the way. A Vucari man bled into the ground, a deep wound through his chest where Walstan had struck him with his blade.

Elena struggled against her bonds violently as Walstan stepped towards the door to peer out.

"Are there more?" Drast asked as he tried to look over Walstan's head.

Walstan backed away from the door, closing it with a forceful shove. With a free hand, he grabbed a chair and wedged it under the handle. "Aye, there are many, Ser Drast. And they heard their fellow's cry."

"Good." He tested the tension on his bowstring, glad the damp had not affected it too much. Walstan gave him an odd look at his excitement, but it did not diminish Drast's eagerness to test his newfound power. He had gotten to play with Peter, but a true test of Koldovstvo would be against the Vucari.

As if his thought were a summons, the door, chair, and all exploded into the room as a great bear surged through. Walstan may as well have left the door open for all the good blocking it had done. Drast fired as soon as the skin-switcher entered, the arrow piercing the beast's thick hide but doing little to slow it.

The pain of the arrow, however, caught its attention and it turned towards him with a roar that made the cabin vibrate. Walstan, unnoticed, thrust his blade into the creature's back, severing its spine. If a bear could show fear, Drast supposed the look on its face would have qualified as the beast's hindquarters buckled.

With half a smile, Drast used Koldovstvo to lift the massive creature and throw it back through the doorway, taking a good portion of the frame with it. The snarls of other Vucari outside told of the effectiveness of the tactic, though the subsequent sagging of the roof made Drast question whether it was wise.

Elena wept, still bound to the floor. "Let me go! I can fight! Don't let me die like this!"

Drast nocked an arrow, unable to stop grinning. "One death is as good as another."

Stepping forward, each twang of his bowstring came in rapid succession. The bear had cleared the entrance and while the various forms of Vucari attempted to regain their feet, Drast wreaked havoc. Arrow after arrow found its mark. Wolf, panther, hawk, and bear were pierced and pierced again.

Drast did not hear the cracking of the roof before it fell on his head. As the rubble buried him, Drast thought his initial use of Koldovstvo against the Vucari bear might have been a little overzealous. That is, until he realized that one of the Vucari had come through the roof in the form of another bear. With the timbers weighing heavily on him and the additional weight of an animal, Drast was feeling more than a little put out.

He embraced Koldovstvo, creating a whirlwind that sent the bear, along with the roof timbers, sailing through one of the remaining walls. The beast took a tree down as it continued on its path with a grunt, a roar, and a whine when the roof collided with it. Drast struggled to his feet to see Walstan facing a trio of panthers. Elena was gone.

How the woman managed to break her bonds, Drast could not say, but he was not particularly interested in solving mysteries at the moment. With a snarl, he pulled a handful of arrows from his quiver and tossed them into the air. Reaching out with Koldovstvo, he sent the arrows into the panthers with as much force as he could muster. Yowls erupted from them and Walstan cast a weary but thankful nod over his shoulder.

"Deal with any others. I need to find Elena." Drast gasped, more winded than he felt.

"She went north, I think," Walstan gulped, adding a belated, "Ser Drast."

Without looking back to see how many of the Vucari remained, Drast set off running down the beach. The fog had begun to clear as the height of day approached and as soon as he came around a copse of yew trees, he saw her running in the distance, stumbling and falling every few steps. It was the saddest attempt to flee he had ever witnessed. She glanced over her shoulder more than a few times to see if she was being pursued.

Drast stopped where he was, a few hundred feet away, and nocked an arrow. Drawing the fletching to his cheek, he measured the distance and let loose the projectile. Shading his eyes from the dim glare of the half-hidden sun, he watched as she stumbled from the impact of the arrow and fell. She stood and attempted to move forward, now dragging her leg behind her, impaled by Drast's shot.

With a sigh, he set forth at a steady jog, his eyes fixed on his prey. She attempted to run for another moment or two, but quickly realized it was futile. Stopping, she turned and Drast felt the effects of Koldovstvo.

The air grew thick and the sand became deep. Drast felt as though he was attempting to run underwater. A snort on his part dissipated her attempts at slowing him. Darkness came next, both blindness and deafness. Drast could not be stopped by such insignificant tricks, and he quickly reversed the effects. In an instant, she was both blind and deaf.

Elena thrashed about in attempts to use Koldovstvo to clear her sight and return her hearing, but Drast resolutely kept her removed from the sights and sounds of the world.

As he neared, he saw that she had begun to panic, her breathing heavy. She spun this way and that with no way of knowing from which direction he came. Vines erupted from the sands and attempted to bind him. Flames and lightning fell from the sky. He walked through it all untouched.

She had aged rapidly from her use of Koldovstvo. She was now an old woman, enfeebled and grey, hardly pretty anymore. She collapsed to the ground, weeping and unable to maintain her use of the life-draining magic any longer. Drast returned her sight and hearing, and she spun about to see him before her.

Though her sight was returned, thick cataracts made her once brilliant green eyes milky so that she likely could see no more than his shape as he approached. "How do you have such power? What are you?"

"I am Stuhia as we were meant to be," Drast sneered. "You weak, sniveling Kluks have drained the Stuhia of their glory and authority. Under the Kaligula name, honor will be restored and the Vucari will tremble under the heel of our boots."

Her head dropped, and she wept unreservedly. She was broken. "I will go. I will flee and cause no more trouble for your family. I am an old woman now. I can do nothing but live out my few remaining days." Her milky eyes found his shape. "Please, let me leave Lairhein and find my kin."

Drast tilted his head to the side. "Unfortunately, my father was quite specific in how I am to deal with Kluks."

Chapter XII

It had been over a week since Tyran had knocked Maelili across the head with the wooden beam and left her in the alleyway. Her limp body lying against the ground still fixed in his mind, blood oozing through her red strands. At least her face had looked peaceful.

Tyran paced in circles around the room, trying to ease his nerves. The tepid sea air that pressed through the curtains only helped in the slightest.

In a dozen battles, he had never been so weak. He had pleaded with Maelili to leave Lairhein. He had shown her mercy. Mercy!

He twisted around circles, dodging the edge of the bed and continuing his march in makeshift circles. He drew deeper breaths as he picked up his speed. His strides lengthened.

Tyran had spent so much time thinking in the past several days that it was a wonder his head did not explode. The worse of all was that he went home after the incident, leaving Isolde at her home, and lied to his father and brother. Tyran could not recall the last time he deceived either one of them. It was likely sometime in childhood. But, no, he had told them that he had killed Maelili Kluk and thrown her body to the sea, and he had done it with a straight face. The two had believed him and he hated himself for it.

The wind pressed harder through the curtains and he sucked in the air through his nostrils before forcing it from between his lips. He circled around again. There would be a path carved in the floor by the time he was finished clearing his head.

Tyran was doing his best to keep track of the lies, and he was drowning. Even now, he was making excuse after excuse to avoid his father's house. He told his father that he was out hunting the other Kluk children, although he was really with Isolde hiding from violence.

Fortunately, there had been no sign of Maelili since the alleyway. It was possible that she really had fled the city. Tyran could only hope that his lie would not come back to haunt him.

He turned on his heel once more, facing a dark shadow that suddenly appeared in the window. It had not been there a moment ago.

"How long before Isolde returns?" Drast stepped out from behind the curtain, his voice hushed.

Tyran took in his brother's wide nose and angled chin. He felt as if this was the first time he had gotten a good look at him since he had returned to Lairhein. He did his best to respond calmly, despite Drast's sudden appearance. He would have used Koldovstvo to enter the room from the streets below. "She will return momentarily. She is downstairs for a moment."

"Her aunt is going out with friends again, is she? It must be peaceful for the two of you to spend the day relaxing in the comfort of her…chambers." Drast's fingers tiptoed through the curtains, pulling them slightly and then letting them go to flutter against the draft.

"Don't try to play mind games with me, Drast. I am not one of your puppets and you are not Father."

His brother's shoulders noticeably drooped as if the words were stinging. His voice raised an octave, giving hint to how deep the statement struck. "That is not my intention."

"Then why are you here?" Tyran asked.

Drast shot back, "Why are you?"

"I told you—"

Drast's hands patted his sides, and he interrupted with a growl. "I know what you told me and what you told father, Tyran. I also know the truth."

Tyran ground his teeth. His brother whispering the words made them that much more dangerous. "Does Father know?"

Drast postponed his response as though the time passed was reprisal for Tyran's deceit. "No. Father doesn't know that Maelili is still alive."

"Good." Tyran could not help but heave a sigh. He almost found himself relieved that Drast had spoken the truth of his lie instead of forcing him to do it himself. That moment was short once Tyran realized Drast was staring at him with the unasked question in his eyes.

His brother shook his head. "It is not for me to tell him. Though you must know that if he learns of it, I will deny ever knowing, and if I ever cross paths with the woman, I will kill her."

Tyran dipped his head. "Fair enough. Listen, I am sorry. I should have said something, but I could not bear the truth of it, not even with myself. I am afraid that I still cannot."

"You are forgiven, so long as you know you never need to lie to me." Drast grinned. "There are plenty of people in this life that I am forced to judge, by Father or for the betterment of the Kaligula bloodline. It is rather…comforting…that I don't need to judge you, as well. I would ask that you don't lie to me, my brother, especially with information as significant as Maelili Kluk. Her being alive is an immediate threat, and one that I would rather know about now than discover as her dagger slides across my throat."

Tyran scratched his head, nodding with discomfort. He understood Drast's concern with Maelili, but he was certain it was all for naught. "She is gone, Drast. She has to be."

"I hope you are right," Drast said. "Still, there is more at risk than the Kluks."

Tyran waited.

Drast turned towards the door as if he heard something that Tyran did not, continuing in a whisper. "The Vucari are drawing nearer to Lairhein. I was handling Elena Kluk when I was attacked by the skin-switchers."

"You killed Elena?"

Drast smiled. "Mm. You are not listening. I will be heading out this evening to find the Vucari camp. They have come awfully close to Lairhein, and I believe that they are readying for an attack."

Tyran bit his inner lip and finally shook his head. "It would be suicide. We are well protected within our walls and our use of Koldovstvo is superior."

"Trust me, Tyran. Something is about to happen. You should come with me tonight."

"Tyran," Isolde's voice yelled from the other side of the door. "Are you okay?"

"Drast," Tyran started, "Father wants us to kill Wolos."

"Wolos?" Drast asked with that damnable grin on his face. "For fun? For the experience? To see if we can? Why in the Netherworld would we kill Wolos?" Drast snorted.

Tyran rubbed his eyes. "It is what Father wants, what he plans. He does not want to die. I think he is afraid."

"Tyran, sweetie," Isolde's voice called.

Drast lifted his eyebrows in amusement.

Tyran ignored him. "We will talk about it later. Be safe."

"Where is the fun in that, *sweetie?*" Drast mocked, a wry twist on his lips. Then, as quickly as he had come, he was back behind the curtain and out the window.

Isolde walked in. "Are you doing okay?"

Tyran turned from the billowing curtains. "Mm."

"Come sit with me on the bed. My aunt will be away for a few hours eating lunch and gossiping with her friends." Isolde's nose wrinkled with her light-hearted laugh. She moved to the bed, taking her own advice, and took a seat.

Tyran joined her. He sat awkwardly on the side of her cot, legs flung over the side, while she stretched out behind him.

"It has been really nice having you here with me." She ran her fingers down his neck. "This is what I imagined it would have been like when you returned from the Shade."

Tyran was not sure how to respond. Guilt pierced at his belly. "I am sorry that I have been preoccupied."

"Don't blame yourself."

He did not turn to look at Isolde. Instead, Tyran looked forward at nothing, thinking of Drast scouting and sneaking in and out of the Vucari encampments without him. "That is easier said than done."

Isolde moved her nails down to his shoulder and back up again. "Is it hard to be away from your family?"

Tyran shivered, goosebumps etching his arms. He was not sure if it was from her nails or the question. It was like she could read his mind.

She had spent the week asking him questions about his family, and he had spent the week avoiding them. The entire time she seemed to look at him like he was an orphan child or a stray dog.

He gawked out the window like a brain-dead corpse, taking in the panoramic view of Lairhein. Being in Isolde's lesser, modest home was much different than his father's estate. There was no view like this at home. He tried to change the topic. "Where is your aunt?"

Isolde's voice was soft, without strain. "I already told you. She is at lunch with friends. You did not answer my question."

Tyran could not be as serene. He did not want to talk about this. "I am fine, Isolde."

Her fingernails scratched into his scalp gently, teasingly. "You don't seem fine."

Tyran hated that he was always on edge, looking for meaning when there was none to be had. Though he could not help think that Isolde was trying to get something out of him, whether it was in him or not. "Is there anything else on your mind, or maybe we could simply sit in silence?"

"I don't want to fight with you, Tyran."

Tyran scrunched up his face, still looking away from her. "I did not know we were fighting. I just don't want to talk about my family anymore."

"Okay." She recoiled her hand. "Would you like to walk through the market?"

Images of Maelili danced in his head. If he saw her or any of her other siblings again, he was not sure that he could keep his promise to Isolde. He told her that he would not be the killer his father wanted him to be, but even now, he felt driven to join Drast in battle instead of watching curtains flutter.

"I would prefer not to go out."

"We could discuss the wedding."

Tyran sighed. It must have been noticeable because Isolde did the same.

"Tyran," she said after a few seconds, "we cannot stay here forever. What are you hiding from?"

Tyran flared his nostrils, sucking in air. "I am not hiding, Isolde. I...I don't know what I am doing. I just need time to think."

"About us?" Tyran could not mistake the pain in her voice.

"About a lot of things, I guess." Tyran answered. It was the honest answer.

Isolde was quiet. He refused to turn around to look at her, afraid that she might have tears in her eyes. After the scene with Maelili in the alleyway, he was afraid of what all she might learn about him.

He relaxed a bit when her fingernails returned to the back of his head. Soothing. Peaceful.

For the next hour or so, she said lovely words to him while his mind meandered. She said things like she "understood him", and she "was there for him", and "he had been through a lot." They were all the comforting things that people said to other people when they had no conception of what to say but were too uncomfortable with silence to keep their mouths shut.

He grunted back when he thought that he should form some kind of response.

The thought crept into his mind that Isolde was plain. He was afraid Isolde was too much like everyone else. His childhood was built around the idea that he was stronger, smarter, and better than others in the world. He had been pushed to perfection. In his fantasies, he imagined his future wife would also be perfect. There was a part of him yearning for her to be perfect.

Isolde was not exactly the epitome of a perfect woman, not to him. She was kind-hearted and beautiful, but she was also naïve and vulnerable. Isolde did not come from a strong bloodline; she was not a battle-hardened warrior. Her family was poor and rarely touched Koldovstvo, even though they were Stuhia. She was not politically or theologically astute. She was ruled by emotion far more than by reason. He was unsure as to whether she really had any opinion of anything beyond weddings, flowers, and love.

Tyran wondered how a woman so far apart from war and death could be with him. He told himself that they balanced each other out. Her oddities are what grounded him to reality. He told himself that love had no bounds. Isolde had enough love in her for both of them. Tyran told himself a lot of things.

But none of those things ever blocked out the scrutinizing voice of Drast. The man was not only his brother but also his closest friend. Drast understood Tyran more than any other person, including Isolde. Tyran knew that he should be wise enough, smart enough, to listen to his brother's advice. But there was a voice nagging him in the back of his head—Drast could never understand.

His brother was too much like his father to understand love.

Then again, it was possible that Drast did not need to understand. Drast knew their father and what the man was capable of doing. Drast focused on survival, and loyalty was the path to living.

Regardless, his father would not allow Tyran to be away for much longer before sending men out to find him. If the Arkhon found him with Isolde, Tyran did not want to think what would happen.

"Are you well?" Isolde's voice broke him from his rambling mind.

In the end, Tyran knew he needed to find peace and to have love. There was no reason why he should succumb forever to war and suffering. "I will be, Isolde. It will just take some time."

"Tyran?" Isolde whispered in his ear.

"Mm." He twisted to see her still lying in the bed. His body had gone numb, nearly forgetting where he was. Her red hair was painted across her cheek, large eyes staring back at him.

"I love you."

Tyran smiled. He was not sure if it was genuine or forced, but he was comforted by a single thought. Whether Isolde was perfect or not, she was his. Maybe that was enough. Maybe that was what love was really about.

"I love you, too."

Chapter XIII

The Vucari army camp was within a thick glade of trees lining the bottom ridge of the Shade Fells. The Vucari only had a handful of tents for shelter or to protect supplies, but no fires. Dark shadowed figures meandered to and fro on the outskirts of the camp a couple hundred yards away.

"Ser Drast," Walstan hissed. "I don't think it is wise to go any farther." He turned to look over his shoulder, then continued. "There are five of us and hundreds of them."

Drast huddled against an alder, unable to keep the excitement from his voice. "Almost a thousand by the looks of them."

One of the soldiers, Nord, croaked, "What are we looking for? We know they are here. Is that not enough? We should return to Lairhein and prepare our forces."

Drast fixed his gaze on Nord. He forgot what a naysayer the man was when he chose him to come along. "We are here to see what exactly we can do. Telling my brother that an army exists is not nearly as helpful as figuring out what they intend. I have to get closer."

"Obviously," Nord's tone scathed, "the Vucari are here for war. Look at the size of their army. We don't even have this many soldiers in our own ranks."

"Which is why we need the advantage of knowing their plans," Drast whispered. "I will not return to Lairhein until I have found something worthwhile."

"Ser Drast," Walstan said, "it may be best if I go ahead. You are far too valuable to risk for simple espionage. I will return to tell you what I find."

"Don't try to steal my fun from me, Walstan." Drast clapped the fellow on his shoulder.

Creeping forward, his knees bent and body hanging low, Drast scrambled from tree to tree. He could hear his men crunching behind him in the foliage. "Move lightly!"

"We are trying, Ser Drast," another man, Mladen, declared. "We can barely see past our noses out here."

Drast peered around the trunk of a tree. The human shadows still stirred in the darkness. He did not see any indication he or his soldiers had yet been seen.

"Stay put and stay hidden. I will be right back."

"Ser Drast?" Walstan objected.

Drast reiterated as if commanding a dog. "Stay."

Without another word, Drast rushed forward, noiseless through the brush. He sprang from tree to tree, staying low and moving quickly. He had been around enough Vucari in battle to know they were perceptive, even at night. Some Stuhia believed that the skin-switchers could see in the dark, which made sense considering the Vucari were seemingly part animal with their perverted magic. Drast decided he was not willing to test the theory.

He extracted his bow and clutched the handful of arrows in his free hand. If he so much as saw a Vucari turn their head in his direction, he was going to put an arrow through their skull.

He stole a look around the trunk again taking measure of the few tents among the trees. Most of the Vucari lay against the dirt, possibly sleeping, while others huddled in factions. The trees gave him some cover, but this was going to be challenging.

Drast crouched with his back parallel to the tree trunk and then spun towards another a few feet away. And another. He peeped again to find that no one had taken notice of him. Luck must be on his side, though he would have preferred to have some moonlight instead of the pale darkness that shrouded the area. Nord was an idiot most of the time, but he was correct in that he could hardly see past his nose.

For a moment, Drast considered touching Koldovstvo to aid him in staying hidden. He could use the magic to shroud himself in darkness, hurry his pace, or eavesdrop from a distance. His fingers twitched momentarily in deliberation before resting against his side.

There was no contest if he used Koldovstvo to help him now. This would be far more enjoyable if he managed to accomplish this feat without the supernatural.

Yes, he would survive this without the use of Koldovstvo. Besides, if a major battle were coming, it was best to save his strength for the real fight.

Movement from the corner of his eye caught his attention. He sank to the ground and twisted towards the shadow. A lightly spotted panther slinked through the trees, sniffing and twisting its head back and forth in the air.

Seeing nothing more in the immediate area, Drast loosed an arrow into the beast's cranium. It plopped down into the dirt with a soft whine and twisted back into human form.

Moving away from the dead Vucari, Drast neared the first tent. He set another arrow upon his bow, ready.

He listened to the murmurs on the opposite side of the tent.

"My da died over here in the early wars. Ma said that he was trying to make peace but the dragon-slayers would have nothing of it. Can you believe the Reds think they are pious?"

"Really? Pious to whom? I have never known the dragon-slayers to worship anyone but themselves."

"Bah!" said a woman in the group. "The Protectors of the Ash Tree said the Reds claimed to worship Wolos in the past. I cannot say who they think Wolos is. The Horned God is too good for their backstabbing ways."

"Mm," hummed the first, a male. "More likely that they adore the Frozen Witch."

Behind Drast, a foot crunched against loose dirt. Twisting quickly, Drast gaped at a male and female who had come as if from nowhere, spears in hand. He fired the nocked arrow, hitting the male in the chest.

The man shouted both in surprise and in pain, grabbing wooden projectile near the fletching.

The woman echoed the outcry, jabbing her spear wildly in Drast's direction. Drast sprang from his squat, swatting the weapon to the side with his bow. He then tumbled sideways to avoid the second thrust. Rolling upright, three more arrows in hand, he fired one into the woman's gut and a rapid second a bit higher up the sternum. She screamed, dropping her weapon, and collapsed to her knees.

The conversation from the other end of the tent had stopped, drowned out by calls and exclamations. The entire camp would be upon him in a matter of moments.

The male and the female on the ground groaned and the male tried to stand. Drast killed him with the last arrow in his hand.

Before he could retrieve any of his spent arrows, another cat-like creature scrambled around the tent towards Drast, growling. With a yowl, it sprang for him. Drast dropped onto his back just in time, squinting as black and orange stripes glided within inches above him.

He forgot his own pact, knowing he had to use Koldovstvo to make it out of the camp alive. The power surged through his veins, skin prickling with its energy. Black shadows swirled swiftly around Drast, propelling him to his feet with more urgency than he could ever manage on his own and sending him a short distance away.

The Vucari was already leaping towards him, too dexterous in animal form for Drast to avoid with the simple tactic.

Flashes of light cackled within the mask of darkness, and forked lightning met the Vucari, tearing through its fur and muscle, splintering bone. Drast intensified his magic, flinging the beast backwards against the earth. Burnt flesh. Blood. In a moment's breath, the creature had been laid to waste.

Drast smiled in satisfaction and gripped his bow a bit tighter. The skirmish would soon alert every nearby enemy if it had not already, he was certain, but he took a moment to savor the singed smell of his small victory.

The elated feeling was short-lived. More Vucari already flooded towards him. Drast did what was necessary.

He ran.

Galloping through the trees, he jumped over underbrush and skipped between the trees. He fired arrows over his shoulder. He had not made it far before his soldiers bound from their hiding place to sprint alongside him.

"Ser Drast!" Walstan shouted.

"Run!" Drast yelled back. Two enemy arrows stuck a tree in front of him. He returned several of his own.

"They are closing! We cannot outrun them!"

His Voivode was right. Drast huffed, footfalls nearing on his left side. There was no way they were going to run more quickly than the skin-switchers. Once they took the form of animals, it would be hopeless.

Walstan pushed himself all the harder on his right side, lengthening his stride to stay with Drast.

"Just keep going." Without looking, Drast twisted and shot three arrows at the closing footfalls. A short yelp sounded as the nearing footfalls ceased.

Walstan turned his head to look behind. "Ser Drast," he panted. "You shot Nord through the head!"

Drast wheezed, taking a double-step to avoid a tree, and looked back. Sure enough, his soldier had one arrow through his cheek and another in his chest. Drast shrugged, finding little choice of words to explain the mishap. "Oops."

The other three soldiers picked up the pace to stay ahead of Drast and his random arrow slinging.

"I don't understand. Why did you go in there, Ser Drast?" Walstan asked.

Drast ran faster. "To see if I could."

The long night was spent running and hiding from the Vucari. They did not only have to outrun their pursuers, but also their own smell.

By morning, Drast had taken the offensive once more.

His boots made cringingly wet suction sounds as he crept through the humid coniferous rainforest. An hour ago, Walstan had indicated a group of Vucari scouts were nearby moving southwards. It was a couple miles from the main camp, which they had been circling throughout the night. He still had hopes of catching wind of how the Vucari planned to take Lairhein.

After speaking with Tyran at Isolde's, he did not want to return to Lairhein empty-handed. Tyran had given him enough trouble about scouting instead of letting his men do the dangerous work, and he certainly did not need to know about his foray into the main army's camp, particularly shooting his own man in the face.

Drast clenched his teeth until they hurt. He slowly lifted his foot and took another step.

He was glad that he had made it out with his skin still intact, which was more than he could say for the few skin-switchers who had gotten in his way. He was disappointed that the whole process had ended up being largely pointless. He had not been able to get close enough to any of the main tents to learn anything of value.

His foot squished down.

He heard Walstan moving behind him and twisted his head around, frowning. He knew he was likely making as much noise as Walstan. There was no cause for both of them to be trying to make their way through this mess towards the three Vucari scouts in the clearing ahead. The rain early that morning had made sneaking far more difficult than last night.

Drast squinted through the branches. The scouts passed around water skins and ate unleavened bread and dried meat. Normal fare for a soldier or scout. He was almost close enough to hear what they were saying. Just a little farther. Squelch.

His oiled boots could no longer keep back the moisture and, worse, he had run out of dry stockings. His feet were soaked through and his toes had begun to chafe from the wetness. It was a struggle to keep his mind off of the burning in his boots. What he would not give to put his feet up by a fire right now. Gritting his teeth, he tried to slide his feet forward so that he did not need to pick them up and could avoid that gut-wrenching sound.

With a stretch, he managed to reach the branch of a thick cedar tree and pulled himself out of the mud and into the tree. Mercifully, the tree did not creak as his weight came to rest on the branch. Easing himself upwards, he began to climb. The next branch up was nearly his undoing, as the combination of slick cedar bark and his muddy boots nearly sent him sailing back to the ground. Quick hands and quicker teeth, which managed to bite his tongue and keep him from shouting, left him dangling in the air.

The tree shook slightly and the Vucari's conversation stopped but resumed after a moment. With painful slowness, he dragged himself to the next branch and softly pulled himself into the next closest tree. Measured breaths that made his chest ache and silent leaps from tree to tree finally brought him within earshot of the scouts.

He could have used Koldovstvo to his benefit in some way, but his encounter on the beach coupled with his adventure in the

Vucari camp had left a streak of silver in his hair that had him feeling more than a little concerned. The ritual with the dragon blood lessened aging effects, but did not eliminate them. Too much Koldovstvo would still kill him. He had been somewhat free with his use of Koldovstvo lately and needed to practice restraint. The coming battle with these fellows was not going to be easy and he needed to keep his strength.

"…the walls. But it will not matter against a hawk or eagle." A younger Vucari male spoke in a deep voice.

A grey-haired female shook her head. "I would not count on such things. The eagle is swift, but a bolt of lightning thrown by a Stuhia is swifter."

A male of equal age nodded in agreement. "Mae is correct. Assume your enemy is wiser than you and knows your weaknesses as well as your strengths. They will look for eagles to dive."

"Then it is the last thing they will see before their deaths!" the young male snarled vehemently.

"It is far more frightening to have death visit without ever having seen its source. It is best to remain unseen until you are ready to strike. An army of mice," he laughed bitterly. "Rodents creeping into the city before our enemy even knows we are there."

Drast blinked. Mice? He hoped that the Vucari tried a full assault rather than such subtle attacks. If they merely snuck into the city and turned from mouse to bear and panther, then the Stuhia would not stand a chance. How could they possible prepare against an enemy who could arrive invisibly and strike whenever it was prepared? He shuddered to think of the chaos that would come from such a clever tactic.

"It is not up to us," the one called Mae said. "We will provide what we know and let the commanders decide the best course of action."

The young male snorted. "A mouse? I will be a wolf or a bear. I will show the Stuhia what it means to fear the Vucari."

"And you will be among the first to die, boy," his senior grunted. "Heed your elders. There will be need for bear and wolf, but I can assure you the first to shift into such forms will be the first to die. Let the black leviathan absorb their hate and drain their years away as they burn Koldovstvo."

A black leviathan could only mean a dragon. Dragons and mice. Drast would have chuckled at the thought if he were not so certain that such a combination spelt out the doom of the Stuhia. He had not expected listening to the scouts would be terribly enlightening, but such news needed to be returned to his father post haste.

"Caution is best. Battles are not a race unless your goal is death." The woman stood. "Come, let us report back to camp."

The other two stood as Drast drew his bow. At the least he could ensure that there would be three fewer Vucari on the field of battle. In a breath, three arrows found their marks, the last cutting off the young male's cry of alarm.

By the time Walstan reached Drast, he was already pulling his arrows free from unmoving corpses. He should have kept one alive to question concerning the dragon, but he did not have the time to spend on such endeavors, and the truth was, he was beginning to grow weary of such bloody means.

"Ser Drast, I heard a scream!" Walstan had his sword drawn, but quickly realized that there was no need for it.

"Walstan, it is time for you to be of use." Drast did not look up as he pulled the last arrow free. "Somewhere in this forest is a dragon." He met his commander's eyes. "Find it."

Chapter XIV

Drem stirred on top of the wall, his breath shallow. "These walls will mean nothing against the skin-switchers. Ser Drast said that their numbers are well beyond our own."

Tyran squinted, trying to penetrate the dampening light. Evening was coming. "It doesn't matter. We will defeat them."

Weeks ago, Tyran had promised his beloved that he would not kill. He would have never guessed that the threat of death would come to his doorstep. Of course, she had to know that his words were slanted. He was a war leader after all. Besides, he had promised his father that he would murder Wolos before he had told Isolde that he would not harm anyone ever again. He was going to have to stop making promises or he would begin to forget his obligations. Did the Vucari even count in the group of "anyone"? He could not imagine that they did.

"I am glad you think so, Ser Tyran. It is comforting to know as much."

"I have never known you to be a man who needed comforting, Drem." Tyran eyed his Voivode, noticing the clean-shaven face and softened gaze.

He hoped that his men had not been gone too long from battle. They had been back home for only three months and already they had seemingly lost their wits.

Drem flared his nostrils. "I know. It may be that I have spent too much time in the arms of my wife. Still, I have never known the Vucari to directly assault a city."

Tyran did not move a muscle. His Voivode was correct. He had also never known the skin-switchers to attack Lairhein either.

The man continued, "It makes me question the will of the gods and our place within their schemes."

"Mm." Tyran swallowed. "We have some role in this world or we would have been wiped from it long ago. I have led you to countless victories. Think of the Shade. We did not falter, did we? Let that give you strength, Drem."

"I understand what you are saying, but I don't think that yesterday has any foretelling over today. Civilizations come and go, do they not?"

"Not this one."

Drem blinked, probably weighing Tyran's words. Tyran knew he did not have the gift of oration like Drast.

"We are lucky to have your father as the Arkhon. Jonafel Kluk would not have been prepared for this. He would have been too caught up in the politics to keep our scouts along the borders and our armies at the ready," Drem said.

Tyran was surprised by the sudden change of topic. Flattery was unlike Drem. But his Voivode appeared genuine.

"I am glad to hear you see the value in Arkhon Kaligula." Tyran said under his breath. He guessed that it was the most appropriate response he could give to such an open statement of loyalty. He had thought as much many times before and considered it now: Drem was a good soldier.

"I forget myself and the task at hand." Drem looked over his shoulder. "It would be wise, Ser Tyran, to give some words of encouragement to the soldiers. Your brother's army gathers as well."

He supressed a grimace. It was like Drast to get his men prepped for battle and not be readied himself. Drast had rushed to the city to tell him an army was marching, pulling Tyran from Isolde's home. Now, the man was nowhere to be found.

"I suppose," he muttered to Drem. Tyran had not prepared anything to say for this moment. "I am not in the mood for speeches. You may do it."

Drem hesitated, perhaps waiting for Tyran to retract his command. After a moment, he stepped forward to address the assembled soldiers.

"Our lives are not measured by a single moment but measured against all moments."

Tyran smiled. Not only was Drem pulling from an ancient Stuhian commander's words, but he did so in the same voice he used to order troops around the battlefield. Commanding, but far from inspiring.

"Don't seek to be remembered by the years you have lived. Seek to be remembered by those you have not. Tonight, we will not hide from the moments beyond death; we will embrace them. War calls to us, men. For glory! For honor! For remembrance!"

Though Drem's speech was short, a roar of approbation soon followed. It was raucous. Armaments were thrust towards the first stars that pierced the night sky. There were fewer than two hundred men prepared to die, and still the sound was vociferous enough that the looming Vucari surely shuddered in its wake.

"An excellent speech, soldier," Drast said with an easy grin. "From *The Ballad of Jalor*, is it not? It is fitting given tomorrow's mourning."

Tyran winced, keen to hearing what most men would not in his brother's caveat. "What grieves you?"

Drem made the effort to seem preoccupied with the laces of his armor. Drast peered at Drem with hesitation but answered anyway.

"The Vucari come with a dragon."

Drem let loose the laces and gawked with disbelief.

Tyran stepped closer to the red stone of the wall, scanning the darkness. He saw nothing. He heard nothing. "How do you know this?"

Drast, the man who grinned at all things, remained solemn. "Walstan. I heard a rumor of the beast and sent him and a small troupe of my men to scout for the truth of it. He reached me in Klukas to verify that there is a dragon among the Vucari."

"And?" Tyran pressed.

"From the description," Drast gritted his teeth, watching Drem, "it sounds like Torn'ash. A black leviathan with eyes burning as yellow as the sun itself."

"Torn'ash. But he is from legend. Ballads a thousand years old!" Drem exclaimed. The concern in his voice could have been the whispers of nightmares.

Tyran would not undermine his brother. To think that a serpent as ancient as Torn'ash could be witnessed by any living man sounded like madness. Yet the dryness of his throat and the stiffness in his chest told him that the words were true.

Few dragons in Stuhian myths were ever mentioned by name. Legend said that Torn'ash was only second in might to the notorious Zyem, the great dragon who guarded the Kalinov Bridge, which led to the path to the Netherworld, hidden deep within the Shade.

Mystics during the time of the Carian Council wrote about Torn'ash. He was referred to as the *Viy*, or the Father of Serpents.

"Beware the eye of Viy." Drem spoke the superstitious rhetoric that Tyran was thinking himself. "I have heard the beast has a hundred heads and a thousand tails."

Drast snorted, "I doubt that Walstan would have left out such pertinent details. That a dragon does come is worrisome enough."

"We have no way of knowing that Torn'ash supports the Vucari in their siege," Tyran reasoned.

Drast scoffed, "Don't start quoting some axiom about assumptions being misleading or any other nonsense, Tyran. I think it is safe to consider that a dragon flying this way is bad and its timing more than simple chance. If you recall, you did kill one recently. Such an action cannot be done without consequence."

Tyran opened his mouth but Drast continued without taking a breath. He did not understand how the man could think—and then speak—faster than he could breathe.

"It would be fortunate if Torn'ash burned the Vucari with equal ferocity as it would any Stuhia, but I doubt that is the case. With that in mind, we will not have the tactical advantage behind this wall. If the army remains here, we will do little but watch Lairhein corrode under the fire breath of a dragon and the corrupted magic of the Vucari. We must move the armies outside of the wall to a battlefield beyond the city."

Drast turned to face the east. "Out there, we will crush them."

Tyran's whiskers scratched against his lips. He knew that time was running thin, and he was certain that Drast was not telling him everything. The man always had a hidden scheme, much like their father.

"What prevents us from being picked off on the open battlefield? Here, within the walls, we can thin out their attack force and strike them with the full force of our legion. Your archers alone have the tactical advantage with their current placement."

Drast had the nerve to laugh out loud. "They have no ability to move behind the walls. An archer has to fire and move. Only children would stand in one spot and keep shooting."

"Not all archers are able to run and shoot at the same time, Ser Drast. Beyond the wall, we will be forced to use Koldovstvo." Drem sided with Tyran. "The Vucari will have to use their magic to breach our walls. With the same tactic we won on the outskirts of the Shade, we will also be victorious in this fight. They will exhaust themselves before they reach us."

"The cost is too great. We would never recover from the damage to the city or to the citizens. Our defenses and morale would be weakened. What happens if more Vucari cross the sea and attack us in a week or even a month?" Drast contended and then answered his own question. "There would be no victory."

Tyran had to admit that his brother's argument was valid. "Yet being spread wide against a dragon will consume both our armies, Drast. We cannot fight in the open against its fire breath."

"Hehehe. Yes, we can," Drast beamed. He pulled a gunny sack from beneath his cloak and widened the opening. Inside were the familiar golden egg-shaped stones.

"The sharishka," Tyran said with disbelief. They were the stones used to protect them at Tekorga during the battle between his father and the late Arkhon. Now his brother had revealed his hidden scheme. "Those are kept and protected within the chambers of the Ninth Council."

"They were." Drast sealed the bag once more and returned it to its holding place on his belt. "I have only borrowed them for the time being. These stones will allow us to cast Koldovstvo and attack the Vucari while protecting our own forces. It should even keep us safe from the dragon's fire breath."

Drem frowned. "Should?"

Drast did not acknowledge the man, but kept his gaze on Tyran like he was waiting for approval or a compliment. "Tyran, you heard the Ninth Council yourself. These stones were created to protect the Stuhia in battle."

Tyran clenched his jaw. "Does our father know? Do we have the approval of the Ninth Council?"

"It is a bit late to call an assembly and ask permission," Drast sniffed. "Our duty is to protect this city. Our victory will stop any questions that could possibly arise concerning the steps taken. Doubly so when we present the body of Torn'ash."

Drem looked to Tyran.

Tyran rumbled his throat in contemplation.

Drast nodded. "We are of an accord, then."

Tyran's eyes widened, but he said nothing to Drast's interpretation of his grunt. He could not muster an argument to halt his older brother. Drast never gave him a chance to think things through properly.

"Open the gates," Drast ordered, using Koldovstvo to lift his gruff voice. "Go, my brothers, and take the field. Do not cower from death. Let the Vucari fear our steadfastness. Our courage does not falter. Our hearts do not wane. Our spears do not break. Our shields do not shatter. So go now, and take the field. Hold it to the last. Defend the sacred blood that flows in your veins. Go forth, my brothers! Tonight, we claim our destiny. Tomorrow, we drink to our fallen!"

The din of the combined armies thundered across the ground. Drem's speech had resolved the men, but Drast's words seem to rouse something deeper within them. The gates opened and the footfalls of the soldiers advanced forward.

Tyran could already hear them singing their death dirge.

The moon was absent, the expanse of the sky glittering with lights, reflected against the rolling waves of the Neabou Sea to the left. A mere two hundred paces from Lairhein's walls, Tyran had always considered it to be a natural barrier against invasion. After his battle with the Vucari coming out of the Shade Fells, he knew his assessment had not been entirely accurate.

Tyran could hardly make out the entirety of the Stuhian forces in the dark. The ground was not level and broke his line of sight. Coupled with gusting winds that made it difficult to hear anything, he might as well have been blind and deaf. Moreover, he was itching with discomfort from having to negotiate strategy with Drast. He still had not decided how wise he was in listening to his brother. Drast was good at many things, but strategy was not among them.

Two columns of about thirty men were positioned near the shoreline, well beyond the protection of the sharishka. Tyran had insisted on the wing guard maintaining their position to keep the rest of the soldiers from being flanked. Meran, one of Tyran's least capable Voivodes, had been left to command the men.

The opposing wing guard on the left was positioned as reinforcement, should the dragon make an appearance. Three columns, one from Drast's army and two from Tyran's, were structured in the shape of a half-arc. Kormish, Tyran's Voivode, commanded them. Sixty paces to his rear were Tyran and Drast with the four columns of archers.

Ahead of Tyran, at the ready, was Drem with the remaining three columns of the Stuhian army. These men formed the front line. Tyran could only hope that the extra men were not needed; besides the wing guards, all the men were within the sharishka.

Meanwhile, Drast had become edgy. And Walstan and the scouting troupe had yet to appear.

"We will do well until the Vucari step within the boundaries of the stones," Drast said. "Do whatever you must to keep them beyond the perimeter."

Tyran tightened his hand around the mace at his belt. The two-foot yew haft felt familiar in his grasp. He suddenly realized that it had been too long since he had held it.

"This is good," Tyran said. It was likely that he was trying to convince himself, but the grunt from his brother indicated that his simple statement was not lost on the wind. Without warning, his older brother's hand clasped his shoulder.

"Come dawn, the power of the Kaligula bloodline will never be questioned again."

Tyran nodded, forcing a smile that did not involve his teeth. He wished that he could think as positively as Drast. The other man may see victory in the coming hours, but Tyran only envisioned his own guts splattered across the grasses.

He blinked several times, erasing the image from his mind.

Drast pointed towards the trees, far from the walls of Lairhein. The Vucari force advanced. "Here they come."

"Ready," Tyran ordered, powered with Koldovstvo. The archers ahead of him nocked their arrows. "Aim."

The arrows were pulled against the strings and angled upwards.

A brief moment passed as the Vucari began to fall into ranks. Drast peered ahead, squinting into the night. "Now."

"Fire!" Tyran bellowed.

Upon release, each archer ignited their arrows with the power of Koldovstvo, and fire blazed towards shadowed shapes that marched across the uneven ground. Shouts of warning echoed from the enemy, but for some it was too late.

Screeches of anguish sounded about the same time that Tyran again shouted, "Fire!"

More arrows rained down. Like a downpour, arrows tore through the heavens and into the flesh of the Vucari.

"Hold," Tyran bellowed. Feeling the dragon blood churn inside of him, Tyran used Koldovstvo to strengthen the flames of the fallen arrows. Fires erupted across the battlefield ahead of them, lighting up the numbers of Vucari soldiers.

Their numbers doubled those of the Stuhia and more, but it mattered little to Tyran. The power of the Stuhia was greater.

He directed the flames to tear in and out of the ranks opposing him, searing the Vucari without restraint. Tyran let the power loose after seconds, killing handfuls. The act would have killed him before the ritual. But drinking the dragon's blood had given him greater strength than he had imagined. Still, he could feel his muscles weaken.

The battalion ranks at the front were invigorated by the display of Koldovstvo cast by their commander. In moments, the soldiers wielded the magic themselves. They did not know that neither Tyran nor his brother would be penalized with the same aging effects that the men would suffer. Still, the men toyed with the flames that had been created, causing them to dance amongst their enemy.

The Vucari barked orders frantically across the field.

Columns of Vucari advanced towards the center, where Drem echoed the command of Tyran to hold their ground. Another set of arrows was released but very few hit their mark. Tyran had heard that the Vucari could see in the dark. He was at a loss for words, watching the way that the skin-switchers hurtled back and forth dodging arrows.

Snarls and growls resounded across the battlefield. Many of the half-naked or fully naked enemy transformed into beasts, some familiar and some not so much.

It was a monstrous man, fortified and nearly a head taller than Tyran, who first breached the front ranks. Unshorn hair, extending the length of his body, slanted like long grass in a heavy wind and rocked as he stamped forward. The hooved feet were forgotten when the pointed broad horns on his skull plowed into the frontline. Several men were split open, their insides spilling out onto the ground.

"Take him down," Drem cried.

Despite its hulking size, the thing moved with the speed of a sparrow. Lightning ricocheted and fire laced through the air within the sharishka towards the Vucari, but the oversized brute avoided each feeble effort. His fists bore into the skulls of the soldiers. More Vucari joined him, slamming into the battalion columns.

The men began to fall back against the strength of the Vucari.

Tyran sneered, leaping over the archers with Koldovstvo in a single bound. Drast's arrows zinged past him, two striking the giant beast of a man, and still the Vucari did not falter.

Tyran pulled his shield from his back and lifted his mace. "Make way! Move!"

Even in the heat of the battle, the Stuhia soldiers were quick to follow Tyran's commands, parting to allow him through. As soon as the way was clear, Tyran flung his mace. The heavy bronze ball slammed into the Vucari, crushing into its chest upon impact, sending the creature stumbling backwards. It grimaced and snarled, taking sight of Tyran sprinting at him in full force.

Using his magic, Tyran pulled his mace back to his hand and entered the vicinity of the beast.

The hulking Vucari lunged forward, a meaty fist propelling itself into Tyran's midsection. He spewed blood as a second fist slammed into the side of his head.

His world rocked, blurred.

He heard Drem scream somewhere in the distance. As if a memory or a dream, he saw the beast reel its shoulder back as three more arrows sank into its chest.

Tyran cursed. This is why he did not go storming into battle like Drast. This is how men were killed.

The creature growled from deep within its chest, preparing another onslaught. Blood oozed from its wounds. The monster was slowed, but hardly done.

Koldovstvo quaked within Tyran as he pulled at the void, capturing the sight of the cosmos, sensing the gap between time and space.

Light seared from the chest of the enemy before him, rupturing the meat of the man, blood spewing, drenching the adjoining fur. The very fabric of the man, the soul of his existence, was torn from him. A horrifying, shrieking wraith was ripped from the flesh. It was a ghostly distortion of what may have been the Vucari before the transformation, with dark eyes and stringy hair. The thing bent and vibrated as energy surged through its core.

Tyran strangled it with the power of Koldovstvo. It exhaled. The screams halted. In haste, it expired like a campfire buried in water.

Fumes of its being, like fog, were taken by the wind as the shell of the monster sank to the ground. Tyran fell to his knees.

He coughed, feeling the impact of the magic he had cast. Even the dragon's blood could not keep the years from touching him after such a powerful spell.

Drast was the first to reach him. "Tyran! What in the Nine Lands was that?"

The multi-faceted roar silenced any response Tyran may have had, as well as the surrounding Stuhian forces. It started low, it rumbled, like the howls of a thousand demons feasting, and ended with a defining explosion of brutality unheard by any living man. The shadow blocked out the light of the stars as a leviathan hurtled over their heads, dropping fire breath upon them.

The blaze washed over the unseen barrier that was created by the sharishka. The fire breath swelled over the invisible dome, harmless to anyone within the protective field. What should have been screams of pain and anguish to reach the ends of time were drowned out by the hollers of Stuhian soldiers, filled with tittering amusement, empowered by their commander's display of power and now the protective elements of the sharishka.

"Torn'ash," Drem said, standing near the brothers.

Drast chortled, his eyes scanning the magnificent leviathan. His red hair curled, falling over his ears. His blue eyes seemed to glow against the distant fires.

"Tyran," he smiled. "You are going to need a larger wagon."

Tyran spit out another mouthful of blood, ignoring the man's humor. He tried to stand but was unable. His insides felt broken and his skull ached.

Drem shouted at the soldiers that had reformed the line and fought back the Vucari soldiers. "We need a healer!"

A soldier, unknown by Tyran, was at his side in seconds. A red-yellow glow pulsed into Tyran, mending him. The man before him wore a bronze helmet that hid much of his features, but his face wrinkled and eyes drooped as he repaired the insides of Tyran.

Tyran felt his body pulsate as the energy of Koldovstvo healed him, not in age, but in injury.

Tyran took a deep breath, inhaling like oxygen had never touched his lungs. The man before him had surrendered hundreds of days of his life so that Tyran could live one more.

Tyran clapped the man's shoulder with respect. "If you survive this night, you will be rewarded greatly, my brother."

The man's voice rasped as he dipped his head. "Thank you, Ser. May the Kaligula bloodline prosper and reign for time without time."

"We are being flanked!" a soldier shouted from the front brigade.

"The northern wing has fallen."

Tyran scrambled to his feet, finding his shield and mace once more. Sure enough, the Vucari had circumvented their plans. Waves of the enemy soldiers filtered from the north. It meant thirty of their soldiers and Meran were already dead.

He should have never listened to Drast's strategy!

Drast shooed the healer. "Back to your column, soldier. The dragon is circling this way once more."

Tyran turned around. Another burst of fire breath was pummeled at the left wing guard. Again, the golden stones prevented the scorching heat from touching the soldiers. Though he was certain it would not be long before they were completely overwhelmed.

"Archers!" Tyran cried, backpedaling towards the southern wing guard. "Attention to the north. Fire at will!"

It would not stop the assault, but it would slow the Vucari.

Drem said, "They have another horned brute in their midst."

"He is right." Drast pointed at the Vucari that marched from the shoreline, stealing Tyran's attention once more. A towering ogre of a man led the enemy troops with the same ferocity as the first.

"If I may, Ser Drast," a voice said from behind.

"Walstan," Drast said, with a cough, eyeing the scouting troupe he had sent forth earlier that day. "Glad you have decided to join us."

"Let me hold the northern line, Ser." Walstan bowed his head.

Drast snorted. "If they bypass you and your men, it better be because you are dead."

The redheaded man gripped his spear. The thirty men at his back grunted in response.

"They will not skirt us, Ser. You have my word." Walstan stalked towards the Vucari, beyond the archers, meeting them head-on.

"Drem," Tyran said, "the frontline is yours to manage. Hold the line. Don't let them divide our company."

"As you command, Ser," Drem said.

Exclamations and cries resounded from the south as the ground quaked. Tyran had to reposition his feet so that he would not fall to his knees all over again.

He watched the leviathan—pitch in color, scales shimmering in darkness—crush the Stuhia like insects beneath a heel. Its three heads, semi-circular with cut-throat horns circled like boars' tusks, were frightening. Several Stuhia leapt and ran as best they were able, only to be snatched up between the fanged jaws. The leviathan was easily as large as a full column of men with its wide breadth and coiled tail. Its wings were overextended, stretched forebodingly, giving Torn'ash the impression of being three times his size.

It had landed within the sharishka. One head roared while another spread its fire breath. The third joined the second in felling fire. This time, there was no protection from the scorching rays of heat. Half of the right guard was burnt to ash in a moment.

"Hehehe," Drast chuckled. "I hear glory sounding its sweet horn, Tyran. Let's lay the beast to waste."

"Mm," Tyran grunted.

Tyran dashed forward with his shield lifted, but Drast was the quicker. The man shoved forward, firing arrows rapidly at the dragon, dodging dead bodies or bounding over them as though he had purposefully laid them there ahead of time.

The sharpened arrows did nothing to Torn'ash, bouncing off or snapping on impact.

Tyran threw his mace. It soared through the air and struck one of the heads. The impact barely upset the creature before his mace returned to his hand.

Drast had slowed his pace as they crossed the field. "Regular armaments are useless. How did you kill the other?"

Tyran kept his stride equal to that of his older brother. "Pierced its heart while it slept."

Drast burst into deep, hearty laughter.

"A leviathan is not an ignorant monster, Drast," Tyran warned. "They have not lived ages to simply die at the hand of men."

"And yet, it will."

Drast, wool-brained as ever, sprang towards Torn'ash, firing another arrow as though this one would do something more spectacular than the last half dozen.

It was no surprise when the result was the same.

The first of Torn'ash's heads picked at the remains of the scattering columns. The second and third turned towards Drast. The first that attempted to assail Drast was caught off-guard as Drast became ethereal, like smoke—black and grey swirls of mist—leaping from the ground to the crescent head of the beast. Drast fired an arrow straight towards the skull. The arrow broke in half, doing nothing to Torn'ash.

The second head swiped towards Drast, and again, he filtered through the air like vapor on water's edge and landed fully solidified on the leviathan's back.

Tyran somersaulted under the dragon and lost sight of Drast. The gloomy scales gleamed above him. Koldovstvo lifted pinpricks on his skin as he channelled the magic through his mace. He swung the yew haft, smashing his weapon into the dragon. The energy caused the leviathan to screech in pain.

Tyran loosed a battle cry and hit Torn'ash for a second time. He may have heard a bone crack; it was likely the scales.

Tyran ducked instinctively as a boulder soared through the air, smashing into the center head of the leviathan. Kormish, his Voivode, bawled from a distance away using Koldovstvo to fling another chunk of land at the dragon.

Kormish had aged twenty years.

With the second rock striking the same head, one of the horns shattered and the neck went limp.

Drast appeared, running along the terrain, calling dark energy, casting forked white bands of light from his fingertips. Silver bolts cackled and tore through Torn'ash's neck, severing a head from the body. Crimson blood doused the landscape.

The other two heads roared in defiance before unleashing fire breath onto the amputated extremity, healing the wound.

Tyran stepped backwards. "Impossible."

"The dragon cannot be beaten, Ser," Kormish said. The Voivode hobbled over to join Tyran beneath the beast.

Tyran maneuvered about as it circled. "It has a heart. It can be beaten!"

He crushed his mace into Torn'ash again. His weapon reverberated against the beast. The sound of the collision was deafening. Tyran was keen to notice the black scale beneath had become dislodged.

The skin of the beast was visible.

The beast howled, feeling the pain; it had become vulnerable.

The sound of the Stuhian soldiers hollering rose from the north as victory was declared over the Vucari. The soldiers had found their columns and were advancing on the dragon from the rear.

Tyran grabbed Kormish. "You pierce that flesh at my command."

"Yes, Ser," Kormish equipped his spear.

"Drast!" Tyran cried out. He ducked into the open, evading the gnashing teeth that sought him. He skimmed over the irregular ground. "Ready your bow!"

Drast sprung to him with Koldovstvo, his bow held outright. "Ready!"

"Kormish, now!"

Torn'ash roared as the spearhead cut into its flesh. The two heads whipped about in anguish, dragon fire lighting the heavens and felling towards Drast and Tyran.

Tyran vaulted with Koldovstvo, his shield forming a barrier between his body and the flame. The heat parched the air on either side of him as he flew towards Torn'ash.

Flinging his shield away, he surged with power and slammed his weapon into the chest cavity of the leviathan. Scales fractured.

Drast needed no direction. His arrow discharged, propelled by Koldovstvo, towards the fleshy opening of the oversized leviathan. The monster of legend sounded its guttural bawl.

As if given bearing by the gods themselves, Torn'ash curled its first head and snapped Drast's arrow between its jaws.

"Fire!" Walstan and Drem cried in unison from the rear. The Stuhian archers loosed their arrows at the mark, but it was too late. Torn'ash wrapped its wings, twisted its bulk, and launched into the night sky.

Drast shouted after the dragon.

Tyran joined his brother in fury. Torn'ash cowered away from the power of the Kaligulas, racing back towards the Shade.

Chapter XV

"How many are dead?" Arkhon Kaligula growled. His face was red and shaded its way towards purple as he paced back and forth in the courtyard. "Mm? Tell me that. How many of our men are dead?"

Drast saw Drem whisper something into Tyran's ear. His brother had aged significantly during the battle and now looked as if he were the older of the two. "Eighty-four men are dead, Father."

"Nearly half of our standing force has been obliterated! What will we do if our enemy renews the assault?" He had stopped pacing and flecks of spittle flew from his lips. "How can we defend our city? How can we survive without soldiers to fight?"

"There was a dragon, Father," Drast said. He cleared his throat. "Torn'ash."

"And you thought the best way to fight a dragon was in an open field?"

"It seemed preferable to the streets of Lairhein."

The blow sent Drast to the ground. His father had not deigned to backhand him, as he was wont to do, but instead punched him solidly in the eye. "Do not get smart! We have city walls! We have defenses in place to protect our city!"

"We do, Father," Tyran said softly while Drast regained his feet. "But those defenses are not meant to stand before a dragon."

"And your concern is that the dragon might tear down our walls? Burn our city?" the Arkhon spat. "Walls can be refortified. Cities can be rebuilt. The dead thank you for saving us the trouble, but now we do not have the men to defend these walls! It takes time to breed men. It takes time to train soldiers. We cannot afford to lose them because you wanted to go play in the field!"

Drast swallowed hard. "It was my fault, Father. I convinced Tyran that foregoing the city's defenses would be best."

His father's imperious glare fell on him. "As reassuring as it is to hear that blame may be laid upon the son who is always most deserving of it," his eyes turned back to Tyran, "I expect that your brother should be capable of recognizing your ineptitude for what it is and make decisions accordingly."

"Would you like for us to extend our condolences to the families that lost loved ones?" Tyran muttered. Drast considered it a weak attempt to change their father's focus.

The Arkhon snorted. "I do not give a whit about the lost or their loved ones. It was their duty and their place to die when I choose. But make no mistake, it is I who make that decision and neither you nor your brother will make such rash choices without my approval." He fixed them both within his glower. "Not only did you alter the planned defense of the city without discussing it with me by your taking to the field, but you failed to tell me that a dragon was among the Vucari. All of the failings of last night can be laid at your feet."

"And the successes?"

Drast cursed under his breath upon recognizing Walstan's voice. The stocky man stepped forward. Like Tyran, Koldovstvo had aged him drastically so that he was old enough to look of a similar age to Dagmar Kaligula. The stocky man quivered with anger. Or, Drast thought, fear. It was difficult to say, but his voice quivered so that he had to repeat himself before the Arkhon heard him.

"Whose man is this?" the Arkhon snarled.

"He is mine, Father." Drast had trouble keeping moisture in his mouth. "I will see that he is doubly punished for his outburst and disrespect."

"Your weakness as a commander and as a son is becoming ever more evident. I am beginning to question your usefulness to me with your many failings."

"I apologize, Father, I will…"

"If I am going to be punished, then I will speak freely," Walstan said shakily. "You give Ser Drast too little credit, Arkhon. He single-handedly kept your position strong while Ser Tyran was away. He secured your position as Arkhon. He dealt with the impending threats of the Kluk children. And his plan secured victory for us last night while saving far more men than hiding behind the walls could have ever done."

Their father did not respond, but Drast sensed the Koldovstvo as Walstan flew backward from the Arkhon and slammed into the wall surrounding the estate. The Voivode hung suspended as the Arkhon looked at him with unveiled wrath. "How dare you question your Arkhon? By what rights can you claim the authority to say such things to me?"

Walstan screamed as a thousand points of blood seeped through his clothes and beaded on his bare skin.

Dagmar's voice was eerily flat. "I should flay you alive and hang you from the battlements. I should let the carrion beasts finish your life. You are not even worthy to die by my hand."

Drast kept his lips sealed. Anything said on his part would certainly mean the man's death. He only hoped that his father would show some restraint. If not, he would shortly be in the market for a new commander.

He turned his gaze from his man to look back at his father. Showing too much interest in Walstan would also mean Drast's death. With a sneer from his father, Walstan was released from the wall and fell where Drast could hear him weeping and shuddering.

Dagmar Kaligula fixed his sons with a disgusted look. "I wash my hands of your incompetence."

Without another word, their father turned and stalked into the estate.

Drast quickly moved to Walstan, Tyran at his back. "You are lucky you are not dead," he murmured.

Walstan shuddered. "I am sorry, Ser Drast. You have done so much for your father. I could not bear to stay silent."

"Well, hopefully this will be a lesson to you," Drast snorted. "Tyran, help me move him. Father only sought to inflict pain, I don't believe his injuries have caused any real damage."

His brother grunted, and together they helped Walstan to his feet. "When will he see how much you have done for him, Ser Drast? How much both of you have done?"

"We will get recognition when he is dead," Drast chortled, helping Walstan walk.

"If even then," Tyran added with a wry smile.

Drast chuckled. "Aye, he will likely reach beyond the grave to tell us of our inadequacies. His spirit will wake us each morning to remind us that the sex we had the night before was not good enough."

Tyran and Walstan laughed, the latter cringing in pain from the effort. "I suppose the sooner you take your father's place the better, Ser Drast."

Drast saw Tyran's significant glance at Walstan's comment and answered, "Such talk is dangerous, Walstan."

Walstan nodded. "I understand, Ser Drast."

"Take my place?" The sound of the Arkhon's voice, faint and precarious, sent a chill up Drast's spine and weakened his knees. Time stilled as he caught Tyran's wide blue eyes and Walstan's gaping teeth. The two beheld his father behind him in horror; Drast had never witnessed such fear, even in the presence of Torn'ash.

Drast could not help but look upon Walstan with pity. It took all his resolve to shift his expression.

Only half a beat behind his father, Drast acted. He compelled himself to appear irate, pretending that he had not heard his father's words. "No! You don't understand, you flea-bitten pile of sheep-dip!" Drast stood as straight as an arrow, blowing his chest up as though he were Tyran, lifting his voice as if he were his father. "Did the Arkhon not deliver you a just punishment for your insolence? And now you speak of treason when he is out of earshot. You attempt to pit me against my father. Despite what you may think, I am loyal to my father. I will not be swayed by your venomous tongue, nor any other's. I cannot stand to have such an ungrateful soldier in my father's army or in my father's city. The law of Lairhein is clear concerning treason. As son of the Arkhon, I am fit to pass judgment and execute your punishment." Drast paused, almost hoping that his father would intervene—or Tyran.

His brother only looked at him coldly, as if carved from stone. The shock had disappeared as quickly as it had surfaced. Tyran dipped his chin, shifting his eyes towards the ground.

"Death," his father supplied.

"Ser Drast?" Walstan fumbled. His face was painted with blood and pain from the Arkhon's *lesson*, but neither the blood nor the physical pain seemed to affect him as much as Drast's words.

Drast nearly faltered as Walstan searched his eyes, pleading. His Voivode was likely the only man whom Drast would ever trust besides Tyran. Yet Walstan asked for the one thing Drast had lost the power to give. "Please, have mercy…"

Drast bit his cheek, tasting the metallic tang of blood. Reaching out with shaking hands, he snapped Walstan's neck. The cracking caused him to catch his breath in his throat. Walstan slumped to the ground, eyes open but lifeless.

Silence ensued. Drast could not look away. The look on his Voivode's face was stained on his memory.

The Arkhon said tersely, "Half a lifetime gone and you finally did something right."

Drast did not move. Did not respond. And after several moments, the sound of his father's footsteps faded into the estate. He did not know how long he sat cradling Walstan's head. He did not remember kneeling. He did not remember taking his Voivode in his embrace. But when he felt Tyran's hand on his shoulder, he departed.

Chapter XVI

Although Tyran marched through the echoing hallway, he could not hear his own footsteps over the thudding of his heart. He felt faint, nauseous, and altogether ill at the thought of speaking to his father about Isolde. His father was not only unkind, but he was also unfeeling. If the incident with Walstan in the courtyard was not enough, Tyran could think of a hundred other examples.

He had not seen or spoken to Drast in days. The man was avoiding all human contact. The last time Tyran had spoken to his brother, he discovered that he had taken Walstan's body to his family. Drast had also given a great deal of coin to offer private funerary rights so that their father would not hear of it.

Tyran reminded himself again that Father had said they would speak again about his wife-to-be. After months of distractions and excuses, it was time to have the conversation once more. He had driven back the Vucari. He had helped defeat the dragon. Autumn was coming. It was time for his wedding.

He scowled at the drawn curtains, red with gold trim, and extended his stride. He felt like he was on a warpath. He needed that level of resolve to face his father. Despite being a war leader, Tyran abhorred conflict, especially when it was personal.

The muscles in his neck twitched; his thoughts were scattered. Tyran took a deep breath, trying desperately to keep his emotions in check, but it was difficult to refrain from feeling. Feelings had a funny way of getting the better of a man when one was not paying attention to them. It was best if he could keep his emotions hidden, especially when talking to his father. He could not be perceived as being weak.

The door to his father's study was suddenly facing him like a demon that held his life in its clutches.

Tyran stood staring at his father's door with his fists against his thighs. The tremors had moved from his neck to his chest. His knees grew weak. Every thought screamed at him to run.

The sound of footsteps approached him from behind at slow pace.

After a moment, Tyran slanted his gaze to see his brother at his side. In spite of the obvious strain around his brother's eyes, he still had a smile on his face. The smile was as strained as his eyes.

"Will you come with me to meet with Father?" He doubted Drast ever showed real concern for anyone, save for their father and him. Somehow, as if a salve had been massaged into his burning heart, Tyran felt calmed by his brother's presence.

"Of course." Drast did not hesitate. He never did when Tyran made a request. "What for?"

"Isolde," Tyran said, knowing that her name would say everything—and then he added, "It is time I start my life with her. I want to settle down, have a family and peace. It is unfair that she should see me as I am, when I only wish to be kind and caring towards her. It is time that I stop acting solely at Father's behest."

A modicum of doubt crept upon Drast's face. His eyes darted to their father's door. "I am not certain if that is wise. I don't think Father will take such news well." He paused, then took a deep breath. "Do you remember the dog?"

Tyran's brow furrowed as he looked at the ground. Drast had to bring up the dog. Walstan seemed to be the more recent example. But, the dog? That had been almost fifteen years ago, and his brother, in all his infinite wisdom, wanted to compare his future wife to the family dog!

"This is not the same, Drast."

"Is it not? You told Father that you loved the dog and what happened?" His brother lifted his eyebrows as though he knew something deeper, more definite, as though he could see the future before it was written.

Tyran grumbled at the rhetorical question but answered all the same. "I had to throw it into the fire pit."

He could still hear the animal bawling in misery as the fire had eaten away at its flesh. It had tried to flee, tried to free itself from the relentless flames. Tyran had been forced to kick it back in. Twice. He shook his head vigorously. "No! This is different. He must see that. He cannot be so cruel that he would make me harm her."

"Can you leave her aside?"

Tyran breathed.

The hallway was silent as death.

"I could." Tyran said finally with a dry throat. The thought made his stomach tighten into knots. "But I do not want to. Father may call me selfish. The world may call me selfish, but I want to have what all men want. I want freedom to think and act for myself." Tyran swallowed. "I do not want to kill Wolos because Father says. Instead, I want to be with Isolde, who loves me."

"Tyran, the more you are told you cannot do a *thing*, the more you want to do it." Drast scrunched his shoulders. "I am like you, my brother. Except I put you and Father above myself. I put aside my wants. It would be better for you—for her—if you could."

Tyran nodded. "You are right, Drast. But I am not you." He forced a smile to his parched lips. "When do I ever choose what is best for me?" He shook his head with a sigh. "But come, let us speak with Father."

Tyran pushed the door open. The room was damp with the morning breeze that heaved itself through the windows on the far wall. Red and gold curtains like those in the hallway waved gently. The smell of saltwater and fish was crushing.

Their father was moving away from the window when they entered. He turned casually with a frown.

"Father," Tyran said, forcing himself to broach the subject immediately. "I need to speak with you about Isolde."

The Arkhon placed his hands behind his back, red and grey hair bouncing as he dipped his head. "What causes such urgency in the matter?"

Tyran kept his eyes off Drast when responding but could not look at his father either. He found himself gazing at the *Varkolak* on top of the alder desk. "I am not acting with urgency. We last spoke months ago and you assured me we would finish the conversation."

"And I thought we had."

Tyran pressed. "The Vucari are driven back. Our family is sovereign." Tyran felt that aching in his neck and back once more. He turned from the tome but still could not look at his father. He noticed the fire pit was heated, red embers sizzling at its base. He tried to focus on the fiery ashes. "All has moved according to your plans. Give me a moment to live my own life."

"It is true that the Vucari have retreated." The Arkhon advanced towards the desk, placing a hand on the smooth surface. "But a wise ruler never stands idle, even during peaceful times. Instead, he increases his resources, becomes stronger for when adversity strikes, and prepares to resist any change in fortune. The Kaligula bloodline still has enemies. The Kluk children are not all dead." Dagmar maintained an even, if somewhat commanding tone. He did not lift his voice, point his finger, or even shift his eyebrow.

"Kindel has fled the city with Habërmani," Tyran said. "There is little threat from them."

"Elena and Peter..." Drast offered while keeping a level tone, "are dead. Ghanimer is all that remains, and my understanding is that he fled as well. He should not pose much of a threat."

"And Maelili, correct?" Dagmar asked.

Drast cleared his throat, lying. "Of course."

"One Kluk is one too many," Dagmar said.

Drast hastily continued, "They will be dealt with quickly enough. I will find them and handle them personally."

"They?" Dagmar shifted in his robes with raised eyebrows.

It was all Tyran could do to not whip his head around in dread. Drast was not usually one to stumble with his words. Walstan's death must have been impacting his brother more than he had thought.

Luckily, Drast was quick to recognize his error. "*He*, Father. I meant to say *he*. I will find *him* and deal with *him*. That is, if *he* even remains in the city."

Dagmar shook his head, obviously annoyed with Drast. "It will take both of you to eliminate the Kluks. They are wolves that threaten our family and more will surface in the city. Within each of us are elements of being a beast and being a man, and it is through the balance of these traits that we find our strength. To battle these wolves, it takes different types of men; it takes those that are the fox and those that are the lion."

"Father," Tyran tried. But his father spoke over him. The man, thoroughly composed, barely took a breath.

"You are a lion, Tyran. You cannot defend yourself against snares. Your brother, Drast, is a fox and cannot defend himself against the wolves. Tyran is needed to frighten the wolves and Drast is needed to discover their snagging snares. Together you can defeat the Kluks, our enemies, and their schemes."

"Father."

Dagmar raised his volume to drown out Tyran. "You fought the Vucari. You fought Torn'ash. Neither as well as you should have, but it remains that our armies are weakened, morale is low, and we have not even begun our campaign to draw out Wolos."

"Campaign to draw out Wolos?" Drast asked.

"Dagmar!" Tyran fumed, speaking over his brother. "I did not come to talk about strategies or campaigns. I will wed Isolde. I will not be going to Rhian or engage in your ruse with death. What good is there in having eternal life if you never get to live?"

"Tyran." Drast rustled from behind him.

He was drowned out by Arkhon Kaligula's shouting. Any equanimity he had was gone. The older man was around the desk, blue eyes peering upward at Tyran like an asp before striking down its prey. "You forget your place, Tyran! You would throw away all that has been gained—sacrificed—for the sake of a weak-blooded girl. She is only another sow fit for spitting out soldiers! Should I bring her into this very room so that you may witness how she will moan like any other whore? I will rape her myself if that will make her less appealing. Would that put some sense into your thick skull?"

"What have you sacrificed?" Tyran was hot. His ears burned with rage. "I battled in the Shade. Drast protected you at Tekorga. We are the ones who shed the years of our life to defeat the Vucari. To turn aside Torn'ash. We have gone to war for you and all you have given in return is pain."

Drast cursed under his breath.

"Pain?" The Arkhon tensed, his expression with matched wrath. "You have not even begun to know pain."

Dagmar was quick. He was much too spry for a man who was far from battle-hardened. Kicking Tyran's legs out from under him, he slammed him into the wooden planks of the floor. Koldovstvo pressed him down.

Air fled from Tyran's lungs. His chest burned against the weight of his father's magic.

He did not fight back. Even in his anger, he would not harm his father. There was no need to carve Znaki into the floorboards. Tyran would not touch Koldovstvo.

The Arkhon was eerily calm in his direction. "Drast. A poker from the fire pit. Now."

Tyran watched Drast turn to look at the metal rod with the curved handle sitting within heated coals. Tyran had not noticed it before.

Drast hesitated.

Their father was unyielding. "Wait another moment and your lesson will be a hundred times worse."

His older brother snatched up the poker and gulped, hands trembling, as Arkhon Dagmar Kaligula uttered his next words.

"Burn him."

"Do you not trust me?" Isolde touched the scalded skin on Tyran's arm. It still oozed blood when he flexed the muscle. "Is that why you will not tell me?"

Tyran took hold of her gentle hand, pulling it away from the blistering flesh. The pine trees within their glade, their special place, comforted him. "Will not and cannot are two very different things."

"If you *cannot* tell me how, then at least tell me why." Tears slowly leaked out of the corners of her eyes, falling over her narrow, girlish cheeks.

Tyran began to pet her hair with his hand, still holding her hand with his other. The emotion in his voice was thick. "If I tell you anything, then it must be a lie. Take assurance in knowing how much I love you because I also cannot tell you a lie."

She pulled away from him. "So I am to trust in you when you will not trust in me? I am to accept your assurances of love when you will not accept mine? Is what you ask of me so different from what I ask of you?"

He clenched his fists, his teeth grating against each other. "What you ask is not mine alone to tell. Can you not see what you ask of me? To tell you is to break the love and trust of another, but to not tell you is to break your love and trust."

"Do you not love me best?"

He answered in a heartbeat, "Of course. I love you more than you can know."

"Then tell me."

Her pleading tone nearly pulled the words from his lips before he could stop himself. Instead, he bit his inner cheek.

Her face became despairing. Irate.

He forestalled her. "I don't want to bring you pain!"

Isolde kissed him, the cold tears on her cheeks pressing against him.

She had to kiss him.

Tyran took the moment to enjoy the taste of her lips. She had so much passion. She did love him, and yet he was not allowed to love her back.

Drast had been right. He hated that his brother had known and Tyran had not believed him. His father had commanded Tyran to treat Isolde as the dog. To die.

The morning would haunt Tyran for the rest of his life. Arkhon Kaligula had reminded him of his duties to their family. To him. To his brother. To Lairhein. If Tyran backed out for love, then everything he strove for was lost. Tyran rejected his father's will and Drast was commanded to burn him.

It lasted longer than Tyran should have let it; the result was inevitable. He should have ended it. Instead, his stubbornness only resulted in his brother being forced to torture him for hours.

The way was set. Tyran must follow the path set before him, and Isolde was not a part of that path. His life had already been written for him. The charge that he must complete did not include the woman. He knew it. In his mind, he knew it, but his heart was slow to listen, beating heavily against her own now so that it was nearly smothered by its thunderous palpitations.

"You are always so far away from me in thought, Tyran." She grasped his hand with the strength of his entire army.

He stroked her hair, feeling the strength in her small hands. Love seemed to be so great of a thing that it was beyond men's capacity to have it in their mortal lives. Maybe no men were allowed to have love and hold on to it.

Still, Tyran found that he could not do it. He could not take the light from Isolde's eyes, which cheerily met his own. He could not steal the breath from her chest, which happily stirred upon his neck, nor the merry beating of her heart, which beat against his own.

"It is not fair," he muttered.

"What is not fair?"

He would tell her. Tell her all and make her hate him so that she would flee this place and be alive and well.

"Isolde," he cooed, his voice cracking, "you have asked about so many things in my past and I must tell you. You were right to ask and I should have shared it with you long ago. Hear me— when I am done, you must go from me and from Lairhein and never return."

Her jaw dropped, clearly hurt. "But why?"

"Because I am not the person you think me to be. I have done terrible things."

"You have had to escape death in war and the Shade! Those things don't define you, Tyran."

He grasped her jaw firmly to stop her speaking. "And all I have done reaches far beyond my days at battle. I have done more evil in my years than most men do in a lifetime. By my death only my brother's capacity for iniquity will be able to match my own." He let go of her face to draw up his sleeve. "The burns you see on my skin are my punishment for loving you."

She gasped, pulling away. "What?"

Tyran spoke over her, lifting his shirt to display another scar. "But this mark is from a knife that a little girl plunged into me after I set her mother on fire because their father had not paid his dues to my father. It was not long before Drast and I slaughtered the whole family." He touched a scar under his right eye. "This scar was acquired when I drowned one of my men to give a lesson to my soldiers in disobedience. The boy hardly had hair on his chin when he died." He shucked his boot and pulled off his stocking to reveal another burn. "This is from when I burned my dog alive because I loved him too much."

Isolde scooted back from him, falling upon a bed of pine needles. "Enough! Enough!" She shook her head, tears falling from her cheeks. "It cannot be!" Her eyes searched him. "You are lying to me! Lying to get me to go away from you! Does your father hate me so much? Does he despise your happiness?"

Tyran schooled his face to stoic calmness. "I only speak the truth to you now."

"No." She was still shaking her head. "It cannot be so. If I must go, then you must go with me. You must escape the tyranny of your father and brother. You are a sweet man who loves me, and I, you!" She crawled nearer him. "No matter what you may have been forced to do, you have shown me kindness and asked forgiveness. I have waited more than a year for your return! For love! You have thought of me, even on your darkest days. Nobody forces you to see me, to spend time with me, or to think of me. You do those things on your own! You do them for love of me!" She wept and screamed, pleading with him now.

Tyran hardened himself to her, struggling against every fiber of his heart to do so. Anger filled his marrow. The burns on his arm ached as though they would never cease.

For who he was, for what he had done, and for what he would do. She had to hate him. He loved her too much for her not to. In that moment, such wrath pervaded him that his mind blanked his actions.

He savagely kicked her in the face to send her sprawling away from him. Leaping upon her, he tore away her dress, and unfastened his pants. He would make her hate him.

He had to.

When it was over, Tyran left Isolde lying in the pine grove, helpless and weeping.

He spent hours meandering outside the city walls and along the coastline. He tried to forget. He screamed. He wept. The pain was more than he could bear.

Before dusk, Tyran decided he could not endure his guilt any longer. He set off to return to the pine glades. He hoped against hope that Isolde was there or would return if she had left. He had to ask forgiveness.

The smell of the pine needles filled his nostrils as he neared the clearing where he had raped Isolde. He heard the mumbling of voices but could not make out the words. Tyran hurried forward towards the opening.

The sight from the tree line stilled Tyran's heart.

Drast stood, his fingers perched on his bottom lip. His eyes were fixated on the woman, Isolde, shaking before him.

Tyran winced, speechless. The beauty of the glade darkened.

The knife flashed in Drast's hand. The blade cut deeply across Isolde's throat. A pierced scream was cut short with a bubbled gurgle.

Tyran did his best to ignore the soreness that throbbed within his stomach, watching Isolde gargle and spit crimson saliva before landing in a heap of her own blood.

Drast held the blade. But Tyran knew his father stood behind the murder of his beloved.

Drast knelt at the girl's side, his eyes heavy, surely seeing Walstan's mask of death in Isolde's slack face. He wiped the blade on her dress slowly, watching her body as blood soaked the green foliage.

Isolde's eyes closed. Tyran smelled the pine.

Tyran did not know how long he stood, unmoving. He watched Drast, who had still not noticed him in the arc of the trees. His older brother crouched with a bent neck as Isolde's face grew paler and her life continued to spill into the earth, though she had long been dead. Drast only moved to sweep back his curled red hair with a quivering hand.

This was death. Tyran had watched hundreds of men die, and nothing had felt this way before.

Where the world may have stopped, it abruptly spun again. Reality hit Tyran hard.

"No. No. No!"

Tyran's voice was deeper than he remembered. Drast turned, mouth gaping and hand trembling. He hastily put the knife back. "I am sorry, Tyran, it had to be done."

"Had to?"

"Yes, 'had to.' Father made me follow you to see that she died." He glanced back at her body. "I know what you tried to do here. What you did do." He licked his lips. "You did what you had to do to separate yourself from Isolde. You had to destroy yourself. I understand that, but this had to be done."

Tyran shook his head.

"I was merciful."

"Merciful?" Tyran screamed, shaking.

Drast hesitated. His eyes dropped to Isolde's motionless body. "You cannot expect that she would have just walked away after you raped her? She would have told someone, and then all the skeletons would have been unearthed. It is better this way."

Tyran loomed forward. "Do not tell me it is better this way. Do not tell me that her death is better!"

Drast stood to meet Tyran's advance. He stood as tall as he could, but Tyran still towered over him.

Drast raised his voice. "No. No, it is not *better*. It would have been *better* if you would have just killed her, Tyran. But you decided to take a path less traveled, and that path would have led to our deaths! I did not want to kill her. I know what she meant to you. Do you not understand how hard this was for me to do?"

"Better the death of the world than what I have done!" Tyran's voice roared in his ears. He could barely hear Drast's excuses. "Better the death of a thousand worlds than what I have done once! I made her hate me, but I hate myself more than she ever could. And I hate you for killing her! And I hate Father for what he has made us!"

Drast snapped. "You did this, Tyran!" He pointed to the pale, bleeding, tattered shape on the ground. "You sought to make her hate you, and you succeeded! And so her last moments on this earth were filled with hatred! And fear! And pain! And you can only blame yourself. You could have kissed her with poison lips to make her feel safe and loved, but instead you chose this path by which you must live and she is dead! You forced my hand! I told you to leave her be!"

Tyran's fist rocked Drast, striking him under the chin. His brother should have fallen to blackness from the attack, but Drast turned his head back around, only to receive a second punch to his ear, followed by a series of blows to the midsection. Possibly the greatest lesson Drast had learned from their father was how to take a beating.

His brother grabbed hold of Tyran's shirt, jerking him forward to offset his balance. He nearly fell when Drast's forehead connected with his cheek, but Tyran managed to throw his brother back to the ground. Tyran stumbled, trying to regain his balance, blood dribbling from the wounds he had received earlier. Drast reached to touch the blood that dripped to his own shirt from the injuries to his face.

"Killing me will not bring her back, Tyran!" he shouted, one eye swollen shut. "I will not fight you."

Tyran found no more use for words. He thundered forward, falling on Drast. Fisted hand after fisted hand pummeled down as though he would make Drast's face one with the soil. His brother attempted to keep his hands lifted to protect his face, growling beneath his breath, but made no move to return the blows. Tyran knew that the man was waiting for his chance to turn the tide. Drast would not let this continue.

Tyran was staggered when Drast kept his hands up but did nothing more. Even as Tyran slowed, Drast held himself at bay.

A final heavy strike to the head caused Drast to cry out.

Tyran crawled backwards, pulling himself to his feet. "Fight me."

Drast stared back, his face awash in his own blood.

Tyran stammered, "Fight me!"

Silent tears ran down his brother's face, turning red with the blood covering it. Drast reached for his knife and threw it towards Tyran's feet.

"Kill me."

Tyran's gaze fell to Isolde's corpse. And then the knife.

He grabbed at his chest, his face, his hair with heavy fists and fell to the ground, weeping. "I cannot do this. Does this world only offer pain and hatred? I cannot be the man that Father wants me to be. I want to be free of him!" His eyes again fell on the knife. "I want to kill you. I want to kill him. But most of all, I want to kill myself. But I cannot."

Drast smiled. Even in his pain, with tears, he grinned. "Tyran, my brother, you don't have to be that man. You don't have to be the man Father wants you to be. I do. I cannot help it. But you have never done his will for power or for glory. You do his will for reasons I could never understand. Maybe a man needs to be able to love something about the world. I can never love it as you do. I do father's will because I must. I will always do his will. If you want to be free of him, you must be free of me." Drast spat blood. "Kill me, my brother. Kill me."

After a moment, Tyran swallowed. "I would rather live with him than without you. I need you to remind me, to refocus me upon the horizon and not the earth beneath my feet. I cannot kill you."

Drast's voice croaked as he glanced at Isolde's body once more. "Then I will live with this as long as I must."

Tyran spoke softly, with care. "Help me bury her. Help me commend her soul to Wolos."

"And then," Drast said, his face grim for perhaps the first time in his life, "we will finally finish this. We will kill the God of the Dead."

Chapter XVII

Slicker than a muddied hog, Drast sat up in bed searching frantically. He clenched his jaw, trying to focus on finding something—anything that would do. His eyes raked the room before giving up and leaning over the side of the bed, balancing himself on the narrow edge. He peered into the bleakness beneath only seconds before his feet flopped over his head, toppling him to the ground. He hit the wooden floorboards in a panic, holding his lips together firmly, grunting. Droplets of vomit spewed despite his desperate attempts.

He swallowed, gurgling and gagging. Drast was too dizzy for these acrobatics. With a grimace, his eyes locked on the chamber pot that he had somehow missed. He clawed at the basin, tearing the bedding from around his waist and feet with his other hand. He was despairing, dragging himself through a hazed, spinning world. The pressure again built up against his chest and throat. Tightening his stomach, and curling his toes, he bent over and retched into the pot until sweat and tears rolled down his face.

He fell backwards onto the ground with a sob and clumsily reached for the bedding to wipe his face clean. He tried not to look at what the blanket took from his face any more than he looked into what he had left in the chamber pot. His stomach was not nearly strong enough to handle any of it.

The room still whirled from last night. He tried to close his eyes to keep his stomach from doing the same, but closing his eyes actually made it worse. Drast was somewhat surprised that the drink was still affecting him like this. He had been having more than his fill for—he did not know how long. How long ago did Tyran leave? His mind was too foggy to remember. And Walstan was gone, too.

Vaguely, Drast saw that the sky was just turning blue with the rising sun. At least he was fairly certain it was sunrise. None of the hues of sunset had begun to color the sky.

"Ser Drast?"

He turned his head to the entrance into his chambers and pulled himself more upright to lean against the nightstand beside his bed. One of the serving women stood at the doorway of his room. "What?"

"The Arkhon wishes to speak with you."

He was not certain what string of curses came from his lips, but the maid blanched and her face grew pink, almost to the color of her hair. The room swirled again while she spoke.

"What?" he asked again.

"I said, Ser Drast, the Arkhon instructed me to remain with you until you came to meet with him." Her voice quivered.

She was right to fear him. Her voice was fuzzy, just like everything else. But he knew he had not been particularly kind to any of the servants of late. He had managed to avoid his father by effectively frightening the servants. Their fear, combined with late nights, ale, and sleeping until the sun set, had allowed him to avoid talking with anyone who did not enjoy a mug or two.

A few of the servants had initially joined him in drinking. He loosely recalled this maid among them. Ura? Mura? Lura?

"Kura," he finally muttered. He had been a little too handsy and she had since avoided him like—he could not clearly comprise a simile. Like. Like? Like the moon avoided the sun? Good enough.

"Yes, Kura," she murmured.

Drast spat at the chamber pot. He was fairly certain he missed. "Well, come on in, Kura." He belched. "I know how we can pass the time."

She retreated so that only her eyes and strawberry blonde hair poked through the door. He chuckled roughly. Leaning back, he closed his eyes.

Kura was still there when he woke again. She now sat in a chair across the room, a disgusted expression pulling at the corners of her mouth. Drast was in his bed with clean bedding, though he had no memory of having gotten into bed nor of anything or anyone in his chambers moving. His head no longer spun, but the pain that made it hurt to open his eyes still pounded in his skull.

He tried to speak, his mouth too dry for him to do much more than grunt like Tyran. With half a smile that quickly turned into a grimace, he humphed and pointed to the jug and basin across the room. Kura seemed to understand and poured water from the jug into a worked pewter chalice, which she brought to him.

When he could speak, he returned the chalice to her and told her to refill it. As she did so, he pulled himself up in his bed. "Why are you still here?"

Her hands shook as she poured the water. "The Arkhon said that I must stay with you until you go to meet him."

"Then you had best be prepared to stay for a while. I have no intention of speaking with my father any time soon." He took the chalice from her.

"As you say, Ser Drast." She returned to her chair, her gaze flitting about until it finally rested on her hands folded in her lap.

Drast placed his chalice on the nightstand and closed his eyes. Now he only needed to find a way to get rid of her for a bit so he could slip off to the mead hall. The cure for too much drink was always more drink and the last thing he wanted to do was hang around so that his father could berate him for Tyran having left. His father had ordered Isolde's death and Drast had been a loyal son. He had to kill Isolde to keep his father's favor. How else would he make amends for his misjudgments in the battle against Torn'ash? And Walstan?

A better question was how could he be the one blamed for Tyran taking his army and leaving? If Drast had his way, Tyran would still be here to share their father's unmitigated wrath.

Tyran's disappearance had occurred right after Isolde's death. Drast rubbed his aching head. This was what he had been trying to avoid. He did not want to think about his brother or his Voivode. He did not want to think about anything. He wanted to go to the mead hall again and drink until the drink consumed all thoughts beyond drinking.

Pulling aside the covers, he quickly found that he had been thoroughly disrobed as well. He schooled his face to as lusty a demeanor as he could manage. "Well, Kura, it appears you are of a mind similar to my own. Come on over and help me stay warm while you wait."

"I cannot, Ser Drast," she said meekly.

"Then you had best step out while I dress myself," he growled, "or I cannot be held responsible for my actions."

With a squeak, she darted out the door, no doubt still lurking on the other side. But with her gone, Drast was certain he could slip away. He rushed to his wardrobe and snagged a pair of trousers and a tunic. While he was still hopping about the room half-dressed and attempting to pull on a boot, a soft knock sounded at the door.

Kura's head poked in, trying not to look in his direction. "Arkhon Dagmar Kaligula," she announced. His father pushed the door the rest of the way open so that he could enter the room.

Drast's father gave him a scathing look before waving a hand behind him dismissively. "That will be all." The Arkhon did not pay any heed to Kura as she bobbed a quick curtsey and closed the door.

Drast finished pulling his boot on, listening to the soft patter of Kura's slippered feet running down the hallway. He was not in the mood to speak with anyone, much less deal with his father. He forced a smile. "Father. It is good to see you. I was just coming to meet with you."

"Undoubtedly," his father remarked dryly. He pulled his samite robes more closely about him, the gold stitching rippling luxuriously over the crimson fabric. "You have work to do. For weeks, you have either had your face pointed at the sky pouring ale down your throat or face down vomiting into your chamber pot."

"Oh, you flatterer!" Drast scanned the room for his other boot while fiddling with his belt. He heard his father grate his teeth.

The Arkhon rubbed his eyes. "Drast, please!" He dropped his hand and pinned him with a glare. "We are at a critical moment in our plans. With your brother gone, the responsibility falls to you, son."

"Funny how that works, Father." Drast finally secured his trousers. By the Nine Lands, his head hurt! "You rely on me when Tyran is gone. Force me to be at your beck and call as I murder and torture for your benefit. And while Tyran is here, chasing around his girls, you treat me like something you stepped in, despite my loyalty never waning. Despite knowing nothing about your intentions. About *your* plans!"

He could not get the smile off his face. Gods, how he wanted to look angry for this!

"Are you finished?" his father asked.

"No, I am not. I want to know what plans are *ours*? Tyran has spilt his blood and the blood of his men running your errands, and you can afford him no happiness. I have worked myself raw trying to earn your kindness and favor and you have repaid my loyalty with derision and despair. What possible responsibility could I have to you?"

His father sighed heavily, looking much older than Drast had ever seen him. He made his way to Kura's vacated chair and sat down heavily. "I know, son. I know. I am neither a kind nor generous father. I have placed great weights upon both you and your brother. I do this because you both possess the potential for greatness, which I do not wish to see wasted." His gaze was now fatherly, understanding. "I am not asking that you forgive me my trespasses, but that you understand the scope of what it is that we—that I am trying to accomplish."

Drast sat on his bed, one boot on, one lost in his chambers somewhere. Why was his father being…human? This was something new. Drast could not think with his head pounding the way it was. He eased his own tone. "Father, you have not explained to me what we are trying to accomplish."

"Your brother told you nothing?"

"Tyran told me everything. He kept nothing from me, Father. But you know that, of course." He sighed, rubbing his eyes. "Are you trying to gain immortality? Killing Wolos, killing death, I don't see what else can be accomplished other than eternal life."

His father nodded. "Yes, immortality. But that is only a piece of it. The Stuhia have a long and complicated history of which few know. The *Varkolak* details the history of the Stuhia and the troubles that have made that history largely unknown." The Arkhon settled himself in the chair. "Our people worshipped Wolos for a long time and were once considered his chosen people, along with the Vucari. Our ancestors came to realize that Wolos was limiting our strength and our potential because of his need to feed upon our deaths. They turned to his enemy, Marheena, in order that all Stuhia might achieve greatness under her name.

"A revolution took place that drove the worshippers of Wolos underground, but they struck back with vengeance. The Carian Council wiped out every person from our bloodline…except for one man. He kept the *Varkolak* safe to pass down the story. Despite the damage done to our bloodline, our blood remained strong, and as our numbers multiplied, we regained power over time until we became one of the most powerful houses in Lairhein. Now, of course, we rule."

"What does this have to do with Wolos? Tyran is now on his way to kill the god. It will be over soon enough."

"Your brother was rash. Too rash. We are not prepared to face Wolos yet, and your brother will die without your help."

Drast's mouth went dry. "He stands no chance?"

"None."

He rubbed his temples. He only wanted to be able to think clearly. He was certain there was a lesson to be learned in all of this, but even the simplest thoughts made his brow wet. "You must tell him. You must reach out to him in Klukas."

"I have tried. He will not respond to me."

Drast pressed harder on his temples. His brother was far too stubborn sometimes, but he knew that his father spoke the truth. Drast had also tried to speak to Tyran in Klukas in the past weeks and had been ignored. "What must be done?"

His father stood. "We have already achieved the means through which we are capable of standing against Wolos. The ritual itself gave each of us untold power, but it also gave us dominion over the blood of dragons. The *Varkolak* tells that only those who command the blood of the dragon can stand before Wolos." He began to pace back and forth.

Drast attempted to follow the movement at first, but it was too painful to move his eyes, so he stared at the floor.

"However, standing before Wolos is not the same as defeating him. In order to do so, we need to clean his presence from Lairhein."

"How is that even possible?"

Drast heard eager excitement in his father's voice. "It is not what you think. We need not destroy believers, only the symbols of belief. I need you to destroy the Temple of Wolos and kill the members of the Ninth Council."

Drast held his aching head in his hands and could not help but laugh. "You want me to murder members of the nine highest ranking bloodlines?"

He felt his father's hand on his shoulder. "If you want Tyran to live, you must. After the Carian Council disbanded, its members accused of heinous crimes by the people of Lairhein, the Ninth Council was formed. It is the same entity in all but name. Just as the Carian Council destroyed our ancestors long ago, the Ninth Council will destroy us. We must end them."

He looked up to his father. His thoughts were still far from being clear. He would have to kill the Ninth Council—Malafej, Grasil—Drast's mind could not pull the other names from its blurred state. Easier said than done, he was sure. "And then Tyran can win? He can kill Wolos?"

Dagmar Kaligula nodded. "With your help, he can. You must physically bring him a message."

"What message?"

"Wolos can only be found at Anaerfell."

Drast gripped his throbbing head, feeling an uncomfortable grin part his lips. "And where is that?"

His father frowned. "I am not sure, but the *Varkolak* is clear about his location. You and your brother must learn of its significance and see that he is found."

Drast groaned. "Maybe it is near the mead hall."

Chapter XVIII

Snow pelted Tyran's face. A strong northern wind whistled through the gorge between the peaks ahead of him, carrying the swirling white flakes. He frowned at the hardy landscape. The mountains were menacing. They were not as nefarious as the Shade Fells, but the terrain made them equally treacherous. It was a rugged wilderness untouched by the cunning hand of mankind.

Drem interrupted the grunts of his soldiers pulling their long boats onto the frozen tundra. "Where do we go, Ser Tyran?"

Tyran sucked the icy air through his nostrils and shivered. "Not this way. The wind funnelling between the mountain ranges would freeze us within weeks. Not to mention, we would also have the threat of avalanches. I can already see the snow building up on those peaks. For now, we will stay south and march east along the coastline. The Vucari cannot be far."

Drem nodded dutifully. "It would be good to have a camp holding stronger than our tents. Winter this far north is not going to be kind."

"No," Tyran agreed. "Already we are disadvantaged, having no knowledge of the land, places, or the past wars that have been fought on Rhian. Our battle expertise is enough to survive this place and maintain a tactical advantage. The element of surprise will be with us as long as we can hide our presence. We don't let any live. No stragglers."

Tyran stopped himself before he echoed his father, who spoke about the importance of imitating illustrious men so that their glory would become his glory. It was a trick to carry one's name into legend. Mimicking the greatness of those before would give a man immortality.

He shook the thoughts from his head. The last voice he wanted to hear right now was his father's.

Drem eyed the soldiers, who tiptoed across the frozen ground in attempts not to fall. His voice cracked. "Several of the new soldiers are younger than those who went with us to the Shade. They will serve as little more than a human shield out here."

"Mm." Tyran would use his soldiers for whichever purpose guaranteed his victory. He expected men to die. This was war.

Drem's face was tight, possibly frozen from the chilled wind. He stared at the countryside. "This is hardly a place for boys."

Tyran followed his gaze through the snowflakes that layered the ground. In a few more months, the snow would be several feet high. Temperatures would plummet. Those that the Vucari did not slaughter would be victims to the weather. "Nor is it a place for men."

"And yet, what choice did we have but to come?"

"Mm," Tyran grumbled in his throat. There was always a choice. But this choice was his to make.

Snow crunched on Tyran's left. He glanced to see Kormish, his only other remaining Voivode. The man looked older than his father since the battle against Torn'ash, the Viy, Father of Serpents.

Kormish's voice was raspy. "The boats have been secured beyond the beach and hidden from sight. It will only be a matter of weeks before the sea freezes over completely. I am afraid they will not carry us back home, Ser Tyran. If we are lucky we can return home on the ice."

Tyran grunted. He was not sure that any of them would be returning home. He had told himself before leaving Lairhein that this would be his last campaign come victory or death.

Kormish cleared his throat. "We could have waited until the spring."

Tyran shook his head. "No. The Vucari will not be expecting us."

"There has been no sign of the bastards since Torn'ash, Ser Tyran. Why must we carry on with this war? They are beaten."

Tyran stayed silent.

He could not tell his Voivodes that killing the Vucari *really* had nothing to do with killing the Vucari. He could not explain to them that this was not a war between races, a war to balance morality, or even a war for glory. He could not say that the end goal was to murder Wolos, the Horned God; the god who the Stuhia and his own soldiers paid honor to in their morning prayers.

Even with all his hate, Tyran would not divulge that this entire plan was devised by Dagmar Kaligula, their Arkhon, to save his own hide from death. But more than anything, Tyran would not admit that he had dragged his army across the sea, without informing his brother or father, to gamble with his own misfortune. He would either kill Wolos, the God of the Dead, or return Isolde to his arms. That was his hope, at least. If he could kill Wolos, maybe Isolde would come back to him. If not, then he would die and be reunited with her in the Beyond. At this point, either option seemed fine to him.

"Excuse my frankness, Ser Tyran," Kormish strained, "but I want peace."

Tyran kept his voice even. "There is no peace for men like us, Kormish. It was taken from us the moment we lifted a weapon. I have yet to lead you astray. Now is not the time to lose hope. Our deeds here may or may not be sung throughout the ages. But regardless of how we are remembered, what we accomplish this winter will free our people forever."

"Free them?" Kormish tensed, hands quaking in the frigid breeze. "From what? Tyranny? War? Pain? These things cannot be avoided no matter how many Vucari we slay or any other creature we wage war against. If all things in the world were dead except the Stuhia, we would turn on each other. It is the nature of the living to prey on each other. Corruption doesn't need to be invited into a man's heart for it to come."

Drem sucked in a breath. "You have no faith. I, too, questioned our fates before we faced the Vucari outside of Lairhein. Ser Tyran will not fail us."

"This is not a question of faith, nor Ser Tyran's abilities as a leader. This is a question of purpose, Drem." Kormish looked as though he would spit in disgust, but he gulped instead. Maybe he remembered it was Tyran with whom he spoke.

Tyran thumbed the yew haft of his weapon. "Are you suggesting passivity? Evil feeds upon indifferent men in the same measure it does the ambitious. Evil does not discriminate, Kormish. All this talk about questions is meaningless. This campaign is about power. The Vucari have demonstrated their might. They came to Lairhein—to our home—and attacked our people. We have been on the defensive for too long. It is time that they recognize our true strength."

Kormish sighed. "Ser Tyran, we are fifty men against a nation. We don't know the full scope of what we face."

"Nor did we in the Shade, Kormish, and we survived there, did we not?" Drem chimed in.

"That is not the same. I am tired of being told that the Shade gives us reason to do more than what we have accomplished. Is there no end to the quest for glory?" Kormish asked. "Traipsing into unmarked lands, wielding swords is an adventure for young men without dreams or virtue. They don't have families, nor do they seek a better future."

Drem continued, "You are telling me that glory is virtuous?"

Kormish did not hesitate. "Not in the same way as love, or peace, or beauty. Glory bespeaks of life lost. By definition that is not good."

Tyran softened. "This campaign is not about glory, but it *is* about life."

"I don't understand."

Tyran lied. "We are here to protect our people from the threat of the Vucari." His Voivodes did not need to know he was here to kill a god for his father's own fears about death.

Kormish dared to say, We may have found victory sooner if your brother's army would have joined us."

"He may yet," Tyran said with a half-smile. The bitter cold burned as his cheeks lifted, wrinkling the skin beneath his eyes. "Let's get moving. I'd rather be dining beside a hearth tonight in celebration than watching you two drive my tent stakes into this frozen wasteland." Tyran reached for the wool cowl across his neck and pulled it over his nose before heading east.

The two men behind him scuffled away to gather the army. Within moments, the entirety of their group was marching eastward along the coast.

What was left of his legion followed Tyran for nearly two hours along the outskirts of the mountains. The flurries that fell from the heavens never ceased. It was around midday when Tyran could not take the burning sensation in his legs any longer. He ordered the army to stop and rest.

Tyran used a copper pot to melt snow over a fire that he had started with Koldovstvo. He had just refilled his waterskin when Drem shouted from a distance.

"Ser Tyran! Ser Tyran!" Drem slogged through the snow towards Tyran.

He removed the waterskin from his lips and swallowed the liquid in his mouth. It still was cool, even coming off the fire. "What is it, Drem?"

"Our men…have caught…a Vucari woman."

Tyran was too cold to spring to his feet. He remained unmoved, gathering the heat from the fire. "A scout?"

Drem heaved, catching his breath. "I am not sure. The men said that she did not put up a fight. She surrendered when our men reached for their weapons."

Tyran tried to gauge his Voivode, whose hands were shaking from what may have been excitement. Yet Tyran could only think about how his teeth ached from the cold. He wondered if they would crack if he bit down hard enough.

"Mm."

His Voivode pressed on. "The men said that she did not even raise a finger and offered her hands for binding."

Tyran took the bait. "What men?"

"Balishul and Viktor."

"I see." The two men were from lesser houses and had been among his ranks for over a year, since leaving for the Shade. Neither was a fool by any measure. Either would have killed the Vucari if they had perceived her to be a threat. "I had said that we were not going to leave any alive, Drem."

"I know, Ser Tyran. But…"

Tyran waited for the man to finish.

"She was wearing clothes."

"Of course she is wearing clothes! What in the Nine Lands are you thinking?" Tyran exclaimed. "It's freezing out here."

"Yes, Ser Tyran," the man said with confusion. "The clothing is bizarre, though. I could not tell you what animals most of the furs come from."

That piqued Tyran's interest. "Where is she?"

Drem pointed across their makeshift camp.

"You brought her here? What if she uses her corrupt Koldovstvo to fry half of our force? What if she escapes and reveals our location?" Tyran was on his feet, composure lost, forgetting the cold momentarily. His hand moved towards his mace with the intention to bash the man's skull into pulp. He had to clench his fists to restrain himself. "Why would you do that?"

Drem took a step back. "Balishul and Viktor thought you would want to question her. She may be able to give us direction in this wilderness. And…you will see when you see her, Ser Tyran."

Tyran rubbed his mustache in thought, snow flaking off against his icy skin.

"Ser Tyran?"

"Very well." He took a deep breath to calm his nerves. "Take me to her but be on guard. I cannot think that this is anything but a trap. It is too convenient."

"Yes," Drem agreed, "except the Vucari did not know that we were coming."

"They could have seen us coming to shore. I am not willing to take any chances. We don't know what they know. In war, it is best to assume your enemy knows your every move."

Drem shrugged.

Tyran followed Drem through the maze of his soldiers until they reached Balishul and Viktor. The two stood among a handful of other soldiers, guarding the Vucari woman.

Drem, the good soldier, was correct about the oddities of the young-looking Vucari woman. She was bundled in colored furs from head to foot. Her dark locks extended from the ends of the skin cap that covered her head. Her hair was uncombed and frayed as though she had not washed it in years.

She sat with a straight back, eyeing the ranks of his men, possibly counting their numbers. Tyran's nostrils flared as he watched her, the woman's sharp brown eyes darting among the faces of his Stuhian army. The woman was expressionless. She appeared as cold as the winter and her skin was as pale as the flakes that settled against the tundra.

Tyran picked up his pace to move past Drem, his eyes locking onto the Vucari. He was certain that he was as straight-faced as she, and he was determined to give her nothing.

The woman looked back. Her lips were sealed, not even splitting to take a breath.

Ignoring his men, Tyran addressed the Vucari. "What is your name?"

He was surprised when she answered without hesitation.

"I am Erzebeth Navenka of Anaerfell, a Warden of the Ash Tree." Her voice was soft yet bold, with a strange accent that sounded like nothing that Tyran had heard before. Then again, he could not think of a time he had actually conversed with a Vucari.

In fact, Tyran realized that he knew very little about the Vucari customs at all. He was not even sure what "Warden of the Ash Tree" meant. It was certainly nothing he had ever heard referenced before. He knew the Ash Tree was a mystical tree that was said to give life to the living, guarded by Wolos in the Beyond. Though he had never known a living being to have seen the tree.

His father would know more. If he were on better terms with the Arkhon, he could travel to Klukas to ask. But he was not on better terms. With anyone.

Tyran realized that his pause had been longer than he intended. "You have seen the Ash Tree?"

"If I say that I have, will you let me go?" She lifted her bound hands.

He breathed easier, recognizing her ploy. She must think he was a simpleton to believe she had been to the fabled Tree of Life. He changed the question. "What are you doing here?"

She dropped her hands back to her lap. "I was going home to Anaerfell. What are you doing here, Stuhia? Are your lands not farther to the south, across the sea, or has there been a change in recent years?" Her voice lifted at the end as though she were genuinely confused by his presence on the oversized island.

"Aren't you Vucari?"

"I am."

Tyran swallowed, holding himself firm so as to not look at the men around him for assistance. "I don't understand your question. You know where my people reside and the war that divides us. You also know that your kin failed to overwhelm us at Lairhein."

"Are we still at war? I had hoped that had been resolved by now." Erzebeth smiled. "You see, I have not been to Rhian or Anaerfell in many years, young Red. I assure you that the war you speak of is not mine."

"Mm." Tyran grimaced. "That is easily enough said, but hard to believe. You *will* answer my questions truthfully. Why didn't you attack my men? Are more of your kind waiting in the hills or up the shoreline?"

Viktor spoke up from behind her. "We have heard enough, Ser Tyran. It's the same droning nonsense that we heard before you arrived. Let's be done with her and move on."

Tyran raised his hand. "It was your idea to question her, was it not? Let her answer."

Viktor snorted, pulling his bow from his back. "I would not have thought her to lie so plainly, especially to you, Ser Tyran."

"I have no reason to lie. Only liars assume others lie as well." Erzebeth clicked her tongue. She looked only at Tyran, paying little attention to the soldiers behind her. "I do not attack men. My wrath is for beasts that cannot think. You can think, can you not?" She huffed, lifting her eyebrows mockingly. "Some of you, at least?"

He ignored her jest. "Again, you did not answer my question. Are there more Vucari nearby?"

Erzebeth shrugged. "I could not tell you. As I said, I recently arrived to Rhian myself."

"You expect me to believe that? If you have not been here, where have you been? Lairhein?"

"Believe what you wish, young Red. The world is much larger than Lairhein and Rhian. I have been traveling south, across Maharia. Thousands of miles away from this place."

"Doing what?" Tyran asked.

Erzebeth eyed the men that surrounded her, steadily breathing as though she feared death as much as love. "You do have a lot of questions, young Red. What is it that you are after? I am not a threat to you or your little war campaign."

"I am tired of her patronizing tone," Viktor interrupted again, leaning down to speak in her ear. "We are here to slaughter your people. You don't care about that?" The man's fingers were white around the grip of his bow.

"Viktor," Tyran warned.

Erzebeth peered over her shoulder at the man and then around at the small army and scoffed. "Fifty men are not going to slaughter the Vucari. You will be lucky to seize Charreni."

Viktor curled his lip from behind her. "You'd be surprised what we are capable of. Ser Tyran is the Dragon Slayer. He defeated the Viy!"

Roars of approval resounded from the gathering men.

"Viktor, stop," Tyran ordered. His voice was flat, emotionless. The soldier should know better than to have his flap flapping.

The Vucari woman watched him with a knowing look. It was like the expression that often haunted his brother's face.

When she spoke, her accent seemed to evaporate from her voice. He heard Isolde. "Let go of your anger, young Red, before it kills you and your men."

"Why do you keep calling me 'young Red'?"

Erzebeth tugged at her own hair with her bound hands. "Because you are not as old as I am and your hair is red as fire, like any other dragon-slayer. To the Vucari, all Stuhia are dragon-slayers. That is nothing to boast about."

"How dare you speak to Ser Tyran that way," Viktor scolded, nocking an arrow.

Tyran clenched his fist. "You have not seen anger, skin-switcher." If pushed, he might show the woman just how much control he had over his anger.

He moved towards the Vucari, but it was Isolde's face that he saw. It may have been Koldovstvo; it may have been his imagination. It did not matter.

"You will get yours," Viktor hit the woman in the back of the head before Tyran reached her.

Tyran fumed, taking an extra step.

At the last moment, he struck Viktor, energy swelling behind his punch. The soldier's skull caved upon impact.

Chapter XIX

"Thanks, Mak," Drast said cheerily, juggling the piping hot bread in his hands.

A grunt issued from the tubby man's folds, his piglet-eyes more focused than Drast had ever seen them.

With a shrug, Drast bit into the yeasty loaf. Crusty on the outside and soft on the inside, it almost made him glad that he was awake early enough in the morning to enjoy it instead of still being half-drunk in his bed. Although, now that he considered it, a nice, warm cup of mulled mead would go quite well with the bread.

The thought was more than he could bear and he wandered off down the street looking for one.

Lairhein was busy at this time of the day, but the disappearance of all the Kluk children had made him something of a social pariah. Drast knew several Kluks had escaped with their lives, but the citizens apparently did not.

When he had first left home that morning, he had attempted his usual cheery greetings to passersby. When the best response he received turned out to be a sniff or snort, he quickly desisted. He soon began to take notice of the glances and heard the muttering behind his back while he walked. Hate undulated down the street with his passage, but he was not about to let such hate ruin his day any more than he was about to let it ruin his bread.

Drast had been drunk. He had no memory of the townsfolk's vile disregard for his family's name while at the mead hall. Oddly enough, the passage of time had apparently done nothing for the mood of the people of Lairhein. He could see the hate fresh in their eyes.

Drast stopped in the middle of the street in sudden realization, his bread forgotten in his hand. The only way the people could actively hate the Kaligulas this much was if someone was inciting the people against them! No matter how much they hated, people would eventually begin to forget. The cares of wives, husbands, children, and the daily grind would push hate from their minds. Hate was difficult to maintain, like trying to hang from a precipice to avoid falling into a fire—a man eventually gave in as the fire died away. That is, unless someone was stoking the fire.

Only the Kluks were capable of causing such trouble, and there were only two who could possibly remain in Lairhein— Maelili and Ghanimer. Drast was certain that Kindel had fled with Habërmani—likely having been tasked with protecting the artifact from Drast's family. But not the other two. Maelili was stubborn and Ghanimer was far from a coward.

Looking around the street as if his realization would force the culprits to reveal themselves, Drast slowly munched on his bread. Here he was skipping down the street surrounded by people who would gladly see him strung up before them. The only reasons they were being docile had to be because they were biding their time or they feared him.

Definitely not fear.

He needed to get off the street.

Dropping the bread, Drast turned in the direction of the Kaligula estate. He needed to speak with his father before the temper of the town was out of control. He may be able to walk down the street without every set of eyes watching him destroy both the Temple of Wolos and the Ninth Council. However, there was no way he could leave Father to find Tyran. He and his brother would return to find their father drawn and quartered.

No one tried to slow or stop Drast as he made his way back to the estate. Once inside the walls, he breathed a sigh of relief. It was not as though he feared them, but hate was a tricky mistress, calamitous and unpredictable to boot. He did not want to be caught in the open with a city full of people who hated him.

Drast found his father in his study with a hot mug of tea and a loaf of bread not dissimilar to Drast's own. He could have eaten here, but he was trying to get back in the habit of being a socialite within Lairhein. It was how he had operated for years and what had ensured that his father was aware of the mood of the city while Tyran had been gone dragon hunting.

"Father!" He realized he was far more winded than he had initially thought, gasping for breath.

His father looked up from his breakfast. "Why are you disturbing me? I do not have time for your nonsense."

Well, at least he was back to normal. "We have trouble. The mood in the city has soured against us greatly."

He quickly went on to describe his morning. As he wrapped up his tale, he began to feel it was perhaps a little thin in terms of real evidence, but he hoped his father had come to trust his instincts.

The Arkhon leaned back in his chair, thumbing his chin. "I see. Well, I think we are in too precarious a position to ignore what may or may not be a potential uprising." He looked up from where he had been staring at his meal, lost in thought. "Are there any we can trust?"

Drast grimaced as he thought of Walstan and shook his head. "Dead or with Tyran's army. I have a few men in my army who are loyal enough, but men's hearts are easily swayed, and I don't have enough confidence in any to trust them with much."

Dagmar stood, his voice as hard as flint. "Perhaps if you had spent more time with your men instead of time with your drink, we would not be facing this issue."

Drast supposed he could not really argue against that point. "Yes, Father, but hindsight will not solve the issue as it presents itself now."

"Yes." The Arkon sat again. "Yes, you are correct. We must turn the public's eye from us, let them hate something else." He mused for a moment. "Continue with the destruction of the temple as planned. Find someone on whom to blame its destruction."

"Who?"

"I do not care," his father snapped. "Blame it on the milkmaid or the Ninth Council. So long as we are not implicated it makes no difference. It will buy us time."

"I believe the Kluk children are still in town."

"Kindel and Ghanimer? Is it possible that the eldest has returned with Habërmani?"

Drast realized his mistake. His father thought that Maelili was dead, but Tyran had not actually done the deed.

"It may just be Ghanimer," he lied. "I cannot think that Kindel would be foolish enough to return with the staff. And who else can inspire the people against us so effectively?" He watched his father. Maybe he did not notice the slip. "But I have no way of finding him."

His father smiled. "I may have a way." He pulled out the *Varkolak*. "Our resource provides more than history, as you may recall. Klukas can be used for more than merely communicating in dreams."

"Of course," Drast said. "We can also use Klukas when awake to scout or call upon others across long distances to gather. But I doubt that Ghanimer Kluk will respond to our callings, and I have no intention of scouting the entire city for him."

"No, no," Dagmar silenced Drast. "You can also use Klukas to pinpoint people or objects with a simple trace of Koldovstvo."

Drast was intrigued. "You can use Koldovstvo in the ethereal plane?"

"Not for protection or to cause harm, but the *Varkolak* teaches one how to scry in Klukas. As long as you know what you seek, it can be found." His father opened the ancient text upon the desk.

Excitement swelled in his stomach, finally having a chance to look at the *Varkolak*. Drast leaned over and smiled.

The small home was one to which Drast could not recall having paid much heed. He was largely familiar with many of the people in Lairhein. As large as the city was, it was not so large that he could not name the majority of its inhabitants. He doubted Tyran could name even one member of the staff working in the estate.

His father had allowed Drast to utilize the methods within the *Varkolak* to determine that Ghanimer and Maelili were within the home. The shutters were closed, but flickering lights escaped through the cracks and crevices.

He smiled and sleuthed closer, grumbling at the hooded cloak about his shoulders. The thing was a nuisance to wear, but he would need it before the night was through. It did not take him long to crouch below a window where he could hear voices. He did not bother to listen to what they had to say. It was enough that they were here. He did not need information, but he did need them. A little work on his part would put this entire affair to an end tonight.

Standing, Drast walked to the front of the home and lazily knocked at the door. The voices stopped abruptly and the sound of footsteps neared the door. Gritting his teeth, Drast forced the smile off his face and raised his hands before him as the door opened.

Maelili stood, stunning as ever, and her brother, Ghanimer, loomed behind. He was a great bear of a man with wild, bright red, shaggy hair. He was everything his brother Peter Kluk was not. Drast would have to play his part perfectly.

Their faces darkened faster than a winter sunset, and he could sense his immediate, unquestioned death.

"Thank Wolos!" he cried. "Thank Wolos! I had heard you were still in Lairhein! I had prayed that the rumors were true!"

"Kill him," Ghanimer rumbled.

Drast fell to his knees. "No! No, please. Hear me out! Please, I only wish to talk to you." He forced his eyes to grow teary. "I know I have wronged your family in ways for which I can never make amends, and I will accept whatever punishment you will place upon me. Just, please, listen to what I have to say first."

Maelili exchanged glances with her brother, who nodded. Ghanimer grabbed Drast by his collar, dragging him to his feet. "Come inside. But you had best watch yourself. One wrong glance, one wrong step, and I will rip your head off."

A chill ran down his spine. Ghanimer's voice was drier than Tyran's wit. How could the man be so emotionless when facing the man who killed two of his siblings? Drast hoped that this would work the way he intended. He was beginning to have a few doubts.

"Of course, of course." He followed them inside, keeping his hands as they were.

"What do you have to say?" Maelili's voice was musical. Drast could see why Tyran lusted after the wench.

"I—" He swallowed audibly and fell back to his knees. "I don't want to try to justify my actions. I only want you to understand the truth of why so many of your family have suffered. Why— why you have suffered."

"Get on with it." Ghanimer was having none of Drast's pleas. Something had to trick this fellow.

"My brother and I have been at our father's boot heels our entire life. The recent happenings with your line has opened our eyes. Tyran fled with those men loyal to him to avoid the corruption my father brings, but I could not." He shook his head. "You will not need to look far to find someone who can tell of my recent habits of drinking. The guilt has been tearing me apart. But I cannot stand the evil my father has done. I want to set it right. When I heard that members of the Kluk family were still in town, I had to come and find you to make amends."

"Amends?" Maelili cried, her voice quivering. She certainly did not have her brother's resolve. "What you did to Peter. What you did—" Tears streamed down her face. "I saw his body. I saw what was left. I cannot imagine a more horrific way to die!"

Ghanimer leered. "Although I am more than willing to try to find one, just for you."

Drast worked up his own tears. He had to make this stick. "Do you think...do you think I wanted that? I was there. By Wolos, I was there!" Drast choked back a sob. "I had him—on—me!"

"Are you saying you had nothing to do with it?" Ghanimer roared, his voice making the walls creak. "I have a dozen men who put you at the table with Peter when it happened!"

"It was a game. Just a drinking game. My father had done something to the coins. I did not know!" Drast bowed his head, half for effect and half because he was having trouble hiding his smile. "This is why I am here. My father has set everything in motion. Tyran and I were used as pawns." Schooling the grin from his lips, he looked at Maelili. "Why do you think Tyran tried to save you? Why do you think he did not kill you when he had the chance? He could have. He could have ended your life, but he is a good man at heart, just as I am. We cannot escape our father's will."

Maelili looked to Ghanimer. "It is true. Tyran could have slain me. He tried to get me to flee Lairhein. I could see it in his eyes." She sighed longingly. "He did not want to kill me."

"Neither do I!" Drast said. "I want to end this madness. I want to see peace restored to Lairhein."

"How?"

"I have summoned the Ninth Council. I have summoned them to the Temple of Wolos. If you will come with me, I will work with you to overthrow my father." He lowered his voice. "And we can do it this very night."

Again, the two exchanged glances. Ghanimer looked at him. "How do we know you are not intending to trap us?"

"Trap you?" Drast exclaimed. "How could I trap you? I—am—alone. My brother is gone. My commander is dead. My father hates and abuses me. I cannot trap you there any more there than I can here."

"The Ninth Council?" Maelili asked.

"Yes. It will take all of us to defeat my father. He has performed heinous rituals to gain power and none of us can do it alone."

"Of course," Ghanimer muttered. "That is how he defeated Father so easily. It was almost effortless."

Drast nodded encouragingly. "And your father had Habërmani. How do you think any of us will fare without the power of that artifact?"

A final exchange of looks between the two siblings resulted in Ghanimer's nod. "Very well. We will accompany you to the Temple of Wolos. Stay in front of us."

Drast stood and turned about, thankful for the chance to finally smile. "We must hurry. I told the council not to stay long. I did not want to chance anything happening to them if my father discovered my complicity."

The three went out into the night. Clouds had rolled in, darkening the sky, so that not a single star gleamed. Drast led them through the city streets towards the temple.

"Drast?"

He was surprised by Maelili's hesitant tone. He glanced over his shoulder. "Yes, Maelili?"

"Where is Tyran? Where did he go?"

"Tyran went north," he said softly. He never thought Tyran was too effective with women, but he had to give him credit.

Perhaps he should threaten more women with death and then let them run free. "He is attacking the Vucari. He knew he could not face Father, but he wanted to make sure the people of Lairhein were safe, Maelili. Tyran cares for us all a great deal."

"I am glad to hear of it."

"Easy, Maelili," her brother muttered.

Silence ensued until they reached the Temple of Wolos. It was a large stone structure, one of the oldest in Lairhein, having been built with the first Carian Council. In the dark, starless night with only a few torches dotting the streets, the temple looked foreboding.

"Come," Drast said quickly. "Let us get inside before anyone sees us."

Suiting his words, he darted up the dozen or so steps and into the door. The Kluk siblings took a moment to follow him in, but Drast had already hidden inside the entryway. The two were left to look about confusedly, seeing neither Drast nor the Ninth Council.

"I knew we should not have come." Ghanimer backed towards the entrance. "The Kaligulas are not to be trusted."

Drast leapt forward and struck the big man in the back of the head.

Ghanimer seemed entirely unaffected. He grunted from the blow but spun around like a cat on hot coals.

With a bit of a yelp—which Drast felt more than a little ashamed at having made—he used Koldovstvo to empower a second strike. He swore he had been a bit overzealous with the magic, but despite crumpling under the blow, Ghanimer stirred as if to stand back up.

He gave a somewhat surprised look to Maelili and, before she could react, Drast hit her brother again using Koldovstvo to strengthen the impact. The man groaned and fell unconscious.

Maelili looked stunned at the betrayal and the sight of her fallen brother. Half a sneer formed on her lips, but Drast met the disparaging look on her face with a savage backhand.

She fell to the ground with a cry. When she looked back up to him, tears already filled her brilliant eyes. "Why?"

Drast looked down at the woman's brother and then kicked Ghanimer in the head for good measure. He laughed. "What kind of question is that? You Kluks seem to be caught up with the *whys* far too often. Why? Because I can."

Rage filled her pretty face as she began to stand. Drast kicked her in the stomach. She gasped, curling in on herself.

"Let us talk, you and me." He smiled, squatting beside her. "You know as well as I do that you are not a match for me, so please cease with the theatrics. My brother spared you, and I will do the same, but only this once." He motioned to Ghanimer, unmoving behind him. "Your brother is going to die here today. You can be a part of that, if you wish, or you can leave Lairhein."

Maelili still hugged her belly. "Why would you let me live?"

"Because Tyran let you live." He could not kill another woman the way he had Isolde. He was the reason Tyran left. He broke his brother. Despite his despair at the thought of his brother, Drast worked to keep his features light and shrugged. "I am tired of death. I am tired of killing. I don't need to kill you both."

"Then kill me." Her eyes were wet, pleading. So much desperation. "Let Ghanimer live, but kill me instead. I have already had my second chance."

"The opportunity stands as is. You can leave and live or stay and die. I am allowing you this chance because Tyran allowed you this chance." Gods, just let her walk away! Although if he were in Maelili's place with Tyran on the ground, he would never leave. He fixed her in his gaze meaningfully. "Know that I can find you. I can always find you. If you are still in Lairhein in the morning, I will kill you." Drast stood. "Now go!"

She pulled herself to her knees, cringing over her stomach. "No. No, please don't kill him!"

Drast smiled. "Last chance."

The smile did its work. A look of horror filled her face, and with a heart-wrenching sob, she turned and fled.

With a wry shake of his head, Drast set to work. Carefully, he positioned Ghanimer just so, kicking him a few times to make sure the big man would not wake up. Drast then went to the rear exit, and with a mighty draw of Koldovstvo, he pulled at the ceiling of the temple so that it crumpled in on itself. Once started, the great building fell with a thunderous crash that likely woke every inhabitant of Lairhein.

Tossing his hood over his head to conceal himself, he darted through the shadows to hide while the crowd began to gather before the temple. The air was filled with the shouts of men and women as they ran to stare. A few more concerned citizens pulled away the rubble to reveal the much crushed and mangled body of Ghanimer Kluk.

Drast eased himself into the rear of the crowd as the voices called out.

"It is Ghanimer!"

"Ghanimer Kluk?"

"Aye, been in town for some time now."

Drast threw out his voice using Koldovstvo so that it came from the other end of the crowd, distinct from his own. "He was here with his sister, aye?"

"Trying to fight against the Kaligulas. I heard they were killing his kin."

Drast created another voice from another location. "He was spitfire mad at the Kaligulas. No telling what he might do to get at them."

"Anything, most likely."

"What are you trying to say?"

Another voice. "Probably trying to make us think the Kaligulas destroyed the temple. He didn't get out in time."

"Maelili in there?"

"Hard to say."

"The Kaligulas do this? I would not be surprised."

Another voice. "Kaligulas are a bad lot but would not offend Wolos."

"Aye, that is true. They are devout worshippers of Wolos."

Another voice. "Besides, one son is gone and the other is a drunk."

"True, and you will never see Dagmar get his hands dirty."

Another voice. "Aye. I would put money on the Kluks doing this to themselves."

"Aye." Additional voices resounded from the crowd in agreement.

"Aye."

"True."

Drast grinned and slunk away.

Chapter XX

"You *had* said no stragglers," Drem agreed with Kormish.

The Voivodes continued to question Tyran's judgment. He had expected as much from Kormish, but never from Drem.

"She will have purpose. She knows these lands better than any of us." Tyran breathed easy, focusing on his footing on the uneven, half-frozen beach.

He suddenly wished Drast were with him. His brother could have redirected the two from the conversation with ease.

Or, more likely, Drast would have simply killed the two with an arrow randomly shot into the clouds.

Kormish pressed, "She knows it so well, she could lead us straight into a sandpit or worse. She has no reason to help us, Ser Tyran."

Drem chuckled, his foot crunching against the frozen ground. "If that Vucari woman can find a sandpit here."

"That is not funny," Kormish said. "This is serious. We have an enemy traipsing about in our ranks. She could touch Koldovstvo at any moment and be burying us by nightfall."

Tyran tried to find an argument to counter Kormish. Nothing immediately came to mind, but Tyran knew that the soldier was right.

"Mm."

"She has not tried anything yet," Drem reasoned. "Honestly, she doesn't seem too interested in killing or having to do anything with us, really."

Kormish slid, catching himself awkwardly. "Yes, she is very clever for a Vucari. You wait until we are comfortable and then she will strike. Mark my words."

"Your concerns are noted. If she kills us, then you can have my head in the world beyond this. As of now, she is our prisoner." Tyran said with finality.

The silence only lasted seconds.

"You killed Viktor, Ser Tyran," Kormish said, nearly at a whisper.

"What?" Tyran slowed, cocking an eyebrow.

His face must have displayed anger, because Kormish cowered back. "You killed Viktor because of that woman. I don't understand why."

Tyran turned to scowl at the man, speaking through gritted teeth. "I did not kill Viktor because of the Vucari, Voivode." He used the man's title as though he were talking to a child that had just been caught stealing a pie from the windowsill. "I killed Viktor because he did not have the sense to shut his trap when the conversation was over."

Kormish paled, his lips suddenly sealed as tight as a virgin's thighs.

Satisfied, Tyran marched onward with Drem alongside him. Kormish remained behind them, trailing like a prisoner being led to his hanging noose.

After less than half a mile, Balishul appeared, trekking back towards the main army. The long-legged scout carried himself with an air of confidence. He approached Tyran with a dip of his head and threw three severed heads to the ground.

The man clearly did not think it was wise to take on any other prisoners.

Balishul's eyebrows angled. "The Vucari village is a mile ahead, Ser Tyran, within the silhouette of the mountains. These three were near the bank, fishing through the ice. I did not see any others."

"Their bodies?" Tyran asked.

"Floating somewhere beneath the ice, Ser Tyran, in the Neabou Sea," Balishul said. "But if we have any element of surprise, it will be lost soon enough."

Drem asked, "Why is that, Balishul?"

"Because the lot of you stand out like a storm cloud against the horizon. You're a black shadow walking across snow-covered tundra. I could almost spot you without Koldovstvo."

Tyran grimaced. He should have considered as much, but really there was little that he could do without killing off his own men or aging himself significantly. Even with the dragon's blood churning in his veins, he could not provide them constant concealment. He had to have enough energy to fight Wolos.

How many priests would he have to kill before the God of the Dead showed his horned head?

"Tell me something I can work with. How many Vucari are in this village?" Tyran demanded.

"It is small. Barely significant. Maybe a few hundred people among the longhouses. No walls or palisades, and no sentries." Balishul smirked. "It'll be like slaughtering lambs."

"The Vucari are hardly people," Kormish grunted.

Balishul sighed. "You know what I mean."

"A fishing village, then," Drem offered.

"No, there must be something more," Tyran said. "Erzebeth said we would have difficulty taking Charreni."

"Maybe this is not Charreni," Drem said.

"I suppose it doesn't matter." Tyran stroked his red beard. "Balishul, how many priests are in the village?"

Wrinkles lined the scout's eyes. "Priests? I cannot say. I did not venture close enough to check."

Tyran shook his head in annoyance. "I will check myself. Kormish?"

"Yes, Ser Tyran." Kormish stepped to Tyran's side. The man looked as thrilled as a cat in a gunny sack.

"Stand guard over my body while I enter Klukas," Tyran explained. "I need to scout the village. Drem will watch Erzebeth."

"How can we take a village with fifty men and guard a prisoner? How will we fight hundreds?" Kormish choked.

Tyran swelled his chest with a deep breath, simply eyeing the Voivode.

Kormish did not need another hint. "Yes, of course, Ser Tyran. I will keep your flesh safe while you enter the world of the spirit. We will be…victorious."

"Yes, we will. When I return, we will lay waste to this settlement." Tyran lifted his mace from its hoop on his belt. "If you find any Vucari priests, you *will* kill them without mercy and… violently."

His men did not respond.

"Understood?" Tyran deepened his voice.

He took their mumblings as acquiescence.

Drem started towards Erzebeth while Tyran settled into a sitting position on the ground in preparation to enter Klukas. The loyal soldier lifted his hands to his lips and cupped them. He blew into them a couple times to warm them. "Ser Tyran, what are we doing here?"

Kormish became rigid. The man was seemingly more interested in the answer than Drem.

Tyran felt his muscles tense in his shoulders, twitching through his biceps. He reminded himself that Drem was a good soldier. Though images of ripping the man's guts out flooded his thoughts. The Voivode was not supposed to question him.

Tyran's voice was as level as his father's. It caused bile to surface against his tongue, warming his own mouth. "Rewriting history. Now, go and secure Erzebeth."

Tyran did not bother to watch Drem scamper off towards Erzebeth. The man would follow direction better than any other among his men. Instead, Tyran closed his eyes gently, his body shivering against the airstream that blustered from the north. Strega the White-Bearded, God of the Nine Winds, was said to power the gales. There was little that a man could do against such power.

Tyran focused on his breathing. In through the nose and out through the mouth. For several minutes, he only thought of breathing in and breathing out. In and out. At times, his mind would start to wander. He thought of Kormish guarding him, and Drem guarding Erzebeth, and of the snow falling around his stilled body. Tyran thought of Isolde: he raped her and Drast killed her. He blamed his father. He hated his father.

No! He would never enter Klukas while charged with emotion. Instead, he redirected his mind back to his breathing. The cold air cycled through his nostrils and out of his mouth. It was frigid, soothing. In and out.

Tyran was not sure how long he remained in this position. Sometimes it took longer than others, but finally he felt his body fall into a deep slumber. His ethereal form jolted, a vibrating current in the center of his forehead.

Next thing Tyran knew, he was standing in the snow next to Kormish. The aged Voivode stood steadfast watching Tyran's physical form still breathing. Relaxed. Asleep.

Tyran watched Kormish watching him, solidifying himself in the spiritual plane. He could not rush himself or he would lose control and slingshot back into his physical form. He did not want to start the process over. Tyran pushed away all emotion.

This is what it meant to be Stuhia. In this form, he had to forget hate, forget fury, and most of all, forget love. He was a shadow of a shadow, and powerful beyond any who remained in the world of the living.

Tyran embraced his newfound senses. It was much different than his physical body. He was alert in the unblemished world of the spirit but had lost his sense of touch, taste, and smell. In fact, he did not need to breathe here. He simply watched and listened. The sound of the living was muffled but understandable, though the words of those who remained in the material plane of existence were of disinterest. Instead, he focused on their emotions. He could feel their feelings. Here, he was not limited by the flesh or time.

Kormish was anxious. That was no surprise to Tyran. The man tried to hide it, but here it was as clear as daylight.

Tyran twisted, hovering above the ground, towards the village in the distance. It was important that he did not forget why he had come here. Sometimes it was hard to maintain memories here – or bring memories back to the physical realm. He had to stay attentive.

He was not as practiced in his ethereal form as Drast. His brother had practiced far more in their younger years than Tyran ever had interest in doing. It was not until Tyran had left for the Shade that he had need of the skill. Even then, it had been challenging, whether he had been speaking to his father or Isolde.

No! He must not put energy towards Drast or his father while he traveled here. It would call to them, encouraging them to find him in Klukas. It would start with an itch in the back of their skulls, images of him flashing in their head. If they entered the spiritual plane, they would propel towards him with the speed of a wave crashing against the water's edge.

He had no interest in speaking with them.

Charreni, if that was the name of the settlement, appeared in very short time. Tyran raced across the expanse in a matter of seconds, having no sense of time in the spiritual plane. He scanned the fishing village through the veil that separated the two planes. He always found it interesting how the physical plane appeared to be sitting behind a thin black curtain.

The village was as Balishul had said. There were about a hundred longhouses scattered in square formations in a valley near the base of the mountain. The snow piled opposite side the peak, giving the Vucari little to worry about in terms of avalanches or falling rocks. Instead, the peak provided them cover and a blockade against the powerful wind.

Tyran raced through the streets, noticing that there were very few people out and about. He assumed that the cold weather must keep them indoors. The sun was already falling in the horizon, having a shorter life this far north with the onset of winter. The people were likely keeping their families warm and away from the pressing frost.

His shadow self glided and weaved past a couple of children with brown eyes and pale skin, being guided by their mothers back to their homesteads.

One of the children tugged at the furs hanging from the mother's waist. "It's not too cold, Ma. We can play a bit longer, can't we?"

The mother rubbed the child's head. "You can play a bit more tomorrow when the sun is at midday. You need some stew in that tummy to keep you warm."

"Yes, Ma."

Tyran felt his wraithlike form tug back towards his body and pushed forward, reminding himself to keep emotions clear from his mind. It did not seem fair that such ugly creatures as these could have mothers while his was taken from him.

Not now!

He trailed away from the Vucari family and discovered a longhouse made of wood. It stood apart from the other homes, having a solid door and smoke filtering from hollowed windows. With haste, Tyran sifted through the wall of the building. He settled, hovering in the air on the opposite side.

The room inside was warmed by a small hearth. He could not feel the heat, but the two men and a woman gathered around looked rather comfortable. They were nestled into furs, sipping from copper mugs, and talking amongst themselves.

"It is a strange age for the priests to be summoned to Anaerfell. What do you think it means, Minsk? Have all of them gone from every village?"

The Vucari man with a grizzled beard and squinted eyes answered, "No. I don't think that is the case. Gonshir and Valees specifically were called, but the traders up the coast said that some of their priests remained behind."

"Bizarre times, indeed," the other man said. "I have not heard of a summoning in our lifetime. Makes you wonder if the Ash Tree is in danger."

The woman nodded. "You echo my own fears, Thoric. It has been the better part of a century since any Vucari has heard from the Wardens."

"They were called too," Minsk said. "I have never thought to question how Wolos delivers his messages."

Thoric choked on his mead. "You mean to say that Wolos summoned the priests to Anaerfell?"

"I am only telling you what Valees said before they departed. I would not say much to the others. No reason to make them afraid, especially with winter coming." Minsk raised his mug. "We have enough to be concerned about without thinking about the summoning."

"Mm," the woman agreed, "but how will we worship without any priests? We cannot lose our faith, and the children must be taught proper tradition."

Minsk's voice was reassuring. "We will guide them. If ever there is a question, we can journey through Rhian to ask the priests that remain here."

Was Wolos aware of his father's plan? Of course, the God of the Dead should be aware of the happenings among the living. Still, Tyran did not come this far to fail.

With no further reason to remain in Charreni, Tyran flew backwards, out of the longhouse and into his body over half a mile away. The shift was almost instantaneous.

"Ser Tyran!" Kormish exclaimed, maintaining his post next to Tyran, who remained in a cross-legged position.

Tyran gasped for air and shuddered, warmth returning to his frozen skin. He shivered, trying to stand. Kormish offered a hand. Tyran swatted away his hand and pulled himself to his feet.

"How long have I been away?"

Kormish replied, "Nearly half an hour. I would have had the men build a fire near you if I thought it were safe."

Tyran waved him off.

"What of the village, Ser Tyran? Should I ready the men for attack?" Kormish asked.

"No. I will handle it myself." Tyran moved to the opposite side of his Voivode. Nothing separated him from his target.

The sun was nearly gone, a crescent on the brink of the world. It gave Tyran enough light to make out the mountain that eclipsed the fishing village. He did not need to see Charreni itself, only the mountain.

Koldovstvo raged through his veins, the energy swelling beneath his flesh, empowered by the dragon blood ritual. The taste of blood burned in his throat as he sucked in more of the magical power.

The ground beneath his feet quaked. Kormish stumbled next to him, barely finding his balance. Again, the world wobbled as Tyran increased the potency of Koldovstvo.

From behind him, he could hear the concerned sound of Kormish raising a question. It was echoed by Drem's voice, who must have come to check on him.

Tyran ignored them, drowning them out with the ringing that resounded against his eardrum. His wrath billowed in his chest. Isolde was dead. Isolde was dead. Dead!

Isolde was dead!

A shockwave erupted in the distance at the base of the mountain. The quake was felt across the makeshift encampment and beyond.

From the peak, snow, ice, and rock fell towards the village. From great heights, the weight of the mountain crushed the longhouses and all within a quarter mile. Blasts of rock and powdery snow were flung into the air, suffocating the atmosphere, stealing the spectacle.

A woman's screech rang from what could have only been Erzebeth. The woman came forward, staring at the village. She collapsed to her knees and watched helplessly.

Tyran stood stone-faced as similar screams from the small village reaffirmed his success.

Erzebeth twisted towards Tyran as though he were the worst of monsters. "You killed innocents. Women and children!"

Tyran merely looked back at her, sensing what he could only identify as hatred, blackening his heart, the fabric of his soul.

"This is not war," Erzebeth tried with desperation. "This is slaughter! There is no glory in what you have done."

"Drem, Kormish," Tyran cracked his knuckles, "take the men and kill anything that comes out of the rubble. Rabbit, mouse, fox, or Vucari. Whatever surfaces, you destroy."

The two Voivodes dipped their heads and left to gather the men.

"You will not be remembered as a heroic man, young Red. There is no greatness in genocide." Erzebeth wept.

Tyran rubbed his nose. "If I am fortunate, I will not be remembered any more than the Vucari."

Chapter XXI

"The Ninth Council has not heard from your family since Claduk. What is it that you desire, young Drast?" The elderly Stuhia's voice shook. Laboriously, Malafej descended into his chair at the apex of a crescent-shaped table with his eight companions. "The fall of the Temple of Wolos has troubled us all and, although we would generally welcome an audience with the imperial family, we are not much for idle conversation at present."

The Ninth Council sat as if prepared for judgment at the arched table. Although they often met with parishioners in the Temple of Wolos, that prospect was obviously no longer possible. Instead, they were gathered in the chamber from where they ruled as religious magistrates. The chamber itself was a singular space with a vaulted ceiling. At the zenith of the ceiling was a keystone with a Znaki drawn to prevent the use of Koldovstvo within the chamber. Such restraints were precautionary in order to keep the peace and ensure unmolested justice.

It had not taken much effort on Drast's part to convene the council. His father's position was enough to allow him an audience with the Ninth Council without too many questions. Dagmar ruled in matters relating to state, and the paths of the two bodies rarely crossed, but the destruction of the temple had afforded Drast the chance to capitalize on the chaos. Though, admittedly, for months to pass without any correspondence was not typical.

Drast bowed his head. He made sure that he did not bow too low given his newfound position within the city, but enough so that he could be seen as deferential. "I am sorry to say we must meet following such a travesty." He gave a self-deprecating grin and motioned towards his face. "I am afraid I don't look quite as young as I used to. The battle with the Vucari was particularly draining. If the war doesn't abate soon, you will see me and think you are looking in a mirror."

A few of the nine chuckled, though Malafej shook his head sadly. "So much death from such a needless war. Alas, none of us dreamed that the sour blood with our neighbors to the north would result in such devastation."

Drast shifted his weight, speaking with precision. "In part, that is why I wished to meet with you today. Our people have long regarded ourselves as the sole arbiters for Wolos, exacting his will on Aenar as both protectors and the protected. Yet," Drast let the word hang in the air for a moment, "the Vucari had a dragon on the field of battle. Torn'ash did not fight for us. Torn'ash attempted to destroy Lairhein and the Stuhian people."

One of the younger members of the council, Grasil, waggled his dark red and gold-streaked beard. "You impart danger with such careless words."

Drast lifted his hands soothingly. "I mean no disrespect. I am merely reporting the facts of the battle."

"Is there a question to accompany your *facts*?" Malafej mused softly.

"Of course." Drast smiled. "I apologize. It is my duty to lead my men against the Vucari, and I don't know how to resolve their discontent. They question our role and relationship with Wolos. How do you advise I address such concerns?"

Grasil snorted. "Address them as we always have. The will of Wolos is impenetrable and complex. Our faith needs to remain strong and all will be revealed upon death."

"Death is a disconcerting thing for men entering into battle, you understand?" Drast said easily. "Men look for signs of reassurance that their faith is not misplaced. It is as if they are marching to war for the Arkhon, only to see the sons of the Arkhon fighting for the enemy."

The members of the council exchanged glances before Malafej spoke. "Drast, you seem to be experiencing some doubt yourself. What is it that you fear?"

Drast could not help but smile. He was beginning to see why Malafej headed the Ninth Council. The old man had effectively changed the topic from one that addressed all the Stuhia to one Drast must be feeling personally. Malafej did not have an answer, and by directing Drast to discuss his own fears, he would keep him occupied and distracted.

Drast could respect the man for entering a game of wit.

"I appreciate your concern for my personal feelings regarding the disturbing fact that our god seems to have abandoned us, but I believe that you can assuage my fears by addressing how or why Wolos supports our enemy." He redirected the question back once again.

From the other end of the table, a bald man with a white beard that extended well below the surface of the table spoke. "Being a member of the Ninth Council doesn't grant us access to Wolos's will. We exist to help our people stay on the path of faith to our god. It is not for us to say why we are faced with such hardships. His purpose may be revealed in time and the appearance of Torn'ash could be nothing more than a test of faith."

"You misunderstand my intent." Malafej picked up the speech and tone where the other council member left off. "I am not attempting to redirect you from your concerns, rather I am attempting to find the root of your concerns. Understand that faith and doubt are constantly at war with each other, young Drast, but when fear arises from such doubts, faith cannot stand. For men of faith, the appearance of Torn'ash is nothing more than a comfort to Wolos's presence. The god we worship is a god of death. Why should we question his intent when he brings that death to us? If we die, we enter his presence, and we should rejoice in that knowledge."

"If death is our end goal, then why live? Why not kill ourselves in pursuit of meeting Wolos? The Stuhia are blessed with agelessness until we touch Koldovstvo. We could remain young forever and never experience death, and yet you tell me that we should worship dying. Why?"

"You ask questions as a child does." Grasil sneered.

"Easy, Grasil." Malafej motioned the other councilman silent with a shaking hand. "Drast has come to us in a moment of doubt. A moment of fear. We exist to help him see and understand the way of the world. It can be comforting—reassuring—to hear the words of our faith from our youth repeated as the passage of time flows over us."

He turned his milky gaze back to Drast. "We worship Wolos for more than simply his protection of our people, for more than his love. The Stuhia recognize that Wolos is a piece of the whole that is essential to all that we know, all that we will come to know on Aenar. The world is not merely comprised of life and death with one being the beginning and one being the ending. Each of us has a charge we must complete during life to reach the Thrice Ten Kingdom in death. It is our task to discover and accomplish our charges. You know well that life comingles with death to create life anew."

The oldest of the Ninth Council continued after a short pause. "The charge of this year's crop is to fuel those who consume it— to fuel the Stuhia. What is left behind dies and rots to fertilize the next year's crop and so on. In this way, the death that Wolos rules over creates all life. Death is the keystone to life. Without it, life would crumble, just as this room would crumble without the keystone at the apex of its dome."

Malafej was correct in at least one aspect—Drast was glad to hear the teachings of his youth again. He rarely gave much thought to what his charge was in this life. He had often heard that those who merely let their life take control would find their purpose more easily than those who attempted to take control themselves. Drast had never felt as though he was in charge. He allowed his father to take charge, and there was something comforting in the realization that his purpose was likely aligned with performing his father's will.

"The keystone," Drast mused, "is marked with the Znaki, keeping us all restricted from the power of Koldovstvo. In a way, it serves to symbolize the death of Koldovstvo. Just as life cannot exist simultaneously with death, Koldovstvo cannot exist simultaneously with the Znaki."

The bald man spoke. "Consider the implications of such a truth. The more a man lives, the closer to death he comes. The more a man uses Koldovstvo, the closer to death he comes as well. Yet it is the death provided by Wolos which allows us to renew ourselves. The Znaki keeps us from Koldovstvo. The Znaki helps us to live just as death helps us to live."

Drast smiled, nodding. "Yes. Yes, I see that. But what happens when death no longer exists? What happens if Wolos no longer exists?"

"We cannot speak towards such blasphemies," Grasil growled.

Malafej cast an unflattering glance at his fellow council member. "Death is the keystone to life, as I said. Does life exist without death? Does an arch exist without a keystone?"

"Well, Koldovstvo exists without the Znaki," Drast said softly. "In fact, Koldovstvo can only exist without the Znaki. Perhaps we don't truly understand what life is because we have only ever experienced it *with* the presence of death. Perhaps what we know is not truly life because death has forever loomed overhead. Just as this keystone looms over our heads. Just as this Znaki looms over Koldovstvo."

With an enormous effort, a strain within his mind that made him feel as though he were going to tear himself in twain, he thrust against the Znaki, against the keystone. Nothing happened.

"What are you saying?" Malafej inquired.

Grasil's eyes widened. "What are you trying to do?"

The bald man gasped. "He is trying to touch Koldovstvo!"

With an audible roar, Drast focused his mind against the Znaki, forcing the power of the dragon blood against the preventative. The keystone scraped roughly against the stones that kept the ceiling of the chamber in place. As soon as it scraped an inch, it flew upwards out of its place and into the sky beyond.

Cries erupted from the men in the room as the ceiling swayed, cracked, and crumbled inwards. Drast let out a victorious cry and leapt backwards, using Koldovstvo freely to keep the falling rubble from striking him. He could see several of the elderly men try to do the same, but their great age along with lacking the added power Drast possessed from the dragon blood made their efforts futile. The ceiling crumbled atop the Ninth Council, silencing their shouts.

Drast looked at the destruction for a moment, letting the words of their conversation sink in. The irony was satisfying.

Chapter XXII

Tyran's stomach growled. He barely noticed it at first. His face and fingers were numb, his toes curled with each step, and the hairs of his beard had frozen together. Yet it was his stomach that bothered him. When his belly rumbled again, he swallowed a mouthful of spit with hopes that it would ease the hunger pangs.

He saw no sign of life across the snow-covered plains. White blanketed the world around them. Tyran's feet sank nearly half a foot deep with every aching stride. The Neabou Sea was completely frozen and covered with the same snowdrifts, making it impossible to tell the difference between land and sea. He relied on the scouts, primarily Balishul, to guide the army to the next settlement and not across the frozen waters.

The mountains, which Erzebeth had named Valarun, had sunk back from the coast nearly a day ago, giving way to open fen; now, Valarun was but an impression in the distance. Tyran was sure that on another day, the sight would have been genuinely beautiful. But today bitterness clouded the view and made the mountains nothing more than a jagged silhouette.

"The days are going to grow shorter, Ser Tyran," Drem panted. "The temperatures will drop too much at night for the army to march."

"It is morning, Drem." Tyran's cracked lips rubbed clumsily against each other, partially frozen. He wanted to lick them in hopes of giving some life back to them, but it was too cold. It was likely they would forever stick together if they were moistened.

"It is mid-afternoon, Ser Tyran," Drem corrected.

Drem was right. The sun hung on the skyline, barely holding over the incline. It was already on its descent even though it had scarcely made it over the mountain ridge an hour ago. They had started late—too late—in the morning because the sun had not risen when it should have.

Tyran had not thought that Rhian would have been much different than Lairhein. Yet it seemed that in just a couple hundred miles, they were worlds apart.

"Perhaps we should move farther inland to the base of the mountains. It would provide some shelter from the wind and the cold."

"No," Tyran said. "The Vucari would not build their cities so close to the mountains, lest they would meet the same fate as Charreni, but naturally."

Drem cleared his throat. "We must do something, Ser Tyran. The men are growing restless, some seemingly going a bit awry."

Tyran did not take the energy to turn his head, really because he did not want the cold air to blow through his cowl. He had finally positioned his head just right to keep his ears warm. "What do you mean?"

"The men believe we are heading to the end of the world, to the Netherworld," Drem answered. "Some think that they will never see their homes again."

Tyran said, "And they may not. But the way to the Netherworld is within the Shade. They should know as much."

"Well, yes," Drem paused, "but we have been to the Shade and did not see the Kalinov Bridge. And here, the farther we travel, the more darkness we find...and everything is frozen."

Tyran did not slow his pace. He was glad that Drem had avoided the argument about them not returning to Lairhein. It was a blessing of sorts not to have to bicker about every little thing. Though Tyran had heard some rumors among the men in the past couple days as well. Some of them had said that Tyran was looking for death, saying he had no desire to live.

Maybe his men were right.

It was not healthy for him to think in that way, but there was a part of him that wondered if he had come here, to Rhian, to die.

He pushed the thought from his mind and instead thought about Drem's last words. He could have spent more time in the Shade Fells looking for the so-called Kalinov Bridge that led to Netherworld. It may have saved him the trouble of having to ease his men's fears in this moment. Then again, Drem's uneasiness did make his stomach churn—unless that feeling was hunger.

Legend said that the Netherworld was a frozen wasteland, full of darkness and demons. In truth, the parallels to Rhian were uncanny with the frozen tundra, shortened days, and Vucari, who may be the worse devils he had ever known.

If that were not enough, Tyran could hear the words of the Vucari man in the longhouse at Charreni: *"Wolos summoned the priests to Anaerfell"* and *"the Ash Tree was in danger."*

Fragmented thoughts showered his mind. He reflected on what the Vucari words could mean. Was it possible that they were heading to the Netherworld? Was the fabled Ash Tree upon this accursed landmass? Wolos was supposed to be the Protector of the Ash Tree. Yet Tyran had never heard any living creature having direct contact with a god. For Wolos to be in the flesh at Anaerfell and to speak with the Vucari... What did it all mean?

He could only speculate that he would find Wolos and the Ash Tree at this place called Anaerfell.

Tyran needed answers, and he knew exactly where to find them. Erzebeth said she was a Warden of the Ash Tree. She was Vucari. The woman had to know these things.

Tyran suddenly realized that Drem was still talking to him. He could only guess at how long the man had been rambling on. "…not that they mean to be disrespectful, Ser. If the men begin to lose themselves, we will have little choice but to execute them to save ourselves. If the cold was not enough, many are hungry. There were talks of eating the dead Vucari at the fishing village just for sustenance."

"Yes, yes," Tyran said, only half listening. "Continue on the path laid before us, and keep an eye out for Balishul. I want a report as soon as he returns. I will be with Erzebeth."

Drem may have been surprised, but his face was practically petrified, stationary from the icy wind. "Um…of course, Ser Tyran."

Tyran adjusted his cowl and retreated to the back of his brigade. The men huddled in small groups as they walked, losing all sense of their station and formation. With the weather, it was not worth his breath to correct them. They were trying to survive. He nearly smiled to himself, considering his own weakness. He may have some humanity left in him after all.

Erzebeth, head hung and shoulders slumped, trudged at the rear of the mass. Next to her was Kormish and a few other men. They were meant to guard her and watch her for the safety of the troop. Though as Tyran approached, he noticed that they were stumbling along with little cohesion whatsoever.

"Kormish, move along," Tyran said. "Take the others with you."

Kormish lifted his dark-circled eyes and nodded as though he might have been holding back a yawn. He reiterated the command to the soldiers in proximity.

Tyran was almost surprised that the man did not put up any argument. First Drem, and now Kormish. He could only suspect that the increased darkness was causing the men to become drowsy and less combative. It was ideal when considering moments like this, but it would be detrimental when they reached the next village.

"What do you want, young Red?" Erzebeth asked, keeping her head down.

Tyran had to admire the woman's brash tone as he fell into step next to her. Her lowered gaze was not respectful, but it was not fearful, either. "I have questions that need to be answered."

She was quick to respond. "I will not help you slaughter my people. We have suffered enough without needing to experience your wrath. I have heard your men talk and the terrible things that they say about the Vucari and me. We are not savages, no more than the lot of you."

Tyran tensed. "It will not do us any good to argue about who is the greater savage."

"I did not drop a mountain on a city of women and children. I imagine that no Vucari has done as much harm to the Stuhia."

"Mm."

"What does that mean?" Erzebeth snorted.

"I told you that I was not going to debate the issue."

"For three days or more I have heard you grunt and grumble without any rhyme or reason. You rumble at your men and even yourself when no one is around. It is not a suitable response in a conversation. Are you mad?"

Tyran withheld the urge to make the same sound. "Maybe I am."

She crossed her arms tightly across her chest, eyes still on the tundra. "It would have been wise for your mother to teach you some manners. I seriously don't know how you have made it this long with that type of attitude. For these men to follow you anywhere, the way you treat them, is beyond me."

Tyran clenched his fist. He had good reason to hit her repeatedly until she fell into the snow and was no more than a puddle of blood and bone. "My mother is dead."

That caught her attention. Brown eyes, turning towards him, digging into him, searching for some sense of humanness within his pathetic soul. He could feel it.

He did not make eye contact. His words came out harsher than he intended. "You will not find any love in me, nor goodness."

Erzebeth wrinkled her nose with doubt. "All men have goodness in them. And love. Some just bury it deeper than others because they don't know how good it can be."

Tyran did not grumble, nor did he make any other sound. This was not the reason he had come back here. He needed to speak to her about the Ash Tree. The rest was irrelevant.

Her intermission seemed to go on for miles even though she said it within a few steps. "Or maybe they do and they want to forget it."

Isolde's face was as clear in Tyran's mind as the slush in front of him. He closed his eyes and breathed. The love of his life, the woman that he was meant to marry, left this world with her last thoughts of him harming her. He hated thinking that she was traipsing about in the frozen Netherworld with a heart teeming with pain.

Erzebeth tilted her chin. "That's it, isn't it?"

"This is not the..." Tyran cleared his throat. His eyes stung. It was likely the cold. "This is not something that we are going to talk about." His jaw clenched, teeth grinding.

Erzebeth unfolded her arms. One of her hands made its way across the emptiness between them and touched his softly.

He held his breath in surprise. Not so much that she touched him, but that he did not pull away.

The gesture only lasted a moment before she pulled back as tenderly as she had invaded his space. It was gentler than anything he had experienced in months.

The tone of her voice was much different, holding less rigidity. "What do you want to talk about?"

Tyran pulled his fist in towards his stomach, away from her reach. "What did you mean when you said that you are the Warden of the Ash Tree?"

Erzebeth widened her brown eyes with interest. "It holds the same meaning as what Warden would mean anywhere, I suppose.

I am charged with protecting the Ash Tree. It is the same charge that many Vucari are meant to fulfill."

Tyran expired his breath louder than he intended, signaling his disbelief. "The real Ash Tree? From legend?"

"It is not legend, young Red. It is very much real." The woman barely blinked.

Tyran pressed, "That gives mortal men immortal life and unmatched power? We are talking about the Ash Tree that stretches into the Beyond, whose roots are nurtured by Wolos?"

Erzebeth was too composed. "Yes."

"It is here? Near Anaerfell?"

The color in Erzebeth's face drained. "No…it is not. Why the sudden interest, young Red?"

"I would really prefer if I asked the questions."

Erzebeth snuffed. "You clearly only intend to bring destruction and chaos and war. I don't see it being worthwhile to tell you much of anything."

Tyran's voice was emotionless. "If you are not helpful to me, then there is no reason to keep you alive, is there?"

Erzebeth noticeably gulped. She stared at her hands for a moment as if considering the kindness she had shown to him moments before.

Tyran hid his satisfaction. "You are afraid of death?"

"Is that why you have come to Rhian? To find the Ash Tree? To escape death?" she asked.

Tyran cocked his head, surprised by the association. "You did not answer my question."

"I may consider answering it, if you were to answer mine, young Red."

Tyran conceded. "No. I did not originally come to Rhian for the Ash Tree. I—"

Erzebeth waited.

"I came to Rhian to defeat death."

"That is something that all living creatures hope to achieve, and I am no different. I admit that I don't want to die," Erzebeth said.

"I need to go to Anaerfell," Tyran said with absolution.

"Anaerfell?" She burst into laughter.

Tyran scowled. "Yes. Why do you find that amusing?"

She looked over her shoulder back the way they had come. "Because that is where I was going myself until you *invited* me to come along on your adventure. I told you as much at our first engagement."

Tyran had just begun to contemplate whether Erzebeth was a priest, destined for Anaerfell, when her next words silenced his drifting thoughts.

"And now, we are going the wrong way."

Chapter XXIII

"Drast!"

His father's voice echoed down the hallway.

"Drast!"

The tone reminded him of when he was young and he had brought half a dozen chickens into his father's study. The results were priceless, but the consequences were dire.

"Drast!"

He had determined at that point that his father completely lacked a sense of humor.

Kura's eyes were wide. He hoped that it was due to him rather than his father. He grimaced. The thought fairly ruined the experience of having finally cornered the busty maid. With a sigh, he withdrew from her and fastened his pants.

"Drast!"

"We can finish this later, Kura."

She gave him a quick, frightened nod and flipped her skirts down. With an awkward curtsey, she scampered from the room, nearly knocking down the Arkhon. A hasty apology, a short dance, and Kura was gone, leaving only Arkhon Dagmar Kaligula and Drast.

"Drast," he growled.

Drast struck his forehead dramatically. "Oh, is that what you were screaming down the hallway? I thought you were saying something about a rash. It sounded quite daft."

"One day you are going to be too quick with your tongue and you are going to lose it!" his father snapped.

Drast was not entirely certain why he felt the need to push his father, but with Tyran gone, he seemed to be able to get away with far more. "I believe, technically, if the tongue is *quick* enough, it would preclude…"

"Be quiet!" His father's voice was icy. The man was visibly struggling to restrain himself. "I did not come to your chambers to play."

"Obviously. I was *playing* with Kura, and you interrupted *that*." He shrugged, unable to keep from grinning. "If I thought you wanted to play too, I would not have made her leave."

In a fit, the Arkhon threw Drast's bed against the wall with Koldovstvo. His face had turned purple. "Why is Maelili Kluk still alive?"

Drast took a moment to school himself. How did he know she was alive? He needed to watch himself or he was going to say something he regretted. Taking a breath, he met his father's gaze. "Tyran did not kill her."

"Clearly! Tell me why!"

Drast bit back the sarcastic comment on his tongue. Tyran let her live because their father refused to allow him to love women. Not to mention their mother dying from birthing Tyran. Now he had a personality-defining soft spot for anything with tits. He kept his voice level. "You would have to ask him, Father."

"And why did *you* let her live?"

"Me?"

His father paced. "Don't play games, Drast. You know as well as I do that she was in Lairhein when you killed her brother."

Drast shrugged. He was hoping his father would not find out about her. "What difference does it make? She left Lairhein. She is gone. Just like Kindel."

"No. She is not gone. Maelili Kluk is outside with half of Lairhein!" He pointed towards Drast's window. "She has created a mob to overthrow us."

"Us?" Drast smiled. "Of course."

A wordless cry rose from outside. The flames of torches flickered against the windows. He shifted to the window and pulled aside the curtain. Sure enough, Maelili stood at the head of the mob, facing them and speaking words he could not hear.

Why did he let Tyran influence him?

"What are you smiling about?" his father bellowed. "If we don't contain this, all that we have worked for is gone. All because you and your brother did not kill one little trull!"

"It is easy enough to blame us," Drast murmured, withdrawing from the window before he was seen.

"You *are* to blame."

Drast shook his head, his smile fading. "If you had simply let Tyran have his girl, he would have slain Maelili. He would be here with us now. His army could turn back this mob. But he is to blame?"

He forestalled his father. "How can you blame us, when you have driven us to this moment? You are Arkhon. You have nearly unlimited power with Koldovstvo. You have had every opportunity to rule Lairhein as you see fit, but you want more. You wanted a dragon. Tyran brought you one. You wanted to be Arkhon. I violated Claduk. You wanted the death of the Kluks. I murdered three. You wanted the destruction of the Temple of Wolos. I destroyed it. You wanted the death of the members of the Ninth Council. I killed them. What has any of it gained you besides the hatred and disgust of those you stepped on to get where you are?"

"How dare you speak to your father in such a way?" Dagmar Kaligula spat. "I am your father. You owe me your very lives should I ask for them. You will deal with this mob," he looked down his nose imperiously, "and you will not return to Lairhein until Wolos is dead."

Drast felt his heart sink in his chest. He could not face his father, turning towards the door to his chamber. "No, Father. I will not deal with the mob. That is your doing." He opened the door. "I must ensure that my brother doesn't die some meaningless death alone chasing the regrets and fears of a heartless old man."

"Drast!"

He closed the door behind him and strode rapidly down the hallway. His father's calls continued as he broke into a jog, darting towards the front of the building. Turning a corner, he saw one of his men.

"Mladen!"

The soldier turned about at his word. Drast was surprised to see such an old face, a face that had been younger than his before the battle with the Vucari. Koldovstvo had not been kind to the fellow. Still, Drast recognized the man from the events at the Vucari main camp. "Are you loyal to me, Mladen?"

The man's eyes darted back towards the mob. "I don't want to kill my friends—my family, Ser Drast." He swallowed. "My da is out there."

Drast clapped him on the shoulder. "I am not asking you to, Mladen. I am leaving and letting the mob do as they will. I am going to find Tyran. No one has to die here."

Mladen nodded fervently. Despite looking older, he still had the heart of a young man.

"Good. Find any other like-minded men and send them to loot the house for supplies and meet me in the stables. Turn the wagon to face the rear and harness the horses." He turned. "I need to slow the mob so that we can leave."

Mladen ran down the hall calling names, while Drast turned to continue in the opposite direction. Maelili had already been exposed to his tricks. He would have to try a different tactic.

After several feet, Drast took a deep breath and pushed open the front doors. The mob stood before him. The din was deafening.

His father would learn from his mistakes.

A ring of soldiers surrounded the estate, attempting to hold back the mob. Apparently, they had made it through the gate before the soldiers were the wiser. The light from the torches was initially blinding, and he raised an arm to help shield his eyes as they adjusted.

After a moment, he flung up his hands as though he would give a great speech. "Listen." He could not even hear himself over the mob, the sound of men and women calling for his head. He lifted his voice with Koldovstvo. "Listen!"

The crowd jeered, emboldened by numbers, pressing forward against the soldiers.

"Listen!" He called once more. Koldovstvo empowered his voice and the ground shook. Maelili, each man and woman in the mob, and each soldier fell to the ground. The estate groaned, the walls grumbled, and silence ensued.

He stepped forward, voice booming. "I have come to offer a peaceful resolution to this situation."

"You killed my brothers!' Maelili screamed, standing. "You murdered Peter in front of half of the town. You framed Ghanimer for the destruction of the Temple of Wolos. Elena is missing. Did you murder her as well?" She did not wait for a response. "There can be no peace!"

Drast kept his face plain, lowering his volume. "I am not here to offer you justice. I am here to offer you your lives. If you want a consolation prize," he waved a hand behind his head, "my father is in the estate behind me. If you want to live, you will move aside. If you stand in my way, you will die. Make no mistake, Koldovstvo runs through my veins and *none* of you can hope to live if you choose to face me."

"How much blood is enough?" Maelili sneered. "How many of your own will you kill to escape your crimes!"

"As many as stand before me." Drast turned his attention to the crowd. "I have wronged many of you. I have spilled the blood of the innocent, made children orphans, made women widows, and made men widowers. I am not interested in your forgiveness. I don't need it."

Drast took on a pleading tone. "Think of yourselves. Think of those you still have. Among these soldiers who serve my father and me are your fathers and brothers. Don't ask them to choose to whom they are loyal. Don't face me and leave your children fatherless or motherless. Allow me to walk free, and I give you my father. Allow me to walk free, and I give you Lairhein."

Mladen called from behind him. "We are ready, Ser Drast. We await you in the stables." When Drast turned to look at the man, Mladen was already gone.

Maelili was speaking, "...the policy of the Stuhia to let murderers walk free? Don't let him frighten you! Don't burden yourselves with what you *might* lose. Consider what has been taken from you! Will you be able to return home tonight and look your children in the eyes knowing that you have done nothing to serve justice upon the man most deserving?"

"I have given you your warning," Drast called and turned about to walk inside the estate. "I suggest you heed it."

Once inside, Drast sprinted down the hallway to enter the stables from the side door. Inside were a dozen men, all from his personal army. He did not have time to gauge whom he trusted and whom he did not.

"If you are here, you are loyal to me and loyal to my brother." He eyed them closely. "If you attribute your loyalty anywhere else, you may leave now."

"Drast!" He could hear his father's voice screaming from somewhere in the estate.

A few shuffled uncomfortably.

Drast continued, ignoring the sound of his father. "I am not asking any of you to harm the men and women outside. My intention is to walk away from Lairhein. The Vucari threat has not gone away, and my brother is in the north fighting them. I am taking you to join his force so that we can end it once and for all."

Again, the Arkhon screamed, "Drast!"

"If we succeed, then we will keep Lairhein safe. We cannot fall to the infighting that has defined our home over the last many months."

Several of the men nodded, reassured.

He walked to the rear of the stables. "Hold the horses and stand back."

Using Koldovstvo, Drast tore boards from the rear of the stable, the creaking of nails and the snapping of boards filling the air. The horses whinnied and the men shrank back. Directly behind the hole in the stables was the rear wall of the estate. His father continued to shout in the background.

Drawing a breath, feeling the aging effects of Koldovstvo, Drast pulled the wall apart. Extraordinary effort was required to keep the process as silent as possible. Stone shuddered and grout crumbled, forming a gap in the wall about ten feet wide.

The roars of the crowd assured him that his actions were still unnoticed. With a sigh, he held the side of the wagon, now filled with a medley of hastily grabbed supplies. "Come. We will be gone before anyone is the wiser." He motioned forward. "Let us go find my brother."

Chapter XXIV

Balishul's body was only recognizable by his red hair. His head rotted in a puddle of frozen blood and ice. The mouth was gaping with the tongue half-bitten off, and the eyes were torn from their sockets. The head was attached by a stretched strand of skin that extended to the crushed neck and flayed chest. The torso was in shreds, with bloody muscle and organs scattered in a fifteen-foot semi-circle. As for Balishul's lower body, it was detached, mangled, and hardly had any meat left against the broken bones.

Tyran knelt to inspect the teeth marks on the femur. He had seen death many times in his short life, but never had he witnessed something as gruesome as Balishul's remains.

Drem stood steadfast at his side, shaking his head. The man clearly had something to share but kept his mouth sealed.

Kormish could not stop himself. "This is madness." The Voivode's chest heaved. Tyran scooted to the side, continuing his assessment, but aware the man was likely going to blow chunks.

Tyran ran his fingers along the bone before peering through the snow-filled gusts that curled and snaked through the mountain pass.

"Wolves? A bear, maybe?" Drem scratched his head. The notion was ridiculous.

"I don't think an animal would be plucking out the bastard's eyes, Drem," Kormish said, rubbing his nose.

"There are no other bodies. This was not a battle," Tyran said. "This had to be an ambush, which suggests that the foes were intelligent."

Kormish agreed. "This had to be the Vucari. I told you the woman prisoner was trouble, Ser Tyran. She is leading us into a trap. We should have never turned around."

Tyran grunted.

Erzebeth had told him that they were going in the wrong direction and he had believed her. Within the hour, he had turned the army back towards the pass through the mountains. Needless to say, it was not well accepted by the men or his Voivodes.

That was three days ago.

The gorge between the mountains was awkward. His army could fit five men across, shoulder-to-shoulder. Man-high snowdrifts flanked their steps and boulders dotted the path. It was likely they were marching atop a river or stream bed of sorts. Yet because of the weather, Tyran guessed it was a good ten to twelve feet beneath them.

Drem spoke in a neutral tone, although his words sided with Kormish. "Erzebeth did stop us before we reached the next settlement. She protected that next village from experiencing what those at Charreni did."

Tyran said nothing. His Voivodes lectured him with the same tone that his father might use. He could not escape the blasted man.

Drem said, "The signs point towards betrayal, Ser Tyran. We are only a few miles beyond the shoreline. It is far colder here than when we headed east, we are running low on food and supplies, and our best scout is dead."

Tyran had to remind himself that Drem was a good soldier, simply so that he would not scream at the man. "I don't need it laid out before me. I can see for myself."

Kormish asked, "Can you see? This Vucari woman is going to kill us. Her Vucari friends are responsible for this…this attack."

Tyran shifted his weight, his foot sinking slightly. "That is quite the stretch. You think she is communicating with the other Vucari?"

"How could we know what they are capable of or what magic she could be using under our very noses? Their Koldovstvo is perverted, Ser Tyran. You know this!"

Tyran opened his mouth to silence the man when Kormish concluded with force.

"She is not Isolde."

The snow hitting Tyran's face may as well have been arrowheads.

Drem took a step backwards.

Tyran practiced serenity, rising to his full height and facing Kormish. He took measure of the man, struggling to mask his sneer. "Are you challenging me for leadership over this company, Kormish? You clearly have had a problem with my *decision-making* since we have come to Rhian."

"No," Kormish hesitated. "I would never challenge you. You know I am a loyal servant of House Kaligula and this army, Ser Tyran."

"Do I know that?" Tyran lifted his eyebrows, shrugging his shoulders. He leaned closer to Drem and whispered, "Do I know that?"

Drem shifted his eyes. "The darkness and the cold are affecting each of us. It will cause us to say and do things that…"

"Don't skirt the question!" Tyran yelled. He could hear the men shuffle around a couple hundred feet away. For sure, they would be taking notice of the commotion among their audacious leaders.

Tyran couldn't care less at this point.

"No, Ser Tyran. No." Drem dithered. His gaze towards Kormish was more than apologetic. It was remorseful.

Kormish glowered in response.

Tyran could feel Koldovstvo tugging at his fingertips. He was going to rip Kormish's soul straight from the pathetic cavity of his chest.

The bawl of a beastly creature resounded through the mountain pass. Tyran barely heard the sound but it cut off the heated conversation and stopped Tyran. When several roars of similar caliber echoed, following the first, Tyran jerked away.

Tyran had never heard the like before near Lairhein or within the Shade.

Valarun, as Erzebeth called it, was the mountain range that erupted on either side of him. It was swathed in snow and ice to the tallest peaks, many of which Tyran could not see due to the great heights and hanging clouds. The sound could be coming from ahead, the rear, or above, and with the resonance, it would be impossible to tell.

Shouts of alarm were heard from the army as they led themselves into formation. Erzebeth was somewhere among their number.

Tyran had only taken a step towards the soldiers when the roars erupted again, closer.

"Ser Tyran," Drem warned.

Tyran's mace was already etching its way out of his belt loop when he noticed the three hulking shadows that emerged from the crevices and cracks on either side of the pass. The creatures were best described as wolf-men. They had layers of shaggy grey hair from their snouts to their oversized paws. Each of them walked upright on their hind legs, shaped like those of an oversized dire wolf.

Growls from the three beasts vibrated with winter's wind.

"Vucari," Kormish yapped. The man sounded as certain as a newly married man on his wedding night.

"Something," Tyran murmured.

Kormish tugged the spear from the leather strapping on his back. As though he was intent on proving his worth, he moved ahead to face the wolf-men.

Drem followed suit, yanking his sword from its holding.

"No," Tyran ordered Drem, watching Kormish stomp towards the enemy, "you organize the men. If it is the Vucari, there will be more than three."

Uncertainty was etched on his Voivode's face watching Kormish march towards certain death, but Drem dipped his head. Without a word, he shuffled across the snow with as much haste as he could muster, two hundred yards back. His voice was hardened as he gave direction to the soldiers. "We are under attack. Defensive formation. Move!"

Tyran advanced to join Kormish.

The wolf-men were swift. If they were limited by the slippery surface, it was not noticeable. Maneuvering between two legs and four legs, the wolf-like creatures bounded into a wide half-circle, snarling and growling. Kormish had his spear extended, held in both hands, at the ready.

The first beast, at the far left, lurched at the same time as the wolf-man at the right. Kormish did not hesitate, flinging the spear forward like he was tossing water out of a bucket. Koldovstvo powered the weapon with the momentum of an arrow, catching the monster in the shoulder. It yelped and twisted backwards, rolling and thrashing against the ground.

Tyran loosed his mace from his hand, striking the second in the skull. The cracking of the monster's pate was only eclipsed by the guttural howls that thundered from farther down the gorge.

As expected, there were many more than three of these monsters. More shadows started to form in the snowy mists.

Tyran wrenched his weapon back to his hand. His target lay unmoving, unconscious or possibly dead already.

The remaining wolf-man dashed at Kormish on two legs while reinforcements swelled from the rear.

Kormish flung fire from his hands at the beast. The painful sound was indescribable as the wolf-man vaulted through the flames, its hair singeing and flesh burning.

"Get down!" Tyran yelled.

His counsel was too late. Kormish stumbled back and the monster barreled into him, knocking him flat to the ground. Kormish barely had time to lift his head, to gain a sense of what had happened, before the monster's teeth were buried in the Voivode's arm.

Kormish screamed. Claws hastily dug into the man's thigh, pinning him to the ground. The wolf-man ripped its snout back, taking heaps of arm flesh from the man. Blood splattered Kormish's face along with the hoary ground.

Another scream, gurgled with pain.

Tyran traveled through space and time with Koldovstvo. Before the beast could spit or swallow the blood-soaked tissue, Tyran was standing with his legs straddling the body of Kormish, his shield pulled from his back and fastened onto his arm. He ignored the massive size of the monster, standing nearly a head taller with more muscle than a team of oxen. With his full strength, Tyran slammed the wooden board into the muzzle of the monster, knocking it backwards and freeing Kormish.

The rumble in the wolf-man's throat was shortened. Tyran advanced, striking the creature again with the shield. Before the beast could react, Tyran pummeled the beast across the jaw with his fist that gripped the yew-haft of the mace. With timing more perfect then the rising sun—if the sun in this accursed country would rise like it was supposed to—Tyran recoiled, striking the mace into the side of the grey-furred face.

The first wolf-man barked as it made its way back to its feet and charged at Tyran. Kormish's spear bobbed against the muscle in its shoulder as it charged. Tyran was at the ready when a husky growl ascended from behind him. He expected the worst, anticipating a throng of wolf-men assailing him. To Tyran's surprise, a massive bear, the largest he had ever laid his eyes on, flashed by him.

Dark fur blurred as the bear roared and tore into the equally robust wolf-man. Teeth gnashed and claws ripped as the fleece of either animal was shredded. Back and forth, bestial sounds boomed off the parallel walls of the mountains.

Tyran twisted from the display to find Drem had approached him with the rest of the army. A handful of men snagged Kormish and pulled him away from the scene. The Voivode had lost blood and his eyes were closed, but his chest was still rising and falling.

"Erzebeth," Drem said, motioning to the bear. "One moment she was sprinting towards you, and in the next, she had changed into…that."

Tyran stared in amazement at the woman, turned monster, who overpowered the wolf-man. Soon she was on top of the creature, tearing her teeth into its jugular and ripping apart its airway.

"At first, I thought she was going to lay you to waste. I had the men prepared to strike her down, but she …"

Tyran gripped his mace. "Speak already, Drem. Time is running short."

The other creatures were closing their distance.

"She called these things Vulkodlak before she charged them."

"So they are not Vucari," Tyran concluded under his breath. He turned to the soldiers lined up behind him. "Tear these beasts limb from limb. No mercy. To Anaerfell! Attack!"

There was no time for grand speeches. The so-called Vulkodlak hurdled across the region, springing from the mountainside and the frozen riverbed. Like a pack of wild wolves, the monsters blitzed the Stuhian army.

Tyran met the first wave wielding his mace with rage. He slammed into monster after monster, listening to cracking bones and yelping bays. Blood and brains splashed and sprayed around him. The creatures were vast in size, rocketing their bodies forward as though they were battering rams, feeling no pain, having no fear.

When regular armaments began to lose their appeal, the soldiers around him embraced Koldovstvo, flinging fire and lightning at the enemy. The monsters kept coming.

Land exploded beneath the charging Vulkodlak. Handfuls of monsters shattered into bits. The Stuhia screamed with power surging through their veins. The Vulkodlak howled in response. Small groups of beasts fell while others turned and twisted in the air, through the snow, and battered into the front ranks repeatedly without restraint. Tyran's men cried out and fought back. It was not long until the Stuhia started collapsing around him. In minutes, dead littered the landscape.

A man near Tyran stumbled forward, a full beard grown and greying from channeling too much Koldovstvo. A Vulkodlak crashed into the soldier, tearing into his flesh. The man was dead before he hit the ground.

Tyran growled, crashing his mace into the back of the Vulkodlak's skull as it feasted on the Stuhia. The beast fell limp. Tyran struck it again, smashing the head into mush against the snow.

"Ser Tyran," Drem shouted, rushing to his side. "There are too many and our numbers are dwindling. At this rate, there will be nothing left to take to Anaerfell."

His Voivode was right. More of the beasts were emerging through the mountain pass. They seemed as thick as the falling snow.

"We need to fall back." Tyran said. His eyes touched the high points of the mountains. There was little that he could do without causing an avalanche to crush the lot of them. "Find a place to make a stand."

Drem pointed. "Some of the soldiers have pulled Kormish into an alcove there. It will have to make due."

"Make haste," Tyran agreed.

As Drem shouted orders to the few living that remained, Tyran turned his attention to Erzebeth, who was in the thick of the wolf-men, her bear form bleeding from several gashes.

He hurried in her direction, barely feeling the cold anymore. Sweat covered his brow from the exertion. In the back of his mind he panicked. He had heard that if a man sweated in the cold, it would turn to ice and he would freeze to death. Ignoring the concern, he focused on Erzebeth.

Koldovstvo flooded his being. A Vulkodlak jumped through the air at him only to be met by Tyran's shield being thrown straight up into the air. It held firm with magic so that the creature thumped into it as though it were hitting a brick wall. Tyran tore lightning into the creature's chest while it fell to the ground. As for the shield, it continued to hover around Tyran's body, circling and protecting him from the attacking Vulkodlak.

Over and over again, he used his craft to cycle the shield on either side of him, pushing back the enemy. His fists were empowered with the Koldovstvo clocking and clobbering the wolf-men that made it past his defenses. Jaws cracked and ribs snapped with every solidified punch.

Almost there.

He could feel the aging affects starting to impact his speed, his dexterity, as he slipped and slid his way to the oversized bear.

"Erzebeth, change back to your human form!" Tyran commanded. "I can save us, but I cannot carry you like that."

She roared, clawing another wolf-man across the midsection. Her brown eyes locked onto Tyran's for a moment. They were the same eyes that had considered his when she had touched his hand so gently.

"Now!" he cried.

Tyran hit the ground with his fist. The shield fell to his feet, useless. In its place, walls of ice sprang upward around them, shielding them both from the onslaught of Vulkodlak. It was not long before the miniature fortress started shaking with the monstrous wolf-men slamming into it with their bodies and their fists.

Erzebeth convulsed. Her fur and skin shed away while she wheeled about on the ground in agony. The bones readjusted and organs reset from beast to human. Where a beast had stood was now the naked figure of Erzebeth. Cuts and scratches patterned her body, but none were fatal.

Tyran had no place for modesty. The Vucari woman, within the privacy of the ice dome, struggled to her feet. Again her dark eyes met his own, filled with compassion.

"You need to be put down, young Red." Her voice was calm as her feet crossed in front of one another, closing the distance between them. "Your power is greater than any I have seen before, even from the Anshedar."

"What?" Tyran said, forehead wrinkled with confusion. He had never heard of the race before, whether beast or otherwise.

"You are like a rabid dog, young Red. You are the perfect companion, loyal and possibly even loving somewhere deep inside." Erzebeth bit her lip. Her breasts, barely covered by her dark hair, touched the front of his chest. She halted her feet. "But you are tainted by a disease that is stronger than the goodness in you. You cannot be left to live in this world, or you will corrupt every living thing around you."

Tyran tilted his chin, lips parting. His free hand touched her pale skin, as whitish as the ice fortress that veiled this moment.

"You would taint me, young Red." She stepped up on her tiptoes. "As with the rabid dog, you need to be put down."

He grabbed her by the back of the neck and pulled her to him. He kissed her with more force than he had ever kissed any woman.

This woman was not Isolde. This woman was battle-hardened and a warrior. She was not plain.

She grabbed his shoulders and returned the embrace, her tongue touching his lips. Her body was far warmer than his own, as if it were heated by the darkness.

He did not know what he was doing in that moment. It may have been the first time that his mind was clear from thought, acting without thinking. Though in time, he may consider that when his death was nigh, he found that this was something he wanted to do before death found him.

The crashing against the ice pulled him from the moment. Tyran pulled back, moving the Vucari's hair from her cheek. "You won't kill me, Erzebeth."

"No," she breathed. Her hands fell to his chest. "But it still needs to be done."

Tyran pulled off his cloak and wrapped it around her shoulders. "Mm."

She gave him a sullen gaze. "None of that, young Red. Say what you mean, but don't grunt."

"Hang on," he muttered.

He jerked the shield back to his forearm and attached it.

The next few moments were a blur. Tyran burst through the ice dome with Erzebeth curled in his arms, skipping through time and space. The Vulkodlak were scattered across the gorge in the hundreds. Tyran and the woman were but a distortion, entwining and interweaving through the masses of Vulkodlak. The monsters barely knew he was passing by until he was beyond them.

When he finally reached the alcove, he found Drem and a dozen men battling off more Vulkodlak than they could manage. The mountain had a slight overhang and a cave settled back into its side that was no bigger than his father's study. It would have to make due.

Tyran zigzagged behind his Voivode and turned Erzebeth loose.

"Pull back," Tyran bellowed.

Drem shuddered. "There is no retreat, Ser Tyran. We are trapped."

Tyran repeated himself. "Now. Pull back or you will be buried with the beasts!"

He touched Koldovstvo without any more caution, sending a boom as loud as ten thousand men bellowing into the ravine between the mountains. The chasm shook with the power of the energy he sent forth.

The Vulkodlak near the cave entrance backpedaled, yowling at the other beasts.

Snow powdered at first. The mountain shook and boomed as the sound carried its way to the clouded tops. The noise started slowly, like the drumming of mugs on a tabletop in an alehouse, but soon it built itself up, like a thousand horses propelling across the plains. The avalanche flattened any Vulkodlak that were visible, but rocks and snow quickly eliminated the view.

Drem shouted, "Move to the back of the cave!" The few remaining men did as they were told along with Erzebeth.

Tyran maintained his hold, using Koldovstvo to raise a shield of force, preventing the falling mountain from crashing into their little holding.

It was over almost as quickly as it had begun, leaving the lot of them in darkness, buried in the side of a mountain.

"We cannot undo this, Ser Tyran," Drem said. It was pitch dark, but Tyran could hear the man's trepidation. "Any efforts to dig out or use Koldovstvo could bring the entire mountain down on top of us."

"Mm."

"On the bright side, we can take the rations off the dead. We should be able to survive for some time," Drem added.

Tyran had thought as much. Plenty of his men were dead or dying around him. There was only one way for them to survive.

Erzebeth asked, "What do we do now?"

Tyran sniffed, admitting his defeat. "I will send for my brother in Klukas."

Month of Slaughter
Fourth of Frost
46 CE

Chapter XXV

Mountains. Snow. Fog.

Drast's heart sank each day when the sun barely rose above the horizon to give him enough light to see the unfeeling, colorless terrain of Rhian. In the dark, he always fell into a trap of believing that the morning would bring some comfort, some escape from the emptiness of the night. Although, he supposed, the landscape was no more dismal in the light than it was in the dark. The land of the Vucari was a pitiful world with nothing to offer.

Mountains. Snow. Fog.

Death.

Drast strove to find something meaningful in the landscape. After several days plodding through the knee-deep snow and ice fog, he felt drained. He wanted to rest, to eat, or even to have Kura there squirming with her skirts lifted. Anything to distract him from the displeasures of this cursed place.

He realized soon after arriving that he had failed to grasp the size of Rhian before departing from Lairhein. The stretch of the frozen Neabou Sea had left the men weary long before they reached Rhian. Weeks of endless trudging across ice piled upon snow piled upon more ice and a nearly absent sun caused the lot of them to consider the wisdom behind the venture. It had only been with constant coaxing and feigned concern for their well-being that Drast had convinced them to stay with him.

Without much warning, a dried strip of salted beef was thrust under his nose. "Ser Drast," Mladen said, handing him the piece.

Wishing he had some sensation in his nose to smell it, Drast took it and tore at it with his teeth. He could not tell if the beef was merely tough or frozen. "Noon already?" he said, trying to smile while he chewed. His face was so frozen he likely looked like a drunkard.

Mladen nodded, scouting the landscape. "Near as we can say. It is a bit brighter right now, but I don't think the sun topped the mountains today."

Drast spent the energy to look over his shoulder at where the sun should have been in the sky. Nothing. He took another bite. "Eh, well, it just means we only have a few more hours of light left. Although the days are finally getting a bit longer."

"Mm," Mladen grunted. The man stared onward as they continued to lead the troop behind him. Drast could tell that the man was lost in his own thoughts. He hoped that his new Voivode was thinking of the task ahead and not what was left behind. Drast had tried to encourage all the men to do as much, though he struggled with the concept himself.

Memories had poked at Drast's mind since Lairhein, especially memories regarding his father. He felt some sense of relief, or justification, at leaving his father to fend for himself against the people of Lairhein. Yet since his flight north, his guilt had plagued him.

Nearly nightly, Drast had tried to contact his father in Klukas. When there was no response, he attempted to find Dagmar Kaligula with the trick he had learned within the *Varkolak*. That had failed him as well.

Now, after weeks of travel, he was certain his father had died. The worst of it came with knowing that his father's blood was on his hands.

When Drast was contacted by Tyran in Klukas while still sailing northwards, his brother had aged so much that Drast had thought he had finally contacted Father. Of course, it did not take him long to realize his mistake, but he could not bring himself to tell Tyran that he believed their father to be dead until only recently. His brother had seemed entirely unmoved, however. Given how Dagmar and Tyran had separated, Drast was still not sure how his brother had taken the news. Did Tyran feel happy or relieved, or the same sense of guilt Drast now felt for having parted on such unhappy terms?

"You said we would find your brother today?"

Drast pushed the last piece of salted beef into his mouth, nodding at Mladen. He took his time to savor the taste, chewing slowly.

He examined the gorge, snow-painted mountains lining both sides. This matched the description of where Tyran said he had been ambushed by the Vulkodlak.

Drast finally swallowed. "Well, we will find the lump of snow Tyran is under. No telling how deep he is. Could take a few days to dig him out."

"How in the Nine Lands did he get buried?"

"His army was attacked by some kind of wolf creatures, I guess. He buried himself to keep them out."

Mladen gave Drast an odd look as he finished off his own strip of beef.

"I did not say it was a good plan." Drast shrugged. "But I don't think he can likely make it until he finally thaws out."

"How has he made it this long?" Mladen squinted at the white surrounding them. "No food, no fresh air, no light. It must be miserable."

Drast nodded.

He had been using the same method of divination his father had taught him to track Ghanimer and Maelili—the same divination with which Drast had failed to locate his father—to pinpoint Tyran's location. However, he was forced to venture into Klukas nearly every day to determine whether the path he had chosen was correct. The mountains, snow, and fog made the entire journey a great maze, and he was trying to find a lump of snow among mountains of snow under which his brother was buried. Miserable was not a strong enough word.

"I have spoken with Tyran a few times in Klukas. They have cut down to half rations or less and most of the men spend their time in Klukas to keep up their spirits, visiting friends and family in Lairhein. Being in that state helps with hunger and such. As to the air, there seems to be a crevice in the back of the alcove that fresh air comes through."

"They cannot get out that way?"

Drast chuckled. "Well, despite it being both too small for any of the men to fit through and leading deeper into the side of the mountain, it smells of those Vulkodlak that attacked them. Tyran sent a few men in through Klukas, but it is black as pitch and they cannot make head or tails of what is on the other side." Drast paused, peering about. "Eh, I think we may have passed him."

Mladen lifted his hand to halt the soldiers behind them.

Drast sighed. "I am going to Klukas to figure this out. Have the men rest for a bit. If this is where Tyran is, I want everyone looking out for those Vulkodlak creatures. The last thing we need is to be under a mountain like my brother. I don't think the odds of finding someone else to come along and dig us both up are too good."

His new Voivode nodded with a grin as if the idea was funny and went off to direct the other soldiers. Drast did not pay him much heed.

Mladen was not as world-wise as Walstan was, but he was easy-going, followed directions, and got along well with the other men. Mladen reminded Drast of himself a bit. Of course, the journey had been so uneventful, Drast could not say if Mladen was any good as an actual Voivode, but that time would come.

Once Drast had lain down and covered himself to ensure that he did not catch his death from cold while he was in Klukas, he eased his breathing to find sleep. It did not take him long to reach the meditative state necessary to enter the incorporeal world.

Being ethereal, Drast schooled himself to calm. It was an exercise he had practiced more often than most, and it made the walk in Klukas much easier. He found that his brother, while outwardly emotionless most of the time, struggled to school his mind to match his body. The two had often considered that Drast, while outwardly rambunctious, was often the more reserved of the two.

He could hear Mladen giving orders and his soldiers' idle conversation, musing about whether they would find Tyran today. Whether or not Tyran was alive—there seemed to be a running conspiracy theory that Drast was going to retrieve his brother's body and did not think the men would go with him unless he lied to them.

While in Klukas, Drast could call to Tyran to let him know that he was needed. Tyran would receive an impression that Drast was present in Klukas and the two could then meet. However, the trick his father taught him involved thinking in a different manner, almost so that Drast forced the impression that Tyran was requesting his presence. From this impression, Drast could place himself at his brother's side immediately.

In a blink, he stood beside his brother in a small alcove. Tyran spoke with a Vucari woman about whom he had told Drast. Tyran looked old, of an age with their father. Whatever else had occurred, Tyran's time on Rhian had taken its toll. Drast thought his brother had even aged since he had last seen him, likely from trying to use Koldovstvo to dig his way out again.

His brother's soldiers, the few left, meandered to and fro, some playing at dice, but many of them appeared to be sleeping.

Having been here daily, Drast noticed several of the soldiers did not appear to move at all, and he supposed being locked in a cave for weeks left little to do other than sleep and venture into Klukas.

One of Tyran's men was in the ethereal world with Drast when he arrived. He appeared to be standing right beside Tyran, listening to what he and the Vucari woman were saying. That was not a good sign.

"Kormish." Drast recalled the man's name.

The fellow would have leapt from his skin if he had not already done so to reach Klukas. "Dr-Drast!"

"How does everyone fare?"

The man's eyes darted back and forth, clearly concerned that Drast had surmised what he had been doing. "Not well, Ser Drast, not well in the least. Spirits are quite low."

Drast nodded. "Well, they should brighten a bit. I am just here pinpointing the location for my men. You should be out by nightfall."

"Truly?" Kormish sang. "Oh, Ser Drast, thank you! I could not spend another minute in this hole."

"Aye, well, there it is," Drast murmured. "I need to speak with my brother. Tell him to enter Klukas."

"Of course, Ser Drast."

"And Kormish?"

"Yes?"

"When we talk next, we are going to discuss your eavesdropping on my brother."

Kormish paled, licking his ethereal lips. "Y-yes."

The soldier winked from existence and a moment later, Drast saw Kormish's corporeal body stand up from a corner in the alcove. Drast did not bother to watch the man go speak with his brother or watch his brother begin the process of entering Klukas. It always took a bit.

Entering Klukas did not involve Koldovstvo in any way. Being Stuhia was enough. Any of Drast's soldiers could do the same as he did, but Drast was always the one to scout ahead using Klukas. He enjoyed being able to see his brother and could not pass up the opportunity to attempt to find his father again.

Once in Klukas, he would be unseen by those around him, though his physical body was in danger since his mind was not present to move it. Growing up, he had heard tales of Stuhia who had ventured into Klukas only to die when their house burned to the ground because their minds were not present to feel the flames.

The obvious danger of being invisible while being able to hear others was the ability of Stuhia to spy on one another, which caused no small degree of concern among certain folk. His father being one of them. It was also believed that evil spirits could inhabit the bodies of the Stuhia if they left them unattended. In either case, symbols of protection could be drawn to prevent those in Klukas, Stuhia or otherwise, from entering certain areas. Drast's father kept nearly the entirety of the estate in such a manner, which is also why Drast continued to check for a response from his father each time he entered Klukas. He supposed that the symbols of protection also prevented him from finding Dagmar; since the finding method that his father taught him was new enough to him, it was truly difficult to say.

Lost in thought, Drast was somewhat taken aback when Tyran was suddenly before him. Tyran had been much quicker than he usually was. Although having nothing to do weeks on end but wander Klukas certainly would make one more proficient in the practice.

"Good to see you, brother."

"You are here for us."

Drast nodded. "I believe we actually walked past you, but I needed to pinpoint your location. I will walk up through the snow and then find my men from there. As soon as I do, we will begin digging you out."

"Good." Tyran rubbed his hands together, as if cold. The impossibility of that sensation was not lost on Drast. In Klukas, nothing could be felt. It was like being somewhere between a dream and being—nothing. It was difficult to describe, but being cold was an impression, not a sensation here.

"Tyran, I have something to ask of you."

His brother grunted noncommittally.

"I—" Drast swallowed, "I want you to reach out to Father so that I can see him. I need to know if he is still alive. You know that I had left him with the mob in Lairhein…I fear that he is dead."

Tyran's expression seemed—pleased. His words were hollow. "What does it matter?"

Drast's mouth went dry. His tongue clove to the roof of his mouth awkwardly. "I want to see him. I must apologize. I know," he hurried on to forestall his brother, "I know you no longer care what happens to him. I know it makes no difference to you whether he is alive or dead, but please, for me, for the love of your brother, set my mind at ease."

"And if he is dead? If he refuses to answer my call?"

"I don't know if he is out there, but if he is, he will not answer my calling. You have been the one he cherishes, not me. If you call to him, I know he will answer. I know he will. Tyran, please."

Tyran's image flickered as though he might leave Klukas, and then re-formed. "For you, brother." Tyran closed his eyes to focus. He had to, Drast knew. His brother was not as strong in Klukas as he was. When he opened his eyes again, they were cold. "Father."

"My sons."

Drast turned to look at his father, the guilt that had haunted him the past weeks washing over him in waves. Drast had left his father to die at the whims of an angry mob. From the moment Drast had walked beyond the walls of the Kaligula estate, he had felt the supreme burden of his decision. Now that he beheld his father before him, the guilt became unbearable, even in lieu of the relief in finding him to be alive.

Dagmar Kaligula was ancient, bespeaking of the hardships he faced in eluding the mob. A beard whiter than the snows covering the ground he stood on. Sunken eyes, now murky with cataracts, peered at Tyran and Drast. Dagmar's hands gnarled so that the fingers seemed to be capable of nothing more than curling in upon themselves, shaking despite the obvious attempts of the displaced Arkhon to keep them steady.

Drast fell to his knees, uncertain how to maintain his connection to Klukas. For a moment, Drast could not speak. His mouth moved, his lips worked, but his voice failed. "Father. I am sorry. I have betrayed you. I have failed you!"

His father's voice shook as badly as his hands, though he did not glance in Drast's direction. "I have had to remain hidden to avoid my enemies in Lairhein. Aged as I am, it has not been easy to outrun those who hunt me. I have had to outwit them as best I can. Now, alas, I am reaching the end of my life and will soon pass on."

"Then Aenar might, at last, be rid of our contemptible line," Tyran growled. "It is unlikely Drast and I will succeed in Anaerfell, and the horrible deeds we have wrought will fade with time."

"No, no, no," their father moaned. "I know you will not fail. You cannot. It is true that our line is reaching its end, but if you succeed, then it doesn't have to be so."

Drast swallowed.

Dagmar leered, his thin, wrinkled skin sagging heavily. "You are my last chance, my sons. You are my last chance at life. You are your last chance. If you fail, we will diminish to nothingness. If you succeed, we will hold a place in the past, present, and future of Aenar. If you love your father, if you are loyal to me, you will see that my will is done."

It was the same claim to action Drast had heard since the time he could walk. He was incited to complete his father's will. It bespoke of the charge he had been given his entire life. Fulfilling this task, he would be given everlasting life either through immortality or eternal life at Thrice Ten Kingdom. He was certain of it.

Drast finally rose to his feet shakily. "I will not fail you again, Father. I will expend my last breath in seeing that Wolos dies." He clenched his fists. "I will not fail."

"And what of you, Tyran?" Dagmar wheezed.

Tyran scowled at his father, not softening his gaze until he looked at Drast. "Mm."

Dagmar's milky eyes darted towards Drast at last "If you can succeed, then there may, perhaps, still remain some forgiveness in your father's heart."

"I will not fail."

Chapter XXVI

Tyran drew closer to the fire. His body shuddered from shoulder to shins, shaking as though it were trying to warm itself. Being back in the gorge was no more comfortable than being in the alcove. Though Tyran did not want to be in a hole in the side of a mountain any longer than needed. He had elected that they build camp in the gorge and erect some coverage from the wind.

It was not this frigid two months ago, but at these temperatures, Tyran deemed cold to be cold. It just did not matter anymore. Regardless, the violent wind gusts had full reign to sway in and out of the gorge, and Tyran was thankful that Drast had used a bit of Koldovstvo to construct a wall of ice to block the icy gale.

"We should get moving," Tyran said, his jaw vibrating, teeth chattering against one another.

Drast's voice was caught by a burst of flurries swirling from the sky into the makeshift ice fortress. Tyran could barely hear his brother's voice. "Give it the night. We did not stop tearing at the mountainside until you were found. The men need rest and food. You, too. You have barely been surviving on what was left of your supplies. You will need all the strength you can muster for what is coming."

Tyran sniffed to no avail. It felt like his nose might be running, but his nostril hairs were frozen solid. He knew that Drast was right in his assessment. Even with most of his men dead by the Vulkodlak, there were few provisions to carry them through the past eight weeks. His body was weak.

"Freezing to death is not my idea of a good death."

Drast smiled. "Then I am glad to have saved you from that fate. Warm up near the fire, brother. Food and rest is what you need."

"I have rested plenty." Tyran did not make any movement towards the heated beef stew the soldiers gathered around a distance behind him.

He pondered his brother's subtle jest: *glad to have saved you.* Tyran had never felt quite as weak as when he had called upon his brother to rescue him, and now Drast was taking the opportunity to poke fun at him. A part of Tyran realized that his brother was suffering equally. His display with their father in Klukas had shown him that much.

Tyran sighed.

"It is no wonder," Drast said, "the Vucari attempt to invade Lairhein each spring. It must be atrocious living in the dark twenty hours a day in the nether of winter. This place is forsaken."

"The darkness doesn't bother the Vucari so much," Tyran said. He had yet to even see the sun since the snow and rock fell away, but according to Drast, even when there should be sun, it was hidden behind the dismal grey clouds.

Drast dropped his jaw. "Oh."

"Mm," Tyran started. "The sayings about them having sight in the dark are true, so it seems. And the cold doesn't bother them much either, so Erzebeth says. They are resilient against the cold."

"So why do they keep attacking us at Lairhein? Have you asked that question?"

Tyran shook his head. "I have not. Erzebeth claims that she is not a part of the war. She says that she has only recently come back to Rhian."

Drast grinned. "And you believe her?"

"Mm."

Tyran shifted closer to the small blaze, trying to soak in the warmth of the fire. He did not have the energy to be the strong one, nor to be stubborn. The heat from the fire pit seemed a thousand miles away, barely touching his nose and cheeks. He grunted and, again, inched closer on the solid ground. Even the fire could not make a dent in the ice and snow beneath his britches.

The murmurs of the soldiers, a mixture from both armies, echoed in the darkness. There were probably about two dozen between the two troops. If they were to be ambushed by the Vulkodlak again, he was certain that they would all be dead in minutes.

Drast looked at him with penetrating eyes. Tyran made a conscious effort to look away from his brother. The man might be thinking about him, or he may be contemplating something else entirely. Right now, Tyran did not care much.

Instead, Tyran strained to hear the hushed tones of the soldiers. The sound was imperceptible with the wind endlessly whistling through the gorge. He idly wondered at the mood of the soldiers, but soon decided he did not care about that either. Besides, the meaningless noises of the gorge seemed to dance in his head like a child's melody; one he had wished he had never learned. It made him lightheaded and dizzy.

The shadows of the firelight danced in such a way they only added to his nausea, making it difficult to focus on anything that was going on around him. The world blurred, and, as usual, his thoughts were fleeting.

Drast was right. He did need food.

Either that or Tyran supposed he was going mad. He found some sense of comfort in the thought. If he were mad, he might be able to forget the horror of his life and the wicked, malicious things he had done.

Tyran hated himself.

The realization was lost when someone touched his arm and sat down next to him in the snow. Tyran did not have to look to know it was Erzebeth. She handed him a small bowl of what appeared to be melted snow and dried meat. "You okay?"

"Mm," he intoned.

Since the battle against the Vulkodlak, she had stayed near him like she owed him something. He supposed that he had saved her but had not really considered what had caused him to do such a thing. Even more surprisingly, Drem and Kormish had not said a word about it, nor had they raised concern that she had been kept alive in the alcove for the past two months.

At the thought, he considered trying to spot his Voivodes in the group of men. Again, the thought was fleeting.

"Eat, Tyran," Drast said. Whatever the man had been wondering at seconds ago was lost to speculation. "Let it sit for too long and it will lose its appeal altogether."

Tyran sipped at his soup.

Erzebeth turned her gaze to Drast, her tone familiar. Equal. "It is good that you arrived when you did. Any longer and these men's stomach pains would have gotten the better of them. Without a doubt, I think I would have been the first to be eaten."

"My sincerest apologies. I think I should have waited a bit longer, then." Drast flashed his teeth, though the smile did not reach his eyes. They were cold.

Erzebeth's face tightened, and her gaze turned away. One of her hands came to rest on Tyran's leg. She meant to be comforting or consoling, but it only reminded him of the kiss they had shared a couple months ago.

He hated to admit that he longed for it a second time. And a third. It had happened too quickly and was over too soon. The secret of his affection for this Vucari woman was nearly as haunting as Isolde's death.

Her eyes looked towards the ground. She had lost her garb in the battle, what with turning into a bear and all, and now she was dressed in the clothes of a Stuhian soldier. But she was far from being a Stuhia. Dark hair. Pale skin. She was not Isolde; she was a fighter.

Tyran tried to remember what he and Drast were talking about, or if they were talking about anything. He looked at his brother casually, the flame dancing between them. The man was watching him and Erzebeth with that blasted *knowing look* that he always had. Thousands of miles from home and he had brought that *knowing look* with him.

"You don't know, Drast."

His brother raised his eyebrows, dimples piercing his cheeks. "I don't know what?"

Tyran tugged at his memories. He was not certain how old he appeared to Drast, but he knew that his age was likely beyond any man among their group. From the battle with Torn'ash, the destruction of Charreni, and the brawl with the Vulkodlak, Tyran had exhausted himself. Like a fool, he had used Koldovstvo as a child might, without restraint and without reason. He had nearly killed himself.

Tyran was certain that death was what he wanted for himself. Though he could not be certain at this moment.

Looking at his wrinkled hand, knuckles, and palms rotating in front of him, the reality of his matured form settled in the pit of his stomach. He was going to die soon. He could feel it in his lungs, the slowness of his heart. Tyran felt as if he carried the weight of the world on his back, and in this moment, it felt too grave for one man to bear.

Maybe this is what his father felt like every day. The sickening image of his father in Klukas flashed in his skull. Dagmar's frailty mortified him.

"What do I not know?" Drast repeated himself. His voice held a strange patience, as a grandchild may have towards his grandfather.

Tyran chortled in spite of himself. His older brother was younger than him. This was not something that men should ever live to experience. It disrupted the natural flow of life.

"Erzebeth," Tyran directed, finally, gripping his pant legs and pulling them from his skin as they softened in the heat, "helped us survive in this hole in the ground. If it were not for her guidance, you may have come to find nothing more than a tomb with your brother inside."

Drast's eyes darted towards the snowy chasm, possibly contemplating the weight of Tyran's words. "I did not question you keeping your prisoner alive, nor did I question her roaming freely without restraint among the men. It would have been equally odd to see her still bound when there was nowhere to go. Survival supersedes war etiquette even amid battle."

"Mm." Tyran was not sure whether to believe his brother or not. The man usually had fancy words for any situation, even if it was not something that he believed.

Drast's breath formed from the shade of the fur-lined hood he wore to keep off the cold. It was clear he was watching Erzebeth, although he addressed Tyran. "Tell me about Wolos and this place called Anaerfell."

Erzebeth shifted on her haunches.

"I know that the Vucari priests were summoned to Anaerfell to meet with the god. I cannot say that there is more than that to tell."

"That is not entirely true, Tyran." Erzebeth bit her lip, brown eyes settled on Drast with the same intensity.

Drast did not hesitate, always being the quicker tongued. "Tell us why Wolos goes to Anaerfell, then, and why the priests follow."

Questions that Tyran had asked before and had forgotten suddenly flooded back. She had said she was going to Anaerfell when they first met and had mentioned being a Warden of the Ash Tree. Of course she would know more. He had spent two months confined with Erzebeth but spent little to no time talking.

At least, no time talking about what was actually important.

Socializing was never Tyran's strong suit.

He licked his lips. They were cracked, blistered from the cold, and yet, several fortnights later, he could somehow still taste her upon them.

"Best I show you." Erzebeth stood and started for the opening of the ice fortress, farther into the gorge and away from the fire.

"If you attempt to flee, be aware that my arrows don't miss," Drast warned.

Erzebeth snorted with derision. "I don't run, young Red. I would have to be missing a limb to even consider fleeing danger."

Tyran stood to follow Erzebeth away from the fire. Drast was inches behind him with his bow held at the ready in his hand. Tyran ignored his brother, his bones aching with each step, again reminding him of his aged body.

Tyran was not certain what he anticipated by stepping farther into the gulch within the vast mountains of Rhian, but the sight that met his eyes was not it. Shades of color—pale green, soft pink, and hints of violet—danced across the sky against the northern horizon.

The only thing he could imagine the sight to be were weaves and flows of Koldovstvo as they might appear if visible to the naked eye. Despite the snow blowing through the ravine, the sky was decorated with magnificent tints, seeming to give life to the blackness of the night.

"What in the Nine Lands?" Tyran mouthed in wonderment.

Drast was not nearly as impressed. "We noticed this spectacle the farther we traveled inland. The men could only guess that it is the work of Czern or Myestera."

Erzebeth replied, "It could be from the Dark God or the Mother of the Stars, but that is not what the Vucari believe. It is unlikely that the light stems from either, doubly so given that Myestera is weakest during the winter months, and Czern has no love for the light."

Tyran was somewhat surprised when Drast did not immediately rattle off some quippy speech or ask a handful of ridiculous questions. Rather, he appeared to listen with interest as Erzebeth continued.

"The lights that you see in the northern sky are from Anaerfell. Wolos has not come to Anaerfell for merely this winter, but comes to the temple every winter until the spring solstice. It is there that he battles against Marheena. I would imagine both of you are as familiar with her as any other god. The Seamstress of Nightmares, the Mother of the Vili, Goddess of the Netherworld becomes warped during the Season of Frost and brings the winter. It is Wolos who must protect us with his magic until Strega comes and sends her back to the Netherworld. It is only then that spring comes each year."

"The story is a familiar one, even to the Stuhia. Marheena furnishes the frost. Wolos shields men from the frost. Strega defeats the frost with the Nine Winds," Drast said with a click of his tongue. The man seemed to have trouble keeping himself quiet for too long. "You are saying that these lights give proof that the tale is more than myth, and it occurs here on Rhian? That would mean we only have about six weeks left until Wolos leaves Anaerfell at the onset of spring. If we don't make it there by then, we would have to wait an entire year until he returns."

Erzebeth took a step back, realization of their intention flooding her features. With a quaver in her voice, she asked, "And why would you want to meet with Wolos?"

"It will hardly be a meeting." Drast smiled under the capering lights. "We will have the Horned God's head."

Erzebeth did not have the complexion to pale, but Tyran was certain the woman nearly swallowed her tongue. She echoed what Tyran had told her months ago. "You came to defeat death. Of course—"

Drast interjected. His voice was as unyielding as the mountains near them. "Explain yourself. *Of course*, what?"

Erzebeth stared at the two brothers as if they were Vulkodlak. "Truly, you are rabid dogs!"

Tyran's heart sank.

Drast twitched, lifting his bow from his side. Despite his physical response, Drast spoke as calm and collected as a group of midwives chatting about their sewing habits while sharing a kettle of tea. "I have had far worse insults thrown my way. Feel free to have another go at it, if you like. Although," he gave a self-deprecating shrug and lifted his bow, "I might warn you that I tend to be a bit impulsive when it comes to being offended."

The look Erzebeth gave Drast could have melted stone. "You are certainly less appealing than your brother."

Drast grinned. "That's better!"

Tyran straightened, interrupting the back and forth. "Tell us what you meant, Erzebeth."

There was no mistaking the pain that she held in her brown eyes, biting her lip in hesitation. "Tyran...I...I had said before that I can find no reason to tell you anything. I stand by that. You want nothing but chaos and destruction and death. I will not be a helping hand in your vile quest."

Tyran turned his head away from the woman, expecting Drast to pull an arrow taut and release it. His heart was split between what he wanted and what must be done: embrace life through love or destroy death through war.

Erzebeth continued, and the words she spoke nearly felled him to his knees. He could not look at her. "You cannot slay me any more than I can you, Tyran Kaligula. We are at an impasse—"

Drast's laughter was loud, rolling out of his throat as though he were riddled with more amusement than he could contain.

Tyran cringed, suddenly wishing he did not know his brother as well as he did. Yet he was comforted that he did not have to verbalize his own emotion towards Erzebeth.

"Maybe he cannot, but do you think the same of me?" Drast snorted, an arrow whisking between his fingers as if by magic and settling against the sinew of his weapon. "Tyran may not have the will to end your life, but nothing would please me more than to wear your skin, skin-switcher, and bathe in your blood for as long as it holds its heat."

From the corner of his eye, Tyran saw Erzebeth's jaw drop. She looked to him for help; he did not have the courage to meet her gaze.

Drast's chortle heightened to a cackle. "You think that my brother will stop me, Vucari scum? You clearly know nothing about the men we have been bred to be. Take note, even diseased hounds don't turn on their own. They will hunt together, kill together, and rip flesh from their prey together. No matter what happened in your little ice cave, you have not been elevated beyond prey. Best you remember your place."

"In that, you are wrong, Drast Kaligula," Erzebeth spat. "Rabid dogs turn upon each other. Destroy each other. The pack, no matter how large, no matter how strong, ends itself."

Tyran breathed, envisioning the air entering and exiting his lungs. His father's words were on the tip of his mind. *Drast is a fox and you are a lion.* This moment was telling of the truth behind the analogy. Even without Drast knowing that Erzebeth's greatest fear was death, he had found the perfect place to settle the snare. And now, Tyran was the muscle to force Erzebeth into its readied teeth.

Tyran spoke evenly, emotion lost, love forfeited to war's calling. His reiteration was waterless. "Tell us what you know, Erzebeth, or my brother will wear your skin to protect himself from frostbite."

Drast's smile may as well have been as wide as the gorge. He pulled the string tighter. "We will share it."

Erzebeth snuffled, a tear forcing itself from the corner of her eye. She glanced at the dancing lights in the northern sky, nodding her head.

"I am a Warden of the Ash Tree," Erzebeth began. Her hand quavered against her side in agitation, and she soon crossed her arms to keep them still. "I am bound to protect the Ash Tree and the Waters of Life under the direction of Wolos. This has long been the onus of my people…it was once the onus of yours, too."

That captured Tyran's attention. "Excuse me?"

"Yes," Erzebeth said. "I had guessed that the Stuhia had forgotten millennia ago that they were also Wardens. At one time, they were considered kin to the Vucari; we were separate sides to the same coin. The Stuhia changed their allegiances, though, and gained Koldovstvo from Marheena, abandoning the ways of Wolos. The Stuhia became hungry for immortality and power. The location of the Ash Tree was hidden from them—from you—by Wolos. In time, they lost their identity as dragon men and became dragon slayers. The Carian Council attempted to burn all the manuscripts to erase the worship of Marheena, to maintain the tradition of worshiping Wolos, but they were executed one by one by Marheena's converts."

The cold was getting to Tyran, standing away from the fire within the ice fortress. He looked at it longingly but said what needed to be said through his ice-covered lips. "That doesn't make much sense. The Carian Council was the first of the Stuhian people." His mind raced to the *Varkolak* that his father treasured with its secrets written in the old language. Tyran really had no clue as to what it said, but his father had said it was the last remaining manuscript of the first bloodlines of Stuhia.

"Not hardly," Erzebeth said, "but I can understand why you would believe as much. The history of your people is as concealed as this frozen river." She tapped her foot against the solid, glossy ground for added effect.

Tyran scowled. Had his father intentionally lied to them, or did he not know either?

"You are a Vucari priest, then?" Drast asked.

She was bold, unflinching. "I am."

Tyran could envision the sneer on Drast's face beneath his fur-lined hood, analyzing the merit of the Vucari who raised question to their entire theology, their upbringing, and their quest.

However, Drast did relax his arms and return the arrow to his hand. "What makes the stories you tell any more sensible than the ones that we have believed and been told since childhood?"

Erzebeth locked onto the shadows created by Drast's hood. "Because I was there, young Red."

Tyran winced. She was patronizing his brother in the same way she had done to him when they first met. Drast was not likely to take such belittlement.

"You were there millennia ago with the Carian Council? With the first bloodlines of the Stuhia people?" Drast said with disbelief.

"Yes," she said without wavering. "As well as with my own people before mysticism divided our people into this fanatical war."

"How is that possible?" Tyran asked.

Erzebeth sighed, her tone shifting from that of a storyteller to that of politician explaining politics to a simpleton. She nearly sounded insulted by having to further explain herself. "Have you not been listening? I protect the Ash Tree. I have access to the Waters of Life. I have lived for a very long time and have seen many things. I was not lying when I said that I have not been to Rhian or Anaerfell in a very, very long time."

"Let us suppose that you are telling the truth." Drast folded his hands into his dark cloak, still clutching his bow. Tyran followed suit, realizing that he could not feel his fingers any longer. "It doesn't explain why you have come here now."

Erzebeth refocused on the light shade of green that danced across the sky, overwhelming the other colors. "In a dream, I was told to return to Anaerfell to speak to Wolos. I was told that the Ash Tree was in danger."

"A dream?" Drast laughed.

"You mean to stop us, then?" Tyran could not hold back his growl, overpowering his brother's mirth.

"No," Erzebeth paused, clearly distressed between her obligation and something else. "I will not stop you. I was told by a man, an Anshedar, and a Highborn—a world apart from here—to be witness to the events at Anaerfell. He encouraged me to follow the message within my dream."

Tyran shuffled at the sound of the unfamiliar word—Anshedar—whether it referred to a creature or a race or something else entirely. "Who is this man?"

"His name is Kinhar Sayan. Though I hardly see how that makes a difference," Erzebeth answered. "Are you done with your hounding questions?"

"Not in the slightest," Drast crooned. "But we should return to the fire before we catch our deaths out here."

"Every answer she gives only leads to more questions," Tyran agreed.

Erzebeth lowered her head.

Drast rubbed his beard within his hood, tilting his chin. "If she is telling the truth," Drast cocked his head at Tyran, "I don't see how her ramblings change anything. Our feet are set in motion and we have our charge to fulfill."

Tyran nodded in agreement. "Yes, we have already come this far."

Erzebeth exhaled, her breath clouding around her. It was unclear as to whether it was relief or disappointment. Maybe she was frustrated that they were talking about her like she was no longer standing there.

"But…" Drast opened, taking a step towards the way they had come.

Tyran filled the silence with a required grunt. "Mm?"

Drast faltered for a moment, refusing to look at Erzebeth, who appeared to wait as eagerly as Tyran did for the revelation.

"Nevermind. We will speak later when I have gathered my thoughts."

If his face had not been frozen solid, Tyran would have raised an eyebrow. Drast was actually thinking before speaking.

Chapter XXVII

"Kormish," Drast wrapped an arm around the fellow's shoulder with an amiable smile. "Come walk with me."

He had let the man stew long enough. Drast had seen the wary glances cast in his direction over the past several days, concern etched deep into Kormish's features while the Voivode waited to learn how Drast planned to address his eavesdropping on Tyran. The time was ripe.

"Certainly, Ser Drast." His eyes darted away. "It is just that I—"

"Nonsense!" he chortled, drawing Kormish away from the rest of the soldiers. "We have put off chatting much too long as it is."

Kormish reluctantly let himself be drawn away from the others, licking his lips nervously. Drem cast an eye on them but said nothing. Drast had to agree with his brother's assessment that Drem was a good soldier. With a grimace, he looked back to Kormish. Drem reminded him far too much of Walstan. Walstan was a good soldier, too.

"Listen," he began, releasing Kormish's shoulder, "we are both fully aware of what it is you were doing in Klukas when I came upon you, so let us dispense with the excuses, yes?"

Kormish looked like a dog caught in the rubbish bin, but he nodded warily.

"Good. Now, why do you not tell me why it is you felt the need to listen to my brother's conversation with Erzebeth?"

Kormish blinked. "She is Vucari."

"And you don't trust your leader?"

Kormish licked his lips again. If the man was not careful, he was going to freeze them together with this cold. He hesitated, his eyes rapidly jumping between Drast, Tyran, and Erzebeth.

Drast took the man's shoulder gently and stopped him. "Kormish, I know you fear to speak honestly with me. Were I in your position, I would be wary as well. But," he clapped his other hand on the man's other shoulder, "I want you to tell me your concerns. You must know that your concerns are important to me because I care for my brother. I trust that you have good reason to betray my brother's privacy. Nothing you say here will induce me to cause you harm. If I decide to kill you, it will be for eavesdropping, not for being honest." Drast laughed aloud. "Come! Speaking now can only save your life, not end it." He laughed again.

Kormish's eyes widened in alarm. "I see, Ser Drast."

"I am glad you do."

Kormish cleared his throat. "I have been with your brother since leaving Lairhein to venture into the Shade, and I have come to know him fairly well, for my part." He coughed. "That is to say, I have come to know his ways. He is hesitant to let others become close."

"True, true." Drast smiled encouragingly. Impatiently.

Kormish continued. "Well, that is to say, except for the fairer sex. He is often passionate for women, and he is passionate for Erzebeth." He shook his head. "I would not normally be so concerned, except that she is Vucari and our current war with the savages makes the relationship discouraging to the troops. Morale is low enough as it is and to see our commander fraternizing with the enemy so openly has caused some of the men to discuss whether or not—I apologize, but you asked for the truth—whether or not your brother's heart is true to the cause, as it were."

Drast nodded. "I see. You say many of the men see this relationship? And the morale issue permeates?"

Kormish dipped his head. "Yes, Ser Drast. I have no desire to listen to your brother's private conversations, but I fear the Vucari witch has put a spell upon him. I have tried to speak with him, but I fear only death can come from any further attempts."

"Death." Drast considered. "Yes, death seems just fine."

The man's eyes widened. "Pardon, Ser Drast?"

Drast chuckled, flashing his teeth. "Ah, Kormish, be at ease. Please. I am talking of her death, not yours."

Kormish's eyes darted. "What did you have in mind?"

Why could it never be easy? Why could his brother simply not be bound up with love nonsense? It was as though Tyran needed to drag after every female who crossed his path. First Maelili, then Isolde, and now Erzebeth.

Drast scowled back at the Vucari as he trudged through the snow. Every few moments he would cast a dark glance in her direction, unable to keep himself from it. He was finally with his brother again and was once again attempting to compete with some tart for Tyran's attention. Tyran spent enough time in his head without thinking about women. Not to mention that Erzebeth was a Vucari. At least Isolde and Maelili were Stuhia. Idly, he wondered if Maelili was still breathing.

Tyran's men were clearly not fans of their Vucari companion either. That much had been clear to Drast from the moment he had dug his brother out of the mountain. Especially his brother's commanders. Drem was too cautious of his brother's wrath, but Kormish seemed to be on board.

Tyran's grunt interrupted his thoughts. He still could not get used to how much his brother had aged since leaving Lairhein.

"Yes, my brother?"

Another grunt.

"Really? Well I always thought my eyes were my best feature, but if you insist."

Tyran gave him a dry look. "You know, we don't have to hold a conversation every time we are near one another."

"The time passes more quickly if we do, though. In addition," Drast ticked off fingers, "I don't have to think about how my hands and feet are numb, or about how our soldiers are tired, or about how we are probably going to die as soon as we reach Anaerfell."

"I didn't realize you found your own company so dreary."

Drast chuckled. "Well, my brother, I think you have gained a wry wit in your old age."

"I have always had a wit. I just don't feel the need to show it off."

"Yes, a crabby, wry old man."

Tyran snorted. "I am still young enough to whip you if I have a mind to."

"At your age?" He shook his head. "No, I don't think you have a *mind* to. If you woke up in the morning with a *mind* to do anything, you would forget it before you had put on your boots." Drast shrugged. "Maybe if you had someone about to re*mind* you."

His brother chortled. "I am beginning to remember why I left. You cannot help yourself, can you?"

"Nonsense!" Drast cried. "I can defy anything—except my appetites."

"I cannot help but feel I have heard something like that before."

"Likely your *mind* wandering in the wilds."

Tyran thinned his lips into a smile that did not quite reach his eyes and did not say anything. Drast said nothing, quite certain that his brother was somewhere inside of his head, and anything that he might happen to say would go unheeded. Only the sound of their boots crunching in the snow and the muttering conversations about them filled the snowy pass they traveled through.

His brother looked at his hands, now covered by great warm mittens. "Drast?"

"Mm?" Drast grunted, mimicking his brother.

"How are they going to remember us?"

"Who?"

Tyran shrugged his heavy shoulders. "The Stuhia. The Vucari. The world, I suppose."

"By our apotheosis."

"Does it always come down to glory?"

Drast snorted. "Yes. If we fail, we will not be remembered. It *must* come to glory."

Tyran shook his head. "But is what we are doing glorious?"

"We are off to kill a god. How could it not be?"

Tyran stopped and turned. "But if we are wrong. If killing Wolos is somehow an evil act. Or if we fail and we are remembered because of our tyrant father—"

"Tyran the *Tyrant*," Drast interrupted, chittering.

"I am serious. How do we know that we should even be doing what we are planning on doing? How do we know it is right? How do we know we can?"

"Tyran, you are overthinking this. Why do you even care how people will remember you to begin with? It will not matter. We will either succeed, in which case we can tell whatever tale of our victory we choose, or we fail and are dead and it doesn't matter. Regardless, people will remember us for the height of our lives, when we faced a god."

"I want to believe that I did something right for this world before I died."

"Well, I want to believe that my father actually cares for me." Drast could feel the heat rising in his neck. "I want to believe that my brother will be there for me instead of wandering off on his own leaving me to cover my own back. I want to believe that I am not alone, that my hard work will pay off. I want to believe that the Stuhia are a chosen people instead of the sniveling hogs that we are. I want to believe a lot of things, but I know the reality. I know who we are and what we have done."

Drast realized he was yelling. Soldiers stared at him, but he could not stop the flow of words. "I have betrayed everyone I have ever known. I nearly killed our father. I killed your bride-to-be. I killed more than half of the Kluks. I have killed for anger, for pleasure, and for pain. I have stepped on the backs of my kith and kin to get where I was told I must go. I am tired, Tyran. I am worn through to the bone, but I will not stop, and as the gods are my witnesses, neither will you. We are brothers and we are together in this, even if we have never been together for anything else in our lives."

Drast clutched Tyran by the shoulders, the wisps of wind so cold they burned into his frozen cheeks. "We survived our father. The God of the Dead doesn't stand a chance."

Chapter XXVIII

Tyran shambled forward with as much energy as he could muster. He tried to find the way to say the words that had been balled up in his throat all day. The silence was nearly deafening as he tried to find a way to speak to his brother.

"Did I thank you?" Tyran asked. He could barely hear his own voice, and it came as a surprise when Drast answered.

"For what?"

Tyran cleared his throat of the cold. Of the uncomfortable sensation of talking with his brother freely. "For being my brother. You are a good friend to me. Always have been."

He and Drast never were ones to share sentiments.

"You did, brother." Drast shuffled his feet minimally, seemingly surprised by Tyran, his eyes sparkling in the watery light of wintry sun. There was youth in his eyes that Tyran had lost since coming to Rhian. "I hope that you know that I am equally grateful to you. I could not have endured this life without you."

"Mm," Tyran rumbled. "Strange that fate put us together in this life as brothers. It is as cruel as it is kind."

Drast raised his eyebrows, his lips already spreading into a smile. "Strange we have gone through what we have had to go through in order to speak plainly to one another."

"It should have been sooner, but I think it was necessary to bring us to this point," Tyran agreed.

"Touching. But I cannot believe you are being wholly truthful." Drast blew the air from his lungs into his hands. "I am in your debt for the pain I have caused you. Rescuing you from this…this hell brings me no satisfaction. I merely saved you from the doom I brought you."

Tyran shook his head.

They slogged side by side across the sleeted ground for several minutes. The small army marched single file behind them with Erzebeth somewhere among their numbers. Another day had come and gone with little ground being covered in the jagged terrain. Trudging between the mountains was a constant challenge in finding suitable passage, whether avoiding large drifts of snow or not getting caught walking in circles.

When he finally found a response, Tyran said, "You did no such thing, Drast." Tyran tilted his head and his hair, now more grey than red, fell over his eyes. "I may have thought to blame you at one time, but I was ignorant to do so. It was Father who did this. If there has ever been a wedge placed between you and me, it was not put there by either of us."

Drast's face was flat, emotionless. Tyran found it to be far too calm for the words that he spoke. "Father did not hold the knife that slit Isolde's throat. I did."

Again, Tyran was speechless. He gulped at the recollection of his beloved. Although he had not forgotten Isolde, he had done well in not speaking about her. In a way, that silence seemed to lessen the grief.

Tyran had no argument against Drast's self-blame. Almost immediately, Tyran's mind wandered to the night he and Drast had questioned Erzebeth in the gorge. He could not even remember how long it had been. Two weeks? A month? "Would you have really killed Erzebeth?"

Drast glanced sideways, looking at Tyran momentarily, and finally shook his head. "No. I could not, especially when knowing the way that you feel about her. I must admit I am surprised you have feelings for the Vucari woman, especially when considering we have killed her kind by the handfuls, but that is not my place to question. I expect your soldiers have better insight into your relationship with her."

"There is no relationship." Tyran stumbled, keeping himself from looking back towards her or his men. "The men have not spoken to me about her since before the alcove."

Drast continued as though Tyran had not said a word. "You must understand that I had to threaten her. I had to know what she knew."

"Mm."

Drast noticeably tensed.

Tyran focused on the path in front of them, hoping that Drast spoke the truth. He had never known his brother to lie to him, though Drast may do things and not tell Tyran the full of it.

Yet it was more than Drast's promise that troubled Tyran. He had not spoken out loud about any feelings he may have for Erzebeth, and still, Drast was right. He could only think that the rest of his army had seen the connection as well.

"Enough of all that," Tyran grunted.

Drast returned the gruff reverberation in his throat and changed the subject. "I wonder if these beasts, the Vulkodlak, fled to the south as the weather worsened. I have not seen any tracks."

Tyran rubbed his fingers together, barely sensing the flesh touching flesh. His fingers were so cold they burned. He was not even certain he could grip his weapon if they were ambushed by the wolf-men. He loosened the amount of pressure he put on them, fearing that they might snap from the joints if he was not careful.

"The snow is so regular that it would likely cover the tracks anyhow," Tyran said.

"Probably," Drast said, gazing across the landscape. "There is no beauty to this land. Even when it is not blanketed in darkness. I imagine that this is what the Netherworld would look like if we were within it."

Tyran dipped his head. "I had similar thoughts when I first arrived. I am still uncertain as to whether we have entered such a place."

"No, I imagine there would be more demons if we had. This place is rather…desolate."

Tyran's feet crunched against the slush. It sounded as loud as a blacksmith's hammer. "Mm."

"At least it stopped snowing for the time being, and the wind has died down," Drast offered.

"I suppose. I still cannot feel my face."

Drast bit off a laugh that caused the subsequent silence to seem all the more oppressive.

The two of them continued onward on the unmarked path for another hour before they built a fire to regain some warmth, and then pressed forward once more.

Darkness settled after a short time, and still they trudged through the snow for as long as they could. They stayed close, following the shadows of one another beneath the lights in the northern sky that ricocheted their light off the white world beneath. Tyran and Drast were keen to not lose each other in the blackness, leading the way closer to Anaerfell. The soldiers behind them spoke in hushed whispers.

It was only Erzebeth who could move through the darkness effortlessly. Occasionally her voice directed the men to stay on track behind the two Kaligula brothers, who were caught up in their own musings.

Tyran ruminated as they lumbered around the base of another mountain. "Drast?"

The man grunted in response, his throat likely as dry as Tyran's. The air had thickened. It was like breathing ice particles.

He could feel them melting in the back of his throat. But he found that conversation steered his mind away from the winter weather, at least for a short time.

"Do you remember when we were young?"

"I try not to," Drast said softly. His voice shook as though the very mention of their youth placed nightmares at the tip of his mind.

"It is what made us," Tyran said.

"What is your point?"

"I—" Tyran started. He bit his inner cheek, reflecting on what he was after. "I wish I had become a farmer."

Tyran heard Drast's soft laugh. The man was quick in his response. It was like he had contemplated the same notion once upon a time. "You wouldn't have been satisfied. Neither would I. I always understood that. I never thought you did."

"No," Tyran acceded, "but I could have been content. I am certain of it. There was always too much drive for satisfaction and not enough acceptance of contentment. It is the curse of youth, I think."

"Well, when I get to be your age I might agree." Drast rumbled his throat. After a moment, he added, "I hate the feeling of power."

Tyran kept his stride even. "Hate?"

"Hate. Hate and love," Drast corrected himself. "It roils in my gut, but I want more. It is like an insatiable lust. I want it to end."

Tyran had probably never heard a more honest and visceral statement from his brother. But it was one that Tyran understood. He had not considered it, but perhaps his power was why he hated himself.

"You know, we had it in the beginning. We must've."

"What is that?" Drast wondered.

"Hope," Tyran said.

Drast adjusted his fur-lined hood. "Ah, I imagine that we did." He paused. "But it reminds me that I had wanted to speak with you. Hope may not be completely lost to us, Tyran."

"What do you mean?"

Drast peered over his shoulder as though he could see as well as the Vucari. The army was not as close as they should have been, a blotch against the darkness plodding behind them.

"We are in agreement that we need to see Father's bidding through." Drast rustled, barely loud enough to be heard. "We have already come this far. Wolos will die; I have no doubt that we will be successful in killing him. But afterwards, I think you and I should seek out the Ash Tree. We should regain our youth as Erzebeth has done."

Tyran was dazed. He had to admit that he had fumbled with the idea, but he would have never thought that Drast would have been of the same mind.

Tyran's hand shook as he lifted it to touch his wrinkled cheek. His greying hair was ice covered and stuck in place over his eyes. As Tyran lowered his arm, he took sight of his wrinkled knuckles.

"I wish I was as confident about killing a god." He examined his ancient hands. "I don't know that I will survive the battle. My bones are already cracking at every step." Tyran was surprised to find his voice break up. For a moment, he thought he actually was going to cry. He swallowed, focusing on the chill against his skin to keep himself from blubbering. He had been a fool expending so much energy, wasting his years away, using Koldovstvo.

"Don't talk like that." Drast raised his voice as though he held the authority to keep Tyran alive. He, for once, sounded like an older brother watching out for the younger. "We will both live through this, Tyran. We have suffered more than any man should in a lifetime. There has to be happiness still waiting for us."

Tyran felt something stirring in him. "I wish that I could believe you, but there is nothing that guarantees happiness. Every living person in this world seeks joy, and instead they find pain. Children die before they have their first kiss. Fathers leave for war and never come home. People embrace hatred and distrust long before they consider peace. We are no different. If anything, we are the epitome of the worst men to walk upon this cursed world. It may be a fitting end for us to suffer, tortured as we are, and have a god put us down."

Drast shook his head. "No, we were created for something greater than what we have achieved. We will endure this; we will be victorious, and then we will find the Ash Tree."

"How?"

Drast slowed his pace. "I don't think that Erzebeth will tell us the location—at least, she will not tell me."

"You want me to ask her, then?" Tyran asked.

"Ask her if you think she will tell you." Drast stopped. "But if you are going to do as much, do it fast."

Tyran stared at his brother in confusion. He said the words as though he knew something that Tyran did not.

Even in the dark, Drast must have seen the expression on his face. "We will be at Anaerfell soon, Tyran. Our time is running short."

Tyran had lost all concept of time when they finally found a spot suitable enough to set up their camp. Valarun was nothing but mountains, abundant in chasms and minor caves. With the help of Erzebeth, they had found a cave facing the south, sheltering them from the wind that blew from the north. Within minutes, a fire was built and smoke rolled out of the mouth of the cavity. Tyran was astonished at how quickly the cave warmed with the simple fire, created with the power of Koldovstvo.

The cave, because of its location, had little to no snow beyond the entrance. The stone space was multi-layered, stretching farther than Tyran cared to venture. The depths of the cave were bound in darkness and ignored by the soldiers, who hurried into the haven, protected from winter's breath. Large boulders, cold to the touch, were scattered in the oblong opening. Several Stuhia fell into them and likely would have kissed them if they thought they could do as much without being judged. Regardless, the cavern was a good size, holding several men comfortably.

It was the perfect resting spot before reaching Anaerfell. It was a place where they could rejuvenate before the battle with Wolos.

Tyran stumbled across the rocky floor. He could not feel his feet or thighs. His hands were numb and a strange pinkish blue.

He had never hated a place as much as he hated Rhian.

Only footsteps ahead of him, Drast had stripped off his hooded cloak and laid it to dry across the stone floor. It was probably the first chance that Tyran had to get a good look at his brother. The man looked twenty years younger than Tyran, even with a silver streak coursing through his hair. Even still, despite his youth, he did not hold as much muscle as Tyran. Drast scanned the cave as he maneuvered about the area.

Tyran did the same and skimmed the soldiers, who crumpled in heaps. "Where's Erzebeth?" Tyran dropped his shield and mace to the ground. He was about to remove his own furs from his back when Drast answered.

"Outside, keeping guard with Drem and Kormish. We still don't know about these Vulkodlak that attacked you, and as we have talked, Erzebeth doesn't have any trouble seeing at night."

"Kormish," Tyran muttered. He no longer trusted Kormish. In fact, he trusted Erzebeth more than he trusted his own Voivode… if he was even worthy of holding the title anymore. Tyran had barely talked to Kormish since the battle with Vulkodlak.

Drem was a good soldier; he would keep Erzebeth safe.

"What about Kormish?" Drast said offhandedly, taking a seat in front of the fire. His fingers picked the snow out of his boots. It looked as though he were considering taking them off to warm his feet near the fire.

"He never apologized for the way he treated Erzebeth," Tyran growled.

"Apologized?" Drast said incredulously. "Why in the Nine Lands would he apologize for how he treated a Vucari? I would pleasure Marheena before I apologized for something I said to a Vucari."

"Never mind," Tyran grimaced, looking over his shoulder towards the outside, trying to avoid Drast's eye. He should have never expected his brother to understand.

He could see little more than darkness and the beginnings of another snowstorm starting fresh.

Tyran was not sure that it was warm enough in the cave to strip down much further than basic armaments. Honestly, he had no interest in looking at his feet or any other part of his skin. He was sure he would only see the green-black of frostbite. He could already feel his skin aching as though it were being scalded with a poker. The rising heat tried desperately to settle itself into his ice-coated skin.

When he turned his attention back to Drast, he noticed the man looking at him, bewildered. "The Vulkodlak have not been seen thus far, and their attack was two months ago. I think we are safe from their kind."

Drast shrugged. "Can't be too careful. We are close enough now that I would hate to fail."

"I suppose precautions are necessary," Tyran agreed. "Yet I don't understand why my two Voivodes and Erzebeth were given first watch. It would likely be a task for someone of lesser rank."

Drast lifted his shoulders again, settling near the fire. "I figured that the finest at the front lines would assure that all is well, eh? Any of these other louts would not do much good standing watch."

"Indeed." Tyran's gut wrenched. "Though I will need my Voivodes equally rested. I will take the first watch." He scooped up his cloak and weapons once more, hoping that Drast did not pick up on his compassion for Erzebeth. Then again, he could not say that he cared much about what Drast thought regarding Erzebeth. The woman had fought next to him as bravely as any of the fighters in his army. That meant something.

Drast tapped his fingers against his knee as Tyran readied himself to brace the cold once more. His brother looked as though he was straining to find words that never came. At length, Drast muttered, "Suit yourself."

Tyran stalked off into Valarun. It was too dark to see the mountains. The chilled airstream and bits of flurries struck him as though he had dipped into a river midwinter, stark naked. It was like experiencing the cold all over again. What warmth had been found in the cave was lost along with his breath.

He sucked in air, his chest tensing. There was no sign of the three who were supposed to be keeping watch. Tyran took a couple of steps before realizing that footprints led the opposite direction.

He followed them.

He had made it about thirty feet from the cave when he noticed something dark lying in the snow ahead of him. A body.

Erzebeth.

Tyran's heart skipped a beat, seeing the overlay of furs. He stiffened, thinking to yell for Drast, but stopped.

It was not Erzebeth. It was too large to be the lithe woman. He rushed forward and rolled the body over. Blood caked his hands, spilling from the man's chest. Dead eyes stared at him under the dancing lights that sparkled through the thin clouds. Kormish.

His Voivode was dead. Heartbeat still. No breath. He hurriedly checked the body, feeling the wound that went from chest to back, or possibly the other way around. The crimson blood colored the snow beneath his feet and he scooted back on impulse.

Tyran could not yell for Drast. Whoever had done this was definitely still in the area, and they would attack again. This was not Vulkodlak though; it was too clean.

The Vucari priests.

Erzebeth.

Tyran's mind was peppered as he sprinted forward, moving with less grace than what Drast might have, squinting to see the imprints in the snow. There were two sets of tracks. Erzebeth and Drem. Running.

After another hundred yards or so, Tyran could no longer see the light from the cave. In short time, the clouds started thickening, blocking out the radiant light from the heavens. The world was quickly becoming as black as the grave.

He heard shuffling ahead, and a woman's cry.

"Die, you Vucari whore! You killed him!"

Someone touched Koldovstvo and a flash of lightning zinged through the darkness, sizzling and crackling. It struck the side of a mountain opposite Tyran, surging shards of snow and ice into the air.

Tyran strained his eyes.

"Stop this, Drem!" Tyran could not see her, but Erzebeth's voice was clear.

Another lightning bolt seared, zigzagging into nothingness, missing its target.

A roar answered, followed by Drem's bloodcurdling shriek. Tyran touched Koldovstvo and threw light as bright as the morning sunrise into the immediate area. The light was blinding at first, but Tyran had been ready—more ready than Erzebeth and Drem, who battled in the snow-covered mountains.

Erzebeth, who could see in the darkness better than her aggressor, stood over Drem with her hand and forearm formed into a massive bear paw.

Before her claws could pierce the Voivode's skin to release his life, a barrier formed of—nothingness. Or, at least, nothing that Tyran could see. Drast was at Tyran's side, his teeth gritted. Tyran did not know his brother had followed.

"Stop her, Tyran," Drast snarled.

Erzebeth was repelled by whatever his brother had constructed to protect Drem. The rest of her body was still in human form.

She twisted to face where Tyran was standing, horror-struck. "You did this!" she accused, slashing against the barrier again.

Her round brown eyes filled with tears, her chin quivering in incredulity. "You sent your best to kill me, Tyran Kaligula. It was not good enough!"

Tyran's jaw quivered. His words were broken. "I did not...tell anyone to harm you, Erzebeth." The light he had cast started to fade. "I would never hurt you. I promise you that."

"Kill her, Tyran," Drast said. "She tried to kill Drem, she will kill us!"

She began to fade into the darkness, backing away. "Rabid dogs!" she spat.

Tyran's heart beat in his chest, he felt anxious, desperate for her to believe him. "I had nothing to do with this, Erzebeth!"

She faded from sight.

"Where is the Ash Tree?" he cried, hoping she would take mercy on him.

Laughter rang out from the darkness, echoing in his ears.

She was gone.

Chapter XXIX

"Tyran, it has been long enough. We need to make a decision."
Drast stared down at Anaerfell, trying to ignore the magnificence
of the temple complex. For some reason, in the back of his mind,
he had thought that Anaerfell would be a town or settlement of
some kind. However, he soon realized that it was merely a temple
to which the Vucari traveled during the winter.

The structure itself nestled against a cliff face, having been
partially built into it. Grey stone and white snow made the thing
almost invisible when they came upon it. Anaerfell was taller than
anything Drast had ever seen, standing more than one hundred
feet tall from the base to the highest tower. The great height was
probably due to the structure being supported by the mountain.

He shook his head, trying to look past the architecture. He
needed to focus on strategy. Of course, strategy was not his strong
suit. He usually left the details up to Walstan. He had Mladen now,
but he soon realized the fellow had no real ability to strategize
either. Which meant that Tyran had to decide the best approach.

His brother had spent the remainder of the journey to
Anaerfell moping and had not more than glanced at the temple
complex when they arrived. Drast had managed to drag him to
the edge of the pine glade they had made camp in to look down
at Anaerfell, but Tyran simply glared at the trees, or the sky, or the
mountain and refused to say much of anything useful.

Tyran had not responded and simply stood staring at nothing. He looked so old and grey that Drast wanted to let the man sink into his despair, but he could not. Drast had made a promise to their father, and he would not fail merely because Tyran could not get over some skin-switcher.

"Tyran, Erzebeth is gone. We can do nothing about that now. You need to focus on Anaerfell." Drast grabbed Tyran's shoulder, forcing his brother to meet his gaze. "We are preparing to kill a god; you can't be distracted by a pair of pretty eyes."

Tyran pulled away from his grasp. "You don't understand, Drast. You never could understand."

By the Nine Lands, his brother was exasperating. "I don't need to understand. I am not trying to. I am trying to get you to help me figure out how to attack Anaerfell and draw out Wolos so we can kill him."

"Mm."

Drast took his brother by the shoulders again. "Listen to me, my brother. You are right. I do not understand your infatuation with a love." He lifted one hand, altering his position. "I understand tits, but I don't understand love." He shook his head. "None of that matters. We need to finish this out. We need to face Wolos. When it is done, my brother, and we are both breathing, I will spend the rest of my life helping you to find Erzebeth or whatever woman you want. But now is not that time." He gave his brother a shake. "Yes?"

Tyran let out a heavy sigh. "How many men do we have left?"

Drast gave a short nod and let his brother loose. "Eighteen in addition to ourselves, of course. We had a couple disappear in the night—deserters—and Ulick fell in a river two days ago and froze to death."

"Who?"

"Good gods, Tyran, he is your man!" Drast exclaimed. "Ulick was with your army for two years."

"Mm."

Drast rubbed his eyes. "You spent two months trapped in the alcove with him. You never bothered to at least learn his name?"

"There was not much use for it."

Tyran was terrible with people. Drast was surprised any of the soldiers had followed him to Anaerfell. "What is the plan?"

Tyran shrugged. "We are not interested in the Vucari or in Anaerfell itself. We are interested in Wolos. So, that is who we need to find."

"Right," Drast said. "How do we do that?"

"Attack the Vucari and Anaerfell."

Drast laughed aloud. Half amusement, half exasperation. "Fine. Good. Would you like to give me more than scraps at a time? Or are you going to make me fight for all of the information?"

Tyran cast a dark glance at him. "Send in our soldiers. All of them. Drem can lead them. We don't have enough to hold any back. It needs to look impressive."

Drast interjected, "*Impressive?* You might have missed the part when I said—and let me quote myself—*we have eighteen men!*"

If it were possible, Tyran's frown deepened, but he continued, "They yell, scream, and use Koldovstvo—whatever they need to do—to make themselves seem wild with bloodlust." Tyran pressed on. "You and I are going to hang back and wait for the show to start and hope it draws out our quarry. As soon as we see something that looks like Wolos, we go in."

"I thought you were the great strategist. I expected something a little more…complex."

"Strategy is about winning, not about getting complicated. Simplicity is best. That is why I win battles."

Chapter XXX

Tyran clutched the yew haft of his mace, the ball of the heavy weapon resting in the snow. His eyes searched the heavens. He could not remember the last time he had seen the sun. Even now, roiling clouds hid the blue of the sky, dampening its brightness. If there was a sun, it was hidden behind the mountain ridge.

He turned and watched the flurries being kicked up by Drast's footsteps ahead of him, swirling in the air like colorless ashes. It was fitting. He and his brother had burned through the world, leaving dead bodies and broken spirits. He never wanted this. Never wanted the world to become a place of hatred, a place of hopelessness. He could only think it was necessary for him to stand on this battlefield today. Live or die, it was for the best.

His father had crafted him into this terrible man. If Tyran failed, then the world was rid of one more demon. If he succeeded, then he rid the world of death. Either was acceptable. Though he wondered if a world like this, with men like him, was even worth saving.

"Tyran?" Drast turned to him, his black cloak a measure of contention against the white background. Anaerfell was grey and lifeless, a spectacle hidden away at the tip of the world, not meant for the eyes of men.

Tyran struggled against his despair. He forced his eyes away from the bleak terrain. "Yes."

Drast wet his lips. "I hope that all we have done has been worth it. When we die, I hope that our charge has been fulfilled. If I don't get immortality, I hope to find the Thrice Ten Kingdom."

Tyran kicked at the ground, sending up a cloud of dust to match Drast's. "As do I." He flipped his mace about so that the end rested on his shoulder and picked up his pace to join his brother. "How long?"

Drast scanned the area. The stone ruins of Anaerfell, possibly grandeur in a distant age, fell against each other, forming a provisional shelter from the cold against the mountain.

They passed by a handful of trees that loomed about them. Drast said, "Not long now. The men should be readied."

"What happens when this is over?" Tyran knew he sounded like the younger brother in this moment, but a part of him wanted the reassurance of Drast. His brother had found words of encouragement many times in their life; there was a part of him that wanted to hear it one more time. It could be the last.

Drast frowned, fingering his bow. "We can finally begin to make amends. We will find peace and happiness. We will find the Ash Tree."

The two moved forward through the thick snows in cascades among the pine trees. Winding through the drifts and slippery slopes, Tyran searched for any movement, waiting for what was to come.

The sounds of combat echoed against the breadth of the mountains before their scrawny Stuhian army was halfway down the hilltop. A warning bell from the temple rang out, followed by fire and lightning falling from the sky. Tyran could make out the Stuhia soldiers racing towards Anaerfell casting their magic against the ancient structure. The display of Koldovstvo was answered with bestial sounds and Vucari flooding from the grey stone of the temple complex.

Figures, shadows against the snow, bounded through the area. The Vucari and Stuhia attacked each other; the war had been waged. Tyran had no doubts that all the remaining soldiers would die. He only hoped that they killed the Vucari priests in the process, drawing out Wolos.

As planned, Tyran and Drast stayed separate from the main battle, watching the fighting unfold below them. Tyran hunted for any sign of the God of the Dead.

Catching sight of a figure moving amongst the trees nearly a hundred yards away, Tyran touched Drast's shoulder, pointing him out. The being, in his first few steps, appeared as an aged man with a white beard and bushy eyebrows. His girth and strength was visibly comparable to Tyran. Strong hands and broad shoulders, covered in pelts and furs, draped over his ashen skin.

"An aged Vucari is all. That cannot be Wolos," Drast said.

Tyran tilted his head with a sense of awe, his chest tensing in preparation. "Don't be so certain."

The old man did not waver or wander as Tyran or Drast had in approaching Anaerfell, but took the most direct route towards the brothers.

Drast lifted his bow and fired an arrow at the old man across the distance. The arrow soared through the air and the man did nothing as it neared. It struck him in the shoulder and snapped in half upon impact.

He continued his walk.

Drast quickly began to mutter under his breath, shrugging out of his heavy winter cloak. Raising his bow, he pulled a handful of arrows from his quiver.

"Your arrow did nothing. What makes you think they will pierce his skin this time?"

Drast scowled, his hands glowing red as he pulled back the sinew. The glow increased to a burn, and the burn to a blaze. His weapon was no longer orange, but a thick crimson. The light infused his body, boiling out of his eyes and mouth. The blood-colored light from his eyes pierced through his lids.

Upon release, the power of Koldovstvo fled from his body and embodied the arrows that flung towards the old man. Upon striking him, each arrow blast into a burst of fire, igniting his skin.

The man howled in pain, the sound ricocheting off the mountains. He quickly patted away the flame and bounded towards them in haste. The distance closed fast.

"I told you it was Wolos," Tyran said.

Tyran stepped forward in front of Drast, his shield pulled from his back. As the god came within striking distance, Tyran did not miss his opening. He swung the weapon upward, catching the man under the chin at the opportune time. Wolos stumbled back from the force of the blow and paused, the intensity fading fast.

At close distance, Tyran noticed twisted, sand-colored horns beneath the man's long white hair.

Drast's eyes narrowed, slivers of scarlet light flashing. "You will die."

Tyran shook his head. "We have been waiting for this, Wolos."

"There are much greater things in this life to cherish besides killing and death, Tyran and Drast Kaligula." The voice was harmonious, far different than anything Tyran had heard before, far kinder, full of pity. "You do not understand what you think you understand. The corruption you have embraced has corrupted your minds. You have no idea what you threaten by killing my priests, by killing me."

"So, the almighty god can die," Drast said, his grin dangerous. "I don't pretend to be wise. That is the game of the gods. The gods have immortality and immense wisdom and then ridicule men for having less. We will see how much men can learn when they are not subjected to death."

"Anything can die, but do you really think that you have the power to kill me? I am the Wolf God, the Protector of the Eternal Spring, the Guardian against the Frost. I am the God of Death. What do you think will happen to this world without me?" Wolos spoke with tenderness. "Nothing will remain but dust and ashes."

Tyran heard his father's voice in his own words. "Sounds like a fate we are already doomed to face."

Screams from the dying priests and Stuhian soldiers in the distance confirmed his words.

Wolos lifted his hands and a great wind rose, sweeping away slush, snowfall, and uprooting dead trees and branches from the area. Tyran stood with his brother, Koldovstvo keeping them from the flying debris and winds threatening to take their feet from beneath them.

Wolos lowered his hands. "There is no power which can overcome me. You have drunk dragon's blood, as your heretical ancestors did, embracing the death magic of Marheena. Who do you think created the dragons? Why do you think I was given reign in the Eternal Fallows and Marheena the Netherworld?"

Tyran grunted. "You may know what we do not and understand more still. Yet it is Marheena you must answer to when you die. I hope she gives you a warm welcome for insulting her name after we rip your heart out."

Tyran lifted his mace, energy channeling into the weapon. A great vortex formed with light swirling about to find the tip of the weapon. A great cry arose from Tyran's lips as he tried to control the influx. Wolos parroted the cry. The scream of the god tore the earth asunder and an earthquake ripped apart the land before Tyran had a chance to attack.

Despite the clearing caused by the god's display of power, snow and ice shelled the area, raining about him.

Tyran faltered backwards from the splitting earth, losing the power of Koldovstvo. Gloom, a darkness he could not see beyond, filled the space between him and his brother. Eddying black clouds danced about Tyran, and the only sound he could hear was the singsong tone of Wolos. Stumbling in the fog, he made his way towards the sound.

"I had hoped our meeting would not come to such an end, but you are as determined as I had feared. Despite what you may think, I do not partake in wanton killing or take part in the lives of lesser beings. But I cannot allow you to kill the guardians of the Ash Tree. It cannot be harmed."

Without hesitation, Tyran found his way to the edge of a smoky wall hanging in the air. And then he saw Wolos mold into something larger, something grander, rising above the obscure bleakness. Something imposing. Indescribable. His height quadrupled, and girth swelled tenfold, with claws as deadly as a Vulkodlak erupting from elongated fingers. The ground cracked and shifted under his might. Even the sky seemed to darken as his new form rumbled into existence. A score of horns, like antlers, thrice as thick as Tyran's yew haft and culminating in points as sharp as pins, sprouted from his skull. The white hair deepened into the dark green of the sea, swirling and sprouting across his body in a thick fur as though it were sprouts springing from spring's crop.

The being was not a monster or a demon, and nothing that Tyran had ever witnessed. It was Wolos, a god, taking the form of the shepherd of the flocks of the underworld.

Somewhere opposite the darkness, Tyran heard Drast moving. His brother must have found his way out from the pitch, too.

Arrows flew from the darkness, penetrating the chest and stomach of Wolos. The oversized creature roared, ripping the arrows free with a swipe from its clawed fingers. Red liquid oozed from the wounds.

Tyran dropped his shield and slammed his mace to the ground, clutching the haft with both hands. The weapon boiled and foamed, as though it were being forged anew. The mace enlarged to the size of his torso, cackling with power. Tyran held onto Koldovstvo, pulling bits of dragon blood through the pores in his skin. The blood raced along his flesh, and wherever it touched, armor appeared. It was harder than the scales of Torn'Ash and crimson in color. In seconds, he was encased from head to foot.

Two more arrows from Drast spewed fire, striking Wolos and burning his fur. Scorching his hide.

With a snarl, Tyran sped towards the beastly creature, his aged body empowered with Koldovstvo. The god, still reeling from his brother's arrows, could not have stopped the descent of Tyran's mace. Landing the weapon on Wolos's thigh, Tyran sent lightning surging through the god. The bone sounded like it was breaking, the flesh searing.

Tyran reared back to hit him again when a woolly fist slammed into him, engulfing his face, chest, and stomach. He instantly lost his grip on the weapon, but his dragon armor withstood the impact, preventing his bones from being crushed. Still, he flew backwards and collided with the mountainside.

"Tyran!" Drast cried.

The wind was knocked from him, but he managed to growl. "I'm fine." He worked at digging himself out of the embankment.

While pulling himself free, he kept his attention on Wolos. The god's magic was impressive. Vines as thick as a man burst from the frozen earth, reaching out with human-like intelligence to snag Drast or knock him flat. His brother was swift and sharp-witted, leaping and skidding across the terrain with the agility of a rabbit in a briar patch.

Drast jumped and bounded and skipped from vine to vine with inhuman agility. All the while, his hand never stopped working, arrow after arrow plunging into Wolos. The flora wrapped and bent and twisted through the area, thorns discharging as rapidly as arrows fired from his bow. The pointed—and likely poisoned—bristles were as large as Drast's head.

Tyran did not think his brother was even looking at Wolos. As monstrous as the god was, Drast may as well have been shooting at the side of a mountain. He doubted his brother could miss Wolos unless he deliberately tried.

Tyran, bones aching beneath his bolstered armor, finally sprang forth with the help of Koldovstvo. Time and space shifted around him as he squeezed through the creeping plants. He neared the god; his hand reached out to call his Koldovstvo-infused mace. His fingers curled around the handle and he came to stop, his momentum transferred into slamming the weight of the weapon into Wolos's kneecap.

Wolos bawled, crumbling to a knee, and Tyran released his weapon. He leapt for the god, running up Wolos's bent leg. Balling up his fists, empowered with Koldovstvo, Tyran struck the god repeatedly up the length of his torso. Ribs fractured beneath his fists, the muscle juddering with every strike. The god seemed stunned by the onslaught, groaning in torment with each successive blow. Arrows from his brother zinged past him, burying themselves in the god's skin, fashioning a ladder for Tyran to continue his ascent.

With a cry as loud as a hundred men on a battlefield, Tyran pulled his mace to his hand once more. Whipping it full circle, the head of the weapon cracked into the Horned God's antler on the left side. The branched tusk fissured and crumbled away from the fawned ears, hitting the ground near Wolos's hooved feet.

Never had an ear-splitting sound been heard in such enormity as the thunderous roar that sounded from Wolos. It boomed, curdling from his throat with such potency, it caused Tyran's chest cavity to vibrate.

He leapt back from the god, finding that the vines had fallen motionless around the clearing, wilting and blackening.

Drast scuffled to Tyran's side, blood covering his left thigh where a thorn must have snagged him. His brother grabbed his shoulder, holding himself upright as best as he was able. Silver streaked through his hair, evidencing the measure of Koldovstvo he had used so far to keep himself from death.

Tyran shivered. If Drast had aged so much, he was likely far worse. Tyran had not been paying any attention, focusing fully on slaughtering the god.

"We can finish this," Drast croaked.

"Mm." Tyran did not have the strength to say much more.

Drast waved his hand towards the ice and formed a solid arrow, an icicle, frozen and razor-sharp, as large as himself. In a flash, he flung it towards the Horned God's crouched form.

Wolos howled, slapping it from the air before it could touch him. "Bah!"

The god's voice was as vivacious as it had been when they started.

A green miasma vented from Wolos's body, whipping and churning over the brothers. Tyran gagged, the gaseous smoke like bark and rotten vegetation, foul as maggots on week-old bread.

Blood spewed from Tyran's lips with each stomach-wrenching heave. Drast followed suit alongside him. Tyran tried to suppress the ill feeling that captured his senses, feeling faint.

He was not certain when he fell to his knees or when his face collided with the ground. A chill swept over his body, sweat pooling on his forehead despite the cold winter weather.

The glade blurred around him.

Wolos's voice occupied his head. It was as clear as his own thoughts. "I was breathed into existence long before mankind was imagined. There was Perom the Thunder-Bearer, and Dahz the Light Bringer, and Svarog the Keeper of Kowin the Deathless. And there was I, Wolos the Protector of the Eternal Spring, with power parallel to any of the three! Did you think I was the weaker while governing over the dead?"

Tyran gurgled on the misty vapor. It burned his skin, seeping through his armor. He could feel blisters forming on his skin. Each sore bubbled and corroded his flesh, popping with heat equal to a fiery pit.

Wolos's voice was full of sadness, overwhelmed with woe, while Drast and Tyran suffered, whimpering on the ground. Tyran coiled and snaked awkwardly as though a demon had embodied him and was bent on ripping him limb from limb. He screamed in misery.

"The Stuhia, like the Vucari, were blessed with Koldovstvo, watched over by the serpents of the Shade. Long have my dragons kept the nefarious races of the east and south from your people. Never would I have thought that you would reject your god, your gifts, and propel yourselves beyond your own position. Do you truly think that you are any more significant than any other?"

Drast's scream came seconds later. It made Tyran weep to hear the sound; blood spewed from his lips again with the sickness that wrought him.

"You will be remembered. You will be an example to all those who would dare test the will of the god. An example to those who miscalculate the might of the beings responsible for your creation and bestowed free will upon you. In your last moments, before I send you to Marheena, the very same to whom you pay homage, understand that even free will has its limitations."

Darkness swept over Tyran, the vapor dispersing, while Wolos transformed for a second time. Tyran could not see fully, but he felt the presence of something significantly superior filling the space near him and Drast.

Tyran wriggled, thrashing to keep his senses about him. Through the slits of his eyes, through the gloom, glowing crystalline eyes stared back at him on the end of a stretched snout. Rows of cutthroat teeth shimmered nearly as bright as the spellbinding, jade-colored scales that flashed in the blackness. Massive wings flailed in an overpowering gush, flattening Tyran to the ground. His eyes teared from the pain that plagued his soul. Yet again, he resisted unconsciousness. His chest and shoulders tightened. His stomach stirred.

He reached for Koldovstvo, calling for his shield a lifetime away. The green beast's throat reverberated, summoning its acid breath.

Wolos had become a dragon.

Chapter XXXI

Drast prepared himself for the outpouring of viperous breath from Wolos. Surely, he and Tyran would die now—nothing stood between them and the draconic god of death. It was the end of the Kaligula line. Drast had failed his brother; he had failed his father.

Behind him, he could hear Tyran wheezing. Maybe he could still save his brother. Choking on his own blood, he stood to face the god. Stumbling, he wiped his lips on the back of his hand. If he was going to die, he would at least do so on his feet in defense of Tyran.

But Wolos did not exhume poison. His deep voice filled the glade. "You are yet young, my once beloved Stuhia. Whereupon once your kind revered me, revered death, you now fear it. Fear is the price of following Marheena. But death is the reward of life. Death is what gives life. One cannot exist without the other. Light cannot exist without dark. Good cannot exist without evil. The Stuhia understood this once, just as the Vucari understand it now." The great green head swayed to and fro as Wolos spoke. "Do not throw away your lives in vain. You have yet to fulfill your purpose, your charge. Understand that it is not yet your time."

Drast exhaled, allowing himself to breathe. If Wolos wanted to talk, then he would talk. "Humor me, Wolos. Tell me what charge I have not completed."

The dragon's voice moaned softly, a deep dirge to tell what might have been. "Your charge has been to protect your brother. As the eldest, it is your purpose to guide him and support him in the ways that a brother should, defending him against the evil that would plague him. You, Drast, were meant to be his champion, to give him the strength needed to overcome hardship and turmoil."

Drast clenched his teeth together, blinking away his emotion. He suppressed the regret, the guilt. How much hardship had been brought upon his brother: burning Tyran upon his father's command, slitting Isolde's neck, and even planning Erzebeth's assassination. He had caused more pain than he had ever prevented. He may have failed his brother in the past, but he could save him now.

He could not help but steal a glance at his fallen brother. "And what of Tyran—" Drast choked. "If you are the wiser, then tell me. What was the charge I should have guided him to complete?"

Wolos's voice remained soft, comforting. "Your brother was meant to walk the path of love, the noblest deed asked of any living being. Tyran should have followed his heart, finding love and holding onto it fast. Thrice he has been given the chance to steer away from his evil ways and to embrace a more wholesome life. Thrice he has denied it."

Drast cringed. Without doubt, the dragon spoke of Maelili, Isolde, and Erzebeth. Wrath swelled within him towards the god, or towards himself, he could not be certain.

Wolos continued, "You have been told more than any living creature. Countless numbers would want to know what you have been told to be given clarity of your purpose. Pursue your charge, Drast Kaligula—tell your brother of his—and walk away from Anaerfell with your lives. This is not your time!"

The winter cold stung Drast. He would not fail his father. He could not. He could do his father's will and save his brother, fulfill both of their charges. "Is that choice not our burden? Whether we should live or die? How we choose to spend our lives?" He slowly began to walk away from Tyran, leading the dragon's gaze from his brother. "If death is our end, why should we not choose when it should occur?"

"For the same reason you should not willingly step into a fire. Death feeds life just as your bones would feed a fire, but there is plenty of kindling in the forest ready for flame. Let the dead wood feed the fire instead of your bones." Wolos spread his wings, adding emphasis to his words. "I am that fire. I am those flames. Let me feed upon the death extant rather than upon your immolation."

Drast continued walking, increasing the distance between him and his brother. He wondered if he could really outwit the god as he had everyone else who had crossed his path. "Perhaps that is the trouble with this world. Your flames are too great. Too strong. It is time that the fire was snuffed out."

Wolos chuckled. "Ah, dear child. You are spitting at a bonfire, hoping that it will not singe your lips. You are a mere snowflake. No, you cannot snuff me out. I *am* too great. I *am* too strong."

"No." Drast pulled an arrow from his quiver. "I am not a snowflake; I am an avalanche." Faster than the eye could follow he nocked, drew, and loosed the arrow, already running towards Wolos.

Koldovstvo flooded him and the single arrow became ten, then a hundred, then a thousand. Taking ten years from his life, the arrows became molten metal as they pierced the dragon's jade hide. Its roar shook the ground beneath his feet and seem to last a lifetime. Drast soon realized that the continued rumbling was snow rushing down from the surrounding mountains.

Despite the direness of the situation, he could not help but grin. How great was it that an avalanche came after his little boast? He wanted to laugh, but the pain in his lungs from Wolos's poison made him choke back his mirth.

Sparing a glance, Drast could see the waves of snow uprooting trees, completely clearing the mountainside in its mad rush to reach the valley. It was impossible to tell if the snow would reach the glade in which they battled Wolos, but he could already tell that Anaerfell would be buried.

Turning his gaze back to his enemy, he fought to keep balance on the rumbling terrain. Yet each stride brought a new arrow to his bow, launching another molten projectile. Though he did not possess the energy to multiply them as he had the first.

Drast could tell that he had injured the god—blood flowed from a myriad of wounds caused by his arrows, but they did nothing to slow it. Wolos inhaled as if preparing to expel its draconic breath, but a great boulder flew into the side of its head, knocking it askew. A second connected with its chest, causing the god to spew its greenish bile harmlessly into the glade.

Although he could not see him, Drast silently thanked his brother for his intervention, as the breath surely would have immobilized him. Coming within a few dozen feet of the creature, Drast leapt into the air, fueling his jump with Koldovstvo to sail through the air and land on Wolos's back.

Before he could fire another shot from his bow, however, the dragon rolled, upsetting his footing. Drast landed hard on his back, knocking the wind from his chest and sending his bow flying from his hand. Wolos, surprisingly agile in this form, rolled upright and snapped at Drast with its razor teeth.

Scrambling to find his feet, Drast sprung backwards, just out of reach. Before he could grasp with Koldovstvo to pull his bow back to his hand, Wolos's mighty claw crushed it into the snow, leaving only splinters behind. Its other foreleg swept forward, the deadly claw catching Drast and sending him sailing through the air. Drast tried to use Koldovstvo to slow his flight. With directed gusts of wind, he avoided several trees before finally slamming into a thick cedar.

He unconsciously appreciated the smell of the wood while he fell to the ground, snapping branches. He did not know how many ribs he broke before he reached the bottom, but he could do no more than groan while Wolos advanced.

The dragon sped towards him like a lizard, its head leading while its tail whipped back and forth behind it, sinuous and deadly. There would be no talking now. Drast had thoroughly angered the god. In retrospect, attacking Wolos in the middle of conversation had likely taught the god better than to try and reason with either of the Kaligulas. Drast wished he had some means of slowing the creature, but his mind was preoccupied by the pain that made his breath come in short, ineffective gasps.

With a cry, he forced himself back to his feet. Touching his quiver, he felt the fletching of a pair of arrows. Two arrows. Just two. He had no bow. A dragon raced towards him. His brother was nearly dead. And he could not breathe.

Fantastic.

Drast was fairly surprised at how far he had flown, but Wolos was closing the distance fast. In a singular smooth motion, he drew one of his remaining arrows and threw it high into the air above. Catching the projectile with Koldovstvo, he sent towards the dragon with lethal accuracy.

The arrow plunged home in Wolos's eye, eliciting a roar of pain. If there had been any snow remaining after the last series of avalanches, it would have come down with his tormented cry. The great dragon stumbled, reacting to the sudden agony, and fell over itself. Crashing to the ground, Wolos tumbled and wiped out a wide swath of the glade, uprooting trees that had stood for centuries.

Drast stood unmoving, still trying to find breath while Wolos labored to its feet. The dragon seemed to be in bad shape—at least as bad as he felt. The god had finally slowed down and looked worn from the constant barrage to his physical form.

"I cannot be destroyed in this world," Wolos rumbled. "Your task is impossible."

Drast laughed wearily. "Yet here I stand, if just barely, and I will continue until I succeed or die."

The god sighed, a great gust of wind from the dragon. "You have turned upon your god, turned upon your people, but it is not in me to kill unnecessarily. I sought to defend the Vucari here today, and in that task, I have failed. Consider this your victory, but I will fight you no longer. I will not give you the opportunity to force my hand."

"No." Drast growled, laboring towards his foe, running as quickly as he could. He had worked too hard, sacrificed too much to be left with an impasse.

The dragon began to fade from sight, shimmering in the dimming light of the day.

No!" he cried.

Drast leapt forward through time and space with Koldovstvo, his final arrow clutched in his hand. A last life-draining burst of Koldovstvo launched him towards the god, his right arm extended with the last arrow, his ethereal form colliding with Wolos's incorporeal one. His arm was inside of Wolos, arrow in hand. The arrow found the heart of the god of death.

Drast returned to the corporeal world, drawing Wolos with him. The dragon solidified, amputating Drast's arm.

And Drast screamed.

Tumbling away, unable to do anything except shriek, he clutched at the stump. Desperate, he hoped it was not real. Confusion. Panicked confusion clouded his mind. Blood poured from the remnant.

He frantically tried to stifle the flow with his left hand. Time passed in a blur as he wept and strained to cover the remainder of his arm with bits and pieces of his clothing. He wept and clawed at the stump, looking to the sky, to the trees, to the god.

Wolos did not move. The body of the dragon lay still, a mountain beside Drast.

He did not know how much time had passed before he finally stood from where he lay, struggling and stumbling to center himself. Slowly, Drast walked around the dragon, around the god, and saw no movement. His mind was veiled with agony, with anger, and he could not think.

Did he kill a god? Was Wolos dead? Or was this merely the physical form and he had not succeeded in killing him.

Shaking his head, he wandered away, faltering steps in which he tripped over his own feet as he made his way across the uneven terrain. He needed to find his brother.

"Tyran?" he called.

The destruction within the glade made it nearly impossible to find from where he had come. Nothing was recognizable. A ruined landscape greeted his eyes, darkening by the moment.

"Tyran?" he cried.

"Drast?" a hoarse voice whispered.

Awkward and hesitant as he had never been, Drast made his way towards the voice. He called out as he moved, adjusting his direction to find his brother. Tyran answered, but it seemed he was growing weaker, even as he came closer.

Finally, Drast saw the prone figure of his brother. In the gathering darkness, he could not see how greatly the aging effects of Koldovstvo had altered Tyran, but a great relief filled his breast.

"Tyran." He smiled. "We did it. We killed him." Did they?

"Mm." The familiar response had a calming hum to it.

Drast produced his stump, blood pouring. Despite the pain, Drast flashed his teeth. "I think you might be able to beat me with the bow now."

Blackness came and Drast fell to the ground.

Chapter XXXII

He had never felt such coldness, inside and out. His muscles convulsed and his lungs burned. Tyran was dying.

"Drast..."

Tyran's own voice was a whisper against the wind, flowing between his teeth like a sword from scabbard, grating and vexing. He gagged as soldiers had before him, writhing on their deathbed. His throat was taut; his vision smudged, but the affliction to his body was crushing.

His brother was near him. He had just been talking to him. How much time had passed? A second? An hour? A day?

"Dr-ast."

He reached for Koldovstvo, whether to heal or even lift his voice, and found it overbearing. The craft was beyond his touch for any more than a moment. He had spent every ounce of his being.

Tyran's wits were rattled. He had to escape this pain.

As a last resort, he allowed his spirit to glide to Klukas.

Tyran's mind first approached Drast but was left empty. His fear was brief, thinking that his older brother was already dead. He could not focus on the fear or he would return to the sting of his dying body.

He redirected his thoughts to his father.

"Dagmar."

The voice that came to him was quick, as if expecting—waiting—for his call.

His father's image formed before him in the ethereal plane, shimmering. Greyed hair, broad shoulders, and more wrinkles than he last remembered frothed into place. "I am glad to see you again, Tyran."

Tyran was certain that he was a close reflection of his father. Old.

He barely heard his father's words. "You knew it would come to this?"

His father's brow wrinkled. "Come to what?"

"I'm dying." His voice was clearer in Klukas, lacking the strain that was found in the physical world. The fabric between the ethereal and the physical, a thin blanket, a shadow of grey that separated him from Anaerfell. Beneath him, he could see his body broken and bloodied, painting the snow.

His father's cheeks tightened as he assessed his son's body through the veil. "You failed me, then."

The words were both judging and ridiculing, a reflection of who his father was at the core, an unloving, hateful man. Tyran, though, played into his father's hatred in his last moments.

"Failed." He said the word blankly, barely capturing its meaning. "Know that where I may have failed, Drast did succeed. Wolos is dead."

"That is impossible." His father, even as a specter of himself, sneered as nastily as he might in the flesh. "If the God of the Dead is *dead*, then there can be no *death*. You would not be permitted to die. Drast must have failed in my instructions. Where is he?"

"I can only guess that he is already gone," Tyran said. He spoke for his brother in a manner he should have long before this moment. "You should mourn what he sacrificed for you, Dagmar. Drast gave up everything to have a moment of your approval, and you denied it to him over and over again."

His father flared his nostrils. "You dare tell me what I should or should not do while insulting me by refusing me the title of Father."

Tyran shimmered, blocking his emotions as best he was able. "How can that be your response? How can you not say a word about your son? Drast is dead because of you. He died for you!"

"He was nothing, Tyran," Dagmar said. "A fool. You had absolute power and immortality in your grasp and you have lost it. The world was ours for the taking. The plan was flawless and you two fools failed me."

"You lied to us," Tyran breathed.

"I did not lie."

"Wolos had already given the Stuhia people immortality by making us ageless." Tyran flared his nostrils. "We abandoned him for Marheena's power, for Koldovstvo. We should have been Wardens, guarding the Ash Tree and protecting the circle of life and death. We should have been standing alongside the Vucari. Our insatiable hunger for Koldovstvo corrupted us!"

Dagmar glared. "You have gorged yourself on the lies of a self-righteous god. The Carian Council were the firsts; our ancestors left us the *Varkolak* to show us the way to true eternal life."

"The book should have been burned with the others."

"Excuse me?"

"Admit you were wrong, Dag-mar." He felt himself slipping away with every word but would have his final say to his father. "I watched Wolos die, and yet, I will journey to the land of the dead. Killing the god did not free us from death, nor did it give us greater power. In moments, I will be trudging through the frozen Netherworld."

"Tyran—"

Tyran interrupted his father, determined to speak a lifetime worth of words. "This fight was futile, reaching for something unattainable. I wasted my life to fulfill the whims of a madman.

You say we failed you? You failed me! You failed Drast! I was given the chance for friendship, and happiness, and love. I have had more opportunities than a thousand men before me, and all of them were taken from me. I came into this world taking the life of my mother," Tyran stammered. "I only wish that I could have left claiming the life of my father!"

Dagmar's ethereal body flickered with energy as emotion seared through his consciousness, clearly conflicted by Tyran's words.

Tyran was unrelenting. "Before long, you will find yourself among the dead, and Drast and I will be there waiting to remind you that you were anything but a father. The title doesn't suit you. You did not teach us kindness; you did not cherish us or nurture us, and nowhere in your counsel did we find love or forgiveness."

"I taught you to be indestructible!"

"Every trespass that we committed against humankind was a reflection of what you made us. The hunger for something more…for immortality…for power…it stole away any chance at a real life. You robbed your sons of their charge, forcing Drast and me to be pawns to your depraved musings. You made us believe we could defeat death! By the Nine Lands, the blood spilt…the evil done…should be weighed against *you* when judgment comes. I pray to the grandfather of gods that it is crushing."

Dagmar sputtered, his body wavering in the ethereal plane.

Tyran was cold, like the ice his dying body impressed. "I hate you."

"You see how far hate gets you in death, my son." Dagmar curled his lip, untouched by Tyran's words. "Fortune has not given up on me; my tale has not ended. I will find the Ash Tree and continue to live while you and your insufferable brother endure your *hate* in the Netherworld."

Tyran flinched, feeling himself being pulled away from Klukas. Death was stealing him away.

"Oh yes," Dagmar turned his nose up at his son, "I am aware of the Ash Tree and its precious gifts. If you wait for me in the Netherworld, know that you will be waiting a long, long time."

Tyran glowered. "Then let the day come when the dead walk among the living."

Tyran jerked, dipping back into reality, dropping out of the ethereal veil of Klukas.

His physical body juddered as he sprang upright, breathless and parched. He spit blood, turning ever so slightly to see his blood gushing onto the snows of Anaerfell.

A handful of feet away, he saw Drast, prone and sprawled out. His older brother's face was pale, and the nearest arm was missing entirely. Tyran flinched, stomach tightening. Darkness came again, swelling fast.

A shadow loomed over him. He strained to see a large bear, gruff and growling, transmute into a dark-haired woman. The naked woman advanced as though she were a visage in a dream, untouched by the cold. Her large brown eyes—familiar—neared his own; their noses nearly touched.

Tyran trembled.

"And so, the rabid dog is put to rest."

ABOUT THE AUTHORS

Joshua Robertson was born in Kingman, Kansas on May 23, 1984. A graduate of Norwich High School, Robertson attended Wichita State University where he received his master's in social work with minors in psychology and sociology. His bestselling novel, *Melkorka*, the first in The Kaelandur Series, was released in 2015. Known most for his Thrice Nine Legends Saga, Robertson enjoys an ever-expanding and extremely loyal following of readers. He counts R.A. Salvatore and J.R.R. Tolkien among his literary influences.

J.C. Boyd lives in the Midwest with his wife and two dogs and has an M.A. in English Literature. The first novel in his world, *Blood and Bile*, was released in 2017. Before completing junior high, J.C. had received his first box set of Dungeons & Dragons and devoured J.R.R. Tolkien's *The Lord of the Rings*. Since, he has been heavily influenced by a myriad of fantasy authors, such as Weis and Hickman, Robert Jordan, and Ed Greenwood.

www.ingramcontent.com/pod-product-compliance
Lightning Source LLC
Chambersburg PA
CBHW050545190726
48283CB00007B/2013